"STOP, MATTHIAS! PLEASE! YOU MUST NOT DEFILE THE GRAVE!"

"How can one defile a grave in which there are no bodies?" I roared between pulls. "Listen to me, please. Earlier you said that I was the investigator and you were my guide, did you not?"

He nodded sadly.

"And you brought me here, after I made that dumb wish on the Carson program, so I could discover the truth for myself, whatever that may be, correct?"

He nodded again and without turning, he pointed back over his shoulder toward the tomb of Lazarus. "And you expect to find the truth in there?"

"I don't know."

"All you will find in there, Matthias, are three empty shelves and a few worms. What are you looking for, my son?"

"I'm looking for the remains of a body."

"A body? Whose body?"

"The body of Jesus."

THE CHRIST COMMISSION

Og Mandino

THE CHRIST COMMISSION
A Bantam Book

PRINTING HISTORY
Lippincott edition published April 1980
2 printings through May 1980
Bantam edition / May 1981

For two men named Silvio,
my father and my brother.

If a man will begin with certainties,
he shall end in doubts;
but if he will be content to begin with doubts,
he shall end in certainties.
Francis Bacon

one

I SETTLED BACK into the crushed ebony velour of the Cadillac limousine's spacious rear seat and checked my Omega. The ride to NBC's Burbank Studios, according to the public relations people handling my tour, would take at least fifty minutes in the late-afternoon traffic.

This was the big one, a perfect climax to three weeks of newspaper interviews, personal appearances on radio and television talk shows, and autograph parties in bookstores from coast to coast. If only I had known how big this night was going to rank in my life, I might have remained in my room at the Century Plaza, double-locked the door, and watched television in my pajamas.

"Ever been on the Carson show before, Mr. Lawrence?"

I shook my head at the inquisitive brown eyes squinting back at me from the distant rearview mirror. Although I was heading for my sixty-first media appearance in twenty days, I felt tense for the first time. I had already managed to conduct myself on the Donahue show with some measure of aplomb, visited with Merv, joked with Snyder, and even held hands with Dinah. So why the butterflies now? I closed my eyes and tried to relax, hoping the Tanner limo people had sent a chauffeur who was not a talker. No such luck.

"I've read a lot of your books, Mr. Lawrence. Ter-r-r-ific! My wife and I, we both love 'em."

"You're very kind," I replied, before I could stop myself. Reflex action. A simple phrase used repeatedly by many authors to acknowledge the heady and often embarrassing praise heaped on them by their fans. I had never realized how banal those words sounded until I shared an autograph session with Erma Bombeck and we caught each other mouthing the same response as we signed our weary signatures. Erma thought it was hilarious, but we both decided to be more creative in the humility department from then on.

My driver skillfully eased his glistening chariot out of the hotel's Mercedes-cluttered circular driveway and onto the

1

Avenue of the Stars. "You must be some kind of smar-r-rt man, Mr. Lawrence, yessir! A genius! Don't know how you think up all those impossible crimes and then put all the pieces together. Never have been able to figure out who the murderer is until the very last pages. Never! Your stuff is even better than those old Sherlock Holmes things—yessir!"

"Thank you."

I tilted my head back and closed my eyes again, taking care not to cross my legs and wrinkle the Calvin Klein brown tweed that my wife, Kitty, had insisted I wear for the "Tonight Show." Sherlock Holmes, did the man say? As we glided on our radial cushions toward Burbank, I tried to keep my mind off the show by recalling all the masters of mystery fiction I had been compared with during the tour. Rex Stout and Agatha Christie had been mentioned often, as well as my favorite, S. S. Van Dine. John Dickson Carr's name had also come up frequently, and Ellery Queen had been suggested by a Chicago *Sun-Times* reporter who didn't know that two cousins, Manfred B. Lee and Frederic Dannay, had written under the Queen pseudonym and that Mr. Lee had now gone on to that great inner sanctum in the sky. One intense young woman from *Writer's Digest* had even compared what she gushingly called the "vivid realism" of my writing to France's best, Georges Simenon. The temptation had been strong to tell her that she was being "very kind," but I resisted. Everyone enjoys a little flattery, even when they know it's not true.

With all twenty-six of my detective novels still available in paperback and selling as well as when they were first published, both Kitty and my publishers had argued against my going on tour. She had insisted that it was an unnecessary intrusion on my time and energy and they agreed, maintaining that every Matt Lawrence book always made the best-seller lists anyway. Still, I prevailed. I had never been on an author's promotional merry-go-round before, and I thought the experience would be a good change of pace. It might even supply me with some fresh story material.

Looking back, I had enjoyed every silly day and night of it, as Elia Kazan had said I would. I had no idea whether my appearances had helped or hurt the sales of my latest effort, *Where Weep the Silver Willows,* but now that it was ending for me, after Carson, I almost regretted having to return to the quiet serenity of our Camelback Mountain home, high above the city of Phoenix.

Exactly forty-eight minutes after I entered the limousine it turned off West Alameda into a forest of high wire fencing, paused at an inner gate long enough for the guard to recognize my driver, and then eased alongside an unmarked door. I thanked my enthusiastic fan behind the steering wheel and went in, immediately recognizing the small, anxious blonde from my publisher's public relations firm. She had almost given me a coronary yesterday morning, by expertly demonstrating the high-speed cornering ability of her Porsche 924 after we had fallen behind schedule for a taped interview in the posh patio coffee shop at the Beverly Hills Hotel.

"Hi, Mary—or should I start calling you Mario?"

She ignored my weak attempt at humor. "Oh, Mr. Lawrence, we were beginning to worry. Gee, you look great! Just like that handsome hunk in the Wind Song perfume commercials!"

"Well, young lady, never having seen those commercials, I don't know whether I'm being complimented or placed in a category that I doubt would appeal to me."

She tossed her head saucily and laughed. "Oh, yes you do! Follow me. I'll take you to the famous green room. The other guests are all there, I think. Taping will begin in about thirty minutes."

Inside the green room—that isn't green—Mary introduced me to a young man on Johnny Carson's staff whose name was Alfred. Then she kissed me lightly on the cheek, wished me luck, and was gone. Alfred asked if I would like to meet the other guests on the show, and I said I would. First I shook hands with Charles Nelson Reilly, comedian and director. Reilly admitted to having been a Lawrence fan for years and proved it by rattling off at least a dozen titles of mine. I responded by complimenting him for his sensitive direction of the Julie Harris tour de force portraying Emily Dickinson's troubled life.

Next, Jimmy Stewart, looking bigger than life, came over and introduced himself. We found our common ground quickly, having both served in the Eighth Air Force during World War II. Finally, I shook hands with a ravishing brunette singer, Donna Theodore, who reminded me very much of our old squadron's favorite pin-up girl, Jane Russell.

Eventually the friends of the guests were courteously asked to leave, and the four of us were left to uplift each other's waning courage. We failed miserably. There's something so mind-boggling, even to show-biz personalities, in knowing that what you say and do will be shown to fifteen million people that only a lunatic or a complete fool would not feel inhibited. Except for a few throwaway remarks about the

3

ubiquitous smog and California's Jerry Brown, little was said by any of us until we heard Ed McMahon exclaim, "He-e-e-re's Johnny!" and everyone gratefully directed their undivided attention toward the huge RCA television set.

Johnny's monologue chided the Los Angeles Dodgers for their long losing streak, needled the current Congress for its inability to pass any legislation except another raise for its members, and unloaded on used-car dealers whose opinion of their own sales abilities is so inflated that they insist on appearing in their own obnoxious television commercials with props ranging from boa constrictors to Dolly Parton look-alikes. Charles Nelson Reilly almost made me forget my nervousness when he described his run-in with a coast guard cutter while desperately trying to bring a runaway engine on his small boat under control. Then Jimmy Stewart showed film clips of a forthcoming special he was hosting, on another network, dealing with unidentified flying objects, and Donna Theodore belted out two rock hits that seemed completely implausible, to me, coming from such a regal and lovely woman.

Alfred startled me. "You're in luck, Mr. Lawrence!"

"Oh? How is that?"

"You're on right after the next two-minute station break, and it looks as if you'll have as much as *fourteen* or *fifteen* minutes with Mr. Carson."

"Wonderful! That will put me right up there with Carl Sagan and Paul Ehrlich!"

"What? Oh, yes . . . that's funny. Fun-ny." He wasn't smiling. "Can you handle that much time okay?"

Having done nearly two hours, only three nights earlier, on Larry King's network radio show, I patted Alfred's fuzzy cheek and replied, "I'll try, son, I'll try."

"Follow me, sir . . . and please watch your step. It's rather dark, backstage."

The band was playing on the other side of the curtain, entertaining the studio audience while the viewers across the nation were being instructed on the benefits of Alpo dog food and Jaymar slacks. Alfred leaned close to my right ear and shouted, "Stand here, please, until I pull back the curtain. Then—step out, take three steps forward, and turn right toward Mr. Carson. Careful you don't stumble when you step up onto that platform around his desk!"

I nodded, wishing as I always did, just before making an appearance on any program, that I was back on Camelback Mountain, sitting by my pool with my basset hound and a

4

good book. Suddenly Alfred, who had his ear close to the curtain separation, tugged at the heavy drapery and patted my back. The lights momentarily blinded me as I stepped forward and smiled. I waved to an audience I still could not see, turned right as instructed, stepped up on the platform, and grasped Johnny's hand. Then I turned, kissed Donna's cheek, and shook hands with Jimmy and Charles and Ed.

"Mr. Lawrence," Johnny said warmly, "I've been a fan of yours for years. Welcome!"

"Thank you. It's a pleasure to be here."

"Why haven't we had you on before?" Johnny frowned, cocking his head so that the question was directed to me and also to director Freddy DeCordova, sitting off camera in the left front row with his headphones and face mike.

"I've never done much radio or television, Johnny. Fortunately for me, the books have always sold so well I think my publishers suspected that all I could possibly do by making personal appearances would be to foul up a good thing. Most authors, from what I've seen, should be locked up as soon as their books are published anyway, because every time they open their mouths their book sales drop."

Johnny grinned and nodded. "I'll buy that. How many of your books have been sold—do you have any idea?"

"Not exactly, because they're also in so many foreign languages, but I would estimate somewhere around eighty million copies in all editions."

The audience moaned admiringly.

"Eighty million? Let's see now." Johnny picked up a pencil and wet its lead tip on his tongue. "If your royalty is a quarter apiece, that would be twenty-five cents times eighty million . . . good heavens!" The audience giggled.

We discussed several of my books that had become motion pictures. Johnny's favorite had been *The Century Plant,* and Jimmy said he had most enjoyed the Academy Award winner, *Scarecrow.* Then Johnny checked his notes and briefly touched on several real-life crimes where police had called me in to act as consultant. My most celebrated case, of course, had been the solution of the terrible Houston hammer murders, five years after they had been committed.

Following another break for commercials, Johnny shifted his discussion and moved to a first-name basis. "Matt, have you ever started a book that you couldn't finish—one where your own plot got so complicated that you couldn't even unravel it yourself?"

I hesitated. All my little internal self-preservation bells

were ringing, warning me that we were approaching perilous waters. My instincts told me to shut up and just answer in the negative, but instead I replied, "Yes, as a matter of fact I've been struggling with that kind of a book since long before I wrote my first murder mystery—for more than twenty years."

"Twenty years! Wow! Can you tell us about it?"

Now it was too late to retreat. "Well, Johnny, I've always been fascinated by biblical novels—you know, *Ben Hur, The Robe, The Silver Chalice*—and for many years I've been studying books dealing with the life of Jesus. I probably have one of the most complete collections of its kind in the world—at least, privately owned. My unfinished work deals with a fictional investigation into the last week in Jesus' life, a week filled with suspense, drama, mystery, and many personalities who either hated him or loved him. Of course, in those times, there were no detectives as we know them now, but history tells us that fact-finding commissions were used often, by both the Romans and the Jews, similar in character and purpose to those we still assemble today for investigative purposes."

"You mean . . . like our Watergate Commission or the Warren Commission?"

"Exactly—and, most recently, the House Committee on Assassinations that re-examined the Kennedy and King deaths. My still incomplete manuscript, a biblical mystery novel if you will, concerns an investigation conducted by a commission comprised of three Roman tribunes, all learned men, into the death of Jesus, and I have it taking place six years after his crucifixion."

"Six years after . . . ?"

"Yes. By then the Roman governor of Syria, Lucius Vitellius, had become greatly concerned about the growing number of Jesus' followers, who were now calling themselves Christians and stirring up the people in the province under his command, a large territory that included Israel—or Judaea, as Rome called the small nation of conquered Jews. In my book I have Vitellius forming a commission which he dispatches to Judaea with one objective: to put to rest, once and for all, the rumors being circulated by this potentially dangerous new wave of troublemakers that their crucified leader has risen from the dead, after his execution, and is the long-awaited Messiah who will soon return to free the people from the chains of Rome."

Johnny frowned, and the audience became as still as if we

6

were in an empty studio. "How on earth would you have them do that?"

"My commission's plan of action is simple. They set out to prove that Jesus did not rise from his tomb but that his body was stolen, instead, by parties unknown, who moved it to another grave, thus enabling his disciples to capitalize on a miraculous event that never took place. I selected the sixth year after his crucifixion for the time setting of my book because history, as well as the New Testament, confirms that most of the main participants and witnesses to the events of the last week were still in Jerusalem. The commission would intend to hear testimony from everyone involved with Jesus and to investigate every possible lead until they finally learn the identity of the culprits who removed the body and where they have hidden it. Then they would obtain signed confessions, by any means necessary, from those who deceived the people, after which they intend to crucify them with their signed confessions posted prominently below their bodies for all to see. The remains of Jesus would also be recovered and displayed, thus destroying this dangerous new movement before it gets completely out of hand and threatens the peace of Rome. In my book I even give the panel of three tribunes a name: the Christ Commission—which, by the way, is also the book's title."

Johnny looked puzzled. For several moments he nervously tapped a pencil on his desk top before he reached over and touched my arm. "Matt, I'm not sure I follow you. Do you mean that for twenty years you've been writing a book where you expect to prove, through the testimony of those who knew Jesus, that he *did not* rise from the dead?"

From out of the corner of my eye I could see Ed McMahon leaning forward. I was certain that the big guy was glaring at me. I shook my head. "No, Johnny. I was writing it so that 'as the plot develops, and the commission examines such witnesses as Pontius Pilate, Peter, Matthew, James, the high priest Caiaphas, and several more, they would gradually begin to realize that the evidence is pointing in a direction other than they had anticipated and they will *never* be able to recover the body of Jesus, or apprehend any culprits involved in a grave robbery, because none has taken place. At the end of my book, according to my original plans, both the Christ Commission and my readers would, I hoped, come to the same conclusion: that Jesus did indeed rise from his tomb in the garden sometime before dawn on that Sunday long ago."

"Fascinating . . . fascinating," Johnny murmured, inter-

7

rupting a smattering of nervous applause. "Why don't you finish it, Matt? It would make a great book, especially with your ability to make complicated facts and clues so easy to understand. It would be the detective mystery to end all detective mysteries."

The applause resumed, much more enthusiastically, and now I knew I was in over my head. There was no place to go, no place to hide, and I had only myself to blame for my predicament. I inhaled deeply and plunged ahead. "I haven't been able to finish that book for one simple reason. The more I studied the events of that last week in the life of Jesus, the more I tried to wrestle with and resolve the strong inconsistencies one finds in the four Gospels, the more I searched the writings of far wiser men than myself who have struggled with this enigma for over nineteen hundred years—the more I became convinced that Jesus *never rose from the dead!*"

A piercing hiss immediately swept across the audience, followed by a crescendo of boos beginning at the rear of the studio. Johnny stared at me openmouthed, his face a frozen mask. To my right, Donna Theodore gasped and Ed McMahon growled. I tried to keep my poise and plunged ahead. "Paul, when he was seeking converts, often said, 'If Jesus has not been raised, then our preaching is in vain and your faith is in vain.' Johnny, the longer I study and research this matter, the more convinced I become that for twenty centuries the faith of billions of people has been in vain. We have been taken in by the greatest hoax ever perpetrated on mankind. There is no solid evidence of any sort that proves Jesus rose from the dead or that he is, as so many want to believe, the Son of God."

Johnny reached into his cigarette box, removed one, and lit it. His small gold lighter sounded like a rifle shot in the foreboding silence that had now settled over the audience. I continued.

"This may sound presumptuous, even insane, but I wish I had a week back there in the same setting I placed my fictional Christ Commission, six years after the crucifixion. I'm positive I could uncover what really happened to Jesus during those climactic days of his last week: what conspiracies were involved and between whom; what facts were covered up and kept from the people; who actually stole the body of Jesus and why; and especially how the truth, whatever it may be, became obliterated so swiftly that we have had nothing to go on, except hearsay, for almost two thousand years. That's about it, Johnny."

8

"Yes," he replied curtly, nodding toward the band. "That certainly is it, all right."

As soon as the music began, a candy bar thrown from the audience landed at my feet. Then an apple crunched against the front of Johnny's desk, and coins began to ricochet across the stage, whining as they flew by our heads. Donna screamed and leaned toward Jimmy Stewart, hiding her face on his chest. An ominous growl bubbled through the crowd, and I saw Freddy DeCordova frantically signaling to the people in the glass-enclosed engineer's booth. A plump gray-haired woman leaped from her seat in the front row, rushed to the edge of the stage, and shook her pudgy fist at me while shouting words I couldn't hear above the clamor. Johnny, obviously shaken, leaned toward me and said, "For your own safety, and ours, why don't you head on out through that curtain, right now!"

I rose and extended my hand, but he pretended not to see it.

"So how did everything go?" The same chauffeur who had brought me was now returning me to the Century Plaza.

"I'm surprised you're taking me back. I thought for a while they were going to tell me to walk—in the middle of the freeway."

"Why? What happened?"

I didn't answer.

"Didn't you get on the show, Mr. Lawrence?"

"Oh, yes, I was on."

"Terrific! I'll see the program when I get home tonight. My Rosie always gets a special thrill when we watch the Carson guests I had in my Caddy. And when she hears I've had you . . . wow!"

In front of the hotel I jumped out and handed him a twenty-dollar bill. "Thanks for two nice rides. And tell Rosie I hope she's not too disappointed in me."

The hotel's entranceway was crowded with overdressed couples either going out for dinner and a show or coming in to attend one function or another in the many banquet rooms. In the lobby a small Mexican combo struggled to be heard above the constant chatter and laughter that welled from the sunken cocktail area. I was positive that the last thing in the world I wanted to do was sit in my room and feel sorry for myself, so I stopped by the desk and left a wake-up call for seven thirty in the morning before hopping on the down escalator in search of a quiet corner and a

9

drink. On the lower floor I found a phone booth and used my credit card to call Kitty. I told her everything that had happened, as best I could remember. All she did at first was repeat, "Matt—you didn't! Matt—you didn't!"

"Kitty, I did," I replied hoarsely.

"What in God's name made you do it? Why didn't you just talk about the new book, turn on your charm and humility, and let Johnny stroke you?"

"I don't know. I've been doing that for three weeks and it was beginning to bore the hell out of me. I just thought I'd stir things up a little, but it kind of got away from me."

"Stir things up a *little*? I can't believe you! Do you have any idea what will happen tomorrow when this gets into the papers? I can just see the headlines now: 'World-famous mystery writer rejects Jesus as hoax!' Every leader of every Christian group in the world will unload on you! There'll be pickets outside the Century Plaza before you even crawl out of bed tomorrow morning. And wait until your beloved publishers hear the news. Things will really hit the fan. My God, you'll be the first author who ever had his books recalled!"

"No, I won't. Four cookbooks were recalled last year for containing recipes with ingredients dangerous to one's health."

"What a lovely time for some good old publishing trivia."

"Kitty, you're blowing this all out of proportion. You're getting hysterical over nothing."

"Over *nothing*, he says."

"Listen, I've already left an early wake-up call so I could play eighteen holes with Lemmon at Hillcrest. Instead, I'll get the first plane out. Be home before noon. Call you from Sky Harbor. Relax. I love you."

"I love you too, idiot. I just don't understand why you would do such a damn dumb thing. It's almost as if you try, every now and then, to destroy everything you've worked so hard to get. You're always tempting fate—skydiving, that crazy speedboat, climbing those stupid mountains—trying to see just how far you can push your luck. Do me one favor, please."

"Of course. Anything."

"You haven't done much drinking, except for one or two at dinner or a party, for a long, long time, thank God. Please don't go hiding in a bottle tonight."

"I promise. Love ya."

"Love you too, Matt."

"Kitty?"

"Yes?"

"One more thing."

"What?"

"Don't miss the Carson show tonight. Great guests!"

I hung up. Hearing a lady swear always upsets me.

The phone booth had been stifling. I wiped my brow and walked into the Plaza's downstairs lounge, a place called the Granada Room. Checked my watch. It was almost three hours before the "Tonight Show" would be aired. I ordered my favorite drink, climbed onto a stool at the empty bar, and settled back to watch prime-time television on the ancient set hanging precariously above rows of half-empty bottles.

With careful nursing of the drinks I was only on my fifth light scotch when Ed McMahon's "He-e-e-re's Johnny!" reminded me why I was sitting alone at a bar, close to midnight, a habit I had broken a long time ago. The room was now filled with bodies and noise, and the bar was three deep with insurance salesmen who had just attended what must have been a lecture on perseverance in the main ballroom, because all of them were now trying very hard to get drunk before "last call."

None of the life underwriters paid much attention to Johnny's monologue or Charles Nelson Reilly's maritime adventures or Jimmy Stewart's U.F.O.s as they guzzled their Coors and compared their sales production. Only when Donna Theodore began singing did the place quiet down enough so that one could hear these community stalwarts making comments about Donna they would have been ashamed to repeat in front of their kids.

At last, above the din, I heard Johnny introducing "one of the world's great criminal authorities as well as the most popular living detective-fiction writer of the century." I ordered another drink. As the bartender was pouring it, he gestured toward the television set and exclaimed, "That's you, isn't it?"

Right then I should have paid the bar tab and hurried upstairs to my room to watch the rest of the show. Instead, I foolishly nodded my head, and word quickly spread from drinker to drinker that the guy they were watching on Carson's show was sitting at the bar. I tried to hear what I had told Johnny about the Houston hammer murders but only managed to catch snatches above the crowd noise. Then the commercials ran, and I could feel myself becoming tense as the "More to come" billboard flashed on the screen.

More, and how! I thought.

It all came across far worse than I had expected. When I

11

finally made my announcement that I had been unable to find any acceptable proof that Jesus had risen from the dead and that billions of Christians, I believed, had been taken in by a hoax for twenty centuries, the cameraman perversely zoomed in for head shots, alternating between my unsmiling face and Johnny's perplexed frown. Even some of the hissing and booing was picked up by the boom mikes before Doc Severinsen and his orchestra mercifully put an end to the segment.

Following the final three commercials, Johnny did his usual wrap-up, first by announcing tomorrow night's guests. Then the camera slowly panned from Reilly to Stewart to Theodore as their host thanked each guest, finally focusing on the empty chair I had occupied before my hasty exit. Johnny muttered something about freedom of speech and the right of every American to express his views, no matter how distasteful they may be to the rest of us, but when the audience began to hiss again, he smiled weakly and waved good night.

I had been concentrating so intently on the program that I hadn't noticed how quiet it had become in the lounge. There was now a rather wide space around me, as if everyone had suddenly discovered that I had leprosy. I was reaching to sign the bar tab when I felt a heavy hand on my shoulder and turned to look up into the bloodshot eyes of a square-jawed giant in a denim leisure suit with sleeves rolled back almost to his elbows. He swayed back and forth uncertainly, and his accent was pure Texas.

"Pardon me, suh, but was that you who just said all those there bad things about Jesus and allowed as how us Christians are all fools for believing in him?"

I've been in a few situations during my checkerboard life when I was able to slug my way out of what had seemed to be no-win situations, but this was one confrontation I knew I couldn't win—or escape. Everyone in the room had turned in our direction except the two bartenders, who had suddenly and conveniently found things to do at the other end of the bar.

I forced a smile. "That was me, all right, but—"

The heavy monogrammed ring on his ham-size fist glinted in the light just before it exploded on the point of my jaw. I felt myself falling and thought I heard cheers as my head hit the floor. . . .

two

THE ANCIENT, LEATHERY FACE staring down at me was etched
with more lines than a geodetic map of North America. His
skin, dark as a pecan shell, contrasted vividly with silver
shoulder-length hair and a full beard that had been carefully
trimmed. Hanging from his neck was a heavy gold amulet
that swayed precariously close to my nose as the old man
leaned forward to look into my eyes.

I opened my mouth, but the voice didn't sound very much
like mine. "Who are you," I rasped, "and where am I?"

The stranger's reply was warm and friendly, and his deep,
rich voice was completely incongruous emanating from such
a frail and antique frame. "My name is Joseph, and you are
on a couch in the dining room of my humble home. Welcome, Matthias!"

Matthias? Gift of God. One of the many variations of
Matthew. I had been christened Matteo, after an Italian
grandfather on my mother's side. Always hated it, so I had
been Matt since grade school.

How did he know my name? The old boy was smiling,
nodding and extending his hand in a silent invitation for me
to sit up. When I did and looked around I almost lapsed back
into unconsciousness.

The room we were in would have done justice to any royal
palace in the world. Above was a vaulted ceiling of dark
azure on which small metallic castings of gold and silver had
been mounted to simulate the stars and planets of the heavens. The rectangular floor was completely inlaid with complex designs of multicolored stone chips, and at the mosaic's
center was a small pool being fed from the open mouth of a
life-size marble lion. Surrounding the oval pool were silver-
embossed flower boxes containing varieties of sweet-smelling
flowers that I could not identify.

The old man who called himself Joseph watched with
unconcealed amusement as I turned my head in awe and instinctively continued with my cataloging. The walls were pan-

13

eled in a dark wood, probably walnut, each serving as a backdrop for highly polished bronze and silver mirrors that hung above tables inlaid with tortoise shell on which were displayed intricate carvings of trees and animals in pale pink ivory. In each corner stood a bronze three-legged brazier banked high with coals, and through the only window, set high from the floor, I could see the tops of cypress trees swaying placidly against a sky of turquoise and copper tints.

Finally I got around to inventorying myself. The gold Omega wristwatch and wide-band wedding ring were missing. All my usual clothing was gone, replaced by a knee-length tunic that felt like linen and was belted at the waist by a thin strip of leather. Down the side of this material was a single purple stripe, approximately one inch wide, running from shoulder to hem, front and back, and underneath this simple outer garment I was wearing a soft loincloth of the same material. On the floor, beside the ornate couch, were two leather-thonged sandals.

So complete was my sense of disorientation that this all struck me as being low comedy, as if I had suddenly become part of a fraternity hazing and was finally getting repaid, in kind, for all the pranks I had pulled through the years. I began to laugh—hysterically, I'm sure. "Well, Joseph, if I've been kidnapped, whoever is doing it certainly has some class, I'll say that for them. This is a lot better than being stuffed in the trunk of an automobile."

"But you have not been kidnapped, Matthias."

"Oh, no? What is it, then? Am I dead? Did that clown really hit me so hard? And if I'm dead, where am I? Is this heaven or—?"

"You are not dead, my son."

"Please don't tell me all I'm having is a drunken dream. Kitty warned me to take it easy, and I did. Is that it, Joseph? Am I dreaming all this?"

Joseph's throaty laugh echoed off the high ceiling. "One from your own profession would have enjoyed answering that question for you."

"One from my own . . . ? Who?"

"Samuel L. Clemens. Mark Twain, as he preferred to call himself. He once wrote that life is only a vision, a dream."

Bless my encyclopedic memory. "*The Mysterious Stranger*! Read it a long time ago. Didn't Twain write that everything is a dream—God, man, the world, the sun—and that nothing exists except some empty space; that all of us are but thoughts?"

14

"Exactly."

"Please, let's forget Twain's problems and concentrate on mine. You tell me I haven't been kidnapped and I'm not dead and this is not a dream. So where am I and what am I doing here? Is someone—one of my friends—playing an expensive joke on me? That's it! Lemmon is behind this, and this time he's really outdone himself. Am I in Caesar's Palace?"

Joseph frowned. "On Capri? No, no, no."

"Not Capri," I replied sarcastically, "Vegas."

Once more Joseph laughed until his eyes watered, but he cut it short when he saw I was serious. "No, Matthias," he said softly, "this is not Las Vegas."

"Then tell me, man, where am I and what am I doing here?"

Joseph heaved a loud sigh and lowered himself to a stone bench near the couch, staring intently at his open hands as if he were trying to read his own palms. His voice was so low that I had to lean forward in order to hear his words. "My son, it is all very complicated and yet very simple. A short time ago you made some very strong pronouncements on a television program that is seen and heard by countless millions."

Sudden chill! Ice cubes down my back. Warily I asked, "You mean my statements about Jesus and the resurrection being nothing more than a hoax?"

His warm brown eyes suddenly became slits of undisguised hostility. "The world has been exposed to ideas such as yours for twenty centuries. Scoffers since the time of Nero have done everything in their power to destroy the faith of those who choose to believe in Jesus. But you, Matthias, because of the age in which you live, are more important than a hundred Neroes. And because of man's amazing progress in the science of communication, it is not unreasonable to conclude that when someone with your widespread reputation and importance speaks out, as you did, his words have an almost instantaneous impact on the entire world."

"How can the truth hurt humanity, Joseph? Shakespeare once wrote, 'While you live, tell the truth and shame the devil.' "

"Excellent advice from a brilliant mind. Of course the truth can never hurt anyone, my friend, for it is the foundation of all knowledge and the cement of all societies. That is exactly why you are here."

15

I felt absolutely helpless. "I don't understand. Where am I?"

"On that program, toward the end of your remarks, you made a specific wish, did you not?"

"I did, and I've made that same wish often, in frustration—usually in the privacy of my studio while I struggled with pieces of the Jesus puzzle that just refused to fit together."

"And what did you wish, on that program?"

"I wished that I could spend a week in the same setting and time frame that I describe in 'The Christ Commission'—Jerusalem, six years after the crucifixion, with all the important witnesses still alive and in the city for me to interrogate and investigate. I said that if I had just a week I was sure I could come up with the truth about Jesus, especially the facts involving the hoax of the empty tomb. So what?"

The old man rose, came forward, and boldly cupped my face between his large soft hands. "Matthias," he said compassionately, "your wish has come true."

"What?"

"You *are* in Jerusalem—and this year, according to your calendar, is A.D. 36, six years after the crucifixion of Jesus!"

I could hear the muted thumping of my heart in the solemn silence that followed Joseph's announcement. Only the arpeggio from water drops, falling into the pool from the immobile lion's open jaws, disturbed the hushed room. I stared incredulously into my host's calm face, searching desperately for a hint—a slightly raised eyebrow or curled lip, the blinking of an eye—anything that would assure me this was all part of a big joke, or even a nightmare. Yes, oh, yes, I'd gladly settle for a nightmare.

"I'm just dreaming all this, aren't I?" I asked weakly.

Joseph cocked his head as if I should have known better than to ask such a question. "Matthias, can you recall ever having a dream during which you *knew* you were only dreaming?"

"I don't remember."

"Of course you cannot. The subconscious mind is incapable of such rationality."

"But this is absolute madness! It's impossible!" I cried, feeling my usual self-assurance ebbing with each exchange.

"Oh, come now, you are much too wise to make such a snap judgment on so little evidence. Certainly none of the fictional heroes you create would make such an arbitrary

16

statement or they would never solve any crimes. And wasn't it Napoleon who said that impossible is a word found only in the dictionary of fools?"

By now I was beginning to think a little more coherently. From his last remark I thought I had him. "How can *you* possibly know about Napoleon, not to mention Mark Twain or the Carson show, if this is, as you say, only the early part of the first century? Aren't you a little ahead of yourself?"

The old man patted my shoulder approvingly. Then he proceeded to lecture me as patiently as a kindly professor would deal with his favorite pupil. "There are a handful of us, too few perhaps, who have been given the power to break through the boundaries of space and time whenever it is considered necessary to do so in the interest of truth. For us, neither the past nor the present nor the future actually exists. Instead, there is a present of things past, a present of things present, and a present of things future."

"That sounds like something from Saint Augustine's *Confessions*."

He patted my shoulder again. "Very good, Matthias! The range of your knowledge is more than I dared to expect. Aurelius Augustinus is one of us. In his own way he has assisted many of the world's finest minds in their struggles with the darkness of uncertainty for almost sixteen centuries. He and I are two of the older messengers, but we still manage to light our share of candles."

Messengers? Candles? Sixteen centuries? Was I hallucinating? Had I gone completely mad after the "Tonight Show"? Did someone slip a drug into my scotch at that bar? Or had I just slipped over the edge of reality into a world of biblical apparitions—ghosts I had struggled so long to capture on the pages of my unfinished manuscript that they had now captured me? Out of habit I reached for a cigarette, but my hand froze in midair.

Joseph chuckled. "Remember, son, it is A.D. 36. Even the Indians in your own hemisphere will not acquire the vice of smoking tobacco for another seventy years or so. And your cigarettes will not evolve from cigars for at least fifteen hundred years. Unfortunately, my powers do have their limitations. I am only able to transpose living tissue back and forth through time and space. Your cigarettes—Golden Lights, I believe they are called—as well as your clothing and valuables, are all back in your room at the Century Plaza."

"Holy cow! What's going to happen when they find all my

17

stuff in that room and no trace of me? And my wife? I almost forgot Kitty. She'll be frantic!"

"Do not concern yourself with such matters, Matthias. Time can be made to retreat or advance or even remain stationary. If you are fortunate, you might be able to fulfill your wish, find the truth you seek here, and still be returned to your hotel in time for breakfast. Unless . . ."

"Unless what?"

"Unless, through some unexpected occurrence beyond my ability to prevent, you should happen to take sick and die here, or . . ."

"Or what?" I didn't like the loopholes he was adding.

". . . or someone slays you to prevent your discovering the facts you seek. In either case your dead body, unfortunately, would have to remain here. I can only work, as I said, with living tissue."

Great! Born in 1923, died in 36. I needed time to think this out. Strange that the old man should have mentioned Mark Twain, who had once written the story of a tough-minded Connecticut Yankee getting cracked over the head with a crowbar in nineteenth-century Connecticut and waking up in the sixth-century England of King Arthur.

"Joseph," I asked, as casually as I could, "who are you, really?"

"You would know me by my full designation. I am certain you came across it often during the twenty years you claim to have devoted to the study of Jesus. I am always referred to as Joseph of Arimathea."

Without thinking, I blurted, "The mystery man of the Gospels!"

Joseph clutched at the folds of his tunic and scowled. "Why do you call me that?"

"Because you are. Certainly you must be aware that some of the world's greatest minds have raised serious doubts that you ever existed. Neither in Matthew, Mark, Luke, nor John does your name appear, even once, until Jesus is crucified. Then all four introduce you into their narratives as the man who goes to Pontius Pilate and petitions him for the dead body of Jesus so it can be buried before sundown, the beginning of the Sabbath. Inexplicably, despite his hatred of all Jews, Pilate releases the body to you after he has assured himself that Jesus is dead on the cross. With the help of another mystery man, Nicodemus, you take down the body, prepare it for burial, and place it in a nearby garden tomb, a tomb that someday would have been yours. Then you disap-

18

pear from the pages of biblical history, never to be mentioned again. That, my friend, is a mystery man!"

Joseph shrugged and grinned. "I am he—and your brief summary of my small efforts is quite accurate."

"Joseph, do you realize that biblical scholars have never even been able to pinpoint Arimathea's original site?"

"Biblical scholars strain too much. My birthplace and first home was in the hill country of Ephraim, Ramathaim-zophim, from which the prophet Samuel sprang."

"Then most of them are correct when they place it at what, in my age, is called Ramah or Ramla or Ramallah, depending on what book is read."

"It is of little importance. Nearly all my life has been spent here in Jerusalem, managing and expanding my many trade caravans that now cover this land from Cappadocia to Egypt."

"Joseph of Arimathea, Joseph of Arimathea . . . is it really you? Am I actually in the same room—and conversing—with the man who buried Jesus?"

"Believe it, Matthias. And you are here with me because I happen to be the only one in all Jerusalem who can help you with your wish. From your research and study you must know that I am on speaking terms with and trusted by not only the followers of Jesus but also the Roman and Jewish authorities. All are in my debt for one favor or another, and with me as your friend and guide they will at least meet and talk with you. I cannot, however, guarantee you any success in your investigation. That will be entirely up to you and your reputed abilities."

I reached out and touched his hand for the first time. "I have many questions for you too, Joseph."

"I'm certain that you do. However, should you not interview your 'witnesses,' shall we call them, in the same order that you had planned to have the Christ Commission hear their testimony in your book? I imagine, from your reputation, that there was a logical reason why you were going to present them to your readers in a specific sequence, was there not?"

"Yes. In my outline I had planned to devote each chapter in the book to the interrogation of a different witness, in the same order that these individuals played a role in Jesus' life. That way, when Rome's governor of Syria, Vitellius, later studied the transcripts of the commission hearings in order to decide on his best course of action, it would be as if he were reading about Jesus from beginning to end—along with all my readers, of course. It was purely a writing device, but it would have been a new and different way to tell the story of Jesus."

The old man extended both hands, palms open. "There, you see. You would not want to question me until after nearly all the others. I was a late arrival on that stage."

"True." I nodded. "According to my outline you would have been quite near the end in giving testimony to the Christ Commission."

"You are a clever man, Matthias. With your talent and reputation, that book would have a profound effect on millions of people."

"Not any more. Not after that Carson show. The book I wanted to write was too big for me to handle. My early years were rough ones, and my faith in Jesus pulled me through some really bad times. I wanted to pay homage to him and all he had meant to me, not with the usual sugar-coated phrases of blind faith and adoration that fill book after book but with the truth—facts, uncompromising evidence, proof, stronger than any in my detective stories, that he was indeed the Son of God. The three tribunes in my story, armed with all their skills and knowledge and power, would plan to attack each witness with unrelenting questions and cross-examinations until one of them cracked, under pressure, and confessed to being involved in the removal of the body of Jesus from his tomb in order for his followers to claim that he had risen from the dead. But, according to my plot, the best efforts of the commission would fail! None of the disciples would crack under pressure, and each testimony would only strengthen those of the others. Thus, when all the facts were compared, the Christ Commission would be forced to conclude that, based on all the evidence they had accumulated, Jesus did rise from that tomb. End of book."

Joseph had returned to his seat on the small bench. He studied me for several moments. "What went wrong with your plan?"

"At first, nothing. I was editing a small magazine in Chicago—hadn't even written my first detective novel—when I got the idea for 'The Christ Commission.' I began to study every book I could lay my hands on dealing with the life of Jesus, preparing long lists of questions that I wanted the members of the commission to ask witnesses such as Peter, Matthew, James, Pilate, Caiaphas, and you."

The old man never moved his eyes from me, only nodding

now and then to encourage me to continue and to indicate that he understood.

"All this reading and note-taking went on for three or four years before I came to two frightening conclusions. By then I had notebooks filled with questions for my tribunes to ask each witness, but in a great many cases I could find *no answers* to these questions—no logical, factual explanations that I could put in the mouths of my witnesses in order to move my book toward the ending I wanted. Now and then I would strike gold, I thought, and uncover a logical explanation to some provocative question in one book, only to find, later, another expert who completely disagreed with the first. Studying the four Gospels drove me up a wall. Inconsistencies everywhere. They couldn't even agree on the hour Jesus died! I read Voltaire and learned that he had struggled with the same problem. I continued researching and studying, and for a change of pace I wrote my first detective novel. It became a best-seller, so big that I could afford to resign from my job and spend all my time writing. That gave me more time to work on 'The Christ Commission,' and I kept at it. Somewhere, I told myself, there had to be answers; I absolutely rejected those who maintained that I had to accept many things on faith alone. Why should I spend weeks and maybe months studying all the facts and specifications before I bought an automobile or a house or a camera and leave the most important thing in my life to blind faith? That seemed ridiculous to me. It still does. Perhaps that was my weakness—a latter-day doubting Thomas who wanted to believe but needed proof. John quotes Jesus as saying, 'Except you see signs and wonders, you will not believe.' Jesus was describing me . . . and I still feel that way."

Joseph said, "Matthias, you mentioned that you came to two frightening conclusions. What were they?"

"The first was the more heartbreaking. Eventually I realized that I would *never* find sources that could supply me with acceptable and logical answers to many of the questions I wanted the Christ Commission to raise. And the second conclusion was that the only way I could possibly finish the book was to publish it as another in the long parade of anti-Christ books, something I just could not bring myself to do."

"Why not?"

"My mother, rest her soul, was a very devout woman. Even though she is gone, I loved her too much to dump dirt on her faith. And I had never before even hinted at my

21

doubts in public until I got carried away on that damn show."

Joseph looked away and shook his head. "Tell me, Matthias, what were some of the questions that proved such stumbling blocks to your efforts?"

I groaned. "Oh, Joseph, there were hundreds of them."

"For example?"

"Okay, if Jesus had actually told his disciples that he would die and then rise from the dead, why did they all flee when he was arrested in the garden and why were they so astonished when Mary Magdalene brought them news of the empty tomb? If Jesus knew that his mission on earth was to suffer and die for the people, how is it that he asked God, from the cross, why he had been forsaken? When Jesus entered Jerusalem on that Sunday before his death, were there really great multitudes to greet him and, if so, why did the Roman authorities allow such a potentially dangerous exhibition to take place? Same question for the Temple, when he threw over the tables of the money-changers. Could he have possibly done such a thing and walked away free and then returned, the next day, without being arrested by the police? More?"

Joseph nodded.

"If John the Baptist recognized Jesus as the 'Lamb of God,' why did John's followers continue their separate way long after Jesus was supposed to have risen from the dead? What really happened at that tomb on Sunday morning? Did an angel actually talk to Mary Magdalene and, if not, how did that story take hold? At Caesarea Philippi, was it Peter who finally sold Jesus on the idea that he was the Messiah, and why did the followers of Jesus decrease in number as time went on? Why didn't he perform more miracles in cosmopolitan Jerusalem, where they would have done him the most good? What did Jesus mean by 'the Kingdom of God'? If the multitude truly believed that Jesus was their Messiah, how could they possibly have allowed him to be crucified when they had demonstrated their willingness to die for lesser causes in the past? Had enough?"

He shook his head.

"What would make a man who had been so close to Jesus, for so long, finally turn on him and betray him? Did the disciples really promote the hoax of the resurrection in order to maintain their status and support from the people? Was he dead, when he was taken from the cross, or just in a coma?"

The old man started at that last question but remained silent.

"What were the real charges on which Jesus was condemned to death? Was there any collusion between the high priest, Caiaphas, and Pontius Pilate, and did they both cooperate in covering up the facts afterward? When Jesus sent out the twelve apostles to announce that the Kingdom of Heaven was at hand, did he tell them that the Son of man would come before they had completed their journey? If he did, what were their true feelings when they returned from their mission and saw that nothing had changed? Why did Matthew, Mark, and Luke ignore such a dramatic and powerful event as the raising of Lazarus from the dead in their writings? Did the Jews expect their Messiah to perform miracles? Why did the family of Jesus ignore him during his ministry? Why was Jesus the only one arrested and tried? What happened to the multitude, on the morning of his trial before Pilate, to cause them to urge his execution and free Barabbas—?"

The old man raised both hands as if in surrender. His eyes were moist and he cleared his throat several times before he spoke. "Matthias, now I can understand why your books are so popular. I'm not so certain that you could find answers to all the questions you have raised even if you spent an eternity here."

"Joseph, finding answers to every question is no longer important to me. I think the assassination of our President Kennedy made me finally realize that if the best brains of modern man, with all our technical gadgetry, cannot completely resolve the truth concerning events that happened only a few years ago in front of thousands of witnesses, how in the name of heaven can I expect to come up with factual explanations of events that happened two thousand years ago? Through the years, the key to my completion of the 'Christ Commission' manuscript has narrowed down to trying to discover the answer to only one question. If I could resolve that one to my satisfaction, all the others would become of no concern."

"Only one question?" Joseph frowned.

"Yes, one. If I had that answer I could finish the book."

"Tell me, Matthias, please."

"I agree with Paul, who went right to the heart of the matter when he said, 'If Jesus has not been raised, then our preaching is in vain and your faith is in vain.' The wish that I expressed on the Carson program hinges on Paul's state-

23

ment—and you certainly must admit that millions share my feeling but would never dare admit their doubts. Joseph, if I could satisfy myself that no one removed the body of Jesus from the tomb, your tomb, and that therefore he did rise from the dead, all other questions would become irrelevant."

Joseph appeared relieved. He walked swiftly to a side table, where he rang a small glass bell. Immediately a servant appeared in the doorway, carrying a silver tray with a flask of white wine and two goblets. The old man poured the liquid carefully, placed a filled glass in my hand, touched his own goblet to it, and raised his drink high above his head.

"May the truth set you free, my son. I have something very special for you to see, but first let us drink to your success. For the next several days I shall be near you always, acting as your guide and confidant. However, you must lead the way. The results you achieve in trying to unravel what is undoubtedly the greatest mystery in the history of the world will depend solely on your own ability, knowledge, and skill in the sifting of evidence and testimony. I shall only stand by to protect you and advise you, as best I can, if the need arises."

We sipped our wine in silence for several minutes. Then he said, "I do not envy you, Matthias. A burden larger than you may realize has now fallen on your shoulders."

I lowered my glass and looked inquiringly at the old man. He shrugged his shoulders and smiled, apparently enjoying my puzzled expression. "Do you not yet realize, Matthias, that you—alone—have now become the force you created in your mind twenty years ago?"

"I don't understand. What do you mean, Joseph?"

"You, my son, are now . . . the Christ Commission!"

three

BEFORE WE HAD DRAINED our glasses, the distant sound of
brass fanfare interrupted our toasts. Joseph placed his half-
empty goblet on the tray and said eagerly, "Put on your sandals and come with me, Matthias. I promised to show you
something very special."

"Those are the seven silver trumpets, aren't they?" I asked.
"Sounded from the Temple, four times a day, to announce
that all the faithful should pause for a moment of prayer and
reflection."

"You have researched very well, my friend. Come."

As we approached a doorway opening onto a long vine-cov-
ered portico, the old man turned to me, his eyes twinkling
with obvious relish. "Kindly close your eyes and give me
your hand so that I may lead you, and please do not look until I tell you."

I did as he requested, and with my hand in his we shuffled
forward slowly. "Joseph, this reminds me of other days," I
told him. "My wife and I always followed this routine with
our two boys on Christmas morning when they were young.
Together we would lead them downstairs into our living room
and stand them right in front of the tree, surrounded by
presents all lovingly wrapped by Kitty. The expressions of
surprise and joy on their small faces when we finally told
them they could open their eyes was our greatest Christmas
gift. With luck we'll soon be doing it again, for our grand-
children."

"You surprise me, Matthias."

"How?"

"That you anticipate, even now, celebrating the birth of
Jesus despite your personal doubts and public allegations."

"Wel-l-l, Christmas has become little more than another
happy holiday in our country. Now, people of all faiths join
in, at least in the exchanging of gifts. Except for an old-fash-
ioned carol or two, one rarely hears the name of Jesus any

25

more, above the clamor of department store crowds and the ringing of cash registers."

"Yes, I know," he said sadly.

Soon I felt a warm breeze on my face, and I knew we were standing in the sun when the light filtering through my closed eyelids changed to a bright apricot. I fought back the temptation to peek and shuffled forward for several more steps before Joseph said, "Now you may look, Matthias!"

At first the harsh desert sun blinded me. Then a loud moan escaped from my throat as I stared down from Joseph's hillside estate at the city of Jerusalem, as Jesus had known it, clinging stubbornly to a rugged plateau of sloping limestone, its uneven profile hovering high above the surrounding fringe of undulating and barren desert. I tried to drink it all in at once: the terraced palaces nearby, the purple valleys, the far-off clusters of limestone hovels with roofs that touched each other, the narrow roads and crowded alleys, and the distant gold-roofed structure I recognized instantly as the great Temple.

I don't know how long I stared before I heard Joseph's voice. "Well, what do you think of David's city?"

At first I couldn't bring myself to speak or take my eyes off the panorama that spread itself at our feet. My eyes swept from elevation to elevation, marked by blue pools, stone spires, green gardens, red-tiled roofs, marble walls and yellow towers, limestone buildings, and endless rows of palm and cypress. Finally I asked dazedly, "Why me, Joseph? With all the truly saintly and believing people in the world who would give their lives for only a minute's glance at what I'm seeing now—why me?"

My host turned and took several steps back toward the villa before he looked over his shoulder at me and said, "Perhaps someday you will understand. For now I shall leave you alone with Jerusalem and your thoughts."

Alone with Jerusalem? If this were all a dream, I had changed my mind. Now the writer in me didn't want to wake up. On steps of saffron-colored stone I descended past cultivated beds of sword lilies and anemones until I found a marble bench with an unobstructed view of the city. There I sat, chin in hand, struggling to comprehend the miracle that lay before my eyes.

The city was small, smaller than I had envisioned, although I did recall reading that it had covered only three hundred acres or so during the first century. To any stranger like myself, viewing it for the first time, Jerusalem appeared to be an invulnerable fortress, surrounded as it was by massive terra-cotta-colored walls studded with huge towers, casting shadows deep down into natural moats formed by one valley toward the east and another on the west and south. Yet, as I well knew from my research, no barriers, either natural or man-made, had ever withstood the endless parades of enemies and devout worshipers, each coming either to destroy or to honor the sanctuary of Yahweh, God of Israel and also, according to the ancient Jewish prophets, God of the entire universe.

Beneath my sandals, Jerusalem's thin soil, veined with strips of tawny flint, was tinged in shades of rose and rust and magenta. Were it not so because of its rich iron content, it could have been because of the blood that had constantly washed over this tortured land ever since David, with Joab's help, had seized the city from the Jebusites and claimed it for his people, the Israelites, centuries before the founding of either Carthage or Rome.

Many cities of the world, I've noticed, have a distinct sound of their own, and so did this one—a guttural but muffled hum interrupted frequently by a human cry or the sound of wooden wheels dancing over cobblestones or the clang of a bell drifting up from below on erratic gusts of dusty air. It was not difficult, as I sat there spellbound and bewildered, to let my mind drift backward to the amazing history of this troubled land I had studied for so long.

Twice, Babylon's King Nebuchadnezzar II had captured and pillaged Jerusalem, and his second plunder reduced the city to what Isaiah had lamented was only "a wilderness of thorns and briars," its walls reduced to rubble along with the magnificent temple built by David and Bath-sheba's son, Solomon. All citizens except the poor and the sick had been removed in chains to a strange and pagan land, where they had endured the humiliation and iniquity of slavery for over half a century, until Persia's Cyrus the Great defeated Babylon and allowed those Jews who had not forgotten, and their descendants, to return to their wasted homeland.

In time, the ruins which had been inhabited by beasts and overrun with wild vegetation were replaced by new buildings, including a small and unimpressive temple. Elders who recalled the elegance and glory of Solomon's structure wept in shame when their new house of worship was completed. Under the reign of Nehemiah the city's walls were rebuilt, and gradually the spirit of the people was rekindled, along with

27

their faith that the heavenly abode of God still existed directly above their humble earthly place.

Jerusalem, according to history, was next brutalized by the tireless armies of Alexander the Great, which surged through the defenseless land after defeating Persia and Syria on their march to Egypt. Later, Alexander's former general, Ptolemy I, who had been selected by his commander to be caretaker king of Egypt, returned to Jerusalem following Alexander's death to seize the hapless city once more, this time for his own budding empire.

Syria's Antiochus III, the Great, was the next to subject the land to foreign oppression, and a reign of terror was instituted by his successor, Antiochus Epiphanes, whose goal was the complete obliteration of every vestige of Jewish religion. He almost succeeded, forcing temple priests to burn diseased and untouchable swine on their holy altar, ordering all copies of the Jewish Law destroyed, and making both circumcision and the observance of the Sabbath a crime punishable by death.

Still the Jews endured, suffering all manner of degradation from this Syrian despot, until he went too far and destroyed their altar of sacrifice. In the revolt that followed, a suicidal band of brave and outnumbered volunteers, under Judas Maccabaeus and his brothers, who assumed leadership when he fell, achieved a blood-drenched independence for their people, a freedom that lasted only until the heel of a new power pressed down upon them—Rome.

When Caesar Augustus selected Herod, the despised Idumaean from the south, as his deputy king of all Judaea, the people of Jerusalem rebelled once more, refusing to recognize or pay homage to this non-Jew who professed to be one of them. Again the city came under siege, and Herod's armies slaughtered thousands of all ages, including the revered high priest and leader, Antigonus. After three months, the starving survivors capitulated.

Herod the Great had ruled with wile and terror for thirty-three years, taxing his subjects almost beyond their endurance in order to please his friends in Rome by building, throughout the land, great theaters and hippodromes and viaducts and palaces of marble and gold as material evidence of his supreme leadership. He also took unto himself ten wives and murdered seven members of his family, including three sons. Since Herod, in keeping with Hebrew Law, at least publicly abstained from eating forbidden meats such as swine, the common joke among the people was that it was much better to be a pig in Herod's court than his son.

When the tyrant's diseased mind and body finally expired, at the age of sixty-nine, his whispered obituary among the Jews was that "he had stolen to the throne like a fox, ruled like a tiger, and died like a dog." One of his last infamous acts, so in keeping with his character, had been to issue an order that every male child under the age of two, living in the tiny neighboring village of Bethlehem and vicinity, be put to the sword. He had heard disquieting rumors that one had been born there who was destined to rule the people as foretold by Jewish prophecy.

Now Herod was dust, as was his patron, Caésar Augustus, and the new emperor of Rome, Tiberius, had divided the little nation between two of Herod's surviving sons and a Roman governor, or procurator, who at the time was Pontius Pilate. Each enjoyed considerable freedom in governing his own allotted domain, but all three were well aware that their actions were always under the scrutiny of the powerful governor of Syria, Lucius Vitellius.

Vitellius had fascinated me since my early days of work on "The Christ Commission." Tough and capable, he was my logical choice from the beginning as the sort of leader who would not have hesitated to deputize a team of tribunes to conduct secret hearings into the activities of anyone who threatened the Pax Romana, even a crucified preacher from Nazareth and his followers, who, illogically, were increasing in number despite the death of their leader.

Lucius Vitellius was not only the governor of Syria but also the highest-ranking officer in the entire eastern sector of Rome's vast empire. From his headquarters in Antioch he commanded four of Rome's twenty-five legions, and he was responsible only to Tiberius for the maintenance of peace and stability in Syria and along its border as well as among the three million Jews to the south.

Pontius Pilate, fifth Roman procurator to the Jewish provinces of Judaea, Idumaea, and Samaria, did not seem to have overly concerned himself with the growing threat to his authority posed by the rapidly multiplying hordes of potential rebels in Jerusalem and vicinity who now called themselves Christians. His superior, Vitellius, on the other hand, realizing that the ultimate responsibility for maintaining law and order rested on his shoulders alone, would have had no compunction in taking matters into his own hands in order to learn, through his own select commission, all that he could

29

about the dead Jesus and the suspected hoax being perpetrated by his followers that he had risen from the dead.

After a long and honorable career, Lucius Vitellius had died of paralysis in A.D. 52, fortunately long before his only son, Aulus, became emperor of Rome on January 2, A.D. 69. Aulus was not the man his father was, and after only a few months in power he was dragged through the streets of Rome by Vespasian's troops and thrown into the Tiber.

Joseph's voice startled me. "What is it that you find so amusing?"

The old man had come up behind me so silently that I hadn't heard him. I shook my head. "I've just been thinking about an emperor of Rome who was dragged through the streets."

Joseph made a wry face. "And you find humor in that, Matthias?"

"No, no, only in the absurdity of my present situation, since that event will not take place for another thirty-three years if this is, as you claim, only A.D. 36. I could really tell that young man's fortune if I met him. You know: advise him to turn down the emperorship when he grew older—and stay out of Rome."

Joseph ignored my nervous flippancy. "That is something you must guard against with great care, my son," he warned. "Armed as you are with the accumulated historical knowledge of twenty centuries, you are capable of accurately prophesying the ultimate fate of nearly everyone you will meet as well as predict the future of this city. You must be extremely tactful and careful in how you interview your witnesses. One slip of your tongue and disaster will befall your mission. Do you understand?"

"I do now. I haven't had much time to think about it."

He patted my head. "I understand. Well," he asked, waving both hands at the city, "is it as you expected it to be?"

"It is—and more. Now I understand why the disciples exclaimed, 'See what manner of stones and buildings are here!' Yet, Joseph, it all looks familiar to me. I have studied so many maps and drawings depicting the Jerusalem of Jesus, in order to make my book as authentic as possible, that I could probably find my way around down there almost as well as you do."

The old man cocked his head and raised both eyebrows. "Truly, how bold a little education makes one. Let us discover how much truth there is in your boast. As I'm certain

30

you have been able to deduce, through the position of the setting sun, this villa is located in the upper city near the southwest corner. Now, to the south of us, on the other side of the wall, is a deep valley as you can see. Tell me, what is its name?"

Without hesitation I replied, "The Valley of Hinnom—sometimes called 'Gehenna' or 'Hell' because children were once burned there in sacrificial ceremonies. Later it became a permanent garbage dump always aflame."

"Excellent! And of course you recognize that magnificent edifice with its roof of gold and alabaster on the summit of the hill across the city?"

"Of course. The great Temple of the Jews. It sits on Mount Moriah and was Herod's supreme legacy to a people whose love and respect he never received. More than ten thousand engineers and laborers toiled day and night during its early stages of construction, and nearly a thousand priests received special training in the art of stone-masonry so that only their holy hands would touch the marble and mortar that eventually formed the sacred inner courts and altar. As we stand here, if this is A.D. 36, it has already been under construction for more than fifty years. Thirty-four years from now, soon after its completion, it will be destroyed completely by Titus and the legions of Rome after the Jewish revolt is suppressed in September, A.D. 70."

Joseph was furious. "Matthias, you must not do that! You must guard carefully against drawing on your knowledge of the future and using it to prophesy. That will get you into the kind of trouble from which there is no salvation."

I couldn't resist. "Jesus also prophesied the destruction of the Temple, and it got him into trouble too."

The old man's jaws tightened. He turned his back on me and pointed. "Beyond the Temple and outside the city, to the east, is a tree-covered hill. What is it called?"

"The Mount of Olives—and it is separated from the city by the Kidron Valley. The Garden of Gethsemane is there, where Jesus was taken prisoner on that Thursday night—"

"To the left, north of the Temple and almost touching it: what is that building?"

At last there was a touch of admiration in his voice. I shaded my eyes in the direction he was pointing and said, "That monstrosity was originally named Baris and erected by the Maccabeans to defend the city. Herod converted it into a sumptuous palace and renamed it Antonia after his powerful friend of earlier times, Mark Antony. Now it is a Roman fortress, under the command of Pontius Pilate, occupied by approximately a thousand troops responsible for the maintenance of law and order here. Pilate's headquarters are in Caesarea, but he usually comes to Antonia for the most important Jewish holidays, bringing with him additional troops to handle the increased number of pilgrims, who usually get carried away with patriotic zeal during their holiest feast days. It was on Antonia's pavement, in the large outer courtyard, that Jesus was brought before Pilate for trial on the morning of his crucifixion."

Joseph nodded and pointed to the area south of the Temple where dark smoke hung permanently above thatched roofs and streets clogged with humanity. "And what is that section called?"

"The lower city. The slums—where two thirds of Jerusalem's population struggle merely to survive as the poor have struggled in every city since the beginning of time. A breeding place for disease, crime, vice, and violence. More than half the infants born there die at birth, and few of them ever manage to break their bonds of poverty, if they survive, to cross over those bridges and eventually become honored residents of this upper city."

"See that valley separating the upper and lower city, running north and south? Would you by chance know its name?" the old man asked, watching me curiously.

"Yes. It is called the Valley of the Cheesemongers, but the people who live there call it the Valley of Dung. Everything from garbage to dead bodies is dumped into it, and that smoke we see is from the ever-replenished marsh of burning scum which spreads its vile stench across the entire lower city, day and night."

Joseph nodded. "Despite your regretfully accurate description, Matthias, is there anything in that area that would attract pilgrims when they come to Jerusalem?"

I tried to keep from smiling at his choice of words. "Oh, I almost forgot. For reasons I could never understand, the most ambitious and varied marketplace in the entire civilized world is located in the heart of all that squalor. Hundreds of shops and bazaars are there, as well as many fine restaurants, all catering primarily to those who come from far off to worship in the Temple."

In rapid succession I identified, for him, the hippodrome, the theater, the Hasmonean palace where Herod Antipas stayed when he visited the city, and the Pool of Siloam. Finally he grasped my shoulders in obvious frustration and turned me so that I was facing directly toward the north. "And what is that place, Matthias?"

"That mighty piece of real estate was the residence of Herod the Great. The wall enclosing the buildings is more than forty-five feet high. In one wing of the palace are at least one hundred bedchambers that Herod filled with guests, each room boasting its own bath complete with fixtures of gold and silver. Those three towers were built to defend the palace. Each soars sixty feet above the wall and is capable of holding a company of soldiers."

A sly expression crept over the old man's face. "Herod gave each tower a name, Matthias. Your extensive research did not, by any chance, uncover what he called them?"

I paused to try to collect my wits. If this was the strangest quiz show of all time, I wanted to win it. I answered slowly, "One is named . . . Hippicus, after a friend of Herod's. Another is called Phasael, after his brother, and the third is . . . is . . ."

"Ah, ha!" chortled Joseph.

"The third is called Mariamne! After the wife he said he loved the most but still executed."

The old man did not give up easily. He led me through the lower garden until we were facing toward the south. Below and slightly to our right stood an architectural eyesore. Unlike most of its graceful neighbors, the main building had two levels. "Whose place is that?" asked Joseph, in the calm tone of a good poker player.

This was going to be a shot in the dark, because I wasn't sure, but by now I realized that there were not many landmarks remaining that would be meaningful to both of us. In my most positive voice I answered, "That is the home of Caiaphas, the high priest of the Jews, the place where Jesus was finally taken, after his arrest, to be judged by the Sanhedrin. And that outer court is where Peter was recognized as he warmed himself by a fire while his master was being tried inside. That's where he denied Jesus three times, as Jesus said he would—before the cock crowed."

"One more," the old man exclaimed as if he were preparing to lay down four aces. He pointed beyond the house of Caiaphas and down the hill to a much smaller dwelling near the south wall, also two stories high, where a young man seemed to be diligently sawing wood close to the back entranceway. I decided to gamble. With my average I could afford to miss one.

"That is the place where Jesus and his disciples celebrated

their last Passover before his arrest. In the upper room, there, on Thursday night, he ate his last meal on earth."

Joseph closed his eyes. His lips were moving as if in silent prayer. Then, with his eyes still shut, he whispered, "And that boy? Who might he be?"

Now there were tears running down my face, tears I could not understand. But I *did* know who that boy was. "He lives in that house with his widowed and wealthy mother, Mary. His uncle is Peter, and later on in his life, after many trials and tribulations, he will write down the first life of Jesus. I have read his words and agonized over them hundreds of times in the past twenty years. His name is Mark—John Mark!"

We embraced for the first time and walked slowly back to the house without speaking another word.

After we had finished our dinner of tender partridge and lentils, washed down with cool Egyptian beer, I asked, "What do we do next, Joseph?"

The old man raised both hands, palms outward. "Tomorrow we begin."

"But there are several things you must explain to me first."

"Such as?"

"Language. How can I speak to these people?"

He chuckled. "Just as you have been doing with me, Matthias. Didn't you realize that we have been conversing in Aramaic, the tongue of the common man here?"

"A-A-Aramaic?"

"You can also speak fluent Greek and Hebrew and, of course, the tongue of your own country."

"English? Why? Who speaks English here when that language doesn't even exist yet?"

"No, no, not English," he replied patiently. "So far as everyone here will be concerned you are an old friend of mine—a writer of history and prose—from Rome!"

This was all getting more and more unbelievable by the minute. "I can speak Aramaic and Greek and Hebrew and Latin?"

"Whichever you need for any particular occasion. Actually, Aramaic and Greek should suffice in most cases. They are both in common use here."

"And I'm a friend of yours from Rome," I repeated uncertainly, "a writer of prose and history?"

"We are completely within the truth, Matthias," Joseph assured me. "You are already a fine writer of many volumes of

34

prose; your long unfinished manuscript, 'The Christ Commission,' most assuredly deals with history; and your late mother's roots, believe me, go back to where she said they did—Rome."

"And how do we explain my reason for being here?"

"Very easily. Many noble citizens of Rome visit this humble place in the course of a year, usually on business involving my trade caravans. So far as everyone need be concerned, you are here researching a history of the people of the eastern provinces and visiting with me because we have mutual friends in the capital. We will explain that your history is also to include the story of Israel's great men and that I had suggested you should include the story of Jesus in your work. Those who were close to Jesus will gladly confide in you, on my recommendation, in the hope that they can convert you to their cause as many other Romans of influence have been converted, both in and out of the military."

"What about the high priest of the Jews, Caiaphas?"

Joseph smiled cynically. "I am, as you probably know from your work, a member of the Sanhedrin, and my contributions to the Temple treasury each year are of some magnitude. He and his subordinates will be eager to meet with you, since they probably will suspect that you are an agent of Vitellius, or even the emperor, here under the subterfuge of writing a history but actually to review the general conditions and current relationships between them and Pilate. They will go to great lengths to keep Vitellius and Tiberius satisfied that everything here is peaceful and under control."

"How about Pilate? Why should he talk with me?"

"Same reason as Caiaphas. He has managed to keep his post here for ten years because of his friendship with Sejanus, who was the closest adviser of Tiberius. But now Sejanus is dead, strangled by orders of the senate after having been implicated in a plot to slay Tiberius. Pilate's future here has grown uncertain, to say the least. He has already stumbled several times, and he is well aware that the Jews have no qualms about going over his head, either to Vitellius or directly to Rome, if they feel mistreated. Pilate, like Caiaphas, will do anything to please you."

It sounded too pat, too easy. "But suppose he begins to suspect that my visit here, and what I might uncover concerning the Jesus matter, might implicate him in some sort of cover-up of an execution that, instead of suppressing a potentially rebellious movement, has been the cause of its great growth,

35

none of whose details he has probably ever bothered to report to Rome?"

Joseph sighed. "There is always that danger, of course. Undoubtedly he will have you followed, if your questioning of witnesses becomes too obvious, and should he decide there is a chance you might uncover facts which could jeopardize his position he would probably arrange to have you slain and your body buried where no one will ever discover it. Pilate would do anything to protect his career. Neither should you take Caiaphas lightly, or any of the original followers of Jesus. All have much to lose, should they be implicated in anything that might displease Vitellius or Rome."

More and more I was getting the feeling that solving an exotic homicide committed behind locked doors would be a simple finger exercise compared to what I was about to face. I sighed. "Well, I asked for it. Can't remember who wrote that fate's saddest joke is the granting of our wishes."

The old man laughed. "Whom do you wish to interview first?"

"If possible, the brother of Jesus—James."

Joseph nodded. "It is possible. James is in the Temple every day, praying and preaching. But why James? Would he have been the first witness called by the Christ Commission in your book?"

"Yes. He would have been their best available source of firsthand information concerning the early years of Jesus. As I mentioned on the Carson show, if the commission then called succeeding witnesses in the order that they played a major role in the life of Jesus, it would enable Vitellius—or my readers, if you will—to move through the pages of testimony as if they were reading a story from beginning to end."

"Ingenious!"

"You're very kind," I replied, before I realized what I was saying.

"Very well then, Matthias, let me show you to your quarters. There will be an orderly there to draw your bath so that you can sleep almost as comfortably as if you were in your own bed."

The bath was luxurious, the room was warm, and the bed was more than comfortable. Still I could not sleep, finally abandoning my soft mattress to pace the floor until dawn.

Soon—within a few hours—I would begin an investigation whose findings could possibly change the world. No one—not even Sherlock Holmes himself—would have slept a wink with that frightening possibility in mind.

four

HE WAS THE LARGEST specimen of manhood I had ever seen.
Wearing only a girdle of some sort of animal hide and huge
boots laced up to his immense scarred knees, his dark oiled
skin glistening with reflected light from the flaming brazier,
the giant stood so rigidly by his master's side that he could
have been cast in bronze.

"This is Shem, my bodyguard and trusted companion,"
Joseph explained after we had breakfasted on warm bread
with honey and cheese. "He will accompany us whenever we
are away from this house."

"We need a bodyguard?"

Joseph nodded regretfully. "Success, as I'm sure you have
discovered, Matthias, makes all of us prisoners of our own
achievements. Kidnapping and extortion through ransom pay-
ments are as common here as they are in your world—and
we have no police force to protect us."

"A slave?"

"No, no, if anything I am a slave of his. Shem was one of
my camel drivers, many years ago, when we were attacked
by a band of brigands near Petra. With only a broadsword he
killed nine of them; the other two he strangled. He has been
close to me ever since, my proud Nabataean, and he speaks
several languages so there will be no communication problems between us." The old man pointed to my cheeks and
neck. "You have several fresh wounds this morning, Matthias."

"Lucky I didn't cut my throat. A bronze straight razor is a
dangerous weapon, Joseph. I'll do better with practice."

"Very good. Come, let us be about our business. My carriage is ready, and Shem will drive us across the city to the
Temple, where we should find James."

Our descent from the upper city was cool and comfortable
in Joseph's sturdy but unpretentious vehicle, and the old man
kept up a running commentary along the route. Too soon,
however, the stately mansions and cedar-shaded pavement

37

were behind us and the ride became teeth-rattling torture. Swirling red dust began filling the interior of the carriage, and forward progress was frequently interrupted by sudden jarring stops. Twice I slid to the floor, and once I gave myself a nasty crack on the head when I dived back on my seat after we swerved to avoid a herd of sheep. Shem skillfully maneuvered the four galloping horses with threats from a wicked-sounding leather whip, guiding the animals along a road choked with wandering cattle, crying children, stray dogs, and hordes of pilgrims shuffling slowly toward the Temple on Mount Moriah.

Finally, from the upward tilt of the wagon, I knew we had passed the lower region of the city and were climbing. The heat was stifling and there was no breeze to dispel the fumes from smoke, rotting garbage, and human waste that now even made my eyes water. I was listening halfheartedly as Joseph tried to direct my attention to the magnificent seating structure of Herod's open theater when the carriage turned into a busy square and headed north. Moments later, because I had neglected to so much as glance at the Hasmonean palace occupied by Herod Antipas on his city visits, the old man grasped my wrists and stared into my eyes.

"Are you ill, my son?"

"No, I'm fine."

"Frightened? Having second thoughts about that wish of yours?"

"No, to both your questions. As we've been riding I've been trying to remember the most important questions I had accumulated, over the years, for my fictitious Christ Commission to ask brother James."

"And?"

I gritted my teeth and forced myself to say, "I'm ready."

But I was not ready—not prepared at all—for the overwhelming and majestic edifice that rose above me when I stepped from the carriage after Shem brought his animals to a halt before one of the gates of the Temple wall. None of the drawings and floor plans and clay models I had ever seen of Herod's wondrous structure did it justice. Speechless, I allowed Joseph to lead me through the arched entranceway, with Shem close behind, until we had entered the crowded courtyard area paved with massive blocks of polished stone. Then I clutched at the old man's arm. I had to stop. I had to give myself time to collect my wits as I tilted my head in touristlike awe at the magnificent peaks of marble and gold

38

that rose, layer upon layer, more than three hundred feet into the air.

Up there somewhere, I knew, were marble steps leading to massive doors overlaid with silver and gold, doors I would never see as a non-Jew. Those doors opened on an area called the Court of Priests, containing an altar exposed to the heavens upon which offerings and sacrifices were consummated. Two bronze doors, more than sixty feet high, opened from that altar to the Sanctuary, which could only be entered by the supreme hierarchy of Temple officials. Above the giant doors, according to my studies, hung a massive vine wrought of solid gold with a value that was incalculable. Inside the dimly lit Sanctuary, two heavy veils embroidered with precious silks of blue, purple, and scarlet were blended with fine twined linen hung from golden hooks and sockets of silver to divide the room. The front portion, called the Holy Place, held the Golden Candlesticks with Seven Branches, the Golden Altar of Incense, and the Table of Shewbread, each an important element of the priestly ceremonies.

Beyond the veils was the Holy of Holies. In Solomon's original temple it had contained the Ark of the Covenant, a gold-lidded box within which had rested the two stone tablets on which God, according to the Jews, had passed the Law to Moses. Now the small room was empty and dark, and no one remembered when or how the Ark had been lost or whether a conqueror had removed it. Still, the Holy of Holies, into which only the high priest was allowed to enter and that but once a year on Yom Kippur, the Day of Atonement, remained to every Jew of good faith the place where the Presence of God abided.

We were too close to the building to see its summit, but I had read that the Temple's exterior sloping roof was formed with huge sheets of hammered gold alternated with slabs of pink marble and pure alabaster, studded with thin spikes of gold sharpened to impale any bird crass enough to attempt to leave its droppings on the holy surface. On an immense arch, outside the wall and facing the city proper, Herod had once hung a monstrous golden eagle, but before his death he had suffered the humiliation of seeing his tasteless tribute to Rome pulled down and destroyed.

Joseph was still testing my knowledge. Leaning close to my ear so that he could be heard above the chanting, screaming, laughing humanity that pushed and shoved from all sides, he shouted, "Do you know the name of this courtyard?"

I did know and I told him. This outside court, the Court of

the Gentiles, was so spacious that it could hold more than 300,000 visitors as well as countless herds of sacrificial animals. Here, both Jew and non-Jew were allowed, free to intermingle, conduct business, or merely rest in the shade of huge cedar beams, supported by long rows of Corinthian marble columns, some fifteen feet in circumference, that completely surrounded the court along each of four walls of more than a thousand feet in length.

No non-Jew was allowed beyond the Court of the Gentiles into any of the elevated inner courts guarded by stone railings. Signs were posted prominently in Hebrew, Greek, and Latin around the entire ornate balustrade with an explicit warning: *Whoever is caught will have himself to blame for his death which follows.*

We had moved no more than a dozen hard-fought steps into the courtyard when we came upon the money-changers. Long, noisy, and impatient lines of worshipers had formed behind irregular rows of crudely built wooden tables piled high with coins. At each table, looking like details from Rembrandt's painting, sat harried officials of the Temple busily engaged in weighing and exchanging tainted foreign coins for the sacred shekels and minas which were the only pieces accepted by the priests in payment of the Temple tax and other sacred obligations. Behind each money-changer stood a bored and imperturbable guard with hairy muscled arms folded across his chest and a large wooden club dangling loosely from his wrist. Beyond the money-changers' tables stood the reeking and flimsy stalls into which were jammed thousands of sheep and rams and he-goats and lambs, their cries and smells dominating the entire area. Near the animals were cages of doves, piled precariously high, around which were gathered the poorer pilgrims who could not afford to buy larger sacrificial offerings.

From where I was standing I could count twenty-one uniformed guards stationed along the interior wall of the courtyard. To my left, high above the Temple's north wall, towered the Roman fortress of Antonia with a wall of its own overlooking the courtyard. Standing on the wall were four Roman soldiers, each dressed in their familiar helmets and body plates and armed with shield, spear, and sword, keeping a watchful eye on all of us.

"Why are you frowning, Matthias?" Joseph asked.

"Was it like this, six years ago, when Jesus was coming here?"

The old man shrugged. "It never changes."

"There were guards behind each money-changer, Temple police along the walls, and Roman soldiers overhead?"

"Yes."

"Yet Jesus, by himself, tipped over the money tables, opened the stalls and freed the animals, smashed the cages and let loose the doves—and no one laid a hand on him?"

"That is what those who were here that morning have reported. I was not witness to the event."

"But how could he? If I were to try that, right now, I'd be unconscious or dead in minutes!"

Joseph smiled mysteriously. "All the apostles were with him, that day, although they did not join in his bold act of protest against the sorry conditions that prevailed—and still do—in this house of God. Save your questions for them. Now let us find James so that you can begin your mission."

As Joseph turned to lead the way I had a sudden urge. "Let *me* show *you* the way, Joseph!"

His dark face turned pale. "*You* know where James is?"

"I think so. We have entered the courtyard from the west, judging from the sun's position. James is probably somewhere along the east wall, preaching or praying in the area called Solomon's Portico, overlooking the Kidron Valley."

The old man reached inside his tunic and removed the leather cord and gold amulet from behind his neck. "You are a joy to be with, Matthias. Here! Take this. Wear it under your tunic while you are with us. It might make your task easier." He smiled. "It may even protect you from evil spirits."

An outline of a fish had been cut into the piece's crudely hammered finish. Resting on the fish was the rough scratching of an anchor. Five Greek letters had been carved on the fish's body. It was, as I knew, one of the earliest symbols of the persecuted followers of Jesus, a predecessor to the cross that Christians later adopted.

"Do you know what the five Greek letters represent, Matthias?"

"Yes. They are the Greek word for 'fish.' Their letters also make an acrostic for the initials of the five Greek words that mean 'Jesus Christ, Son of God, Savior.'"

"And the anchor?"

He had me. I was sure I knew, but I just couldn't remember. I shook my head.

Joseph gleefully clenched his hands together in prayer and raised them toward the Temple in an exaggerated act of gratitude. "Finally I have managed to confound this brilliant

41

master of words and history. Perhaps I may be able to contribute some small share to his efforts, after all." He placed both hands on my shoulders, leaned forward, and whispered, "The anchor is our symbol of hope—hope that someday man will realize the truth that was crucified but not destroyed here in Jerusalem, six years ago."

I hefted the amulet in my hand. "It must be very valuable, Joseph, and I appreciate your generosity but I cannot accept it. I'm not one of you, not any longer."

He was insistent. "Take it anyway. Wear it as a charm—a piece of good-luck jewelry—or, if you must, just to please an old man."

I rubbed my hand softly against the rough surface. It felt warm and pliable, almost as if it were alive. Maybe it would come in handy in a tight spot. After all, some of these original Christians were pretty rough characters. This might be my passport from danger if I should ever slip and let any of them suspect that my real motive was to expose their crucified leader.

I nodded my thanks, passed the leather cord over my head, and carefully tucked the "sign of the fish" beneath my tunic, out of sight.

His return was expected at any moment.

Each day the followers of Jesus, increasing in number, gathered beneath the shaded colonnades of Solomon's Portico along the east wall of the Temple courtyard, praying and waiting. Soon he would come in glory. Maybe today!

Of course Jesus would come to the Temple first. Had not the prophet Malachi, five centuries ago, foretold that "the Lord whom you seek will suddenly come to his Temple." And where would Jesus come, within the Temple area, if not to the porch of Solomon where he had walked and taught, so often, among the people?

In my eager anticipation to find James I raced ahead of Joseph, who, with Shem protecting him, had fallen behind in his efforts to penetrate the crushing mob that spilled into the portico area from all directions. I stopped and waited. To keep from being swept forward I braced my feet on pavement recently drenched with pungent animal urine and extended my elbows to protect my ribs against the ebb and flow of man and beast. Psalm-singing pilgrims, praying priests, surly soldiers of Rome, alms-seeking cripples, crudely painted harlots, and innumerable coarse peasants, obviously from rural areas, all joined in producing a chorus of sounds and a kaleidoscope of colors that were numbing to the senses.

Joseph finally arrived at my side, breathing heavily and leaning against the sweat-covered body of Shem. "See, Matthias," he panted, "see how they wait!"

"Wait for whom?"

"For the Lord—for Jesus!"

I had to say it. "Why don't you put them out of their misery? You, more than anyone, know that they are waiting in vain."

He pretended not to hear. "We should find James near the south tower," he shouted, pointing to the tall steeple high above the fluted marble columns at the junction of the southern and eastern walls. "Come!"

Finally we reached an impregnable wall of humanity that refused to part, and I sensed that we were on the outer edges of the crowd that had gathered to hear James. Shielding my eyes with my hands, I stood on my toes until I could see a robed figure, at least two hundred feet away, gesturing wildly with his hands as he paced back and forth on a raised platform. Although the throng was comparatively quiet, I could only hear snatches of what he was saying.

". . . you have condemned and killed the just and he did not resist you . . . be patient, brothers, for the coming of the Lord . . . prepare . . . prepare . . ."

The old man tugged at my tunic. "Follow me. There is a better way." He led me to a shaded cubicle against the south wall, near the Royal Porch and away from the mob. His face was flushed and he was breathing heavily. "Let us sit here and rest. Shem will deliver James to us in due time."

A tall blue-robed figure passed nearby, miniature golden bells tinkling softly from the hem of his robe with each step. He bowed respectfully in our direction and continued on.

"A Temple priest?" I wondered aloud.

"Yes, from one of the many lower orders. More than seven thousand priests are needed to serve God and his people in this Temple, Matthias."

"Bureaucracy, even here?"

He chuckled. "Oh, yes."

"Tell me, Joseph, why do the authorities allow James, of all people, to address the crowds? Aren't they asking for more trouble?"

Joseph shrugged. "This outer court is for everyone's use, Jew and gentile alike. Any man can speak his mind here so

43

long as he does not blaspheme or incite the people to riot. As a strict observer of Jewish Law, James has as much right as anyone else to come here and be heard. You must never forget, during your inquiries, that the disciples and other close followers of Jesus are all pious Jews. This Temple, for them, is still the most holy place on earth, just as it always was for Jesus. And even if James did not accept the yoke of the Torah, including its most burdensome restrictions, he would still be allowed to speak."

"But from what I could gather, just now, he's telling that crowd that if they have patience they will soon have their Messiah!"

"Anyone can proclaim that he, or another, is the Messiah," Joseph explained patiently. "Surely your research has disclosed that the expected Messiah was to be a normal man, imbued with the spirit of God, who would come one day to deliver our people from oppression. The Messiah would not be God, only God's instrument; therefore it is not blasphemy that James practices. Scores have claimed the Messiahship for themselves or another, throughout our history. Even now, a new one appears at least once a month, quickly fading into hasty oblivion when his deeds fail to match his words. Only when one of these self-anointed charlatans attempts to organize the people into rebellion against our governing body will the high priests act, with all their power, before the wrath of Rome is visited upon our nation and the innocent are made to suffer along with the guilty."

"And what of James? Isn't he promoting his dead brother's cause in a way that could upset the establishment? Look at that crowd! If they were organized and armed they'd be tough to handle."

Joseph sighed. "Ever since he arrived in Jerusalem, soon after the crucifixion of Jesus, James has been treading an exceedingly fine line. He has attracted a large following among the common people and converted many to Jesus because of his courage and stout convictions. Fortunately, for his own safety, he has also managed to recruit several priests and Pharisees, and so the hierarchy tends to turn a deaf ear toward his more inflammatory remarks. Still, I have it on firsthand knowledge that his words have provoked the high priest on more than one occasion, and this could eventually lead to serious charges being brought against him."

"Joseph." A hoarse voice interrupted us. "Joseph, my dear friend!"

44

At the sound of his name the old man's face brightened and he leaped from the bench. I did likewise, and my knees felt weak as the onrushing figure came ever closer until I was, at last, face to face with the man whose brother I had condemned to the world as a hoax.

five

AT FIRST GLANCE, James was a disappointment to me. Watching the two old friends embrace, it was difficult to realize that the powerful head of a great trade caravan, richly costumed Joseph of Arimathea, was paying homage to this unimpressive-looking individual whose shabby appearance fell far short of the image I had built in my mind.

I was disappointed and yet I welcomed the disappointment as if his unkempt looks and self-effacing manner indicated a weakness that I might be able to exploit through my questions. I should have known better. I've been around too long to let first impressions deceive me, but they still do.

James was short in stature, like most of his countrymen, with long, untended strands of black hair hanging loosely over his jowls and down his broad back. His dark square face, dominated by a wide forehead above heavy eyebrows and light brown eyes, was framed by a full but untrimmed beard, glistening with perspiration and partially covering a barrel-like chest. The front of his faded linen tunic was frayed, exposing knees so raw and calloused from constant praying that they really did look like those of a camel, as I had remembered reading.

At last Joseph turned and extended his palm in my direction. "Here is a friend of mine, Matthias by name, from Rome. He is preparing, for his countrymen, a history of our nation and our great leaders and prophets."

James came close enough to give me a brief embrace. I opened my mouth but the voice box refused to cooperate. Could it be? Was I actually in the Temple built by Herod, and was this the brother of Jesus who had put his hands on me?

It was obvious, now that we were only at arm's length, that this man was close to exhaustion after his long and strenuous sermon to the people. His eyes were streaked with blood, and he blinked his puffy lids frequently as if it took great effort to keep them open. Even so, he smiled cordially and said,

46

"Peace be with you, Matthias, and with your work. Another history for the mighty eagle to chew? Livy's great work was sufficient for Augustus. Tiberius wants more?"

I felt like a tongue-tied first grader struggling to say his lines in a classroom play, and the question did little for my self-confidence. How did this rural and supposedly uneducated Galilean know about Rome's finest historian? I explained that Livy's supreme work had dealt primarily with Rome since its founding, but there was a strong need to tell the story of the other great people who were now part of the empire and I had selected the eastern provinces as my project.

"But how can I help you? If it is the authentic story of our nation and prophets you seek, I would suggest that you talk with them," he said, nodding toward the Temple.

I glanced at Joseph and he nodded his encouragement. "You are the brother of Jesus, are you not?"

James cocked his head and stared at me until I felt uncomfortable. "I am."

"I want to know about Jesus."

"Why?" he asked, his weary eyes roaming up and down the purple stripe on my tunic. "Jesus was never a king or a general. He never won a battle or headed a government or wrote a learned discourse. Why would you—or Rome, for that matter—care about him?"

"Forgive me, sir, but I have heard many stories about Jesus, stories that I cannot bring myself to accept, especially the rumor that he rose from the dead on the third day after his crucifixion. Because Roman authority was involved with his execution, I believe it is within my province, as a citizen and a writer, to learn the truth about this man, for your brother's life remains an enigma to many."

I paused to clear my throat. Both James and Joseph remained silent, so I continued.

"I do not wear Caesar's harness. I am not here to spread whitewash on events of the past as the laborers cover the sides of buildings to hide old scars. I seek nothing but the truth about Jesus, and as his brother you are in a unique position to supply me with information it would be impossible to learn from any other source. Will you help me, James?"

My voice trembled, but there was nothing I could do about it. Feeling absolutely helpless, I waited for his reaction, positive that I could state my case in a more diplomatic way if I had another chance.

James glared at me, and my heart sank. Then he groaned,

turned his back, limped slowly to the shaded bench, and patted the place next to him. "Come and sit, Matthias. I suspect that what you have in mind may take some time, and my bones are already tired."

I had a sudden urge to jump up and down and cheer that must have shown on my face, but Joseph's stern glance quickly calmed me. He accompanied me to the bench and sat on the other side of James while Shem continued to pace back and forth nearby, his awesome presence a perfect buffer to any strangers who might happen to come too close.

I had little expectation of learning anything about the last days in the life of Jesus, or where his body was hidden, from James. From all I had read, he had been in Nazareth during that entire final, fateful week, and anything he told me would be hearsay. I wanted only firsthand accounts. However, following the plans of my fictional Christ Commission, I needed the background of the early years, not only to have a complete picture of Jesus but also to rummage among the events of his youth in the hope that somewhere I might find a clue or two that would help me to better understand his motivations and later actions—actions that led him unswervingly to the cross, a fate he could have avoided so easily.

"Proceed with your questions, historian," James urged. "Since God is always my witness, be assured that I shall not lie to you."

I exhaled and began as tritely as any rookie detective or reporter. "What is your age?"

"I am in my thirty-ninth year."

"My information is that your parents are no longer living."

James nodded, clasping his hands loosely in his lap. "My father has been dead for many years, and my beloved mother was laid to rest, here in Jerusalem, only a year ago."

"You have other brothers and sisters?"

"Three brothers, still alive, and two sisters."

"They are still in Nazareth?"

"Or nearby there."

"Jesus was the oldest child, was he not?"

James' eyes widened with surprise that I would know such a relatively unimportant detail, but he nodded and replied, "Yes, he was my elder by three years."

I could sense that he already was becoming more relaxed and his guard was gradually lowering. Now it was up to me to keep him talking with as little prompting as possible. The truth always surfaced faster when that happened. I asked him what he could recall of the early years of Jesus.

"There is little to tell. Our father's profession was that of *naggara,* a builder of many things with wood and stone, and both Jesus and I served as his apprentices. When we were not in school we were with our father, in his shop or elsewhere in the village or countryside, repairing a roof or a plow or even, on occasions, building a house. The days were long and hard, especially in the heat of summer, yet while we were poor in material things there was always enough to eat, a soft bed at night, and faith in our God to sustain us. In truth, as our mother often said, we were wealthier and happier than Herod."

"Your family did not move to Nazareth until after Jesus was born. Why did they go there?"

"I do not know why Nazareth, except that my father had no love for the land or the people here in the south. Often we heard him say that it was easier to raise a whole forest of olive trees in Galilee than one child in Judaea."

I decided to tease him a little, hoping to relax him further. "But James, is it not true that the people of Jerusalem refer to all Galileans as fools?"

James laughed for the first time. "Worse than that, Matthias. They have even been known to inquire as to whether anything good could ever come from our village of Nazareth."

Regarding the formal education of Jesus, James explained that school in the synagogue was compulsory for all children beginning at the age of six. There they were taught the scrolls of the Law and the history of their people until the age of ten, after which they studied the Mishnah, or traditional law, for five years.

"After the age of fifteen, what teaching did Jesus receive?"

"None, except that which he imparted to himself by studying the holy scriptures whenever he was not occupied with an awl or a saw or a mallet and chisel. Jesus did the work of two, since my father's health was not good, and for him to attend the advanced rabbinical schools would have worked a great hardship on our family. Then my father died and Jesus, as the firstborn son, became the head of the family, feeding us, clothing us, and warming us with his labor, from sunrise to sundown."

I probed a little. "During those early years, what was your brother's behavior when he was near anyone with infirmities or disease in your village? Did he go out of his way to provide relief or comfort to those who were handicapped with afflictions of the mind or body?"

"No more than any of us. Nazareth is a small place. We are all our brothers' keepers. No one went hungry, no one suffered bodily curses without care and attention, and no one died unattended."

"Did he, to the best of your recollection, ever lay his hands upon anyone or recite any chant or prayer over anyone who was crippled, diseased, or without sight in an effort to make them whole again?"

"Never! If he had, the villagers would have mocked him, or worse. Still, for two days and nights while our father burned with fever, I remember Jesus sitting with him, holding his hands, ministering to his needs, and praying. Yet . . . my father died."

"And how did Jesus act when your father died?"

"As did all of us. He wept."

I tried to keep the disappointment out of my voice. "In those early years, before your father's death, was Jesus involved in any situations that seemed unusual to you?"

James closed his eyes. "During the past six years I have meditated on our youth for days on end. Only one occasion would perhaps fit your description. When Jesus had attained his twelfth year he was permitted to accompany our parents to Jerusalem and participate in the holy ceremonies, here in the Temple, for the first time. His strange behavior during those feast days was the subject of many whispered discussions between our parents for months to follow."

Suddenly I thought of my mother. Luke's narrative of the youthful Jesus in the Temple had been her favorite, one she had read to me often after she tucked her little guy into bed. Now I was about to learn exactly what had happened during that milestone event in his life.

James continued. "The journey to Jerusalem had been without incident, as was their first day's visit to the Temple, when our family delivered their Paschal lamb to the high priests for sacrifice. On the second day, after they brought their sheaf of barley to the Temple, they began their homeward journey on roads crowded with pilgrims and animals, believing that Jesus was behind in the company of our neighbors. Not until the next morning did they realize that my brother was not with any of our friends. In haste they returned to Jerusalem and searched for three days before they finally found him, in one of these cubicles, sitting as we are now, among some of our most respected rabbis and teachers, not only asking questions like the other children present but answering many, to the amazement of the crowd. As only a

50

mother would act, ours broke through the throng, seized Jesus, and angrily demanded an explanation as to why he had treated them so and caused both her and our father such anguish."

"What was his response?" I asked, almost too eagerly.

"We shall never know for a certainty. Not once was this incident ever openly discussed in our home, but just before her death my mother confided some of the details to me as best she could remember. It seems that after she had embarrassed Jesus by chastising him in the presence of the rabbis, he placed his hands on her face and asked, 'What reason had you to search for me? Could you not tell that I must needs be in the place that belongs to my Father?' However, the noise from the crowded courtyard made it difficult for her to hear, especially in her distraught condition. My father, standing close by, later told her that he believed Jesus had said, 'What reason had you to search for me? Could you not tell that I must be about my Father's business?' "

"Let me understand. Your mother believed she heard Jesus say that he must be in the place which belongs to his Father. Yet your father heard him say that he must be about his Father's business. Is that correct?"

"That is so."

"Did they later ask Jesus to repeat the actual words he had spoken?"

"If they had, I believe my mother would have told me. Apparently they sealed the matter in their hearts and never discussed it later with anyone, even him."

Cross-examination. I waved my hand at the architectural wonder before our eyes and said, "James, every Jew considers this Temple to be the place of his only god, which he also calls 'Father,' is that not true?"

"Yes."

"There was nothing unusual, then, in Jesus referring to the Temple as the place of his Father?"

"You are correct. I believe it was in part the other remark, that which my father thought he heard Jesus utter, which frightened them."

"You mean if he said that he must be about his Father's business?"

He nodded.

"But why should those words have alarmed them? Here was a young boy from the country being exposed to the sounds and excitement of a crowded Jerusalem for the first time, followed by the pomp and fervor and general bedlam

51

of this Temple during feast days. Could he not, in this atmosphere, have been so impressed by all he saw that he decided to devote his life to his Father's business, meaning religious pursuits, just as a Roman child might dream of becoming a gladiator after his first visit to the games in the Coliseum?"

James shrugged his shoulders. "Look around you, Matthias. Can you conceive of any youth from the country, one who had always been very close to his parents, suddenly deciding to abandon their love and protection in order to spend his days here, among total strangers?"

He had me. "Very well," I conceded, "but there is another strange aspect to this mysterious behavior of your brother. According to your mother, Jesus said, 'I must needs be in the place which belongs to my Father,' and according to your father he said, 'I must be about my Father's business.' Are you positive that, whichever were his true words, both parents recall his use of the word 'must'?"

"Of that I am certain."

"Doesn't that sound to you as if Jesus believed he was under a mandate or order of some kind to be in the Temple? Perhaps it was this, most of all, that concerned your parents?"

His brown eyes flickered and he placed one hand gently on my knee. "Matthias, you are a rarity among men."

"He is indeed!" contributed Joseph, who had remained silent until now.

"Why?" I asked.

"You have eyes to see—and you see. You have ears to hear—and you hear. Blessed be the womb that bore you."

"Thank you," I mumbled, but I just couldn't let that important event get closed out with only a few kind words. I probed again. "James, you were the brother closest to Jesus in age. Brothers are always confiding in each other. Didn't the two of you ever speak of this matter?"

"I plagued him often about it, as a child might do, but all he would ever discuss was the sacrifice of our lamb in the Temple."

"Oh? And how did he speak of that?"

"With great sadness and distaste for the entire ceremony. He could not forget the bloodstained robes of the priests when they presented our lamb for God's blessing by slitting its throat, draining its blood in a cup, and pouring it upon the altar. And after the animal's small body had been returned to our family, Jesus could not bring himself to assist our father with the lamb's special preparation for roasting at sunset. What he later talked about, with disgust, was the manner

52

prescribed by our laws for the hanging of the sacrificial lamb above the roasting coals."

"I don't understand."

"He said that he watched our father push two pomegranate skewers through the lamb's flesh, one through the breast and the other through the front legs, for support over the flames. These two pieces of wood, embedded to form a cross, reminded him of Rome's method of executing those who oppose the rule of Caesar. He had never forgotten the crucified rebel we had seen, a few years before, while visiting our kin in Capernaum. The sight and smell of that rotting body, its vulture-plucked flesh hanging on two crossed beams of wood, had frightened us both so much that we awoke sobbing for many nights afterward."

I rubbed my sweating palms on my tunic. Those internal alarm bells were ringing again. All my instincts warned me that I was close to uncovering something meaningful: a road sign, a clue with strange implications, a rare fossil that had never surfaced before in all my digging into the tons of literature devoted to Jesus. I couldn't let it rest. "James, is there more to this story?"

He sounded almost grateful for my persistence. Head down, he addressed the polished slab of marble beneath our feet. "Isaiah was one of our great prophets and my brother's favorite. Often, in the months that followed his Temple visit, Jesus compared what he had seen here with words from that prophet—words that I was too young to understand at that time."

"Do you recall them?"

James stood and clasped his hands to his chest. His voice broke when he replied, "They are burned in my heart, forever. Isaiah said, when describing the Messiah who was to come to save the Jews, 'He was oppressed, and he was afflicted, yet he opened not his mouth: he is brought as a lamb to the slaughter, and as a sheep before her shearers is dumb, so he openeth not his mouth.' "

I felt the hair rising on the back of my neck. "James, was he comparing your family's sacrificial lamb to . . . a Roman crucifixion and also to Isaiah's description of the Jewish Messiah?"

There was no reply, and for good reason. Stern, bold, fiery James, respected and feared by all manner of men, had buried his face in his hands and was sobbing! Joseph leaped to his feet and wrapped his arms around his slumping friend while Shem stood by, scowling at me again.

No more than a few minutes passed before James and Joseph returned to the bench. I was ready with an apology, but the proud and defiant look on James' face warned me that it would be wiser to ignore what had happened and proceed. I changed the subject. "Jesus never took himself a wife?"

His voice was growing more hoarse. "No, and whenever the elders of our village chided him on his bachelorhood, reminding him of the prophet's words that the Lord God had said it was not good for man to be alone, Jesus would laugh and reply that since he was wed to an entire household he would certainly be stoned to death for adultery if he were to offer himself to another."

"And yet the day came when he divorced himself from his entire family, is that not true?"

James nodded.

"What caused this great change to take place in your brother's life?"

"It happened in his thirty-fourth year. By then our other brothers and I had all married and were living with our families in the village while Jesus remained with our mother and sisters. One evening he came to my door and invited me to walk with him, a strange request, since he usually spent so many hours alone in the nearby hills, when he was not at his bench, that he had become the butt of many jokes among the people. As we walked, he with his hand on my shoulder, Jesus asked that I look after our mother and sisters so that he might go to hear John the Baptist, who was preaching at Bethabara, no more than a day's journey from Nazareth."

"This was he who eventually died under the blade of Herod Antipas?"

"The same. More than nine hundred years ago one of our greatest prophets, Elijah, worked many wonders against the evil forces of Queen Jezebel and Ahab before he was swept up into heaven by a whirlwind. It has been the belief of our people that someday Elijah would reappear to prepare and restore our land for the coming of the Lord. Some were now claiming that John was Elijah, while others believed that he was only a forerunner for Elijah, who was yet to come. Jesus wanted to hear what John was saying to the multitudes on the banks of the river."

This was as good a time as any to clarify a definition that had always puzzled me in its scores of variations. "James," I asked, "help me to understand. What is a prophet?"

"A prophet is a messenger from God, the word in Hebrew

meaning 'one who speaks for another.' He can be rich or destitute, educated or unlearned, from noble ranks or the fields. Elijah was a poor shepherd, Isaiah was a teacher, and Jeremiah came from a priestly family. Prophets always speak with no concern for their own welfare or safety, warning men and nations, kings and beggars, that only doom and misery await those who turn away from the laws of God and fall into habits of evil and sin. No new prophet had come forth unto Israel in nearly two hundred years, and so John's appearance had caused great joy among the people while creating apprehension in Herod, the priests, and others in authority."

"Jesus went to hear this prophet?"

"He did, but he failed to return within the time he had allotted, and my mother was soon beside herself with worry. Finally I went in search of John, who told me that he remembered Jesus when he came and asked to be baptized although he had not seen him afterward."

"Describe this service that Jesus asked John to perform for him."

"The baptism? John was proclaiming that everyone should repent, change their ways, and cleanse their mind and soul and body in order to make themselves ready for the Kingdom of Heaven that was close at hand. To prepare for that day when the anointed one would come to judge all mankind, each of the faithful who came to John on the banks of the Jordan was immersed in its water as a symbol of his willingness to receive the ... the ... "

"The Jewish Messiah? He who would bring universal peace and under whom all nations would serve in a dominion that was from sea to sea?"

James appeared shocked by my words. "How is it that a Roman is acquainted with words from an ancient psalm of the Jews?"

Behind James I saw Joseph's look of concern. "To write the history of your people," I replied, "without studying your psalms and their meanings would be an insult to all Jews."

James appeared satisfied. "Then you must know, Matthias, that the words you repeated were sung in tribute to our great King Solomon, who ruled this land nearly a thousand years ago."

"And those words from that psalm of old had no special significance to the crowds who flocked to hear John announce, day after day, that the Kingdom of Heaven was at hand—a kingdom that would certainly need a king?"

55

He knew how to handle himself. Instead of taking offense at my obvious sarcasm he merely shrugged those broad shoulders and replied, "Who can ever know what is in the hearts and minds of an oppressed people?"

"Finally Jesus returned home from his wanderings?"

"Yes, after more than forty days had passed. His appearance was so frightening that none of us had any heart to chastise him for remaining away so long without so much as a word. His clothes were covered with thistles and half torn from his body, his hair was a mass of snarls, his face and hands were burned nearly black from the sun, his eyes were little more than two glowing cinders, and his body was so thin we scarcely knew him."

"Did he explain the cause of his condition and long absence?"

"He told us that for two days he had listened to John preach on the banks of the Jordan before coming forth to be baptized. Afterward, almost as if he had been given leave of his senses, he found himself wandering in the desert and wilderness beyond the river. There he remained for weeks, with no food and little water, drunk not with wine but the words of John that echoed as loud as thunder, over and over inside his head: 'Repent ye: for the Kingdom of Heaven is at hand. . . . I baptize you people in water unto repentance: but he that cometh after me is mightier than I, whose shoe's latchet I am not worthy to unloose, and he shall baptize you with the Holy Ghost, and with fire!' "

"Jesus had returned directly to Nazareth after his time in the wilderness?"

"No. He found himself one day, after being alone so long, walking along the banks of the Jordan again until he came upon John. Ashamed because of his appearance, he remained on the outskirts of the crowd and listened, but even from that great distance John saw him, pointed in his direction, and shouted, 'Behold, there is the lamb of God! Look, this is he who takes away the sin of the world!' Upon hearing those words, Jesus said he turned and ran until he fell from exhaustion, and the next thing he could remember was arriving at the door of our mother's house, in Nazareth."

I stood. Looking down on him, I tried to choose my words very carefully. "James, do you know whether your brother attached any special significance to John's acclaiming him as the lamb of God, recalling Isaiah's prophecy and how he felt regarding the lamb that was sacrificed and skewered on a cross of wood at his first Passover?"

He answered immediately, as if the same idea had often entered his mind. "I do not know. In retrospect, it is easier to see and understand things which, when they take place, provide no inkling of their hidden meanings."

"When his health returned, did Jesus once again resume his trade?"

"Only for a short while—until news came that John had been arrested by Herod and was a prisoner in the castle at Machaerus. Soon afterward my mother came to my house in tears and begged that I return with her to reason with Jesus, who had not eaten or lifted a hammer or saw since he had been told of John's capture. I found him sitting on his cot, his head bowed. I called his name several times but received no response. Then I seized him by both shoulders and shook him gently, and when he looked up at me I could see he was weeping. He leaned forward and embraced me around my waist, and I could feel his body trembling against mine. Then he rose, kissed me on both cheeks, and said, 'James, tend to our mother and sisters. I must go. I must continue that which John has begun.' "

"He used the word 'must' again?"

"He did. Then he kissed my mother and sisters and departed from us before we could convince him to stay. He took nothing with him—only the clothes on his back."

"Do you know where he went?"

"Word soon came that he was going from village to village, preaching the word of John and calling for repentance by all in preparation for the coming Kingdom of Heaven. Most of the villagers, as well as my brothers, gossiped that the time he had spent in the desert sun, after John had baptized him, must have affected his mind. For more than two months not a single message came from him, and our concern for his safety, with Herod's spies everywhere, grew each day. Then one afternoon he returned to the village, and on the following day, our Sabbath, he accompanied us to the synagogue. I shall never forget that morning."

That famous day of confrontation when Jesus shocked the congregation, the village, and his family. "Please tell me," I urged.

"The service of worship went on as usual during the first part. We were led in prayer by the minister, we recited the Shema, and the benedictions were spoken. After the raising of hands and the singing of certain eulogies, the minister approached the ark and withdrew a roll of Law. This was the moment for the words of our prophets to be read to us by

57

one selected from the people. The minister looked around for a brief moment, stepped down among us, and handed the scroll to Jesus. There was some grumbling and even a few shouts from those who looked with great disfavor on Jesus' being so honored after having abandoned his mother and family. I was sitting next to him, and I remember feeling a sudden premonition of danger. Apparently my mother also felt it, for I caught sight of her, in the women's section, shaking her head at me as if to give me a sign. I knew not what to do."

James inhaled deeply before continuing.

"Jesus clutched the scroll to his breast and closed his eyes. Then he walked deliberately to the front of the ark. Carefully he unrolled the scroll and read words from his favorite, Isaiah: 'The Spirit of the Lord God is upon me; because the Lord hath anointed me to preach good tidings unto the meek; he hath sent me to bind up the broken-hearted, to proclaim liberty to the captives . . . to proclaim the acceptable year of the Lord, and the day of vengeance of our God.' "

Those special words! Biblical scholars had argued and discussed the possibility of their actual use on that Sabbath morning for centuries. I had to find out. "Let me interrupt you for a moment, James. Were there a great number of scrolls from which your minister could have selected that which was to be read?"

"There are many scrolls; however, the minister has no choice. Our sacred texts are divided into more than one hundred and seventy segments, one to be read on each Sabbath, always in sequence until all are read, after which they are repeated. Three years and more are required to complete a single cycle."

"So this particular text which Jesus delivered was neither chosen by the minister nor by Jesus but was, indeed, the proper one for that Sabbath?"

"That is correct. When Jesus completed his reading, he handed the open scroll back to the minister and returned to my side. All eyes were upon him, and the synagogue had grown as quiet as a tomb. Jesus raised his head and in a strong voice that could be heard by everyone present he announced, 'This day is this scripture fulfilled in your ears!' "

James' voice had subsided to nearly a whisper, and I had difficulty hearing him above the clamor of the courtyard.

"I remember a woman's scream, her cry reviving the crowd, who had been transfixed by the announcement from my brother's lips. The people jumped to their feet, and from the rear I heard a voice ask, 'Who is this man who pretends to be our savior?' Another asked, 'Is this not the carpenter, the son of Mary, the brother of James and Joses and of Judas and Simon? Are not his sisters here with us?' "

I couldn't help noticing the intense concentration with which Joseph of Arimathea was hanging on every word—as if he had never heard this particular incident in the life of Jesus described before. "What did Jesus do?" he asked eagerly; then he looked toward me and murmured, "I'm sorry."

James smiled at the old man and continued. "Jesus was still on his feet, and although I dared not look at him I heard his deep voice, bold and unafraid. 'A prophet has no honor in his own country, and among his own kin, and in his own house.' His words both shocked and angered me. All of us were included in his condemnation. Suddenly the people rushed toward him, throwing me to the floor. As they seized my brother I could still hear him shouting something about our prophets Elijah and Elisha, and his words seemed to further incite the mob. While still on my knees I saw him break free from many hands and run behind the ark. Then he was gone, through the back doorway, with the crowd in pursuit. I hurried to my mother, who had collapsed, lifted her into my arms, and carried her home. Later we learned that the people had tried to push Jesus from the cliff at the edge of our village but he escaped."

I feigned ignorance. "What exactly had Jesus said to offend them to such a degree that they tried to take his life?"

James inhaled and clapped his hands together. "He was one of us, a common man of the earth who earned his daily bread with the sweat of his brow and the muscles of his back. He had grown up in Nazareth, played in our streets, and the only schooling he had ever received had been from the villagers themselves, in our small synagogue that had no rabbi. How could they possibly accept his outrageous announcement that God had anointed him, of all the great and wise men in Israel, to be his special messenger of liberty and vengeance—the Messiah?"

"And you?" I asked. "Did you believe he was something special? If not the Messiah, at least a prophet perhaps, such as John or Elijah or the others who had come before?"

"No. Jesus was my brother, whom I had always loved and respected—at least until that morning, when he rebuked all of us. Then I was glad to be rid of him, despite my mother's anguish when he ran off."

"Later, did you or any of the family go to hear him preach while he traveled through Galilee?"

"Only once, after we had received a visit from four men of the Law, called Pharisees, from the Temple here. They asked many questions about him, just as you have today, and we became fearful that if Herod did not move against him there was now a new danger that he might be called to explain his words and actions before the Sanhedrin, our chief judicial court. Although the Sanhedrin has no authority in Galilee, only here in the province of Judaea, my mother was desperate to warn Jesus that he was in grave trouble. When we heard that he was in nearby Capernaum she prevailed on my brother and me to accompany her there, so that she could plead with him to return home before it was too late."

Another famous scene, one that had been discussed and sermonized and twisted to fit various points of view so often, through the years, that it had lost all sense of reality. "Did Jesus respond to your warning?" I asked.

"He would not even see us! He was preaching in a house that was so filled with fishermen and the poor of the streets and harbor that the crowd overflowed into the yard so that we were unable to enter. When I sent word in to him that his mother and brothers were outside, he replied in a voice that all could hear, 'Who are my mother and my brothers? Behold, here are my mother and my brothers, for whoever does the will of God, he is my brother and sister and mother.' That time my mother did not cry. She grasped my arm and said, 'Let us go home.' "

"Did Jesus ever return to Nazareth?"

"Only once more. He passed through the village to pay his respects to our mother, several months later. By then he had gathered a small following of disciples, who were with him."

"How was he received by your family?"

"As always, my mother and sisters treated him with special care, love, and attention while my brothers and I, when the women were not present, accorded him nothing but disrespect. We taunted him, saying that we had heard many tales of how he performed miracles by healing the lame, making the blind see again, and even driving out evil spirits. We told him that we believed none of the stories. We even challenged him, saying that if he truly did such wondrous things he should not keep them a secret by performing in the smallest of villages but should go to Jerusalem so that the great crowds, as well as the Temple priests, would see his mighty works and know that he spoke as a true prophet of God."

"And what did Jesus say to you?"

"His only reply was that his time had not yet come. We laughed and jeered and left him to himself."

Now we were getting close to the most important question James would hear from me. I moved to return to my seat but instead, for some inexplicable reason, I bent one knee and knelt in front of him, boldly placing both my hands in his lap. "James, I believe you said you were married by this time. Had there been no family responsibilities, would you have considered joining your brother's group?"

"No!" he roared, sounding as he had from the platform. "While I endeavored, as best I could, to live my life within the laws of our Torah and practice the injunctions of our prophets, Jesus, according to those who saw and heard him, violated some of our most sacred laws openly. He drank and ate with publicans and harlots, he violated our Sabbath with disdain, he derided our great scribes and the wisdom of the Pharisees, he washed not his hands before the breaking of bread, and—worst of all—he dared to *forgive* sinners! Not even Moses or Abraham or Elijah had that power. Only our Father in heaven can remove the curse of sin. I was convinced that Jesus was on a path that would lead to his shame and destruction, and I wanted no part of it."

Beads of perspiration dropped from the face of James onto my wrists. His lower lip was quivering, and deep furrows of anguish creased his forehead. I almost hated myself for putting him through the torture of recollection that he was willingly enduring as if it were some sort of penance. "You never saw your brother bring anyone back from the dead or cure the affliction of blindness or cause a cripple to walk again or make a leper whole, as others claimed he did?"

"Never."

"Did you ever see him perform any feat which you might consider a miracle, something contrary to the normal laws of nature?"

"No."

"Did you ever hear him claim to be the Messiah, that Jewish savior and king for whom you all wait?"

"No."

"Did you ever hear him say that he was the Son of God?"

"No."

"You were not with him during that last week in Jerusalem, prior to his execution?"

"No. I was in Nazareth with our family."

61

"Then you were not with him in the garden on the night he was taken prisoner?"

"No."

"You were not present when he was tried and condemned to death by your respected jury of eminent citizens, the Sanhedrin?"

"No."

"You were not among the crowd, there in the yard of the Antonia Fortress, on the morning when Pilate tried him, scourged him, and condemned him to die on the cross?"

"No."

"You did not observe his crucifixion?"

"No," he sobbed.

"You did not assist this man, Joseph, in the burial?"

"No."

I took hold of both his hands and looked directly up into his eyes. "Yet even now, here in this courtyard, the followers of your brother gather and recruit each day, and they are multiplying in numbers faster than flies. And who is it that is being acclaimed and honored as one of the leaders of this mob, six years after the death of Jesus? You, James! You!"

He lowered his eyes.

"While your brother stirred up the people and broke the laws, you were so ashamed of him that you would have nothing to do with him. But ever since his crucifixion you have risked the same punishment that he received by preaching his philosophy in the streets and even here, in your Temple, under the very noses of those who tried and condemned him! You refused to join him while he lived and preached, you said, because you were so convinced that he was on a path that would lead to his shame and destruction. Why are *you* now on that same path, James?"

There was no response.

"Why, James?"

Still no response. I closed my eyes in frustration. James had already endured too much in his Jerusalem years to be intimidated by a mere writer when the ever-present threat of Roman swords and priestly injunctions had not affected him.

Suddenly I felt both his hands on my head, his strong fingers and thumbs cradling my neck as if I were a child. When I opened my eyes, his were only a few inches away. There was not the slightest hint of anger or hate in his fatigue-lined face for the grilling I had just given him—only compassion.

"Matthias, in truth you have not asked all these questions

for a mere history book, have you? Can it be that your own peace of mind and soul wait on my reply?"

I could feel the blood pounding in my temples. I tried to answer but couldn't.

"Matthias, is it your intention to question others about Jesus?"

I nodded.

"Very well. Let us meet again, you and I, after you have finished speaking with all of them. By then you will understand, I am certain, far more than you do now and you will also be better prepared for my answer to your last question."

He kissed me on the forehead, released me, and turned to embrace Joseph. Then he was gone, but not before he turned and shouted, above the tumult around him, a single word.

"Mizpah!"

The Lord watch between me and thee, when we are absent one from another.

Emotionally drained, I turned to the old man from Arimathea and said wearily, "Joseph, please take me home."

six

JERUSALEM HAD THE PERFECT community wake-up service. Every morning, as soon as the rising sun's first shaft of light appeared on the distant eastern horizon beyond the lavender and gray ranges of Moab and Gilead, surging blasts of priestly trumpets from the Temple announced the birth of a new day. Not even the soundest sleeper in the most remote corner of the walled city could ignore their strident and persistent message that the first hour had commenced. Those horns were all the reveille I needed on the morning following my first visit to the Temple.

Matthew, the next on my list of "witnesses," proved as easy to locate as James. His habits were well known to Joseph, and we found him, soon after sunrise, exactly where the old man said he would be—praying in the Garden of Gethsemane.

Outside the city's east wall, jagged limestone cliffs descended several hundred feet into the Valley of Kidron. Beyond the valley sprawled a green uneven ridge, the Mount of Olives. The garden lay at the foot of the mount, only a short walk across a stone bridge from the city's gates yet concealed from the curious eyes of passersby and those looking down from the Temple courtyard by thick clusters of cypress, fig, almond, pomegranate, and—especially—olive trees, from which it had derived its name, Gethsemane, meaning "olive press."

Leaving Shem with the carriage, Joseph and I entered the garden, dodging several low-hanging silver-leafed olive boughs as we made our way along a narrow path that wormed its way between bushes and partially submerged boulders. Untended beds of flowers had overflowed their once prim borders and now struggled for survival against lush dew-covered grass that grew almost to our knees, while dead lower branches of fir trees still clung tenaciously to living green trunks. Above our heads each tree seemed to be sheltering its own family of swallows, which were all letting us know, with shrill angry cries, that they did not appreciate this early morning intrusion.

"Jesus came here often, didn't he, Joseph?"

"Yes. It was his favorite place except for the hills of Nazareth. He spent many hours here, alone and with his flock, praying, instructing, or just refreshing himself after the heat of the city."

"He came here once too often."

The old man refused to be baited. "You mean on that night when he was arrested? Matthias, never forget that he was here, that evening, of his own free will. Knowing the grave danger he was in, he could have easily vanished north into Galilee and escaped from the clutches of all his enemies. But those are things you must learn for yourself, my son."

Shem had now joined us, walking several paces behind as we moved through the garden, which was more orchard than anything else. Suddenly the old man halted and placed his hand against my chest. "Look!" he whispered.

Up ahead and to our right was a small clearing. In its center was a kneeling figure with head raised toward the heavens and hands clasped tightly together as they rested on a large chalky boulder.

"Remain here," Joseph instructed. "Let me go to him alone so as not to startle him. I'll inform him of the purpose of your mission, and if he is willing to talk with you I shall signal."

Joseph approached the praying apostle hesitantly until Matthew turned and saw his old friend. His face immediately brightened, and he bowed his head once more before leaping to his feet. Watching from my hiding place as the two old friends greeted each other, I had all I could do to keep from breaking and running. But to where? How could I get from *here* back to Phoenix?

Finally I could see Joseph pointing in my direction. Matthew was nodding his head, pausing occasionally to interrupt the old man. Then he raised his hands, palms upward, and I heard Joseph call my name. I stumbled twice before reaching the clearing.

Matthew's head was crowned with short brown hair that barely reached his frail shoulders. His beard was neatly trimmed, covering an angular jaw below exceedingly high and protruding cheekbones, and his widely spaced gray eyes seemed unnaturally large against a skin so fair that it appeared never to have been exposed to the merciless Judaean wind and sun. A light-blue woolen cloak was draped loosely over his tall frame, partially covering a white linen tunic that parted only at his ankles to expose wooden sandals laced with heavy cord. He came forward to greet me, both hands extended in friendly greeting.

"You have a good name, Matthias."

I smiled feebly and mumbled, "You too, Matthew."

"Joseph tells me that you are writing a history of the Jews and wish to include the role that Jesus played in our lives."

"Yes," I replied, "and I am also seeking the truth about his death."

Matthew smiled indulgently. "But Jesus is not dead. That fact you can verify without my help. Only a few hundred cubits from here, beyond the wall to the west of the city, is the place where he was buried. Have Joseph take you there so that you may view the empty tomb with your own eyes."

If I wasn't careful I could doom this interview before it ever began. "Forgive me, Matthew, but even when I see the tomb it will not be enough to satisfy me. Like your friend Thomas, I need more facts, more verification. To me an empty tomb is just a hole in the ground. It proves nothing. Joseph said that you might help me in my search for the truth, wherever it may lead."

Matthew hesitated and then gestured toward Joseph. "You have a powerful advocate here in the Arimathean. However"—his eyes twinkled momentarily—"you must be on your guard with him, I warn you. Many doubters such as yourself have fallen under his spell and are now among our most loyal supporters. I shall be happy to answer your questions; however, all of us who live for Jesus must support ourselves as well as contribute to the central fund, and so I must be in the market by the third hour, to assist Obadiah the silversmith after he opens his shop for business. The poor man is an excellent craftsman but a terrible keeper of ledgers, and he was badly in need of a bookkeeper before we found each other."

"I am most grateful for your assistance. Let us sit here and be comfortable while we talk." I gestured toward the huge flat-topped boulder alongside which I had seen Matthew praying. I turned to sit—

"No!" they both screamed, their anguished cries echoing through the garden.

I froze, in a half crouch. Feeling silly, I stood erect again and looked toward Joseph for guidance. Instead, Matthew came forward and grasped my hand.

"Forgive us, Matthias. How were you to know that this

66

common-looking slab of stone is sacred to us? It was on this rock that Jesus prayed on his last night here before he was arrested."

I reached down and rubbed my hand against the hard chalky surface, remembering the idealistic paintings I had seen of Jesus praying in the garden. White dust still clung to my moist palm as we followed Matthew to a smooth patch of grass beneath an ancient olive tree and made ourselves comfortable. Shem moved nearer, squatting close to the path up which we had come, his dark body slowly turning in full circles as he constantly studied the shifting shadows within the garden. I began from square one. Although we had just been introduced, I asked nervously, "What are you called?"

Matthew smiled. "That depends on who is addressing me, friend or foe. I am Matthew, sometimes called Levi, a son of Alpheus of Capernaum."

"And what is your age?"

"This is my forty-seventh year."

"You were a close friend of Jesus?"

"I was the fifth to be called by him after he began to teach in Capernaum, where I lived and worked."

I purposely worded my next question as I did to test his reaction. "From what I've been told, I understand that you deserted your prosperous post of tax collector, to which you had been appointed by the tetrarch of Galilee, Herod Antipas, to go with Jesus. Why would any man abandon family, friends, and profession to run off with a penniless band of gypsies?"

The apostle stared at me with more disbelief than anger. Finally he began to chuckle, half to himself. "Matthias, certainly the source who has supplied you with the other facts about me must have also informed you that what you generously refer to as my profession is considered by our people to be a more sinful life than that of a harlot. I was not only a tax collector but the lowest of tax collectors, a little *mokhes*, which is the name of one who stands in the toll gate himself, rather than hire others to do his dirty work. By personally suffering the taunts and curses of all who passed, I was able to keep a larger percentage of the tolls before I remitted the balance to Herod, who in turn passed on a share to your emperor in Rome. Friends I had none, except my own family and other tax collectors from nearby."

"But you were one of the wealthiest men in Capernaum."

"Many of us pay too much for our gold. As a publican I was forbidden to bear my money to the Temple for any pur-

67

pose. I was not allowed to serve as judge, or even a witness, in any proceedings, and there is hardly a rabbi living who does not preach that repentance for publicans is a waste of time in the eyes of God."

"Then why did you become a tax collector?"

He shrugged. "Who can say why we become what we are? Why do you write? For me, not competent in any craft or trade, tax collecting was a living."

"How did you first come in contact with Jesus?"

"He had come to Capernaum alone, bringing with him a message of hope for our people the likes of which we had never heard. Sometimes he would speak in our small synagogue, but more often he was on the waterfront, from sunrise to sundown, teaching and comforting the poor and the sick of the harbor whose ignorance of the laws of Moses made them feel unworthy to enter our neighborhood house of God. One morning, when he was close by, I left my booth unattended and went to listen to him. The words he spoke, that day, changed my life forever."

"His words had such power?"

"Yes. I had abandoned all hope of ever erasing my sin of being a publican from God's ledger. But here was a man who said there was still a chance for me and for all other miserable sinners. He told those of us who crowded close to him that the Kingdom of God was at hand and that all of us—all of us!—could prepare for that day. Salvation, he taught, was available to everyone, and even the worst of sinners could be born again in the eyes of God, providing they acquired the faith and humility of little children. He even taught us what to say, in our prayer for salvation, and he warned us always to pray in secret, not like the hypocrites who stand in synagogues where they may be seen and heard by men. Their reward, he promised, would only come from men, while ours would come from the Father who, seeing our needs in secret, would reward us openly."

"When did you become one of his followers?"

"Soon thereafter. I went to hear him whenever I could, hoping I might find the courage to approach him—touch him—have him speak a few words to me. But always my shame held me back. Then one morning, after Jesus had preached to a large crowd from the deck of a small boat, he passed near my booth with four of his followers. He came close—so close I could have reached out and touched his robe. I struggled to say what was in my heart, but the words stuck in my throat. As he walked away I began to weep, certain that I would never again have such an opportunity. Suddenly he stopped and turned until he was facing me. I shall never forget that look of love and sympathy and sadness in his gentle brown eyes, as if he understood everything I was thinking. He motioned to me and said only, 'Follow me!' "

"And what did you do?" I heard myself prompting, unnecessarily.

"I left everything behind—my records, the money I had collected that day, my home, my brothers and parents—and remained with him for the rest of his earthly life until that terrible night he was arrested here, in this garden."

"Have you any regrets?"

"Regrets? I have many. That I became a coward and fled with the others, as Jesus said we would, when he was seized. That I did not fully understand the meaning of all his parables and prophecies when he first spoke them. That I did not fight, with everything I had in me, against those who sought to discredit him almost from the first. That I did not comfort him more or serve him better. Most of all that I was too blind and ignorant to recognize him as the Son of God until after he was crucified. Still, my chance will come again."

"You, too, expect him to return?"

"Matthias, he has never departed. He is with me always. He guides me even this moment, as I speak with you. He promised that when we were brought before gentiles, for his sake, we were to give no thought as to the words we spoke, for they would be given us in that same hour by the spirit of our Father, who would speak through us."

Somehow the meaning seemed different, coming directly from Matthew, than it had read in any of the biblical translations I owned. "He is speaking through you now?"

"Yes. I believe it!"

"From all I have been able to learn, Jesus was unquestionably a wise man. If that is true, why did he recruit the most despised of Jews, a tax collector, to help him in his mission? Were you not a millstone around his neck?"

"That very same evening of the day I was called, before I had time to ponder such questions, I learned of his plans for me directly from his own lips."

"Will you share them with me?"

"After the sun had set, on that day I became a follower, I tendered a feast in my home to celebrate the most happy event of my life. Jesus and his few disciples were my guests of honor. After we had dined and the hour had grown late, three respected men of the law, Pharisees, passed through the

69

crowd and approached the disciples Peter, Andrew, James, and John. They inquired of the four why their master made himself unclean by eating in my defiled house among publicans and sinners. Jesus, who was sitting next to me, overheard their question and raised both hands until the room was silent. He repeated what the Pharisees had asked, loud enough for all to hear, and then he answered by saying, 'Those that are whole do not need a physician, but they that are sick do. Go and learn what is meant by the prophet who said, "I will have mercy and not sacrifice, for I have not come to call the righteous, but sinners to repentance." ' "

"Did that satisfy the Pharisees?"

Matthew sighed. "They are never satisfied. They murmured among themselves, and then the boldest asked Jesus directly, 'Why do the disciples of John the Baptist fast often and make prayers, as do we and our disciples, while you and yours fast not?' I remember Jesus replying patiently, 'Can you make the children of the bedchamber fast, while the bridegroom is with them? As long as they have the bridegroom with them they cannot fast. But the days will come when the bridegroom shall be taken away from them, and then shall they fast in those days.' Hearing this the Pharisees quickly departed from my home."

"You are positive that he said the bridegroom would eventually be taken away from them? You heard him?"

"I am positive."

"When did he tell you of his plans for you?"

"Later, when only Jesus and his disciples remained, he asked me to go out with him, alone, into my yard. We sat on a large rock, beneath the only tree on my property. With his arm on my shoulder, he began by reminding me of our great prophet, Isaiah, who more than seven hundred years ago spoke the word of God despite the persecutions of his enemy, King Manasseh. Isaiah had wisely foretold that some day Manasseh would put him to death, a prophecy that eventually came true when Isaiah was tied under the blade of a saw and cut in two. Yet the mighty words of Isaiah are preserved even to this day, for he had selected and instructed certain disciples to carry on his work and put their master's words on papyrus and leather so they might live forever. Isaiah had said, 'I will bind up my testimony and seal my teaching in the heart of my disciples.' This, Jesus explained, was also *his* intention, and he would accomplish it through me."

"You were to record his words for future generations?"

"Yes. And his deeds."

"Including—miracles?"

"He said nothing about miracles. As we sat in the darkness, he told me that soon he would select twelve from among his followers to be his special apostles in alerting the people that the Kingdom of God was at hand. I was to be one of the twelve; however, my duty was to remain always by his side in order to record everything that transpired. He said, 'As you have witnessed this night, in your own home, already they spy on me and seek reasons to put me away as they did John the Baptist. Even now my days are numbered. Herod, Pilate, and the officers of the Temple lie in wait with their traps, and there is no place to hide. The foxes have holes and the birds of the air have nests, but the Son of man has no place to lay his head.' "

"He did say that his days were numbered?"

Matthew nodded.

"When did you commence keeping a record of his words and acts?"

"The very next morning."

"Did you ever record Jesus personally using the word 'messiah' to describe himself, either to the crowds or in private?"

"No."

"Did you ever make note of a time when Jesus called himself the 'Son of God'?"

"No."

"You've just quoted Jesus as referring to himself as the 'Son of man.' This is a common expression among the Jews, is it not, meaning simply a man—or any man born of men?"

Matthew smiled. "That is true. Still, those who are wise in the words of our prophet Daniel can read another meaning into that phrase if they choose, a meaning far different from its common use in the streets."

I tried to act annoyed, slapping the grass in exasperation. "You Jews call the Romans a heathen people because of their abundance of gods, and yet your own supply of prophets is unlimited. One can always be paraded forth whose words will fit any condition. What did your Daniel say, please tell me?"

"Daniel had many visions regarding our people. After one of these, he said, 'I saw in the night visions, and, behold, one like the Son of man came with the clouds of heaven, and came to the Ancient of Days, and they brought him near before him. And there was given him dominion, and glory, and a kingdom, that all people, nations, and languages should serve him: his dominion is an everlasting dominion, which

71

shall not pass away, and his kingdom that which shall not be destroyed.' "

"Is that a good description of what the Jews expect from their Messiah?"

"There are many different expectations from the Messiah."

He was much tougher than he looked and had obviously been through this sort of interrogation before. "Are you suggesting that Jesus imagined himself to be the 'Son of man' of Daniel's prophecy and that he purposely used that phrase as some sort of secret code that he knew would be recognized by those he wanted to rally to his cause without placing himself in any danger from Pilate or Herod?"

A furtive glance passed between Matthew and Joseph.

"But that makes no sense at all," I argued. "Wouldn't the uneducated masses be as unlikely to recognize or understand the hidden meaning behind those words, if there was one, as any spy of Pilate or Herod?"

"Perhaps," Matthew agreed reluctantly.

"And yet it was before those who were unschooled in the words of most prophets that Jesus taught and preached, nearly every day of his public life. How do you explain this?"

"He loved the poor and—"

"Yes, yes," I interrupted, "but if he loved them so much and wanted to lead them to a better life, why didn't he just come out and tell them he was their long-expected Messiah— or even, as many now claim, the Son of God? Why did he hide behind mysterious pronouncements of old prophets or speak in complex parables with messages so disguised that even you, who were so close to him, have admitted that you did not understand many of them?"

Matthew, at least on the exterior, remained undaunted by my badgering. He replied, "Jesus told us, once, when we asked him why he spoke in parables, 'Unto you it is given to know the mysteries of the Kingdom of God: but to others in parables; that seeing they might not see, and hearing they might not understand.' "

"Hardly the best way to prepare the masses for a new kingdom," I said maliciously.

Standing, to stretch my legs, I could feel Joseph of Arimathea's angry eyes on me. So be it, I thought. If the old boy has the power to bring me here, he should also have the wisdom and intelligence not to underestimate his captive from the twentieth century.

I shifted gears. "Matthew, do you still possess the notes you made while you were with Jesus?"

"Yes. They are locked in a chest and held in safekeeping for me by a trusted friend."

"Are they on papyrus or leather?"

"Both."

"Why are you saving them?"

"Why should I not treasure the master's words?" he asked in dismay.

"Well, are you not frequently in the Temple courtyard with James and the others promising the people that the Kingdom of God is at hand and that it will arrive even before many who hear you are in their graves? If that great event is to take place so soon, what need is there to preserve his words if they soon will be heard again, directly from his very own lips?"

"I have done that which the Son of God asked me to—"

I exploded, "Son of God indeed! You have already told me that you *never* recorded Jesus calling himself the Son of God! Why do you put lies in a dead man's mouth?"

The garden grew very still. Even the quarrelsome birds momentarily ceased their piping, and only the leaves in the top boughs of the eucalyptus trees rustled softly in the light breeze.

I waited until I realized there would be no reply. Then, in a far less belligerent tone, I asked, "Matthew, if Jesus has not returned within the next five or ten or twenty years and you have survived the danger that surrounds all of you who followed him, what will you do with your notes?"

"I do not know." The disciple shrugged. "I live only one day at a time. Jesus told us to take no thought for the morrow, for the morrow shall take thought for the things of itself. Sufficient unto the day is the evil thereof."

I persisted. "But already six years have passed and your crucified leader has not reappeared. Let us assume that six more years pass and then another six pass by and still he has not returned. You possess the only written record of his teachings. Might not those who still revere his memory, at that time, place great value on copies of his words if you were to provide them?"

He sounded almost patronizing when he replied, "I say unto you, again, that not far from here is an empty tomb. He who was raised from that place, by God, will return. On that certainty I am willing to wager my life."

Unconsciously I raised my left wrist to check the time. Foolish move. Joseph smiled and looked away. There was still so much I wanted to learn from Matthew: the miracles, the journeys through Galilee, the celebrated entry of Jesus into Jerusalem on the beginning of his last week, the cleansing of the Temple. If I were just writing this, I realized, instead of living it, I could let my Christ Commission take as much time and as many pages as necessary to question Matthew on specific events in their proper sequence. But this was for real.

"How much longer can we talk, Matthew?"

The apostle turned and squinted through the branches at the sun. "Perhaps for another hour or so, but then I must leave. Whenever I am late, the silversmith worries. He is certain that my life is in jeopardy because of my past association with Jesus. However, I can be found here every morning, God willing, should you need additional testimony in your search for the truth."

His poise and manner amazed me. Despite all my barbs and needles he was ready for more. Were all the others like Matthew and the brother of Jesus, so accustomed to taunts, harassment, and ridicule that adversity had become a way of life they could only endure by turning their other cheek with a smile? Was their equanimity genuine or only a shield they wore to protect them from the slings and arrows of their most powerful foes? Or were they really doing no more than practicing what they preached—destroying their enemies by loving them until they became friends?

I needed time to gather my thoughts. Excusing myself, I stepped out into the sunlight and inhaled deeply. I could smell wild flowers, and they reminded me of Kitty. Would she believe all this if I ever got the chance to tell her? Who would?

I had no illusions about my chances of success. It was the longest of long shots. In order to learn the truth about the resurrection hoax I had to track the movements of perhaps fifteen individuals, from the time the body was taken down from the cross to the discovery of the empty tomb on Sunday morning. Somewhere among that group was an alibi, or maybe more than one, that wouldn't hold up, but the almost impossible challenge I faced was checking them out six years after the crime.

When I turned, both Joseph and Matthew were watching me curiously. I smiled bravely and walked back to them, hoping I looked more confident than I felt. "Matthew, early on the night that Jesus was arrested, he and you twelve apostles ate the Passover supper alone in a place here in Jerusalem, did you not?"

"Yes."

"Where did this take place?"

Matthew hesitated until Joseph said, "It will do no harm to tell him."

"In the upper room of the house belonging to the widow Mary, a sister of Peter and mother of John Mark."

"According to my information, there were also several women in your party, among them the mother of Jesus and also Mary Magdalene. Where did they take the Paschal supper?"

"With the widow Mary, her son, and a few neighbors on the lower floor of the house."

"Matthew, I realize that you have had six years to think about and discuss the events of that night with the others who were involved. By now you probably have a much clearer picture of everything that was said and done. I don't know if this is possible, but I would like you to try to answer my questions only from what you personally remember seeing and hearing and living through during and after that supper. For example, early in the meal, I've been told, Jesus gave an order to Judas, who immediately left the room. Did you, from your position at the supper table, hear what was said?"

"No, but—"

"At the time did you consider it unusual that Judas should leave during the meal?"

"No. Judas was always running errands or purchasing supplies or making arrangements for sleeping quarters on our behalf. I remember thinking that perhaps Jesus had sent him downstairs to the widow Mary for some purpose connected with the food, but truly his absence was not unusual."

"The supper that night was a long one, was it not?"

"Yes, longer than any meal we had ever taken together. Besides the customary rituals of the Passover supper, Jesus had much to tell us about the future. Some of what he said gladdened our hearts, while many of his words frightened us."

I fought against the strong temptation to get into the message of the Last Supper and asked instead, "Where did your group go when the supper was finally ended and all of you left the house?"

"We believed that we were returning to the home of Martha and Mary in Bethany, while the women were to remain with the widow until we came back into the city in the morning. With Jesus at the head of our small procession, we passed through the lower city and out the Fountain Gate and followed the path north, outside the city's wall, until we finally arrived here in the garden."

"Had Jesus said anything that led you to believe you were going to spend the night here?"

"No. There was too much of a chill in the air to sleep outside, and it is only a short journey from here over the Mount of Olives to the home in Bethany where we had slept for the past five nights. We assumed we would only wait until Judas rejoined us after completing whatever Jesus had asked him to do. Then we could all return to Bethany together."

"Matthew, I know that time here is calculated from both sunrise and sundown. At about what hour would you say you arrived here in Gethsemane?"

He looked up and frowned, "At about the fourth hour after sundown."

"And the supper had commenced soon after sundown?"

"Yes, as is our Passover custom—as soon as the first three stars became visible and we heard the three fanfares from the Temple trumpets."

"Then by the time you arrived here, Judas had already been absent from your party for nearly four hours?"

"More or less."

"Didn't that concern anyone—his long delay in rejoining the group?"

Matthew shook his head. "It had been a long evening, and our only concern was returning to the warmth of our cots in Bethany. There was some grumbling against Judas for his tardiness, although all of us realized that his time was never his own as the keeper of our purse."

"What happened when you arrived here in the garden?"

Matthew led Joseph and me back to the boulder on which he had been resting his hands when we found him. "Jesus told us to wait while he prayed. He knelt here, against this rock, and there"—he pointed only a few paces away—"there Peter and James and John remained, close to him as he requested. The rest of us walked on, up this path, to a familiar cave we hoped would protect us from the dampness until Judas returned. There! See?"

I could barely make it out. Almost hidden from view, behind a cluster of olive trees, was a smooth outcropping of limestone, its side hollowed by the elements into a deep rounded cavity. Matthew paused on what had become a rather steep uphill climb and said, "The eight of us sat inside there, huddled together, and waited. Soon, because of the lateness of the hour and the fullness of our stomachs, not to mention the wine that had flowed freely during the meal, all of us were fast asleep on the damp floor of the cave."

"And how long did you sleep?"

"I don't know. The next thing I remember was the strong hand of James, the brother of John, shaking me and whispering in my ear that our master was being taken prisoner by the agents of the Temple. At first I thought I was having a bad dream, and it took some time for the import of his words to sink in. By then all the others, including James, had rushed from the cave and disappeared uphill in the darkness."

Normal reaction under such conditions. Run in the opposite direction from the danger, up over the hill and down the other side toward the home in Bethany.

"And you?" I asked.

"I had been as close to Jesus as his shadow ever since he called me from my toll booth. That habit was too much a part of me. Instead of running away I fell to my knees and began crawling through this tall grass, until I could see the many torches and hear angry shouts from a mob so large that I was unable to identify Jesus or Peter or John among them, despite the bright light. Then one of the torches separated from the others and began moving through the garden in my direction."

"What did you do?"

"I turned into a coward, like all the others, and ran through the darkness up the mount. I remember stopping, near the top, to catch my breath, and when I looked down into the moonlit garden I fell to my knees in shame, grieving at my lack of courage. No torch had followed me through the trees. I was alone, and I could see the lights of the arrest party as they headed south outside the city's wall. Then I heard my name being whispered and I saw Bartholomew. Together we followed the path over the mount and down the slope until we arrived at the home of Martha and Mary in Bethany."

"And what of the others?"

"Before dawn, all nine—James and the eight of us who had slept through our master's arrest—had returned alone or in pairs to that home where we had spent so many happy hours with Jesus."

"After you were all reunited, what did you do?"

The apostle shrugged helplessly. "We knew not what to do. We were stricken with both grief and terror. Martha and Mary and some of the men were weeping. The rest of us sat around in stunned silence. Remember, most of us were not of the city, so that even under the best of conditions Jerusalem intimidated us. To have our rabbi—and Peter and John as well, for all we knew—seized by the authorities was the end of everything. Thomas kept saying he was certain he had seen Roman soldiers among the arresting party, and that possibility added to our terror. Someone, I forget who, wanted to start out immediately for Galilee before we were all arrested, but how could we? How could we abandon Jesus and Peter and John and the women who were still in the city? Yet how could we hide for very long in the house of Martha and Mary when it was common knowledge that they had housed us for the past week?"

"So now all of you were certain that you were fugitives from the law. What did you finally decide to do?"

"My suggestion was accepted, such as it was. We took blankets and hid in the woods behind the house while the two women watched the road from their front windows. If any torches or lanterns were seen approaching in number from the city, they were to hang an oil lamp in a rear window as a signal for us to flee. The night passed quietly, however."

"And when morning came?"

"By then we were exhausted from lack of sleep. There was some talk about making an attempt to get back into the city to warn the women at the house of the widow, but none had either the courage or the strength to undertake such a venture and risk being captured by patrols—not even the three whose mothers were there. Martha, I remember, brought us some bread and cheese soon after daybreak, and we arranged a daytime signal of bleached cloth, hung from the window, should she or Mary see any approaching soldiers."

This was it! Now I would know. "How long did all of you remain in hiding in the woods?"

"For more than two days—until the sixth hour, or thereabouts, on the day following our Sabbath."

"All *nine* of you? No one left the woods, for any reason, even for a little while?"

If he was lying he was doing a superb job of it. He looked directly into my eyes and waved his hands helplessly. "Where would we go? What could we do? Rescue Jesus and the others from the high priest and his guards? Or from Pilate and his thousand armed legionaries? Us? Nine cowards with one dagger among us? Nine sheep who had been sheared of their faith and fled in the night just as Jesus said we would when the shepherd was struck down?"

"Then none of you knew that Jesus had been tried and

78

found guilty of sedition and crucified and buried in the tomb of Joseph and that Peter and John were still free? Bethany is only a short distance from Jerusalem. How could such terrible news not have reached you?"

"Jesus died on the cross while most of the city was preparing for the Sabbath, which was to commence at sundown. On the Sabbath there is little or no traffic on any roads. Word of what had happened did not begin to spread throughout the land until that first day after our holy day of worship."

Easter Sunday!

"How did you and the others finally learn of the execution?"

"From John—who, expecting to find us with Martha and Mary, had come directly from the tomb of Joseph of Arimathea after he had seen the empty grave with the stone rolled away, just as Mary Magdalene had reported it to them. John told us everything he knew, from the trials of Jesus before the high priest and Pilate to the horrible crucifixion and the burial by Joseph. But as John spoke, there was something in his manner that puzzled us. Instead of tears and recriminations he seemed joyful, and even in our sorry condition of self-pity and heartbreak we looked at each other with consternation. Then John told us that Jesus had risen from his tomb, but none of us believed him. We scoffed at his warning that we should tell no man, for who would pay heed to such madness anyway? I remember John tried to remind us of what Jesus had said about his death at the hands of the authorities and how he would rise on the third day, but we taunted him until he went away."

"And what did all of you do?"

"We remained where we were until dark and then returned to the city and went to the house where we had celebrated the Passover supper, in order to extend our sympathy to the brave mother of Jesus, who, according to John, had witnessed her son's crucifixion at his side. But his mother would have none of our condolences. She told us that the living Jesus needed no tears. Peter was in the house, and he, too, was filled with joy—urging all of us to go to the tomb to see for ourselves that our Lord had risen from the dead as he had said he would."

"Matthew! Joseph!" A harsh booming voice interrupted us. I turned to see a heavily muscled man, wearing only a leather girdle and sandals, rushing up the path in our direction. He slapped a smiling Shem on his rump as he passed and, throwing down his wooden staff, raised Joseph from the ground in a crushing embrace. Then he turned to Matthew and apologized for not coming at sunrise.

"Matthias," panted the old man when his breath returned, "this is James."

He had been the fourth to be called by Jesus, this strapping son of Salome and Zebedee who had fished the Galilean waters with his brother and father since childhood. Impetuous and short-tempered, he more than John had earned for the two of them the title "sons of thunder." Once, when a village of Samaritans did not show what he considered proper respect for Jesus, he had begged his master to call down the fires of heaven in order to consume them, only to be reminded by Jesus that the "Son of man is not come to destroy men's lives, but to save them." Jesus must have seen much that was admirable in this fierce-looking extrovert, for he had been almost as much a favorite as his brother, John, who had been called "the beloved disciple."

Joseph of Arimathea, bless him, made it easy for me. After introducing us, he told James of my mission and explained that Matthew had already been of great help in my search for the truth about Jesus. Then he went directly to the question he thought I would probably ask first.

"James," the old man said, "recalling that terrible night here, when they arrested Jesus, where did you go when you ran off into the darkness after alerting the others that Jesus had been taken prisoner?"

James scowled angrily at Joseph, clenching and unclenching his fists.

The old man raised his hand and said reassuringly, "There is no danger in your telling Matthias. He is my friend. Ignore his purple stripe and instead look on him only as a possible recruit to our cause. Have we not heard the Lord's brother, in the courtyard, telling the people many times that he which converteth the sinner from the error of his way shall save a soul from death?"

Joseph's words didn't thrill me too much, but they had their desired effect on James. The big man ran his thick stubby fingers nervously through his long black hair and said, "You want to know where I, the coward, escaped to on that night we abandoned the Lord?"

"Yes," the old man said gently.

"I—I went through the woods and over the mount to the house of Martha and Mary, running as if Satan himself pursued me."

At last I found my voice and asked, "Were you the first to arrive?"

"No," he replied, still eyeing me suspiciously. "Andrew and Simon had preceded me. But long before dawn all the others had placed their timid knuckles on the sisters' door."

"All *nine* of you were there? Are you positive?"

James avoided my eyes. "How could I ever forget?"

"And what did all of you do after you came together?"

"We went out into the woods, behind the house, and lay in the weeds like the worms we were."

"And how long did you remain there?"

"For more than two days. Until John brought us the news that Jesus had been crucified and buried but that the tomb where he had been laid was now empty. He was trying to convince us that our Lord had risen from the dead."

I moved closer to James until he could not avoid my eyes. "No one left your group, even for a short time, during those two days and nights in the woods?"

"No one!"

The "son of thunder" never blinked.

seven

THE HARSH SUN BLINDED US momentarily when we made our exit from Gethsemane's cool green canopy of leaves and vines. Shem was already waiting with the carriage, near the garden entrance, but before we climbed aboard, Joseph moved closer to me and said quietly, "Try not to be obvious, but look directly across the road and tell me what you see."

I turned my head slowly, pretending to inspect the dusty spoked wheels at the rear of the carriage. "I see a very small man with a bald head, sitting on a rock. He has a large knife with which he seems to be slicing thin strips of wood from a small tree trunk that he is holding between his knees."

"He is neither collecting wood chips, Matthias, nor is he carving a cane. You are looking at an agent who is in the employ of either Pilate or Caiaphas. Although you have been with me only two days, your actions are already under surveillance."

"Are you sure, Joseph? That one doesn't look as if he had enough intelligence to come in out of the sun, and I'll bet he hasn't had a bath in weeks."

"You surprise me, Matthias. As a creator of mystery stories, surely you realize that a spy who looks like everyone's conception of a spy is useless."

I still couldn't believe that such a scruffy character would be tailing us. After we were seated in the wagon, I kept glancing out the window at him, whittling away as if it were the most important function he would perform all day. Joseph showed little concern. Apparently things like this were a common occurrence in his life. He said, "You were undoubtedly seen in the Temple with me yesterday. Someone in authority is probably wondering why a new visitor to the city, obviously a citizen of Rome with some standing, has not taken the time to pay his respects."

"Is that usual protocol?"

"It is for anyone planning to engage in trade here."

"How about writers and historians?"

82

"Because you are in my company you have probably been mistaken for a merchant, and merchants planning to do business here are expected to make generous contributions to two treasuries, Pilate's and the Temple."

"Graft in the city of David?"

Joseph smiled. "It was invented here. However, I'm certain that a courtesy visit by us, to both Pilate and Caiaphas, will clear up any misunderstanding."

"Oh, no! I want to pay them more than a courtesy visit. I've got some very special questions for those two."

The old man nodded, his eyes shining. "I thought you might have a few. We can arrange it whenever you are ready. And now, since it is still early in the day, who is next on your list?"

"Martha and Mary."

"The sisters of Bethany? You need to further verify what you have just heard from Matthew and James?" he asked incredulously.

I said nothing. Had I told him my real reason for wanting to go to Bethany, he might have turned me over to Shem with instructions to lose me in the wilderness.

Joseph scratched at the creases in his forehead. "A visit to Martha and Mary, at this time, would not be in your best interest."

"Why?"

He pointed, almost imperceptibly, toward the roadside whittler, who never once looked up at us although we were only thirty feet away. "Undoubtedly our little friend has a horse tied nearby," Joseph explained, "and he is certain to follow us. Consider this simple problem in deduction, Matthias. Assume that we were seen yesterday, talking to James in the Temple courtyard. This morning we met with Matthew, and then James, the brother of John, joined us. Now we go to the home of Martha and Mary. What do these five have in common?"

It didn't take me long. "Their close connection to Jesus."

"Exactly. Now if you were either the high priest or the procurator, who both serve at the whim of Vitellius, what sort of suspicious thoughts might run through your mind if you received reports that a Roman citizen had arrived in the city and was meeting with no one except those who had been closely associated with Jesus—and to compound matters was staying at the home of the man who had claimed his body for burial?"

"If I had anything to hide I guess I'd begin to lose some

sleep. But I've only got five more days, Joseph, and I want to make every minute count. Tomorrow I had hoped we could visit Peter and John, but I'd really like to complete this part of the investigation first, and the only way I can close it out to my satisfaction is through a visit to Bethany."

"Now, now, do not abandon hope. I never said the trip was impossible."

He stepped out of the carriage and walked to the front, where he and Shem had a brief and discreet discussion while they pretended to check the harnesses and reins. Then he returned, and as soon as he slammed the carriage door we were off. After we had traveled only a few hundred yards, he nudged me and pointed his thumb out the rear window. Our whittler was no longer sitting on his rock, nor was he anywhere in sight. Complications like this I didn't need. What I was trying to do would be tough enough even if nobody interfered. Joseph reached behind and pulled down the dark linen curtain that hung above the rear open window, preventing anyone who might be following us from seeing into the carriage. I learned why, soon enough.

Our four galloping horses scarcely slowed their gait when they turned left and headed east, placing the city at our backs. "Follow this road far enough and it will take you to Jericho," the old man yelled above the creaks and groans from the carriage body as it was being bent and twisted by unsprung axles that scraped against deep wheel ruts in the single-lane dirt road that circled around the base of the Mount of Olives.

I was struggling too hard to keep my seat to do much sightseeing, but every now and then my head would snap low enough for me to catch a glimpse of bilious green meadows sloping off to my right from which slabs of pale limestone protruded with so much frequency that it was difficult to recognize the sheep and goats wandering aimlessly among them. Occasionally Joseph would move aside the rear curtain and nod with satisfaction. Apparently our "tail" was not in sight. Then the old man would lean over in front of me, intently studying the terrain as we jounced and bounced from side to side. We rode on for several more minutes before he yelled, "Get ready!"

Now I was not only hurting but confused. "Get ready for what?"

"We shall soon be approaching a sharp turn in the road. When we make that turn, Shem will slow down momentarily.

Open the door as soon as he does and jump out. I shall be right behind you."

Dust or no dust, my mouth flew open. "You've got to be kidding!"

He shook his head. He wasn't kidding at all. "Get ready!" Suddenly the wagon turned abruptly to the right and there was a loud moan of wood against metal as Shem applied his hand brake. Joseph reached over in front of me and threw open the door. "Jump, Matthias!"

I did as I was told, rolling over in the soft grass and watching from my knees as the old man, with surprising agility, followed. He landed on his feet and ran toward me, hand extended. "Come. . . . Hurry!"

He pulled me over to a patch of olive trees still too young to be more than overgrown bushes. We waded into the middle of them and fell on our stomachs. After catching my breath I edged forward and carefully parted the branches just enough to see our transportation disappearing around a bend in the road.

Joseph was obviously enjoying himself. He wasn't even breathing hard as he lay next to me in the bushes and explained his plan of action. "If our friend is following us, he should be going by soon, so keep your head down. Poor man, he's in for a most difficult and frustrating day. Shem will take our carriage all the way to Jericho, and on this miserable road that is a two-hour ride. Then he will turn around and come back the same way, picking us up right here, approximately four hours from now. Will that give you sufficient time for your Bethany visit?"

"Yes, but how far is—?"

"Bethany is just over that hill to our right. Only a short walk."

"You old fox. Shem is our decoy?"

"He is, and so far as anyone following us knows, we're still in the back seat of that carriage. It will be . . ."

His voice trailed off. Small patches of floating sand and dust were moving toward us along the road from the city. Eventually a single rider appeared, wearing a long black robe and headcloth. He trotted by on a gray stallion, less than fifty feet from where we lay, carefully adjusting his pace so that he could keep the dust clouds from Joseph's carriage in sight.

"He is not such a fool, that one," muttered the old man. "Back there, outside the garden, we saw a bald head that might make us suspicious if we saw it again, so now the skin is covered. No matter. Shem will make him earn his wages, this day. Let us be up and about out business, Matthias."

The Mount of Olives, or Olivet, is a mile-long undulating range of hills running north and south, parallel to Jerusalem's eastern wall. It rises more than three thousand feet to a flat summit before sloping down toward the east, the River Jordan and the Dead Sea, more than twelve miles away.

Bethany, in Aramaic, means "house of poverty." It was aptly named. Arriving at the crest of a rock-strewn hillock in the meadow, Joseph pointed to a small cluster of flat-roofed hovels, perhaps fifty in all, on both sides of the descending road. "As you can see," he said, "to travel from there over the top of Olivet on the footpath is a much shorter journey to and from the city than circling the mount as we have just done."

"And probably a lot easier on the body," I groaned, rubbing my now tender rear.

Joseph grinned. "Breathe the air. Clean. No smoke. No stench from the rivers. And one cannot see the city from here. Peace." He sighed. "No noise, no distractions. Do you wonder that Jesus preferred staying here whenever he came to Jerusalem?"

With an assist from the declining terrain, our pace quickened as we neared the village. To my right I could see a solid limestone cliff rising twenty feet or so and extending along the base of a small hill for more than a hundred yards.

"The tomb where Lazarus was raised is there," Joseph said casually, nodding toward the miniature gray range streaked with rusty veins of iron.

I stopped in my tracks and stared. How many times had I agonized over that famous resurrection scene? How often had I read and reread each sentence in that eleventh chapter from John that reported, in powerful and unequivocal terms, how Jesus had brought a dead man back to life? How long did I search for a clue among those simple words—some whisper that only I might hear that would help me to relate that resurrection story to the one that followed a few months later?

"Matthias, are you coming?"

I hurried to catch up. "No need to try to see the tomb site from here," Joseph assured me. "If we have time, after you have finished with Martha and Mary, I'm certain they would have no objection if we visited it up close."

If we had time? I had to see that tomb up close—very close! "Joseph, whatever happened to Lazarus? All I've been able to locate on him are some old traditions concerning his visits to the south of Gaul."

"Lazarus has not rested since Jesus was crucified. Always he travels and always alone, from Hebron to Antioch, preaching in the synagogues and the streets and telling the people how Jesus raised him from the dead. Of course he is his own best witness." Joseph laughed. "He tells them, 'Look at me, feel me, touch my skin. Once I was dead and now I live through the grace and power of Jesus and his Father who is in heaven.' Ah," Joseph exclaimed, "at last we have arrived."

The home of Martha and Mary was larger than most of their neighbors' although constructed in the same boxlike shape and of the same rough stone that was so abundant in the meadows and hills. Two small latticed windows flanked a solid wooden door, and nailed to the doorpost was a thin brass *mezuzah*. Before he knocked, Joseph said, "This was the house of Simon, a man of considerable wealth, to whom Martha was wed. Simon contracted leprosy of the worst kind and died before the two were ever blessed with child. Martha's brother and sister, Lazarus and Mary, came here to live soon after Simon's passing."

Before I could reply I heard the distinct sound of a sliding bolt. The door, hung with three leather hinges, opened a few cautious inches at first. Then came a muffled shout of joy from inside.

"Oh, Joseph, Joseph—it has been so long!"

"Martha, Martha!"

Both sisters fitted the sketchy personality profiles I had once constructed from their scant descriptions in Luke and John. Martha was stern, strong-willed, and assertive while her younger sister, Mary, remained timidly in the background, nervously flexing her long thin fingers and nodding frequently in unspoken affirmation of whatever Martha was saying. Both had lovely olive skin and wore their jet-black hair tightly bound at their necks. Their dresses were also alike, made from a dark blue, rough-textured material that reached to the ankles and also covered their arms to the wrists. Martha, I guessed, was around forty years of age; Mary, thirty-five.

We followed the sisters through a narrow entrance hall into a large room that was obviously their central living area. Although it was sparsely furnished, its dimensions were large enough so that it wasn't difficult for me to imagine all the apostles sleeping in it, if necessary, when their master had visited Bethany. Three curtained openings led into what were probably bedrooms. The house was dark and damp, and Martha apologized for its condition as she heaped charcoal on the red coals of a sunken pit in the center of the tiled floor.

After the typical litany of questions concerning health and relatives that reunited friends always seem to observe, Joseph deftly brought the conversation around to me and the purpose of our visit. To my happy surprise, Martha, with her sister nodding, seemed eager to cooperate, as if she felt it was her duty to tell everyone all that she could about Jesus. I would have bet that she spent many hours of her life in the Temple courtyard seeking out potential converts. Conscious of our scheduled rendezvous with Shem, I scuttled all the background questions I had planned to ask and plunged right into the resurrection of Lazarus, addressing all my questions to Martha.

"When your brother took sick, how did you know where to contact Jesus?"

She was sitting next to me on a long polished bench in front of the fire, with Mary on her left and Joseph on my right. Apparently my question was not the sort she was expecting. Her jaws clenched and she gave me that stare that grade-school teachers reserve for their most hopeless pupils. Finally she leaned forward and looked beyond me toward the old man for guidance. Without turning my head, I knew he'd be nodding his okay to answer.

Martha began, "During our winter Feast of Dedication, called Hanukkah, there had been trouble in the Temple between Jesus and the Pharisees. They had approached him, while he was walking alone in Solomon's Portico, and challenged him to stop talking in riddles and to come right out and tell them if he was the Messiah. He refused, telling them that the works he did in his Father's name should be all the witness they needed, but he realized that, since they were not his sheep, they would never believe him. When he said, 'I and my Father are one,' they began to pick up stones to destroy him for his blasphemy, but he stopped them by asking, 'Many good deeds have I shown you from my Father; for which of these do you intend to stone me?' Enraged, they tried to seize him, but he escaped and returned directly here. All this he told me before he departed, saying that he was taking his sheep beyond the Jordan, to safety, into the land of Peraea, but that he would return to our home in time for Passover. I was frightened for him. I pleaded that he not return so soon, but he said that he must."

"He used the word 'must'?"

"Yes."

"Peraea is a large land. How did your messenger find Jesus when your brother took sick?"

"The road from here to Jericho continues across the Jordan and also across Peraea. Jesus had confided to Lazarus that he and his apostles would never be far from that road should anything occur in the city that we believed he should know. When my messenger, Joel, a neighbor's son, rode off, he had been instructed by me to inquire of the master's whereabouts along the Jericho Road, and when he found him he was only to say, 'Lord, behold, he whom thou lovest is sick.' "

"When did Lazarus die?"

"Only a few hours after I dispatched the messenger."

"Then it is likely that by the time Jesus received your message, Lazarus was already dead?"

"Yes."

"And how many days passed before Jesus finally appeared?"

Martha lowered her head. "We were already in the fourth day of mourning. Mary and I were sitting in this room with our friends, neighbors, and many representatives from the Temple who had come out of respect for Lazarus and the generous contributions we had made over the years. Thomas, one of the apostles, entered the room and whispered in my ear that Jesus was outside the village, waiting. I went with him immediately."

"Why didn't Jesus come as soon as he was told that Lazarus was sick?"

"When Joel delivered my message to Jesus, he said that the Lord had responded by saying that the sickness was not unto death but for the glory of God. Since Lazarus was already dead by the time Joel returned and repeated the Lord's words to me, I was mystified by them. I even, God forgive me, began to have doubts about my master for the first time."

"But Jesus finally came."

"He did, and as I accompanied Thomas along the road, outside the village, I asked what had caused Jesus to change his mind. He said that he did not know, but after they had remained in Peraea for two more days Jesus had surprised them by saying, 'Let us go into Judaea again.' All the apostles were afraid to go, reminding Jesus of the danger they faced from those who had tried to stone him in the Temple so recently. Jesus told them that their friend Lazarus was sleeping and he wanted to go to awaken him from his sleep, but they

89

reminded him that sleep was beneficial to any illness. Then he announced that Lazarus was dead and struck fear into all their hearts by saying that he was glad, for their sakes, that he had not been there, for now what they were about to witness would increase their faith in him. Thomas said he told Jesus that he would go with him, and he urged the others to accompany them so that if there was any danger they could all die with their master."

"Why was Jesus waiting outside the village instead of coming directly here to the house?"

"He must have realized that there were many in our mourning party from the Temple, and he wished to cause no trouble. When I saw him, standing apart from the others, I ran toward him and cried, 'Lord, if you had been here Lazarus would not have died, but I know that even now, whatever you ask of God will be given to you.'"

"You expected him to perform a miracle?"

"No, no. I only prayed that our Lord would intercede with God in behalf of our beloved brother. Jesus took my hands and said, 'Your brother shall rise again.' I told him that I knew he would rise again in the resurrection at the last day, and the Lord replied with words I shall never forget."

"Please repeat them for me."

"Jesus said, 'I am the resurrection and the life, and he that believes in me, though he were dead, yet shall he live, and he that lives and believes in me shall never die. Do you believe this?' I replied, 'Yes, Lord, I believe that you are the Christ, the Son of God, which should come into the world.' Then he asked to see Mary, and I went back to the house and told her in secret."

I leaned toward Mary. "And what did you do?"

Mary's voice trembled, as if she had been reliving, once more, the events of that afternoon. "When I rose to go to him," she said, "those who had been comforting me, thinking perhaps that I was returning to the tomb to pray again, came with me, and I could not avoid them. I ran to Jesus and fell at his feet and cried, just as Martha had, 'Lord, if you had been here, my brother would not have died.'"

"What did Jesus do?"

"He reached down and lifted me up, a strange moan coming from his lips as he did so. Then he asked where Lazarus was laid and I took his hand and led him to the tomb. By this time all the mourners from the house had joined us. When I pointed to the stone that had been rolled across the grave opening, Jesus put both hands to his face, and when he removed them I saw that he had been weeping. My Lord—weeping! I turned my back, unable to look at his countenance dark with sorrow. Someone in the crowd, I know not who, said loudly, 'Could not this man, who opened the eyes of the blind, have prevented this man from dying?' Jesus, I am certain, heard the question, for he moaned again as if he was in great agony. Then he said, 'Take away the stone!' "

Martha immediately interrupted. "Like a fool, I tried to stop him. I told Jesus that the body must surely stink by now, since our brother had already been dead four days. He placed his hand on my shoulder and reminded me, again, that if I believed, I would see the glory of God. At that I surrendered myself completely to his will and asked some of the men who were nearby to remove the stone from the opening."

"And after the stone was removed?"

"Jesus stepped in front of the opening while the crowd backed away. Some even ran off. Then he looked up into the heavens and said, 'Father, I thank you for hearing me. And I know that you hear me always, but because of these people who are watching and listening I say it so that they may believe that you have sent me.' Then he cried out in a loud voice, 'Lazarus come forth,' and his words echoed off the stone, and lo! our brother came forth from the small opening, still bound hand and foot in his grave cloth and with his face and head covered by a linen napkin, just as he had been laid to rest. Jesus said, 'Loose him, and let him go,' and our beloved brother was returned to us whole."

"What did the people do?"

"Many cheered and praised his name and believed. But some departed swiftly, especially those from the Temple, and I am certain that they reported all they had seen to the authorities."

I had to raise the most obvious of questions, if only to see the women's reaction. Concentrating on Martha, I said, "Every now and then someone is buried accidentally who is not dead. Could this have happened in the case of your brother?"

Both Martha's eyes and lips wrinkled into the beginning of a smile. Apparently I had not been the first to suggest such a possibility.

"Sir, even if Lazarus had been alive when he was placed in his tomb, he would have expired from the burial rituals and his entombment. His body was dressed and wrapped tightly in linen, by my sister and me, from neck to feet. After he was laid in the tomb, a napkin was placed over his face, and the linens were covered with myrtle, aloes, hyssop, rose oil, and rose water. Then he was sealed in that damp cave where there is little air. No human could endure those conditions for four days or survive without any food or water."

"How large is that tomb, inside?"

"There are only three shelves within, carved into the stone. One is for Lazarus, one for Mary, and one for me."

"What did Jesus do afterward?"

"He rested in our house for a day before he departed, telling us that he would return for the Passover. Then he withdrew into Peraea again, but not before we had received word that the Sanhedrin had met and the high priest, Caiaphas, had announced that Jesus must die before everyone believed in his miracles wrought through what Caiaphas called the power of Satan. The Sanhedrin agreed that if Jesus were allowed to continue, all the people would soon join him, and the Romans would be forced to put them down by destroying the nation. Caiaphas had said, 'It is expedient for us, that one man should die for the people, and that the whole nation perish not.'"

"Martha, tell me, who would dare to bring news of such a meeting to Jesus? Certainly it would have had to be someone from within the Sanhedrin itself."

Martha flinched. I saw fear in her gray eyes for the first time. Her lips quivered.

"Go ahead, Martha, tell him," urged Joseph.

"It was he," she whispered, pointing to the old man.

I didn't dare look at him. "When did you see Jesus again?" I asked her.

"He returned to us, with his apostles, one week before the Passover—his last. We celebrated with a supper in his honor and many came to honor him, as well as to marvel at our brother, who had been dead but now was not."

"Did anything unusual occur at this supper?"

Martha turned to Mary and said sternly, "You tell him."

Mary paled and rubbed her hands together so savagely that I was afraid she would peel skin if she continued. She finally clasped them tenderly, as if in prayer, and said, "I had been saving an alabaster flask filled with precious spikenard for my wedding. But since Jesus had come into my life I had no desire to be with and serve any man except the Lord. I waited on his every need, through supper, and then went to my room and returned with the flask. I broke the glass in my hand and poured the perfume first over his head and then over his feet and I knelt and wiped off his feet with my hair to show him how much I loved him. The spikenard was mine, to do with as I chose, but one of the apostles, Judas, came forward and shamed me before everyone by asking why the ointment had not been sold and the money given to the poor. I began to weep until I felt the master's hand on my head and heard him say, 'Why do you trouble her? Let her alone. She has wrought a good work upon me. You have the poor with you always and whenever you can you should do them good; but me you will not have always. She has done what she could, for in casting this ointment on my body she prepared me for my burying.' "

Mary leaned against her sister, hiding her face in the curve of Martha's neck as a child seeking comfort would do. Liking myself less and less each minute, I turned to Martha again. "Did anyone ask Jesus what he meant when he spoke of his own burial?"

"No one. We were all afraid, even the likes of Peter and James. Only later did we understand."

I swept my hand around the spacious room. "Each night, during that Passover week, Jesus and the twelve slept here?"

"Yes. Until the night he was arrested."

"Was it usual for all the apostles to make their home with you when they came to the city with Jesus?"

"Oh, no. Usually they split up into pairs and stayed with different families of our village. But during the Passover holidays every house is always filled with visiting relatives from other parts, so the twelve all slept here, in this room, some on cots and some on the floor with blankets to protect them from the cold. Lazarus occupied one bedroom, Mary and I shared another, and the Lord slept in the third—that one there." She pointed.

"On that night when Jesus was arrested in the garden, had you been expecting him and the others to return here after they had taken the Paschal supper in the city?"

"Yes, although Jesus had warned us they would be late, and so we did not become concerned until—until perhaps the sixth hour after sundown."

That would be midnight. "And where was your brother, Lazarus?"

"In the city, taking the supper with our cousins."

"Where is Lazarus now?"

Martha sighed. "I do not know. Somewhere in Israel, witnessing for the Lord. But wherever his journeys take him, he always returns to celebrate the Passover with us."

"When Jesus was arrested, how did you learn the news?"

Martha shut her eyes and shivered. With the warm red

glow from the coals reflecting on her strong face, I was reminded of Tintoretto's painting of her chastising Mary for sitting at the feet of Jesus instead of helping with the dinner preparation. She replied, "Mary and I were resting here, our eyes heavy with sleep, when we were startled by heavy pounding on our door and heard someone outside calling our names. When I unbolted the lock, Andrew rushed in, red-faced and out of breath. At first he spoke so swiftly that we could not understand his words. Finally he calmed down enough to tell us the terrible news that our Lord had been taken prisoner by the Temple authorities while praying in Gethsemane. Soon afterward, Thomas arrived, and then Matthew and Bartholomew. Before sunrise, nine of them were sitting here. Only Peter and John and Judas were absent. No one knew of the whereabouts of Judas, but all were certain that Peter and John had been arrested with Jesus."

I looked around the room. It wasn't difficult to picture nine frightened, rural Galileans, sitting in this dark room, panic-stricken and leaderless.

"What were they doing and saying as they sat here?"

There was scorn in Martha's voice. "Nothing. Nothing except babble and sob and wring their hands in despair. They were all like frightened little boys. I remember Matthew repeating, over and over, 'He said it would happen, he said it would happen.' Philip kept insisting that they all flee north, without delay, into the safety of Galilee, until Matthew asked him, in anger, if he would desert the mother of three of them and the mother of Jesus who were all still in the city without protection. Thomas said he was certain there had been Roman soldiers among the Temple police who arrested Jesus. James agreed and said that they would all be taken if they remained in this house, since it was well known that we had sheltered them for almost a week. It was Matthew who finally suggested that they take blankets and hide in the woods behind the house while Mary and I watched the road from the city. If we saw any torches approaching, we were to hang a lantern in the back window facing the woods as a warning for them to flee."

"May I see the woods?"

Martha nodded. The four of us went out the front door and around to the back of the house. Approximately a hundred yards away, in the middle of a boulder-studded meadow, was a stand of trees no larger than a half acre but certainly dense enough to conceal nine men. I turned and checked. There was a window at the back of the house from

94

which a lantern could be seen while hiding in that small patch of woods. Once again I had arrived at the moment of supreme truth so far as my investigation was concerned.

"How long did the men remain in the woods?"

"For two days!" Martha cried, her voice filled with anger and disapproval at the behavior of the nine. "Until the fifth or sixth hour of the day after our Sabbath, when John arrived with the news that Pilate had crucified our Lord and that his body was already missing from the tomb where Joseph and Nicodemus had laid him because he had risen from the dead as he had prophesied."

I could feel Joseph of Arimathea's eyes on me as he waited to see how I would react to Martha's story.

"Did anyone leave the woods and later return, during those two days?"

Both sisters shook their heads in unison. Negative. Mary spoke up. "Martha and I took turns taking them food and water through the days and the nights. Always they were huddled together, all nine—sometimes crying, sometimes sleeping."

"And none of you had been aware of the events in the city until John arrived?"

"By the time we knew, our Lord no longer needed our help," Mary sobbed.

I wasn't finished with Bethany yet. With the sisters' permission to visit the tomb, Joseph and I hurried through the meadow toward the limestone cliff. The old man said little as we walked, but he looked pleased with himself. "Did you have something you wanted to add to what we have just heard?" I asked sarcastically.

He shook his head. "No, no, it is *you* who are conducting the investigation, and it is *you* who must reach your own conclusion. I am only your guide, remember?"

I put my arm around him and hugged him. "Come on, old man, I know you're dying to say more."

He laughed. "However, if your Christ Commission had spoken to the same witnesses that you already have, I am certain they would agree that they had heard testimony of the strongest kind—testimony affirming without doubt that none of the nine who fled from the garden could have possibly removed the body of Jesus from the tomb. Matthew told you that they had all fled from the garden and eventually hid in the woods for two days. Then James, the son of thunder, corroborated Matthew's testimony, and the sisters have corroborated that of both men. Now you have two reasons why the nine could not possibly have been involved in the act that you suspect them of committing. First, they had no knowledge that Jesus was dead and buried until after the empty tomb was discovered and, second, they were too terrified and broken in spirit to do anything about it even if they had known."

"I thought you told me that *I* was the Christ Commission."

"You are, my son, you are."

"Well, I'd like to reserve judgment until after I've checked out this tomb. It may offer some testimony that could destroy a few alibis and all your fine logic."

"Testimony? From a tomb?"

I didn't elaborate.

Flush against the smooth wall of the cliff stood a heavy piece of chiseled stone, rounded in such a way that it reminded me of the old American Indian millstones used for the grinding of grain. It was approximately nine inches thick and stood four feet high, with small boulders wedged against the curvature of its bottom to keep it from rolling.

Dismayed, I asked, "Is this it?"

"What were you expecting? This is a grave, no more, no less. See there, how the stone still shows signs of the white paint that was applied to it, after Lazarus was laid to rest, in order to warn trespassers against defilement."

"No other marks? No inscriptions?"

"What for? Can the dead read? Do not the owners of tombs know who is buried within? Certainly God needs no identifying signs."

"Why aren't there any other tombs along this cliff? I would think this is an ideal burying place for the dead of Bethany."

"All this land was owned by Simon and now belongs to Martha. This family grave is on private property."

"And where is the tomb's opening?"

"It is covered by the round stone."

As I had suspected it might be. I could feel myself growing tense.

"From what we know, Joseph, that stone was rolled away at the request of Jesus before he commanded Lazarus to come forth."

"That is correct."

"But now the tomb is empty, is it not?"

"Of course it is empty. You heard Martha, did you not? It is for the three of them and they are all still alive. Therefore the tomb is empty."

"Then why is it closed? Why is that stone against the opening since there are no bodies inside to protect? Why would anyone bother to seal the tomb again after Lazarus came forth?"

The old man stood absolutely immobile. He was looking at me, but I knew he couldn't see me. "I d-d-d-don't know, Matthias, I don't know. . . ."

The meadow was so still that I could almost feel the silence as one feels the clinging moisture of a heavy fog. My left sandal accidentally dislodged a small rock. It rolled along the crusty limestone beneath our feet until its clatter reverberated off the stone wall. After several steps I was directly in front of the round paint-flecked stone. Was this the spot where Jesus had finally put his life on the line? If he failed to raise Lazarus after he had said he would, even his apostles would have probably deserted him. If he did raise Lazarus, those who hated him and feared his growing popularity among the masses would surely mark him for an early execution. Only a few weeks earlier he had escaped from those who tried to stone him in the Temple. Why had he returned to place himself in a situation from which there could be no retreat?

How had Jesus sounded when he issued his famous command to the dead man? Was his voice amplified by the natural acoustics of this place so that it carried beyond the cliff's distant edge and washed back over the village of Bethany?

I cupped my hands around my mouth, drew a deep breath, and yelled as loudly as I could, "Lazarus, come forth!" The words rolled like charging thunder along the wall of stone. Once more I shouted, "Lazarus, come forth!" and there was another clap of thunder, chasing vainly after the first. "Lazarus, come forth!" I cried, again and again until I felt Joseph shaking me from behind.

"Stop, Matthias! Enough! Let us be gone from here."

"No," I bellowed, breaking loose from his grip and racing toward the branchless trunk of a small dead tree that had been propped against the cliff's wall. Seizing the makeshift pole I plunged its fatter end beneath the base of the gravestone and pulled back with all my strength.

"Stop, Matthias! Please! You must not defile the grave!"

"How can one defile a grave in which there are no bodies?" I roared between pulls. I ignored his repeated pleas, tugging back on the wood, again and again, until the huge stone began to rock on its cradle of small supporting boulders. I kicked away some of the stones and pulled again. The stone budged, just a little. I pulled and strained. It trembled a few inches and then a few more. I dropped the pole and leaned against the stone with my shoulder. Sweat, salty and hot, ran into my eyes and down my cheeks and into my mouth. I was gasping for air. My chest hurt. I pushed. I grunted. I slipped and fell to my knees, still putting all my weight against the stubborn stone until it yielded reluctantly—six inches, then a foot, two feet—until at last I had managed to roll it completely aside from the mouth of the grave. Then I slid down the cliff's smooth wall, spent.

Joseph stood over me, his two hands pressed tightly against both sides of his face. "Matthias, what have you done? May God forgive you. May God forgive *me* for bringing you here."

I patted the hard stone beneath me. "Joseph, sit here, please."

He knelt on one knee instead, with his head turned so that he could not see into the tomb. I reached out and touched his cheek, gently.

"Listen to me, please. Earlier you said that I was the investigator and you were my guide, did you not?"

He nodded sadly.

"And you brought me here, after I made that dumb wish on the Carson program, so that I could discover the truth for myself, whatever that may be, correct?"

He nodded again.

"There were no loopholes in that deal, were there? I could go anywhere, look at anything, and talk to anyone in my search for the truth, right?"

Without turning, he pointed back over his shoulder toward the tomb. "And you expect to find the truth in there?"

"I don't know."

"All you will find in there, Matthias, are three empty shelves and a few worms."

"Perhaps—perhaps not."

"But what else could possibly be in there? What are you looking for, my son?"

"I'm looking for the remains of a body."

"A body? Whose body?"

"The body of Jesus."

For a moment I thought he was going to faint. "Jesus?" he cried. "Why would you expect to find his remains here? Why?"

"Because if any of the apostles were the culprits who removed it from your tomb, this would have been the most logical place for them to hide it. My studies, almost from the beginning, led me to suspect that a few of the apostles, or others closely associated with him did what they believed had to be done in order to make it appear that his prophecy had come true. One of the possibilities I considered was that sometime after dark but before dawn of the third day, his body was removed from the tomb and carried here, either in a stretcher or some sort of small wagon, and placed in the empty grave that once held Lazarus. Then this tomb was sealed again, with reasonable certainty that the body would be safe from discovery since it is on Martha's private land. Circulating and feeding the rumor that Jesus had risen from the dead would be easy with that empty tomb of yours serving as a star witness—and, best of all, a silent one."

"But there were soldiers guarding my tomb."

"When I know who took the body then I'll know how the soldiers were handled."

"And how about the nine who were hiding in the woods behind the home of the sisters? How could any of them have carried off such a thing when, from what you have learned, none of them even knew that Jesus was dead, much less the location of his tomb?"

"All right, for the sake of argument let's delete those nine names from my list of suspects. But that still leaves Peter and John, who were in Jerusalem and knew of the crucifixion and burial. And then there's the high priest, Caiaphas, and even Pilate, who could have easily arranged to remove the body and hide it somewhere so that your tomb would not become a dangerous rallying point for those who still believed in Jesus. Of course, if either of those two were involved, they committed a colossal blunder. They actually helped promote the resurrection myth with their theft of the body, and now it is too late for either of them to admit to their error. Last on my list, but not least, are the two who buried Jesus."

"You mean Nicodemus—and me? You even suspect me?"

"Wouldn't you, if you were the Christ Commission?"

He sighed. "Well, at least we have managed to narrow down the list of suspects considerably."

"Yes, and four of those still on the list could very possibly have hidden the body right here, in this tomb."

I turned away from Joseph and crawled the few feet to the mouth of the grave. With reflected light from the pale stone I could see inside, directly ahead of me, the outline of a shelf carved in the rock, long enough and wide enough to hold a body. It was bare. To my left was another shelf. It, too, was bare. And to my right was the third shelf. Nothing! Still kneeling, in a four-point stance, I lowered my head and cursed. A faint smell of rose water clung to the stone floor. There was no other clue, of any sort, that even one dead body had ever occupied the small chamber.

I backed out of the cave slowly. Disappointment had quickly turned to weariness. I began to shake until I pushed myself to a standing position. Joseph was watching me anxiously, still kneeling exactly where I had left him.

"What have you discovered, Matthias, tell me?"

"Only a few worms, Joseph," I cried, "just as you said. Only a few worms."

eight

I HADN'T HEARD A ROOSTER crow since my youth, but I opened my eyes, positive that I had just heard one. How symbolic, I thought, that the crowing of a cock should wake me on the morning I hoped to meet and talk with Peter.

I had already bathed and shaved when the first timid knock on my bedroom door announced the arrival of my morning meal. Nicholas, the Syrian orderly assigned to me by Joseph, was standing outside, flashing his usual obsequious smile, but today he wasn't pushing his bronze cart stacked with covered serving dishes.

"Master Joseph apologizes for any inconvenience," he said timidly, "but he would like to have you join him in the peristyle, this morning, to dine with him and his guest."

"Guest? Let's go."

Joseph's villa, built on the side of a hill, was actually two octagon-shaped wings connected by the long statue-lined hall we were now descending. All the sleeping and dining quarters were located in the upper wing. Our destination, the lower wing, housed what Joseph had modestly called his cultural center. Two rooms contained his collection of sculptures, and in one of them the old man had introduced me, yesterday evening, to Hermogenes, according to Joseph one of the most talented sculptors ever produced by Greece. The small head of a child was coming alive in marble under Hermogenes' gentle hammer and chisel, and I had asked my host how all his precious possessions in stone were condoned by the priests despite the Second Commandment's injunction, 'Thou shalt not make unto thee any graven image, or any likeness of anything that is in heaven above, or that is in the earth beneath, or that is in the water under the earth.' Joseph had only smiled and reminded me that *he* didn't make the images himself, and there was no law against one's being a patron of the arts.

Three other rooms in the lower wing were filled with scrolls, large and small, in parchment, leather, and papyrus.

101

Another two contained his collection of paintings. There was an eighth room in the lower wing, but the old man purposely avoided its closed door when he was showing me around and I purposely avoided asking him about it.

The rooms surrounded an expansive peristyle, open to the sky and yet protected from direct sunlight by a latticed roof that allowed some of the sun's rays to filter down on more than two hundred varieties of desert flowers that Joseph had collected over many years. Nicholas guided me through one of the libraries, opened a door leading to the plant-filled courtyard, and pointed toward the old man and his guest, sitting at a circular glass table with their heads together in animated conversation. Joseph stood when he saw us and extended his arms until I arrived at the table. Then he gently stroked my cheek and exclaimed, "No more cuts! Each day your mastery of that treacherous weapon increases."

Still more asleep than awake, I replied, "Thank you. Progress of any sort is sweet at this point."

He smiled and said, very casually, "Matthias, this is Peter."

That woke me up! Peter! Simon! Cephas! The rock! Closest friend of Jesus. With his master from the earliest days—until he lost his courage at the very end. Or had he? Impulsive. Loyal. Chief spokesman for the apostles. Bold. Tough. The driving force behind the increasing number of converts. Acknowledged even by the brilliant Paul as the most powerful and respected Christian. The leader.

When we embraced, his biceps felt like thick strands of twisted steel. His smile was warm and open, but those deep-set black eyes told me what I already knew from my studies: that he could be a very rough opponent for anyone, even the chief priests, as they had learned to their sorrow. Peter's darkly tanned square face was unlined and unmarked except for deep furrows in his wide forehead, and his thick auburn hair nearly covered his broad shoulders. The beard was full and laced with streaks of gray. His loose-hanging tunic, cut from unbleached linen, came to just above his corded, muscular calves. Around his massive right wrist was a thick, studded leather strap.

I tried to concentrate on what Joseph was saying: ". . . telling Peter that we had planned to search him out today, and lo! he appears at my door to bid me farewell before he journeys to his old home in Capernaum to visit his wife's family. Matthias, I have already taken it upon myself to explain the purpose of your mission, and Peter is willing to answer your questions providing he can be on his way before the sun is too high."

I could feel the apostle's eyes on me as I listened to the old man, and I had all I could do to keep my composure. I had some very harsh questions to ask this man whom Jesus had aptly named "the rock," and I was beginning to wonder where I'd find the courage. If he had once dared to contradict Jesus, to whom he had devoted his life, how would he react with me if I began probing into areas where memories must still cause pain, anguish, and regret?

There was so much Peter could tell me. How many thousands of books had been written about him, how many questions raised, how many conclusions reached, how many mysteries were still hanging over his years with Jesus? Last night, before falling to sleep, I knew exactly how I would conduct my interview with him. After all, my purpose here was not to write the definitive life of Jesus but specifically to discover what had happened to his body after he was buried. I had reviewed, in my mind, those questions that I had the three tribunes asking Peter in my book, and I had decided to follow the same course I had plotted for them in my unfinished manuscript. But that was last night. Now, eyeball to eyeball with the man, I realized how much that game plan might have to be flexible, to say the least.

Peter was waiting patiently, both elbows resting on the glistening tabletop, his huge hands clasped loosely together beneath his beard. He seemed completely relaxed, unconcerned about anything I might ask him. I decided to blast through that equanimity early. If I could knock him off balance, he might say things I would never hear under normal conditions.

"And how is your mother-in-law?"

"What?" he bellowed. Then, in a softer but still disbelieving voice, "What did you say?"

"I asked how your mother-in-law was. Her health? She is feeling well?"

My question had its intended effect. Obviously disarmed, Peter replied, "She is in good health, sir," Now he was smiling. Warily. "But what has an old woman's condition in Capernaum to do with your search for the truth about Jesus?"

"Did he not save her life once?"

Equanimity out, astonishment in. "Your search for the truth has been exceedingly thorough, my friend," he replied. "Yes, the Lord saved her life when she was near death."

"How?"

"It happened not long after my brother, Andrew, and I had abandoned our nets and our boats to follow him. We were still in our own village and Jesus was preaching in our synagogue. My wife's mother, only a few days before, had become afflicted with the burning fever, a deadly sickness common to people of the waterfront. We had already tried the remedy of magic recommended in our Talmud and repeated the prescribed four verses from Exodus, day after day, but her condition grew worse and there was little hope. We shared our sadness with Jesus, but instead of just consoling us he made us take him to our home, and when we walked into the room where the dying woman slept, he knelt beside her bed and took her hand. Then he reached out and lifted her to a sitting position and she opened her eyes. Soon her feet were on the floor and the fever had passed and she went directly to the kitchen, after kissing Jesus, and prepared supper for all of us."

"Would you call that a miracle?"

Peter cocked his head defiantly. "What would you call it?"

He had obviously dealt with people like me before. "I don't know," I replied. "I've not had as much experience with miracles as you are reported to have had. Now, let me take you to another time and place. Almost from the beginning, the words and actions of Jesus angered those in authority—Herod, the high priest, the Pharisees and Sadducees—so that on many occasions, in order to escape their taunts and challenges, he led those closest to him away from Judaea and Galilee to places where you would be out of harm's way. Is that correct?"

"That is so. Those hypocrites in power, feeling the sting of the Lord's words every day, were constantly plotting to entrap Jesus in their nets and destroy him. He called them 'a generation of vipers' who, being evil, could never speak or do good things anyway."

"But didn't their constant harassment eventually take its toll? Did not many who had been loyal followers of Jesus begin to fall away, after a while, because they feared those in authority?"

Peter rubbed the back of his hairy hand across his eyes. "There was a time," he said regretfully, "when Jesus asked me and the other eleven if we were planning to desert him too."

"Caesarea Philippi!"

The apostle's body stiffened. "What?"

"Caesarea Philippi!" I repeated.

"What of it?"

"What happened there?"

"How do you know about Caesarea Philippi?" he asked, scowling furtively at Joseph.

"I have been given to understand that something very important took place near Caesarea Philippi—something that none of the apostles have ever forgotten, even to this day."

"Especially this apostle." Peter sighed.

"Tell me, Peter, was the situation with the authorities becoming so intolerable for Jesus that he had to take you far north into a strange, gentile city where the people had little love for the Jews and no one knew who you were?"

I held my breath when he dipped his head. After all, he wasn't under any obligation to me. He could just as well stand up, say goodbye to us, and leave. But from all I had read, this rugged apostle had never avoided confrontations of any sort after the crucifixion, and I was gambling that he wouldn't run now. He didn't. Pointing to the purple stripe on my tunic, he said, "I'll tell you, Matthias, but I am certain you will not comprehend the consequences behind the story."

"Try me."

"Jesus was speaking to a crowd in Magdala, on the shores of Galilee, when the Pharisees and Sadducees interrupted him, as they had done so often, and demanded that he show them a sign, direct from heaven, to attest to his words and deeds. They accused him of many things: that he preached a kingdom to come far different from what they had been taught to expect by our prophets, that he mocked our customs and traditions, that he violated the Law without shame, and that he spoke with authority that was not his. 'A sign from heaven,' they demanded, 'show us a sign so that we will know you are not a false prophet.' "

"What did Jesus do?"

"He remained calm and waited until they grew weary of their own voices. Then he answered his tormentors by saying, 'When it is evening, you say, it will be fair weather: for the sky is red. And in the morning, you say, it will be foul today: for the sky is red and threatening. Oh, you hypocrites, you can read the face of the sky, but you cannot read the signs of the times. This wicked and adulterous generation wants a sign, and there shall be no sign given other than the sign of the prophet Jonah.' "

"The sign of Jonah?"

"More than six hundred years ago Jonah warned the people of Nineveh to repent their sinful ways swiftly, for soon they would be facing judgment. His words were ignored and the city was eventually destroyed."

"What happened after Jesus chastised the Pharisees and Sadducees?"

"He left them standing in the crowd and brought us to the waterfront, where we boarded a small boat and sailed north to Bethsaida. On that journey he warned us to be on our guard and never allow the doctrines of the Pharisees and Sadducees to leaven our beliefs. When we landed at Bethsaida we traveled farther north on land, for a day, until we arrived in the hills near Caesarea Philippi. There, far from the crowds and his tormentors, Jesus was able to teach us for many days in peace and tranquility."

"And then something happened?"

Peter nodded ruefully. "I opened my big mouth once too often."

"Tell me."

"One morning we were sitting on the slopes, watching the clouds sail slowly past the peak of Mount Hermon, to the north, when Jesus interrupted our thoughts by asking us who the people thought he was. Andrew replied that some said he was John the Baptist, and Thomas said that others believed he was Elijah or Jeremiah or one of the other prophets. Then Jesus said, 'And how about all of you? Who do you say I am?' I remember the strange looks that passed from one to another but no one dared to answer the master, so finally I stood up and said, 'You are the Christ!'"

"The Christ—meaning the Messiah who would come to deliver the Jews from their enemies and restore the nation? The anointed one?"

"Yes."

"Had you ever heard Jesus claim, in public or private, that he was the Messiah?"

"No."

"In other words, *you* told *him* something that he had never admitted to any of you, himself?"

"Yes."

"How did he take your declaration?"

"He seemed both shocked and pleased by my words, telling me that flesh and blood had not revealed it to me, but his Father who was in heaven. Then he charged all the apostles to tell no man what they had heard and told us that soon he must go to Jerusalem and suffer many things of the elders and chief priests and scribes, and they would kill him but he would be raised again on the third day. That's when my

106

mouth brought down his wrath on me. I had listened, with heavy heart, to his prophecies of agony and shame and death. How could such terrible evil befall the Messiah? 'God forbid, Lord!' I said. 'None of those things will ever happen to you!' "

"Jesus had said that he *must* go to Jerusalem?"

"Yes."

"And he became angry at your refusal to accept his words?"

"More than that. He laid his hands on me and shook me and shouted, 'Get thee behind me, Satan! You are a hindrance and an offense to me, for your thoughts are not of God but of man!' "

"As if he knew what was ahead, for him, and your denial of his prophecy would only make it more difficult for him to bear?"

"Yes, but I did not realize it at that time. Then, because all the others had been filled with fear by his rare display of temper, the master put his arms around me as if to apologize and said, 'If any man will come after me, let him deny himself and take up his cross, and follow me. For whosoever will save his life shall lose it: and whosoever will lose his life for my sake shall find it. For what does it profit a man if he gains the whole world and loses his own soul?' "

I happened to glance at Joseph. The old man was watching and waiting—waiting with obvious trepidation for me to abandon the reporter's role and assume the part of a probing Roman tribune bent on discovering the truth for his Christ Commission. Joseph's waiting was over.

"Peter, you were undoubtedly the closest to Jesus of all the apostles, were you not?"

He nodded.

"But Jesus had never told even you, in so many words, that he was the Messiah, before you spoke up at Caesarea Philippi, isn't that true?"

"That is true," he admitted, sitting back in his chair as if he suddenly felt a need to increase the space between us. As he retreated, I moved forward and planted *my* elbows on the tabletop.

"Peter, I think I can understand why Jesus would not want the people to be told that he was the Messiah. His life was already in jeopardy, and such an announcement from any of you would have surely hastened his end. But why didn't he tell you, his closest and most trusted friend, who he was? Why did it finally fall upon you to tell *him?*"

He didn't reply. I tried again.

"Just as important, how did you know he was the Christ since he had never told you so? Obviously none of the other apostles thought he was, or they would have spoken when he asked them. How did you know, Peter—or were you just speaking words of flattery that you thought would please him and lift his spirits?"

"I knew!"

"How?"

"Had you heard him speak or seen his miracles, Matthias, you too would have believed. Had you been witness when he cured the man with leprosy and the centurion's servant with palsy and the woman who suffered twelve years with an issue of blood and the daughter of Jairus and the man with the withered hand and so many others that their names would fill your book—then you too would have known that he was the Messiah!"

"And the others who accompanied him and observed the same deeds and works that you did: why did they not know what you professed to know?"

"In time, all their eyes were opened to the truth," he said.

"Including Judas?"

His shoulders sagged. No answer. But he was hanging tough and I couldn't help admiring his patience. Careful, I thought. Remember why you're here. I said, "Throughout the history of the Jewish people there have been many unusual tricks of magic performed that were called miracles by the people. Tell me, how do you describe a miracle?"

Peter pondered my question for several minutes before replying. "A true miracle is not a trick of magic that anyone can learn to perform. It is a demonstration of God's unlimited power, and it usually runs contrary to the laws of nature as we know them to be. A miracle is an expression of God's will and purpose, and when we are witness to one it provides us with renewed faith that he is with us always."

"By that definition, did Jesus perform miracles?"

"The miracles were wrought by Jesus," Peter corrected me, "but the power to perform them came from God."

"From your God—or mine?"

"Romans or Jews, Matthias, there is only one God!"

"Tell me, Peter, did Moses perform miracles when he transformed a rod into a serpent at the command of the pharaoh and later when he parted the sea of reeds so that your people could escape from the armies of Egypt?"

"Yes."

108

"Did Elijah perform miracles when he raised the widow's son from the dead and when he had the troops of Ahaziah consumed by fire?"

"Yes."

Joseph was glaring at me, and I was sure the old fox thought he knew where I was going with my questions. "Peter," I continued, "when Elisha supplied water to King Jehoshaphat in the wilderness of Edom and cured a leper and caused an axhead to float in the water—were these things tricks of magic or miracles?"

"Miracles."

"When Daniel was sealed in the den of lions by King Darius and emerged the next morning unharmed—had he performed a miracle?"

"Yes."

I ran my finger slowly across the glass tabletop. "Did any of these great miracle workers of the Jews ever claim to be a god—or the Son of God—or the Messiah?"

At last Peter realized where I had been leading him. "No." He sighed.

"Miracles, then, of themselves, have never been considered by your people as a sign that he who worked them was anything more than a prophet at the very most, is that correct?"

"Yes."

"Was the Jewish Messiah—he who would someday come to free your people from bondage, deliver them from their enemies, and establish the Kingdom of God here on earth—was he expected to prove his authority by performing miracles for the people?"

"No."

"Then how is it that you called Jesus the Christ, the Messiah, based on the miracles you said he performed, when the long-awaited Christ was not expected to perform any?"

The big man nervously clenched and unclenched his fists. "Matthias," he almost whispered, "I would have believed that Jesus was the Christ without a single miracle. His words alone set him far above any prophet who has ever lived."

We had now come full circle. "And yet the wisest of your sages, the Pharisees and Sadducees, were always challenging Jesus to show them a sign to attest to his words. Why is that?"

"They tried, in their evil ways, to discredit his every word and move. When one has little faith, one must survive from day to day on signs. As Jesus said, 'Blessed is he who does not need to see the red of an evening sky to know that to-morrow will be fair.' "

"Speaking of faith, I understand that one day, as Jesus was entering Capernaum, a centurion begged him to heal a servant who was sick with palsy. Do you remember what happened?"

Peter nodded. "As if it were yesterday. Jesus said, 'I will come and heal him,' but the centurion answered, 'I am not worthy that you should come under my roof: speak the word only and my servant shall be healed.' When Jesus heard this he said, 'Verily I say unto you, I have not found so great a faith in Israel.' "

"Jesus used the word 'faith'?"

"He did."

"And the servant was cured?"

"Jesus told the centurion, 'Go thy way; and as you have believed, so be it done unto thee.' And the servant was cured that very same hour. He lives in Capernaum to this day, should you wish to verify my story."

I said, "There was a time on the lake when you and the other apostles became terrified by a tempest which tossed waves over your boat. Some of you went to Jesus, who was sleeping, and said, 'Lord, save us or we perish.' What did he reply?"

Peter actually blushed. "How is it that you know such things?"

"What did Jesus say when you woke him?" I persisted.

"He was angry at us and asked, 'Why are you fearful, you of little faith?' "

"The word 'faith' was used by him again?"

"Yes. Then he stood in the pitching boat and rebuked the winds and the sea, and there came a great calm which frightened us more than the storm, for we wondered what manner of man this was that even the winds and the sea obeyed him."

"That sea, Peter, as you know, is notorious for its sudden squalls caused by the desert winds that sweep over the mountains near its shore and descend into the middle of the water, pushing waves in all directions. Do not those storms on Galilee usually subside as swiftly as they begin?"

Peter smiled tolerantly. "I have been a fisherman all my life. No summer squall such as you describe would have caused me any concern, for I have survived hundreds of them. But that storm had me convinced that we would all

110

sleep, that night, at the bottom of the sea—until Jesus saved us."

"There was another occasion, one you have already mentioned, when a woman who had been afflicted with an issue of blood for twelve years came close to Jesus and touched his garment. I understand he turned to her and said, 'Daughter, be of good comfort, your faith has made you whole.' He did use that word 'faith' again?"

"Your sources are good, Matthias. I was standing next to him when that woman came forward, and those were his exact words to her."

"Do you recall the two blind men?"

"I do. They came to Jesus, in Capernaum, crying, 'Son of David, have mercy on us.' When they asked to be cured, he said, 'Do you believe I am able to do this?' They answered that they did believe, and he touched their eyes, saying, 'According to your faith, be it unto you,' and their eyes were opened."

"Those who believed—those who had faith that he could perform miracles—were cured of their infirmities, and those who did not believe were not cured. Is that a reasonable conclusion?"

Peter objected. "That is not reasonable. There was far more to his works than what you are ascribing to them. You do not understand—"

"Peter, Peter, be logical. Certainly you can separate truth from the passion of hysteria after all these years. I have been told that Jesus never performed a miracle in his home village of Nazareth. Why? Because the people there knew him as a carpenter—and carpenters, no matter how skilled, cannot perform miracles. His own townspeople did not believe in his power; therefore he could perform no mighty works for them! Do you recall another incident, one involving a fig tree in Bethany?"

His eyes grew large. "How could you know of that? Who are you, Matthias?"

"Tell me about the fig tree."

"Jesus was hungry and went out to a fig tree in a meadow. It had no fruit because it was not the season, and so he cursed it and it withered away. Then he turned to us who were with him and said, 'Verily, I say unto you, if you have faith and doubt not, you shall not only do this which is done to the fig tree, but also, if you shall say to this mountain, remove yourself and be cast into the sea, it shall be done. And

111

all things, whatsoever you shall ask in prayer, believing, you shall receive.' "

I repeated his last words slowly. " 'Believing, you shall receive'?"

"That is what he said."

"On one occasion did you and some of the other apostles try to cure a lunatic youth and fail?"

"Yes," he murmured. "And when we were unable to do any good, the boy's father went to Jesus."

"What did Jesus do?"

"He said, 'O faithless and perverse generation, how long shall I be with you? How long shall I suffer you? Bring the boy to me.' "

"Jesuus called all of you 'faithless'?"

"To our shame."

"Then what did he do?"

"He cured the boy. Later, we went to him and asked why none of us had been able to heal the afflicted one, and he replied, 'Because of your unbelief, for verily I say unto you that if you have faith as a grain of mustard seed you shall say to this mountain, remove to yonder place and it shall remove; and nothing shall be impossible to you.' "

"Faith, again?"

"As little as a mustard seed."

"Peter, by now you have had several years to reflect on those events which took place during the last week of his life. Tell me, was the faith of Jesus so strong that he truly believed he could do more than move mountains after he entered Jerusalem, a week before Passover?"

"I do not understand your question."

"Did Jesus believe that with only the twelve of you he could liberate the people from Roman rule despite Pilate's soldiers and even the mighty legions of Vitellius, only two days' march away, in Antioch? Did he expect to perform the miracle of miracles against all the forces that were arrayed against him?"

Peter, like the others, had shown no signs of losing control of himself or his temper through all my questioning. Now he replied, "Matthias, I fear that you still do not understand the nature of miracles. The power to perform them does not come from one's faith but from God. However, faith must be present in order for your heart and soul to be open so that God may enter. Only then, when the Kingdom of God is within you, can mountains be moved."

"And governments overthrown!" I replied caustically.

At that moment a servant silently approached our table and placed an ornate silver goblet before each of · us. Then the young man filled them with red wine, placed the carafe before Joseph, and departed. The interruption couldn't have come at a better time for me. Although Peter had been more than indulgent, I knew I was running out of time with him, and I needed that pause in order to plan my remaining questions so that they would lead Peter into explaining his whereabouts after Jesus was arrested. Inexplicably, not one of the four Gospels mentions his name even once, during all those drama-filled hours between the trials of Jesus and his hurried visit to the empty tomb with John, approximately fifty-six hours later. Where had he been and what was he doing while his master was being tried and crucified?

I drained my goblet and said, "Peter, I know that those days surrounding the crucifixion and burial of Jesus must be filled with painful memories for you but—"

He reached across the table and patted my arm. "They are no longer drenched in sorrow, Matthias. Now I know what I was too ignorant and blind to understand at the time."

"Good. Sometime before Jesus arrested, he made a certain prophecy to you concerning the crowing of a cock?"

His face clouded momentarily. "He did. We had completed the Passover supper at the house of my sister and nephew, Mary and Mark, and the twelve of us had departed from the house singing hymns. Young Mark accompanied us as far as the city gate before I sent him home."

"All of you believed you were returning to your beds in Bethany?"

"Yes, but as we walked, Jesus told us certain things that slowed our steps. He said that we would fall away from him that very night, for it was written that the shepherd would be smitten and the sheep of the flock would be scattered abroad. We crowded around him in the dark, pleading for an explanation, but all he would tell us was that after he was risen he would go before us into Galilee. Some thought he planned to awake before us, in the morning, and travel north by himself until we joined him later, but I could not accept his words so I spoke out, again to my everlasting sorrow."

Peter's eyes were moist and his voice trembled. The interrogation was beginning to take its toll. "What did you say?" I asked softly.

"First, I placed my arm around him as if to protect him. Then I boasted that though all the others should fall away from him I would never desert him. He pulled my face close to his until I could feel the tears that covered his cheeks, and he whispered in my ear, 'Verily, I say unto you, that this night, before the cock crows you will deny me three times.' I replied, 'Never! Even though I die with you I will not deny you!' He kissed my cheek and smiled sadly."

"He led you and the others to Gethsemane?"

"Yes. A small path crosses through the garden and goes up the Mount of Olives and down the other side to Bethany. We had walked it often, rather than circle around the mount on a much longer route."

"I've seen it, Peter. Were you surprised when Jesus said he wanted to stop in the garden to pray?"

"I was, especially after his prophecy of terrible things to come that very night. Bethany seemed a much safer place to be than a dark garden if he was in any danger. It was also very late and cold, and all of us were drowsy from the food and wine. Still, we always did his bidding, and when he asked James and John and me to remain near him, the others moved farther into the garden up the path toward a large cave that had sheltered us on many other occasions. Then Jesus said, 'My soul is heavy with sorrow, even unto death. Stay here and keep watch with me.' "

"For what were you watching?"

Peter raised his wide shoulders. "He never told us before he walked away and knelt, with his arms resting on a large flat rock. The clouds no longer hid the moon so I could see him clearly. Then we heard him say, 'Oh, Father, if it be possible, let this cup pass from me; nevertheless not my wishes but yours be done.' The next thing I remember he was shaking my head gently and saying, 'Could you not watch with me one hour? The spirit is willing but the flesh is weak.' Before I was fully awake he was gone again, and soon I heard him cry out, 'Oh, my Father, if this cup may not pass away from me, except I drink it, thy will be done.' I soon fell asleep again, next to James and John, who were both snoring from the wine they had consumed. When next Jesus woke me, he said, 'Behold, the hour is at hand, and the Son of man is betrayed into the hands of sinners. Rise, let us be going; he who will betray me is here.' "

"Peter," I interrupted, "during the past six years you must have relived that night many times, in your mind."

"Both awake and in my dreams."

"Has it ever occurred to you that Jesus was actually waiting there, in that garden, to be arrested, and if need be he would have remained there all night—or until he was taken?"

114

Joseph of Arimathea gasped, but Peter's face brightened as if he was pleased to find someone who shared what must have been a minority viewpoint. "I reached that conclusion long ago, Matthias! Everything I can recall Jesus doing in the city, during that last week, seemed to have but one purpose, that of challenging the authorities to arrest him. He upset the tables of the money-changers in the Temple, but the guards were afraid to seize him since rumors had already circulated in Jerusalem that he had raised a dead man in Bethany. Then he scolded the chief priests and elders, insulted the respected Pharisees in front of the crowds, baited the scribes and Herodians, and yet they dared not touch him while he walked among the people, for fear of an uprising that would have brought down the sword of Rome on all of them. It was plain to me, if not to the others, that Jesus had made himself a man marked for execution—and the only question remaining was when and where it would take place."

"In truth, Peter, he committed suicide, didn't he?"

"No! He did not! He offered his life, in sacrifice, for all mankind, as a ransom to hasten the coming Kingdom of Heaven!"

I sidestepped that one. If I got myself involved in that theological maze I'd never get untracked. "Was there a large arresting party?"

Peter smiled bitterly. "With all their torches and lanterns, the garden was brighter than at any hour of the day. Chief priests, Pharisees, Sadducees, Temple guards, and even a contingent of Roman soldiers from the Antonia garrison: two hundred or more, at least, were in that mob, including—Judas."

"Do you know why Judas betrayed his master?"

"No. It is still a great mystery to me, Matthias."

"Something else puzzles me about the Judas situation, Peter. According to the others he was excused by Jesus from the supper just as it began, supposedly, as everyone thought, to perform some errand. Now, if he went directly from the house of your sister to the authorities and told them where they could find Jesus, why did they not go and arrest him there immediately? Instead, it was almost six hours later before they took Jesus into custody. Do you know what caused the long delay?"

"No, I do not. I do know that the arresting party first went to the house where we had taken the Paschal supper, but by then many hours had passed and we had already departed."

"Why was only Jesus arrested?"

"John and I were also seized, but as the three of us were being led from the garden a priest held his lantern close to our faces and spit on us before he told the guards that Jesus was the only one Caiaphas wanted. Our hands were untied and we were thrown to the ground and kicked, especially by the soldiers, before they took our Lord away. When we could finally stand we went back into the garden and called for James and the others, but the place was deserted."

"I know you didn't return to Bethany. Tell me what you did."

"We started up that path, and then I remembered my boast to Jesus that I would never desert him even though the others did. I stopped and told John that I was going with Jesus. He turned and followed me. Although most of the lanterns and torches of the mob had been extinguished, so as not to alarm people of the city who might still be awake, it was not difficult to follow the arrest party. First they went to the house of Annas, who had been high priest for many years and was the father-in-law of Caiaphas. When they arrived there, the Roman cohort marched back to Antonia as if their work was done. After Jesus was in the house of Annas for only a short while, the Temple guards brought him here, to the upper city, to the house of Caiaphas."

"What did you and John do?"

"Do? What could we do? Our faces and bodies ached and bled from the Roman boots, we were nearly exhausted from lack of sleep, and our hearts were numb with sadness. Our beloved master, whom we loved more than life itself, had just been dragged through the streets like the most despised of criminals and we were powerless to help him. We huddled around a small fire that burned in the high priest's courtyard and waited for some word from inside. Soon several members of the great Sanhedrin arrived, one or two at a time. What were they doing to our master? Later, one of the servants of the priest came out into the yard and accused me of having been with Jesus of Galilee. Did I stand up and proudly admit that I was his friend and follower? No! Instead I denied any knowledge of Jesus and moved closer to the porch, hoping I might catch sight of him. Before long another maid passed nearby and cried that I was a friend of Jesus. Again I denied that I knew him, but her words attracted the attention of some of the guards who had delivered the Lord to Caiaphas and they approached me, saying that I surely must be an accomplice of the prisoner since I spoke as a Galilean. I cursed them and said that I didn't even know him."

Even though I knew what was coming, I wanted to hear it from Peter. But I had to wait. The big man had buried his head in his hands, and the wrenching moans that escaped from his barrel chest were almost more than I could take. Joseph of Arimathea turned his head.

At last, Peter spread his huge fingers and squinted at me from between them, asking plaintively, "Do you want to know what happened next, Matthias? I'll tell you! After I had denied my Lord for the third time, as he said I would, I swear to you I heard the crowing of a cock just before I felt myself falling—falling to the ground and into the blessed escape of dark sleep."

Shock? The mind's ultimate escape from physical pain or the shattering blow of an unexpected, overwhelming event that comes as a surprise to the psyche. Characterized usually by a decrease in blood pressure, a weak and rapid pulse, and, very often, unconsciousness.

"What is your next recollection?" I asked gently.

"I remember hearing the terrible sound of wailing and lamenting women, such as one cannot escape during those days of mourning after a burial. I opened my eyes and saw John leaning over me and was relieved by his presence, but when I tried to ask him for what reason the women wept I could not move my jaws. I recognized the room in which I lay as that of my nephew, Mark, and I knew I was in the house of my sister and then I must have slept again."

"How had you managed to get there from the high priest's courtyard where you fell?"

Peter smiled sheepishly. "John later told me that he had been unable to lift me from the ground, much less carry me, so he ran here to Joseph for help and with Shem's strong arms they managed to place me in Joseph's carriage and take me to Mary's home—the place where we had taken our supper with the Lord not many hours before."

"What else do you remember?"

"A dream. While I slept I could see myself fishing from my old boat and Jesus came to me, walking on the water, and when I saw it was the Lord I leaped into the sea to go to him and felt myself sinking beneath the waves before he took my hands and held me up and then I awoke, soaked with sweat, screaming his name, and then John wiped my brow and spoke to me until I slept again."

"At that time you still did not know that Jesus had been tried, crucified, and buried?"

"I knew of nothing that transpired until that first morning

117

after the Sabbath, when I awoke and told John that I hungered and soon my sister brought me a bowl of hot soup. Only after it was empty did John tell me that our Lord was dead—crucified at the hands of Pilate and the high priest. We shed many tears together before I fell back on the cot and began to pray for the strength we would need to survive without our beloved master. I would have welcomed death, that very moment, for I had no wish to face life without Jesus by my side."

Now I was back, once more, to that morning after the Jewish Sabbath, that fateful day of discovery: Easter Sunday. "What happened next, Peter?"

He raised one of his massive fists and said, "Suddenly I heard loud screaming in the room and felt a body fall across me. I opened my eyes to see Mary Magdalene's terrified face, close to mine, and she was clawing at my shoulders with her nails, crying, 'They have taken away the Lord out of the tomb and we know not where they have laid him!' Again and again she said the words, shaking me all the while, until John lifted her from me and my sister came and took her away. My thoughts were still cloudy from sleep and the fever, but I suspected that the poor woman's mind must have come loose again. She had once been possessed of seven devils before the Lord had laid hands on her, and I reasoned that the events of the past few days had brought about a relapse of her old condition."

"What did you do?"

"Somehow I found the strength to crawl from my cot and put on my tunic and sandals. Then I asked John if he knew where Jesus had been buried, and he nodded, and I told him we should go to the grave and see for ourselves if what Mary had said was true. We both ran but John, being younger, arrived at the tomb long before me. When I finally entered the garden, not far from the hill of Golgotha where John had told me that Jesus had been crucified, John was standing beside the opening of the tomb, waiting. Resting against the sepulchre was a huge round stone that had been rolled away from the mouth of the grave. John's voice sounded like a small child's. 'The tomb is empty!' he said, and immediately I went inside."

"Had you noticed any soldiers in the vicinity, any guards from the Temple, anyone at all?"

"No one. Once inside the tomb I could almost stand, and there, on a shelf hewn from the rock, I saw the sheet that had covered the body and smelled the heavy fragrance of spices. The sheet was the usual long and narrow piece of linen that is used in burial, wound around the body many times with spices and herbs inserted between the layers to prevent the body's corruption. This sheet appeared to be still wrapped around something, but when I dared to place my hand on the cloth it collapsed and some of the spices fell from its folds to the floor of the cave. On the same shelf, only an arm's length away from the sheet, lay the napkin that is always placed on the dead one's head. When I backed out of the tomb, John went in, and he soon emerged, crying, 'Now I believe!' and we both knelt in prayers of gratitude to God for raising our Lord from his grave."

"You both believed he had been resurrected from the dead?"

"We knew it! I told John to hasten to Bethany, to the house of Martha and Mary, for I was certain the others were hiding there and would be overjoyed with the news that our precious Lord had done that which he had prophesied. I also told John to warn the others to say nothing to any man for fear that the authorities would claim that we had removed the body and cause us more trouble. Then I returned to my sister's house."

"Peter, when you first entered the tomb did you notice a great supply of spices and herbs on the floor of the tomb?"

"No, only their odor filled the place."

I turned to Joseph, who was scowling at me as if my last question had offended him. "You and Nicodemus prepared the body for burial. You used the prescribed amount of myrrh and aloe?"

"Of course we did, Matthias," the old man replied testily. "More than the prescribed amount, all placed with care between the folds of the long sheet as we wrapped the body."

"You were not hurried because of the approaching Sabbath, commencing at sundown?"

"We were hurried, but there was sufficient time to prepare the body according to the Law. Why do you ask?"

"I was wondering why, if anyone stole the body of Jesus from the tomb, they would go to all the trouble of unwinding the yards of linen from his body, carefully remove all the spices that were packed between each layer so that they did not fall to the floor, remove the napkin from his face, and carry a naked body from the tomb? Then, having done all that, why would they carefully rewind the sheet, replace it on the shelf after inserting all the spices in its folds again, put the napkin back where his head had rested, and leave *without*

119

rolling the stone back across the opening to hide their crime? Why didn't they just roll the stone away, take his body—grave cloth, spices, and all—roll the stone back to conceal their theft, and be gone? Seems much more logical, doesn't it? As you describe the scene at the tomb, Peter, it's exactly as one would leave it in order to fool the public into believing that Jesus had risen from the dead."

Peter fell back in his chair as if I had struck him. He stared at me glassy-eyed, looking more betrayed and disappointed than angry. "I have told you nothing but the truth—and you respond with rumors that still will not die because they are fed constantly by the vipers of this city! Historian of great integrity and talent you may be, Matthias, but you remain blind to the truth where it concerns Jesus!"

He began to rise, but I tentatively placed my hand on his shoulder and he settled back in his chair. With his heavy voice resounding against the walls of the peristyle and his dark eyes snapping in cadence to his words, it was difficult to picture this man ever denying his master three times in one night.

"Forgive me, Peter. I am merely trying to understand a very complicated matter, and I am more confused now than ever. I have heard from many, including yourself, that Jesus offered his life in sacrifice for all mankind, as a ransom to hasten the coming Kingdom of Heaven. Am I to conclude that Jesus hoped to accomplish, through his own death, that which he had been unable to bring about with his teachings? Was there not a better way to accomplish his goal, a way that would have left no doubt in anyone's mind as to who he was and what he intended to do for his people?"

"How?"

"In the course of my investigation I have been unable to uncover a single report of any miracle performed by Jesus during his last week in this city. With the vast crowds in Jerusalem and the Temple for Passover week, instead of attacking the money-changers, the high priests, the Pharisees, and other authorities, would it not have been far wiser for Jesus to perform a single miracle for the multitude, a miracle so majestic and inspiring that all manner of men, even the chief priests, would have recognized that he was truly their Messiah—and even the Son of God?"

Peter leaped to his feet and leaned toward me until his perspiring face was only a few inches from mine.

"He did!"

"He did what?"

120

"He did perform such a miracle as you have just described!"

"How? What miracle?"

"Jesus allowed himself to be tried and tormented and scourged and crucified and buried as a man. On the third day he walked out of his tomb as the Son of God, and the special conditions in the tomb were as *he* left them—not to fool the people but as a sign to them that he truly had been raised from the dead by his Father!"

Long after Peter had departed, Joseph and I continued to sit at the table, sipping wine but saying little. Peter's aura and charisma still lingered around us. Finally the old man said, "Matthias, despite the disappointment you may be experiencing, I believe you have made great progress."

When I didn't reply he continued.

"You have already spoken with James, the brother of Jesus; with Matthew; with James, the son of thunder . . . and now Peter. Tell me, do you still believe that these men you have met are the kind who would risk their lives, every day in this city, preaching a resurrection of Jesus that they know is a lie? And for personal gain and power?"

Frustrated at the possibility of having to cross two more names from my dwindling list of suspects, I replied impatiently, "Joseph, the history of this world is filled with men and women who have lived a life of lies in order to line their pockets or to seize power or hold it once they have it."

"How about you, Matthias? Could you live a life based on a lie?"

"Perhaps," I heard myself saying, "under certain circumstances."

Joseph scratched his left nostril and studied me closely. "You say you could live your life based on a lie, and I will admit this is possible for any of us. But could you lay down your life for a lie?"

"No, of course not," I snapped. "Not even a fool would do that."

Check! As soon as the words left my mouth I knew I had been trapped. I waited helplessly for Joseph of Arimathea to close me out.

"Matthias, would you consider any of those you have met, so far, to be fools?"

"No," I admitted.

"And in your extensive research, did you ever learn the ultimate fate of James, the brother of Jesus?"

121

Checkmate! "Yes," I answered reluctantly. "He will be stoned to death by orders of the high priest Ananus in A.D. 62."

"And Matthew?"

"Tradition has it that he will die a martyr in Ethiopia."

"And James, the son of thunder?"

"He will be beheaded by Herod Agrippa, in A.D. 44."

"And Peter? What fate will befall our friend Peter?"

"Peter will be crucified in Rome in A.D. 68, with his head at the bottom of a wooden cross. He will request that he be crucified in that manner since he does not believe he is worthy of dying in the same position as his Lord."

"Yes," the old man said as he rose, "I would say you had made great progress, considering this is only your third day. Now, if it will not disturb your schedule too much, would you like to accompany me after lunch when I deliver my annual Temple tithe to the high priest, Caiaphas, at his home? I'm certain he can add a fact or two to your collection."

"I can ask him anything, without getting you in trouble?"

"So long as he agrees to meet with you in private, yes."

"Even why he has a black-hooded man following us?"

The old man chuckled. "You can save your breath on that one. I've learned we are being spied on by Pilate, not Caiaphas."

"And we'll get to Pilate eventually, won't we?"

"If he doesn't get to us first."

nine

"JESUS?"

"Yes."

"Jesus . . . Jesus," he murmured. "It is such a common name. . . ."

"A young preacher—from Galilee. Crucified. By Pilate, about six years ago."

His rust-colored eyes narrowed. "Ah, yes, yes, him I remember. A troublemaker! Our patience is tested by many false prophets, every year. That one actually believed he had been sent by God to personally redeem everyone's sins. Went around stirring up the crowds with promises of a new kingdom here on earth—a flagrant act of sedition against Rome. I had no choice, in accord with my sworn oath to protect the safety of my people, but to turn him over to your esteemed procurator, Pilate, for punishment well deserved."

I was alone with the high priest of the Jews, Joseph Caiaphas, in a second-floor room of the palace where Jesus had been tried and condemned to death, and I was sitting only a few feet away from the man who, according to Matthew, Mark, Luke, and John, had engineered the whole thing. Listening to the cultured enunciation of Caiaphas, I almost pitied him. How could he possibly envision, in his wildest dreams, that his name was destined, along with Herod's and Pilate's, to live forever in infamy?

Joseph of Arimathea, bless him, had somehow managed to promote a private audience for me. After delivering his tithe, a massive chest carried into the palace's underground vaults by a straining Shem, the old man had graciously endured the effusive gratitude from scores of young priests who dutifully formed a reception line to embrace him, one at a time, with an accompanying kiss on both his cheeks. Then he was ushered upstairs to meet with Caiaphas while I waited nervously in the busy lobby and pretended not to notice the double takes from passersby when they caught sight of the purple

123

stripe on my tunic. Roman citizens, I gathered, were not frequent visitors in the house of the high priest.

Joseph finally descended the worn marble steps, after what had seemed like hours, and patted my shoulder. "You are in luck, Matthias. His excellency has agreed to meet with you immediately. I shall wait for you here. Since I am still a member of the Sanhedrin, over which he presides as always, I fear that my presence might inhibit his responses. However, I have told him many things about you, and he seems more than willing to answer your questions." He winked, and on his dignified features the act looked almost grotesque. "May you find the truth," he said, shoving me gently.

Climbing the long stairway, I kept wondering what the old man had told the spiritual leader of the Jewish people that was impressive enough for Caiaphas to interrupt his busy schedule in order to be interviewed by an unknown historian. I wasn't long in finding out.

"And how are things in Rome, sir?"

Careful! Remember, it's A.D. 36. How were things, that year, in the ancient city on the Tiber? I forced a smile and said, "Your excellency, I have been traveling for many months, but everything was quiet and peaceful, at least for Rome, when I was last there."

"And Tiberius? How is your emperor's health?"

"Tiberius is still on Capri, of course, so we don't hear very much except rumors. I imagine that things must be very difficult for him now that Sejanus is no longer alive to oversee things in the capital."

Caiaphas made a clucking sound with his tongue. "Terrible thing, that Sejanus affair. To think that he would betray his emperor after so much trust had been placed in him."

I had a sudden impulse to ask how he felt about a man named Judas Iscariot, but that would come later.

"Did you know that Pilate was a friend of Sejanus?" he asked.

"Yes, so I've heard."

"I'm surprised that the procurator has not been replaced, now that his mentor has been strangled by the senate."

Was he testing me? I shrugged and said, "Pilate has already served ten years here, so I assume that Vitellius must have great faith in him."

His expression never changed. "And how is our governor? Enjoying the climate of Antioch, no doubt. Joseph tells me that you two are old friends, neighbors when you were children?"

124

So that's how I got in so easily! The Arimathean had probably laced his description of me with so many hints and innuendos that he's got Caiaphas suspecting just what he wants him to suspect: that I might be nosing around for more than historical background material. And of course any friend of the governor is certain to receive tender loving care in this palace. I tried to sound noncommittal. "The governor is in the best of health, as always."

I didn't hear the knock on the door, but when Caiaphas turned and shouted, "Enter!" a black-robed youth appeared, bowing and apologizing, carrying several scrolls in a wicker basket.

"Please excuse me . . . Matthias, is it? I must sign these so that they can be posted in the Temple today."

I sat back, grateful for the opportunity to study the man. Nothing in his calm manner and low-pitched, almost gentle voice gave any hint of the cold-blooded and devious human being that my research, from a majority of admittedly biased writers and historians, had led me to believe must be encased in those soft linen clothes. High priests before him had come and gone so rapidly that fifteen had served in the past sixty-five years, three for less than twelve months, and yet this seemingly harmless and meek little man had already survived for seven years under the procurator Valerius Gratus and for the past ten under his successor, Pontius Pilate.

Except for exceedingly thin and pale lips, his small unlined face had no distinguishing features and his pointed pure-white beard looked like many others I had seen in the lobby and the Temple. Across his chest was a tight-fitting vest, woven of gold and blue threads tied over a shirt of lustrous red-dyed linen above matching breeches. On his child-sized feet were gold mesh slippers. An ascetic in the garb of royalty.

When the clerk finally retreated from the room, Caiaphas immediately resumed our conversation as if it had never been interrupted. A developed skill of the good executive. "How long is it since you have seen Vitellius?" he asked casually.

"Three months—four, perhaps." I lied uneasily, wondering how I could change the subject before I trapped myself.

"He has been a fair and understanding governor to our people. It must give him great pleasure to know that the provinces under his command, including this one, will finally get the recognition they deserve throughout the empire, when your work is circulated."

"I hope that I do not disappoint him," I said.

"But Matthias, with all the great kings and warriors and

125

prophets that fill this nation's past, I cannot understand why a man like this Jesus is deserving of even a single word from your pen."

I started to reply but hesitated. Joseph had taken me this far with his fictions about me; should I go the rest of the way? And would it work? I inhaled and said, with my best straight face, "It was at the suggestion of Vitellius that I initiated my inquiry about Jesus."

"Vitellius?" His voice broke. "But why? For what reason? The name of Jesus is no more than a flyspeck beside the names of our great prophets."

"Your excellency, I know that Vitellius values your opinions highly, but on this matter he apparently differs. He explained, when I last visited him, that always in the past, whenever a rebel movement got out of hand in this country, the most certain way to put an end to it was to hang its leader on a wooden cross. He said this had not happened when Jesus was executed; on the contrary, six years after Pilate crucified him the movement has grown so large that it even overflows this country's borders and thrives in Antioch, beneath the governor's nose. He said that any man who could inspire that kind of following, long after his death, may have been the greatest prophet ever born here, and so he suggested that I might want to include the Jesus story along with the others I write."

For a fleeting moment I thought I saw a flash of fear in the eyes of my host. He leaned on the small onyx tabletop and asked, "What have you managed to learn so far about this . . . this Jesus?"

I shook my head hopelessly. "The more I learn, the more confused I become. Some claim that he is your Messiah and they now await his return each day, as you are certainly aware, in the Temple courtyard. Others deny that he was any more than a charlatan and a sorcerer. Some claim to be witnesses to his curing the sick, healing the blind, and even raising the dead. Others insist he was only a magician and a rabble-rouser. Many even believe that he himself rose from the dead on the third day after his burial, while others say that his body was removed from the tomb in order to fool the people. This is why I prevailed on my old friend Joseph to try to arrange a meeting between us. From you, the holiest and most respected man in all Israel, I knew I would hear the truth."

Caiaphas nodded and pretended to study the woven designs on his vest. He tugged on one earlobe and then the other.

"Very well," he said, "I'll do whatever I can to help you learn the truth about this man. However, you must remember that we are dealing with events that took place six years ago, and memories, especially unpleasant ones, tend to fade away. Exactly what is it you want to know?"

"Let us begin, if you are willing, sir, by your telling me when you first became aware of Jesus. And, to simplify our discussions, let us base all our times on their relationship to his crucifixion."

The high priest stroked his beard and spoke slowly, choosing his words with great care. "As best I can recall, we began to hear stories about this Jesus perhaps ten months before his execution. They were the usual sort of thing. As you know, every Jew is waiting for the coming of the Messiah who will deliver our people to a perpetual Kingdom of God here on earth. God had once promised our ancestor Abraham that in him and his descendants all the world would be blessed and that someday we would enjoy the fruits of peace and plenty. It is our belief that God has continued to remind us of his promise through the words of those we call prophets, men such as Isaiah, Jeremiah, Samuel, Ezekiel, and Moses. As one might expect, it is inevitable that a land which brings forth so many true messengers of God's word also spawns countless false prophets, motivated by selfish and base interests. One of my most important duties, as high priest, is to protect the purity and integrity of Israel against the poison of such imposters by any means at my disposal."

"You considered Jesus another false prophet?"

"I did not consider him at all, in the beginning. There were several reports from friends in Galilee stating that this man had cured one affliction or another, but I paid little attention to them since they involved an uneducated carpenter from a poor little village called Nazareth."

"A man reported to have the power of healing and you were not even curious?"

"Why should I be? We have many magicians and sorcerers who travel across our land deceiving the people. Such reports are common. However, a few weeks after the first report, I received another that aroused my anger as well as my curiosity."

I nodded for him to continue.

"It seems that a family whose son was sick with palsy brought him in his cot to a house in Capernaum where Jesus was preaching, but the crowd was so great that they could not enter so they carried the boy in his bed up to the roof, parted the straw, and lowered him by rope into the room where Jesus was speaking. When Jesus saw this he was so taken with their faith that he said, 'Son, thy sins be forgiven you.' Several scribes were present, including he who eventually reported this incident to me, and they all wondered to themselves how Jesus dared to speak such blasphemy since only God can forgive sins. Though they had uttered not a word of protest, because they feared the crowd, Jesus turned to the scribes and asked why they were thinking such things in their hearts. Then he asked them whether it was easier to tell the youth that his sins were forgiven than it was to tell him to get up and walk. He said that to prove that the Son of man had power to forgive sins on earth he would speak to the boy again and he did, saying, 'Arise, and take up your cot, and go back to your own house.' And the boy, according to my witness, rose up, took his bed, and departed from the crowd, who were all amazed."

"Caiaphas," I said, purposely addressing him by name, "is such a healing common among the magicians you say are everywhere?"

"No. Those who were present said they had never seen one like it, especially when dealing with palsy."

"What did Jesus mean when he referred to himself as the 'Son of man'?"

The high priest shrugged. "It is a phrase found in many of our writings and psalms, meaning a man of simplicity and purity."

I just couldn't help myself. "But didn't your prophet Daniel write that 'one like the Son of man came with the clouds of heaven . . . and there was given him dominion . . . an everlasting dominion'?"

Caiaphas straightened up in his chair, eyeing me suspiciously. "Yes," he acknowledged weakly, but there was no explanation or rebuttal.

"Then didn't the use of the phrase 'Son of man,' by Jesus, cause you any concern?"

"No," he said recovering his full voice, "but his blasphemy did. To pretend to forgive sins is a grave offense against God and punishable under our laws by death through stoning. I immediately dispatched messages to many Temple associates and priests who live in the north country, requesting that they keep me informed of exactly what this man said as well as what he did. Our supreme court here, the Sanhedrin, has no authority outside this province of Judaea. However, I wished

128

to be prepared for the time when Jesus came to Jerusalem, as he was certain to do for the feast days."

"In the months that followed, what did you learn about his activities?"

"In truth they were a mixture of good and evil. We would hear that Jesus had cured a leper and two blind men, and all the while he was eating and drinking with publicans and sinners. He would make a dumb man talk and cure one possessed of demons, and then he would harvest corn on the Sabbath and sea without washing. Once he even cured a man with a withered hand—and he was brazen enough to do it before a crowd on the Sabbath!"

"But wasn't he chastised for his Sabbath activities on both occasions by the Pharisees, and didn't he respond to them with such logic that they were unable to deal with his reasoning, so they went away and began plotting how to destroy him?"

Caiaphas looked at me aghast. "What are you saying?"

"Didn't your reports tell you that when the Pharisees criticized Jesus and his disciples for picking corn on the Sabbath he reminded them of David, who, when he was once hungry, went into the Temple's sacred altar and ate the holy shewbread and also gave some to those who were with him? Jesus said that the Sabbath was made for man and not man for the Sabbath. And then, when he cured the man with the withered hand on the Sabbath, he asked those who chastised him if it was lawful to do good on the Sabbath or to do evil, to save a life or kill—and the Pharisees could find no answer to give him."

"How do you know these things? How long have you been collecting such information?"

I started to say twenty years. That would have lowered the curtain on everything in a hurry! "For many months, off and on. Tell me, Caiaphas, did you ever initiate a more active investigation into his activities?"

"Active investigation?"

"I mean did you ever instruct any of your priests or others who were proficient in your law to try to entrap Jesus into responding to their questions with answers that would condemn him as a lawbreaker or, at the very least, turn the people against him?"

"Sir!" He bristled, raising both fists: clenched. "I am the high priest of my people, and my integrity in all affairs is a matter of record. Ask your procurator if you suspect otherwise. I find your question insulting and offensive. Among

other things I am also a Sadducee. No member of the Sadducee, who all live strictly by the precepts of our holy written
Law, would ever consider resorting to such vile subterfuge."

"Forgive me. And the Pharisees?"

"I cannot speak for them. I know many in that party who
are honorable men and many who are not. Unlike us, they
also observe unwritten codes and alter the laws of Moses
whenever selfish conditions favor a change in their behavior—usually for the worst."

"Then you were not among those who asked Jesus, once
when he was in the Temple, whether or not it was lawful to
give tribute to Caesar?"

"I was not, although it was reported to me that in reply he
asked to be shown a coin, and when they did he inquired
whose image was on it, and after they said it was Caesar he
told them to render unto Caesar the things which are Caesar's; and unto God the things that are God's."

"Were you present, by chance," I asked, "when Jesus was
asked if it was unlawful for a man to put away his wife for
any cause?"

"No, although I understand his answer was that what God
had joined together, no man should put asunder. There was
more to his reply, but I cannot recall it."

"Did you know, Caiaphas, that wise men sought to implicate him with his own testimony on many other occasions
and always failed?"

He nodded. "Jesus was a wily and dangerous man, undoubtedly guided in his words and deeds by Satan. His death
came none too soon for our nation."

"What finally made you decide to move against him? Apparently he condemned those of you in authority at every opportunity, and yet you seem to have displayed great patience
and tolerance for a long time." Trading sympathy for information was a new role for me.

"I practiced more patience than you will ever know." He
sighed. "There was pressure from the Pharisees constantly,
also from many in my own party, and even from friends in
the priesthood and our high court, the Sanhedrin. All of
them wanted me to stop this sorcerer before he incited the
people to commit acts of violence and rebellion that would
bring the wrath of Pilate down on all of us and turn our
streets into rivers of blood."

"And then something happened to force your hand?"

"Yes, one night I received several reports, all from unim-
peachable sources, that Jesus had succeeded in raising a dead

130

man from his tomb in Bethany after the man had been buried for three or four days. By the next morning everyone in the streets and the Temple courtyards spoke of little else. I called an informal meeting of the Sanhedrin and the leading members of both parties and asked their counsel as to what we should do with this man who worked miracles."

"Miracles? Not tricks of magic?"

"No, no, by now we were convinced that he was indeed working miracles, but we were certain that they were with the help of Satan."

"But, Caiaphas, I've been told that once a person who was blind and dumb and possessed with a devil was brought to Jesus and he healed him, but the Pharisees said that it was with the help of Beelzebub, the prince of the devils, and Jesus asked them how he could possibly exorcise the devil with the devil's own help and they were speechless. In any event, what came of your meeting regarding his miracle at Bethany?"

The high priest stared up at the dark ceiling as if to focus his thoughts. "I remember nearly everyone expressing the same fear, that if this man were allowed to continue he would have all the people seduced into following him and the Romans would intercede and take everything, even our nation, away from us. At the end of our discussion I announced my decision: that it was expedient for us that one man should die rather than the whole nation perish. The others cheered and orders were issued, throughout the land, that if any man knew where Jesus could be found, because he was no longer in Bethany, we of the Sanhedrin were to be notified immediately. I was certain, however, that we would not have long to wait for his return to the city. The Passover holidays were fast approaching, and from my experience with other rabble-rousers I was convinced that Jesus would not be able to resist the lure of flaunting himself before the great crowds that would gather in the Temple during those days."

"And you were correct."

"Yes," he said grimly, "but also careless. It was the afternoon of the first day of the week, six days before our Passover holidays were to begin, and already the Temple courtyards were choked with pilgrims. The captain of our guard came to my chambers there, disturbed my afternoon sleep, and informed me that Jesus had just entered the Temple with a group of his followers, tipped over the tables of our money-changers, driven them off, and freed the doves from their cages while shouting, 'It is written that my house shall be called the house of prayer, but you have made it a den of thieves!' When I asked the captain in which of the Temple's many rooms he had imprisoned Jesus for his abominable crime, he cringed and replied that because of the great crowds that encouraged and praised Jesus, neither he nor his men had dared lay hands on him. I became so enraged at the cowardice of this lout that I struck him across the face. Had he been serving under Pilate he would have been executed for malfeasance of duty."

"What happened next, as you recall?"

"After Jesus committed his offense against the Temple he immediately removed himself from the premises and the city and went, with his accomplices, to the Bethany home of Mary and Martha and Lazarus, the man he had raised from the dead."

"You *knew* where Jesus was staying?"

"Of course. There were a dozen or more in his party, so he was not difficult to track."

"I don't understand, sir. If you knew where he was, why didn't you send your police to Bethany that very afternoon, to arrest him for his criminal actions in the Temple?"

Caiaphas rubbed his soft hands together and looked away. "Because, I regret to say, there were many lacking in courage among us. Less than an hour after Jesus had departed from the Temple, I summoned a meeting of those same men who had cheered my decision that Jesus should die, only a few weeks prior. I informed them of his assault against the money-changers and also that I knew where we could find him. Their permission was not necessary for me to act; however, I thought it unwise to make any move, considering the mood of the people, without the approval of leaders from all factions."

Caiaphas was now speaking the same kind of gibberish used by most individuals in authority. Translated, he was telling me that he didn't want the responsibility for the death of Jesus laid at his door.

"High priests who abuse their power," he continued, "usually end up by losing everything. I asked for their advice once again, and now I learned, to my dismay, that many were having second thoughts about doing away with Jesus. One man, a Pharisee, said that if Jesus had dared to throw over the tables of the money-changers, with Temple guards everywhere in the courtyard, he must have done so knowing that they had no power to lay hands on him. Another warned us that if he could raise a man from his tomb he might not hesitate in striking us all dead if we ordered his arrest. I was beside myself. These men of power, the most affluent and respected in our city, had turned into frightened old women, urging me to postpone any action against Jesus until they could further evaluate the situation. I chastised them for their weakness and told them that if Jesus were allowed to work his spell on the people for the entire week of Passover, all would be lost. But they turned a deaf ear to my pleas. None wished to get involved."

"I understand that Jesus returned to the Temple on the very next day."

"He did—acting as if he had done no wrong and had nothing to fear. This time even the little children gathered around him and shouted the salutation reserved for our Messiah, 'Hosanna to the son of David!' I watched from an upper window until I could bear the sight and sounds no longer, and then I went down into the courtyard alone and confronted him. I should never have stooped so low."

"Why?"

"When the crowd saw me approaching him they all gathered around us. I stepped close to Jesus, in order to be heard above the tumult, and asked him if he realized what the children were chanting. He just smiled at me and raised his arms and said, 'Out of the mouths of babes and sucklings. . . .' I was furious. He was taunting me! I pointed in the direction of the money-changers he had molested, who were once again conducting their necessary business, and asked by what authority he did such things. He said he would ask me a question first and if I answered his then he would tell me his authority. I told him to proceed, and he wanted to know if the baptism that John had dispensed was from heaven or men. I didn't know what to say, in front of that mob. If I told him that it was from heaven he would have asked me why I had not believed in John. But if I said it was from men, all those who still believed in John would turn against me. Finally I told Jesus that I could not tell him, and he replied, 'Neither will I tell you by what authority I do these things.' I turned in order to summon the guards to arrest him, but when I saw the mood of the crowd I held my tongue and went inside. And then that very same day, Judas Iscariot came to me as if he had been sent by God to resolve my terrible dilemma."

"This is the man who was the keeper of the purse for Jesus and his party?"

"Yes, and formerly one of his most ardent followers. His confession to me provided all the tinder I needed to light a

133

fire under those who feared Jesus. Judas, bless him, made a seemingly impossible task no more difficult than arresting any other common criminal."

"I don't—don't understand," I stammered. "All I have heard about Judas, from the followers of Jesus, is that he was responsible for betraying Jesus into your hands by leading your people to Gethsemane and identifying him."

Caiaphas shook his head. "He did much more. He was the key."

"The key?"

"When God directed him to me, three days before our Passover was to commence, Judas was a disillusioned and broken man. He told me that in the beginning he had gone with Jesus because he believed he had seen, in this man, a leader who would deliver our people from under the heel of Rome."

"A messiah with a sword—a great deliverer like David?"

"Yes. But he said that as the months passed he began to realize that he had been gravely mistaken. Jesus continued to speak of a 'Kingdom to come' but one 'not of this world,' and instead of rallying the people to join with each other to overthrow Caesar he preached that one should love his enemies, which David would never have said. I remember Judas' falling to his knees and clutching at my robe, sobbing and asking if there was anything he could do to atone for his terrible mistake. I inquired if he had ever heard Jesus claim that he was the Messiah."

"No one, I take it, had reported to you that Jesus was ever heard making such a claim."

"That is correct. It was then that Judas confided in me that when their party was far north, in a place called Caesarea Philippi, Jesus had asked the apostles who they thought he was and Peter had announced that he was the Messiah and Jesus warned them to tell no man."

"And you considered this to be an admission, on the part of Jesus, that he was the Messiah?"

"Yes, although one witness is not enough to convict before the Sanhedrin. But Judas proved invaluable when he told me that Jesus, especially during the most recent weeks, had prophesied his own death many times at the hands of the authorities, and he was now beginning to act as if he would offer no resistance if an arrest attempt was made. Even though that did not sound much like the man I had confronted in the Temple, it was all I needed to hear. I called a third meeting of the same parties who had been reluctant to move against

Jesus and made Judas repeat, for them, all the prophecies that Jesus was making about his own demise. When the council heard his words their courage returned, and I once again had a large majority who favored his immediate arrest and trial, providing we could do so quietly without stirring up the people. The decision as to the most favorable time and place was left with me. I then rewarded Judas with some pieces of silver and instructed him to return to Jesus, where he could serve us best by keeping me informed of any unusual activities or movements that took place."

I suddenly thought of Kitty. Soon after I had started research on "The Christ Commission," she had presented me with a copy of Albert Schweitzer's *The Quest of the Historical Jesus*. I remember Schweitzer's insistence that the main question regarding Judas was not *why* he had betrayed his master but *what* he had betrayed. Schweitzer apparently had been correct. Judas not only had betrayed the possibility that Jesus believed he was the Messiah but, even more damaging, had assured his enemies that there was no danger in arresting him since he was ready to sacrifice his life anyway. I heard myself asking, "What happened next?"

"Judas came to me, in a state of frenzy, early on the night of the Paschal supper and told me that Jesus was eating the lamb, with his apostles, in the house of the widow Mary and once again talking as if he was resigned to his death at the hands of the authorities. More than that, Judas babbled, Jesus was now saying that it would take place very soon. With the city at holy supper and no one in the streets to interfere, I knew that I would never have a better opportunity. I decided to take him that very night."

"Pontius Pilate cooperated with you in the arrest and trial, did he not?"

"He did. I needed Pilate's authority and backing so that the people would not accuse the Sanhedrin or me of unfair prejudice against their new favorite. I also required his approval in order to carry out the death sentence, if one should be forthcoming from the trial. With Judas waiting here, I was driven swiftly to the Fortress Antonia, where the procurator was headquartered during our Passover. I asked Pilate for his immediate assistance in arresting a dangerous imposter who could cause us both many anxious moments during the feast days if allowed to remain free to incite the people. At first he refused, telling me that false prophets were my province and I should attend to Jesus myself. However, Pilate and I, despite our many differences, had managed to work together on Judaea's behalf for ten years, and so he finally agreed to dispatch some of his troops to this palace, from which they would accompany my Temple guards, a few priests, Judas, and me to the house of the widow Mary to consummate the arrest."

"To the house of the widow Mary?"

"Yes, where Judas had said Jesus was taking supper."

"What happened next?"

"I returned here and waited in the courtyard, with the others, for Pilate's soldiers to arrive. I remember there was a chill in the air, and I gave my men permission to light fires. We waited for more than three hours! Pilate was having his usual little joke with me, I thought, but when his men finally arrived I was furious. It was not a little joke on the procurator's part but a big one. For instead of sending me a dozen soldiers or so, enough to lend Roman sanction to our proceedings, he had dispatched three centuries—more than two hundred armed legionaries—headed by a chief centurion whom I knew. When I asked Fabius why so many soldiers, he, not knowing the circumstances, replied that the procurator had sent him with instructions to assist in the arrest of a dangerous rebel who was at the head of an armed band of unknown strength and who threatened to take over the nation and proclaim himself 'King of the Jews.' That Pilate! By now I was nearly beside myself, for I was in a race against time and knew I was losing."

"Why were you concerned about time so long as you knew, or thought you knew, where Jesus was?"

"Matthias, at sundown on the following day, our Passover would commence, as well as the Sabbath, and all trials and punishments are expressly forbidden by our laws for the seven days of the feast. For my mission to be a success I had to arrest Jesus, try him before the Sanhedrin, and carry out the verdict of the court before the sun set in approximately seventeen hours. Otherwise disaster: we would have had to hold him in custody during the entire week of Passover, and once the news of his arrest spread we were certain to have trouble with the people, especially those Galilean ruffians who infested the city. So with an unnecessary army large enough to capture Peraea at our backs, Judas and I went to the house of Mary to seize a single unarmed man who, according to Judas, was already waiting to be taken."

"And when you arrived, no one was there."

"Only some women and a young man. Pilate's spiteful delay, I was certain, had cost me dearly, and the people

136

would laugh at me and the Sanhedrin as soon as it became common knowledge that Jesus had disappeared from under our noses. Of course they would attribute the escape to his miraculous powers."

"What did you do?"

"I was frantic. In despair I seized Judas and shook him until he cried, 'Gethsemane, he must have gone to Gethsemane! If not there, waiting for me as he has done before, he must have returned to his bed in Bethany, with the others.' I knew that my legs could never endure the trek to Gethsemane or beyond, so I summoned Fabius and two of my assistants and told them to take Judas and the soldiers to the garden, and if Jesus was not there to proceed directly to the house in Bethany. I reminded them that only Jesus was to be arrested and that Judas would identify him so there would be no mistake."

"Why only Jesus?"

"I reasoned that the others were of no consequence and would flee to their villages in the north as soon as their leader was dead and buried."

"A mistake."

"Yes, we should have put them all away when they were only a dozen or so. Now there are thousands! In any event, the party was to deliver the prisoner to me, here in the palace, but Fabius objected. Pilate's orders, he said, were only to assist in the capture and arrest; once the prisoner was taken, the soldiers were to return to the fortress immediately. We finally compromised, with Fabius reluctantly agreeing to deliver Jesus to the home of Annas, my father-in-law, who lives near Roman headquarters. From there my Temple guard would be responsible for taking Jesus across the city to this place.

"The arrest party went out through the city's south gate, their torches aflame, and I returned here to dispatch messages to those witnesses who had previously agreed to testify against Jesus whenever he was finally brought to trial. Then I notified the members of the Sanhedrin to report to me immediately, instructing my messengers to say only that we were about to remove a thorn from the side of Israel. In less than an hour one of my officers notified me that the prisoner was under my roof and being held in the large hall, only a few steps down the corridor from this room, and that the members of the Sanhedrin had already taken their seats there, waiting for me to initiate trial proceedings."

"Sir," I said, "would you indulge a small whim of mine?"

"If it is in my power."

"Historians have this constant need to gaze on the actual sites where the events they are trying to describe took place. I have already visited your magnificent Temple, the garden at Gethsemane, and the tomb where Lazarus came forth. May I see the room where Jesus was tried?"

He hesitated briefly, shrugged, and said, "Come with me."

The room we entered, off the dark corridor, had obviously not been the scene of any formal functions for some time. Wicker barrels, huge packing crates, chests, and broken furniture were piled haphazardly against one of its yellow-stained marble walls, and on the opposite side of the room were three rows of unfinished wooden benches squatting in irregular half-moon configurations. No other furnishings were in the musty-smelling meeting hall, and the stone floor was so thick with dust that my sandals made dark imprints with each step.

I nodded in the direction of the benches. "The members of the Sanhedrin were sitting there, on that night?"

"Yes."

"And your prisoner, where was he during the trial?"

Caiaphas' slippers raised small clouds of dust as he noisily stomped across the floor. I could see that he was growing impatient with my questions. "Jesus stood here, so that he could face the court and the witnesses. Behind him was a guard. The witnesses were brought in from the corridor and made to stand near Jesus and also facing the court. I occupied that center bench in the front row, with assistants, scribes schooled in the law, on each side."

I walked to where Jesus had stood while Caiaphas, perhaps from habit, moved to the center front bench, wiped away the dust with his hand, and sat facing me, eyes half closed. Standing on the spot where Jesus had been brought before his enemies, I tried to imagine that early morning scene. Foul-smelling oil lamps and candles casting their meager light over the proceedings. Dark, elongated shadows sliding ghostlike across the floor and walls. Men of affluence and power, called from their warm beds after an evening of feasting and drinking, their mood more that of a lynch mob than a supreme court, especially in that chilled setting. And the prisoner, looking anything but what a Messiah should look like, with his hands bound tightly and his face reflecting both the weariness from a long day and night and the abuse from those who had arrested him.

I fought with myself to remain calm and dispassionate as I

138

stood in the invisible footprints of Jesus. It wasn't easy. Caiaphas did not take his eyes off me, nervously crossing and uncrossing his legs, folding and unfolding his arms. I waved toward the benches. "The Sanhedrin has seventy members, does it not?"

"Yes, with me as presiding officer of the court who cannot cast his vote on any verdict."

"Were they all here that night?"

"Oh, no. Distance and the lateness of the hour prevented many from attending. However, only twenty-three are necessary for a quorum, and we had at least thirty present before our interrogation of witnesses commenced."

"Had you notified them all?"

"I cannot recall. Certainly all who lived nearby were summoned."

"The home of Joseph of Arimathea is only a short walk from here, and yet he tells me that he was not called," I said. "Neither was his friend Nicodemus. You didn't, by chance, purposely omit notifying any members whom you suspected of having friendly leanings toward the prisoner?"

Even by the light from a single shaft of dusty sunlight I could see the high priest's face turning livid. His voice trembled. "As a friend of Vitellius you should know better than to utter such slander about me. I resent your implications, sir. Considering the late hour, our attendance was excellent."

"Forgive me, sir. I was merely repeating a rumor I had heard. Tell me about the trial, please."

"There is little to tell," he said haughtily. "It was brief. Jesus finally admitted his crime of blasphemy, and according to our law the Sanhedrin found him deserving of death."

"Your witnesses convinced the court?"

"Ah-h, they were a waste of our time. The first seven or eight who were called told stories that conflicted so much, one with the other, that we had no choice except to excuse their testimony as worthless, and the priest whom I had entrusted to select them was relieved from office that very night, for his incompetence."

"Caiaphas, I have heard allegations that you bribed those witnesses to appear and that the reason their stories did not agree, as required for conviction, was because you failed to rehearse them properly."

His thin lips curled contemptuously. "Even to consider such a falsehood indicates that you must have this court's high integrity confused with what I understand is common legal practice in Rome."

I bowed slightly and smiled. The high priest knew how to counterpunch. "What happened after you rejected all those witnesses?"

"An old man was brought in, a seller of trinkets outside the Temple whom we all knew. He testified that Jesus had once told a crowd, near the Temple's west wall, 'I will destroy this Temple that is made with hands, and in three days I will build another made without hands.'"

"That was the kind of testimony you needed in order to convict, was it not?"

"It was. Those words were obviously a blasphemy against the house of God, and our law demands that whoever vilifies or profanes the Temple is to be punished by death. Still, the testimony of one witness is not sufficient to convict; two are necessary. We called another to testify on the same matter, but he repeated the words of Jesus as being, 'I am able to destroy the Temple of God and to build it in three days.' Immediately there were angry cries of disappointment from members of the court, for the two stories did not agree. According to the first witness, Jesus had said 'I will destroy,' while according to the second he said 'I am *able* to destroy,' and in that statement there was no blasphemy—only vain boasting."

"Do you know that his apostles are now claiming that when Jesus made that remark, outside the Temple, he was not speaking of the building but of his own body, and the three days referred to the time he would spend in the tomb before he rose?"

Caiaphas nodded. "I have heard that perversion of his words. The apostles are already quite proficient in distorting his sayings to suit their outlandish claims that he returned from the dead."

"Then you had to reject the testimony of those two witnesses also?"

"Yes, and I did so with a heavy heart for they were my final pair. I could sense, from the looks of the members, that already I had lost much respect in their eyes for bringing them out on a cold night to be a party to the acquittal of Jesus instead of his conviction. I rose from my seat and said to the prisoner, 'Have you nothing to say for yourself? Haven't you heard all these witnesses speaking against you?'"

"What did he say?"

"He said nothing. He just stood there, watching me, knowing that he stood unconvicted of any offense according to our

140

trial laws. When I turned to face the Sanhedrin I saw that some of them had risen as if to leave, several of them whispering loudly among themselves. I knew what they were saying. They had placed the responsibility for ridding the nation of this criminal in my hands, and I had failed them. Even my position in the Temple, I feared, would be in jeopardy when news of this was leaked to Vitellius by my enemies. Suddenly I remembered our Oath of Testimony, the most fearful and powerful form of oath under our law. Anyone to whom it is applied is bound by our constitution to answer. I rushed over to the prisoner and shouted, 'I adjure you by the living God that you tell me whether you are the Christ, the Son of God!' "

Caiaphas was warming to his story, and I hated to interrupt him but I had to. "Why did you combine the title 'Christ,' meaning Messiah, with 'Son of God' in your question? The Messiah, according to my understanding of what your people believe, is only expected to be one sent from God, not his Son."

"Matthias, so many false claims had been raised about Jesus that I felt it proper, in this case, to include both titles in my adjuration. That way we might discover what delusions he truly had about himself."

"Did he respond?"

"He was well versed in our law. He had to answer the adjuration and he knew it. I asked him again, 'Are you the Christ, the Son of God?' and he replied, 'I am—and you shall see the Son of man sitting on the right hand of power and coming in the clouds of heaven!' His words made my spirits soar. Victory was finally mine over this plague on our people. Quickly I performed the ritual that one is bound to do when confronted by blasphemy, tearing my shirt between the seams so it could not be repaired. Then I said to the council, who had all reclaimed their seats, 'You have heard the blasphemy; what think you, gentlemen?' and they all answered as one voice, 'For death!' I ordered the prisoner to be removed to a lower room and held there, under heavy guard, until sunrise, not many hours away. Then we would take Jesus to Pilate."

"Why?"

"For many years Rome has not allowed us to inflict capital punishment, for any crime, without permission from the procurator. When I had called on Pilate the previous evening, I had extracted from him not only his legionaries to assist us in the arrest but also his agreement to an early morning sanctioning of the anticipated death sentence so that we could complete the execution before sundown."

The high priest paused, almost as if expecting praise for a job well done, one certainly deserving of several pages in my history book. Reliving those events with me seemed to have drained him of energy and confidence. He sat slumped on the bench, hands clenched tightly in his lap, more an object of pity than hate—never to know that his handling of the Jesus affair, whether motivated by selfish reasons or national duty, would bring undeserved slander and contempt and death to so many of his people for the next twenty centuries.

"Caiaphas," I said, "the Sanhedrin and you found Jesus guilty of blasphemy, and for that offense, according to your laws, the punishment is death by stoning."

"That is correct."

"And this punishment is usually inflicted by those witnesses who come forth to testify against the guilty one?"

"It is written that they should throw the first stones, and then the crowd usually joins in."

"But Jesus was not stoned to death; he was crucified on a cross! And he was executed not for blasphemy but sedition! And not by your witnesses and the crowd but by Roman soldiers! What happened that morning, when Jesus was brought before Pilate, that caused the procurator to take the case completely out of your hands?"

There was no reply.

"I have heard rumors, Caiaphas, that you had planned for it to go that way, although there are differences of opinion as to whether or not you were in collusion with Pilate."

The only occupant of the benches licked his lips nervously but remained silent.

"What really happened, Caiaphas?"

"You will have to discuss that with the procurator, sir. My jurisdiction in that matter ended at the gates of Antonia."

"Why can't you tell me? Jesus was your prisoner when he was taken to Pilate. Didn't you expect him to remain in your custody until the execution?"

"I did. As soon as we had Pilate's sanction, Jesus was to be taken to a hill outside the city's walls, stoned until dead, and his body thrown in a pauper's grave."

"But Jesus was never remanded to you. Why?"

"I have no comment on what transpired at the fortress. You will have to seek your explanation from Pilate."

I tried again. "According to what you have told me, Pilate had already agreed, even before you had Jesus under arrest, that he would grant permission for *you* to execute your prisoner. What made him change his mind and do it himself?"

He shook his head but said nothing. I walked toward him until I was almost leaning over his bench.

"Caiaphas, during my stay here in the city, I have met and talked with several men of wisdom, knowledgeable in your laws. Some of them have confided in me, secretly because they fear for their safety, that the entire action against Jesus was illegal and broke many laws of the sacred codes that you, as high priest, are sworn to observe and enforce. Some even go so far as to accuse you and the Sanhedrin of the murder of an innocent man and say that Pilate was merely the instrument of his death."

"Murder? Me? Illegal? Who would dare utter such vile untruths about their high priest?" he gasped.

"Are you so withdrawn from your people, here in your palace and the Temple suites, that you have never heard these accusations? Has not anyone close to you, responsible for keeping you informed of the moods of your people, ever dared to recite, in your presence, all the illegalities you are suspected of having committed that night and early morning in order to do away with Jesus?"

"No one here would have the courage or audacity to speak to me as you are doing," he mumbled, holding both hands against his blood-drained cheeks. "You tell me. I demand to know. What are they saying about me?"

Authenticity in points of law has always been a proud hallmark of my detective mysteries, and I had spent long hours researching the ancient Hebrew codes of criminal law while working on "The Christ Commission," with growing awe and respect for their fairness and thoroughness. Of one thing I had become certain, despite my doubts about Jesus. If the versions of that nighttime trial, as told in the New Testament, were accurate, a terrible miscarriage of justice had taken place in this very room. Since Caiaphas' account had not differed to any extent from the Gospels, I decided it was time to unload on him.

"First of all, sir, Jesus' arrest was illegal according to your own laws. No formal criminal charges were ever brought before the Sanhedrin for the issuance of a warrant, so the arrest took place without one, and when Jesus was arrested he was not informed of his crime, the arrest took place at night, and it involved the treachery of another—all forbidden by your codes."

Caiaphas opened his mouth as if to reply but apparently thought better of it and nodded for me to continue.

"You tried Jesus at night, and in your Mishnah it is written that a capital offense may be tried during the day but must be suspended at night. It also specifies that no case involving a man's life can be tried on the day before the Sabbath, but Jesus was tried in the early hours of the day before the Sabbath. Next, you have a law that forbids a relation or a friend or an enemy of the accused to sit in judgment of him, and yet, according to your own words, many of those present on that night, including yourself, had plotted for weeks to destroy Jesus."

I walked back to the spot where Jesus had stood and pointed to the floor in front of me.

"Witnesses?" I shouted, and my voice echoed in that stone cube. "According to your law it is written, 'At the mouth of two witnesses, or three, shall he that is worthy of death be put to death; but at the mouth of one witness, he shall not be put to death.' By your own admission you had been unable to find two witnesses to agree on anything, and since the power of accusation is vested solely in witnesses you had no case at all!"

"But the man confessed—"

"His confession was of no use to you, and you know it! Your law says that no one can bring an accusation against himself, but if he does, it still cannot be used against him unless it is properly attested by two other witnesses. Furthermore, you were in violation of another law when you put your question to Jesus, for your code expressly forbids any question to a witness that would condemn him if he answered. Am I correct?"

I didn't wait for an answer.

"You told me that when you asked the Sanhedrin for a verdict, after Jesus responded, they all cried, 'For death!' A majority of one vote is required for acquittal, two for conviction, but your holy Mishnah also stipulates that a unanimous verdict of guilty has the effect of an acquittal and a sentence of death is forbidden!"

I still wasn't finished.

"Jesus was tried and convicted in one sitting of the Sanhedrin. That, too, was illegal. Your Mishnah says that a criminal case resulting in an acquittal of the accused may end on the day it begins, but if the sentence is death the trial cannot be concluded before the following day so that a full review of the evidence may be made. And then, according to your own story, after you had found Jesus guilty you neglected to impose formal sentence on him. From beginning to end, Caiaphas, all of it was illegal—the arrest, the lack of witnesses who could agree, the trial on the day before the Sabbath, enemies on the bench, using the prisoner's own words to condemn him, the unanimous verdict, the lack of formal sentencing, all of it—illegal! According to your own laws you brought an innocent man to Pilate!"

The high priest cocked his head and returned my stare. I could hear laughter, alien in such a setting, floating up from the lobby. Caiaphas twisted his body so that his back was facing me and asked a question that nearly floored me. "Does Vitellius know what you have just told me?"

"Everyone knows," I said, as positively as I could. "How could they not know with so many noisy Christians out there, even in your Temple courtyards, repeating their story over and over?"

"I agree," he said despairingly, "and they are too ignorant to realize that what I did was to save all of them from being impaled on Pilate's sword."

"Caiaphas, did you ever consider, even for a moment, after the crucifixion that you might have murdered the Son of God by mistake?"

"Never! When the father of our people, Abraham, prepared to sacrifice his beloved son, Isaac, God interfered and delivered a ram to be killed instead. If God would not even permit the sacrifice of Isaac, would he permit the murder of his Son without destroying the world? The world, as you can see, Matthias, still exists."

"Will you tell me, now, what happened at Pilate's hearing?"

"No! Ask him."

"Did you witness the crucifixion?"

"I did not," he said. "When the soldiers led Jesus away, I returned to the Temple to make preparations for the approaching Passover. A few of my assistants did go in my stead and reported to me when it was finished."

"Were you surprised when you learned that Jesus had expired only a few hours after being hung on the cross?"

He shrugged. "Some endure for so long that their legs are finally broken to put them out of their misery, while others die immediately, perhaps from shock. But why am I telling you? Crucifixion, after all, is a Roman punishment, not ours. I was more surprised to hear that one of our own Sanhedrin, your friend Joseph, had gone to Pilate without consulting any of us and claimed the body and laid it in a new tomb, carved

145

for his own eventual interment, in a garden near the place of execution."

"Joseph's act must have offended many of his fellow Sanhedrin members after they had condemned Jesus to death. Did you take any action against him or that other member—Nicodemus, I believe—who seems to have assisted Joseph in the burial?"

"Those two are very independent men, honored and respected by the people for their many charitable deeds. When we chastised them severely for their behavior, they offered to resign from the court rather than cause us any further embarrassment. They insisted that nothing they had done was unlawful and said that no Jew who spoke and lived as Jesus lived deserved to have his body tossed in a common grave with criminals of the street."

"Have you ever looked back, Caiaphas, and reflected that had Joseph not claimed the body there would have been no empty tomb—"

"Every day," he moaned, "and many sleepless nights. Without that empty tomb for them to gloat over, there would probably be no Christians at all today."

"I understand that you even took some measures to guard the tomb."

"As it turned out, not enough, Matthias," he lamented. "Reminded by one of my priests that Jesus had not only prophesied his death but promised he would rise again on the third day, I went to Pilate early in the afternoon of our Sabbath, the day after the crucifixion, and told him what Jesus had said. I asked that he have the tomb sealed and guarded until the end of the third day, to prevent Jesus' disciples from stealing his body and telling the people that Jesus had risen as he said he would."

"Pilate agreed?"

"He laughed in my face and said he wanted nothing more to do with the matter. The procurator told me that I had many guards in my Temple, and if I wanted the tomb guarded I would have to see to it myself since he needed every soldier to attend to the Passover crowd that overran the city. I returned to the Temple and ordered Shobi, one of my most experienced officers, to take three of his best men to the garden, seal the tomb, and stand watch through the night and until sundown of the following day."

"When did you learn that the tomb was empty?"

"Sometime before dawn I was awakened by my orderly, who said that the guard had returned from the tomb and insisted on seeing me immediately. Alarmed, I dressed hurriedly and went down to the lobby, to find the four of them acting as if they had all taken leave of their senses. Shobi, who is a huge man, rushed toward me and fell to his knees sobbing. He clutched at my garment, begging for forgiveness, crying that he and the others had grown weary of guarding a dead man, after their long day in the Temple, and so they had fallen asleep. While they all slept, he wailed, someone must have come to the tomb, removed the great stone, and taken the body away."

"What did you do?"

"What could I do? I ordered Shobi and the others to wait in their quarters until I had decided on their punishment. I then returned to my bed and lay in the dark and tried to resolve how to deal with Pilate and the Sanhedrin when they heard the news."

"Your Temple officer, Shobi, is he still with you? May I speak with him?"

The high priest shook his head. "Shobi disappeared that very night. According to his orderly he never returned to his quarters. We have not seen him for six years."

"The other three guards—are they still in your service?"

"They were all found in their quarters shortly after sunrise, dead by their own hands, unable, I imagine, to live with the disgrace of being derelict in their duty."

How convenient for someone, I thought. Of four possible eyewitnesses to what really happened at that tomb, three were dead and one was missing. "And how did Pilate and the Sanhedrin react when they heard the news?"

"Pilate, I've been told, displayed his usual contempt for all of us. He said that one could expect no more from Jewish guards who play at being soldiers by keeping peace between old men and women in the Temple courtyard. The Sanhedrin, called into immediate emergency session by me that morning, deliberated for only a short while before voting to make no public announcement of any kind. They reasoned that the followers of Jesus must already be in flight, to avoid arrest and worse, and they probably had taken the body of Jesus with them to be buried in his native Galilee. So far as they were concerned, the matter was closed and the less said about it the better."

"How wrong they were."

"Yes. Hindsight is the greatest prophet of all, Matthias. For the next seven weeks the city was quiet. We assumed that Jesus had been forgotten like all the other false prophets be-

147

fore him. Then, on the morning of our feast for Pentecost, signifying the end of our early harvest season, news came to me that more than a hundred disciples of Jesus had gathered outside the house of the widow Mary, and Peter, a man who had been close to Jesus, had announced to the crowd that the Holy Spirit had appeared to them while they had been at prayer and that Jesus had been loosed from the pains of death and raised up by God and made both Lord and Christ. Before the day had ended, it was reported to me that two or three thousand had believed Peter's words and gone to him to be baptized as a sign of their new loyalty to Jesus, the Messiah, who would soon return on the clouds of heaven."

"If the tomb was empty on the third morning, why do you suppose they waited seven weeks to tell the people that Jesus had risen?"

Caiaphas shrugged again. "I do not know. One of my priests suggested that after seven weeks the body would be so corrupted that even if it was found it could not be identified, so that by Pentecost perhaps Peter felt safe in making his false announcement."

"What did you do when you heard about Peter's claim?"

"I had notices posted throughout the city and inside the Temple courtyard, offering a reward of ten thousand silver shekels for information leading to the location of the body and the apprehension of those culprits who had removed it from the tomb."

I made some hasty calculations. As I remembered, one silver shekel was worth approximately sixty-five cents. Six thousand five hundred dollars, in A.D. 36, would have been enough to tempt the holiest of angels. "No one claimed the reward?" I asked.

"No one." He sighed.

"Would you like to know where the body is hidden?" I heard myself asking.

Caiaphas leaped from the bench. He seized both my arms and clutched them to his frail chest. "You know, Matthias? You know where it is? Tell me, I beg of you, and I shall double the reward! Twenty thousand silver shekels! Think of it! Enough to live all your days in more luxury than you ever dreamed, in the finest villa in Rome. Tell me!"

And now I knew I could scratch the high priest from my list. Caiaphas had definitely not removed the body from the tomb of Joseph in order to prevent that place from becoming the scene of embarrassing demonstrations against him and the Sanhedrin. "I'm sorry, sir, but I do not know where the body is hidden as yet. But I hope to find it before I'm finished here."

"Thirty thousand—thirty thousand silver shekels when you tell me!"

I turned away so that he could not see the disgust on my face. How ironic, I thought, as he led me downstairs to the lobby. Six years ago Caiaphas had paid Judas thirty silver shekels for the living body of Jesus. Now he was willing to pay a thousand times that amount for the dead one!

Joseph and I were both silent during the short ride back to his mansion, until the old man said softly, "I believe it would be wise if you plan to see Pilate early in the morning. It will not be difficult for me to arrange."

"Why?" I asked absentmindedly, still reviewing all I had learned from Caiaphas.

When he didn't reply I turned to face him. He tilted his head backward several times before I understood and looked out through our rear carriage window.

Not far behind, on a gray stallion, was the black-hooded rider I thought we had lost on the road to Bethany.

ten

TWO SENTINELS, high atop flagstone walls, stared down at us suspiciously as we emerged from the carriage and approached the gates to Rome's military headquarters in Jerusalem. Shields, body armor, and even their long supple spears glinted menacingly in the early morning sun.

"Our welcoming committee," Joseph said casually.

"What would it take for them to let those javelins fly?"

The old man chuckled. "They are only Syrian auxiliaries, Matthias, and would undoubtedly miss their mark by several cubits from that height."

"How comforting."

"We are no more than a momentary diversion for them. Their main concern is in that direction." He nodded toward the adjoining great Temple, whose marble and gold facade glowed in vivid contrast to its flinty-gray, dingy neighbor.

I had once read that during his later years as puppet king of Israel, Herod had erected a huge golden eagle on the foremost part of the Temple roof so that it could be viewed from anywhere in the city. Before his death he had suffered the ultimate humiliation of seeing his tasteless and sacrilegious tribute to Rome pulled down and destroyed by a small band of Jewish scholars.

Thirty or more years had passed since the eagle had fallen, but now a far more intimidating and deadly symbol cast its degrading shadow across the people and their holy place of worship. Squatting on a domelike hill of hard limestone that soared high above the Temple's tallest pinnacle was the fortress called Antonia, presently occupied by more than a thousand Roman legionaires and auxiliaries.

Ignoring the curious soldiers immediately above our heads, Joseph said, "Note the smoothness of the walls' outer surface, Matthias, constructed so as to prevent any uninvited guests from ascending its steep sides. The old palace of Herod, inside the wall, is three stories high and surrounds spacious parade grounds paved entirely with stone. There is, as you can see, a tower above each of the four corners of the outer wall, and the base of this one nearest to us actually encroaches into the Temple courtyard, with passageways leading directly to the Court of the Gentiles for easy access by the soldiers in the event of trouble. Antonia has become, without question, a Roman fortress of the highest rating, capable of sustaining a full legion, if necessary. It has its own cisterns for water storage, a large granary, hospital, baths, and countless rows of barracks on the north side of the grounds. Pilate and his officers are always quartered in the south wing, whenever he is in the city, and fortunately for us he has only just recently arrived for our Feast of Tabernacles, which commences next week. The procurator always makes it his duty to be here in Jerusalem for each of our three great holidays, usually bringing with him an additional cohort of soldiers from his headquarters in Caesarea to assist in controlling the crowds and maintaining peace."

The old man gripped my arm as we passed beneath the thick wall's arched gateway, guiding me to the right along a wide dirt path that separated wall and fortress until we arrived at a heavy bronze door already being held open for us by a smiling legionary approximately my age.

"Greetings, Centurion Cornelius," Joseph said.

"Welcome, Joseph. It has been a long time. The procurator is awaiting you in his quarters. Come, follow me."

As we were being led through a damp passageway illuminated by small hanging oil lamps, I tapped Joseph's shoulder and whispered, "He is expecting us?"

"It is the very least I can do to assist you in your quest, Matthias. After all, this is already your fourth day here, and you did announce to the world that a week was all you needed to discover the truth about Jesus. My gold may be tainted by commerce but it does open many doors."

I pointed to the centurion walking ahead. "How is it that you know him?"

"It is a long story, Matthias. Later, perhaps."

We began climbing stairs, many of them, until we had to step around several life-size marble statues pressed close to each other on a wide landing before we proceeded down a long carpeted hallway whose walls were decorated with multi-colored standards, rusting shields, and swords of various lengths and shapes. At the end of the hall, outside an elaborately carved wooden door, a helmeted guard stiffly snapped his javelin forward to what I assumed was the salute position. Cornelius knocked four times, and at an unintelligible bellow

151

from inside he pushed down on the latch and waved us into the presence of Pontius Pilate, fifth procurator of Judaea, Samaria, and Idumaea.

Pilate was a man of medium size with white hair clipped short. His features were sharp, especially his ears, and there was a deep cleft in his chin. He was beardless, like all Romans of status, and his swarthy complexion suggested that perhaps those writers were correct who had deduced, through the centuries, that Pilate's roots had been in Spain. I was pleased to see that he considered our meeting an informal one, for he was wearing none of the trappings of his office. Covering his body was a light tunic, similar to mine, and his feet were barely encased in brief leather sandals. He poured white wine for us, from a flask at his elbow, and replenished his own goblet while he and Joseph discussed politics and conditions in the city as if I were not even present.

From all I had been able to research on the man, Pilate was uneducated, uncouth, cold, and surly. Josephus, the first-century historian, had described him as haughty, obstinate, coarse, and tactless, and the Jewish prince Agrippa, in a letter to the Emperor Gaius, had called him inflexible, stubborn, and relentless. As I watched, it would have been difficult for me to attach any of those adjectives to this relaxed and polite individual who was listening to Joseph's opinions with attention and respect. Whenever he spoke he would wave his hands to emphasize a point, and I couldn't help noticing the heavy gold ring on his right middle finger. It must be, I assumed, that treasure so highly prized throughout the Roman empire, the ring signifying that Pilate was a "friend of Caesar's," an honor granted to only a special few of high status and carrying with it many prerogatives and privileges. Shakespeare was correct when he wrote that heaven hides the book of fate from all creatures. Who would have dared to predict that of all the great Romans who ever lived, this man, never more than a procurator in a tiny province that Cicero had called "a hole in the corner" of a vast empire, would one day be better remembered than any of his countrymen? And how many millions of children throughout the centuries had learned to despise his name by reciting those lines from a prayer: "suffered under Pontius Pilate"?

I didn't realize anyone was speaking to me until I looked up and saw both Pilate and Joseph looking in my direction expectantly. "I'm sorry."

Pilate shrugged his shoulders and smiled. "Joseph informs me that you are preparing a history of these eastern provinces. Sometimes I feel as if the citizens of Rome are unaware that our empire's boundary extends beyond Sparta to their east. I commend you for undertaking to shed some light on these lands for those who cannot see beyond their Colosseum."

"Thank you," I mumbled, nervously rubbing moist palms against my tunic.

"Joseph also tells me that you wish to include, in your history of the Jews, the story of that rebel from Galilee?"

"Yes."

"Your efforts will consume the remainder of your life and fill an entire library if you waste your time recounting the foolish exploits of every rabble-rouser these people have embraced." Pilate's voice hardened. "And even then I would think that this . . . this Jesus would merit no more than a sentence or two, if anything."

I glanced toward Joseph for support, but the old man sat impassively staring down at his hands. He had done his part. I was in the presence of Pontius Pilate. The rest was up to me. "When I complete my research on the man, sir, I may well decide that your assessment of him is correct. Until then I must continue to seek the truth."

"Truth? What is truth? No one has ever answered that question for me. And how does one know when one finds it?"

"I'll know, sir."

"Where has your investigation taken you so far, in your search for the . . . the truth about that dead troublemaker?"

Careful! Booby trap! Remember that he has had you followed and knows exactly where you've been and with whom you have met, with the possible exception of the Bethany sisters. Lie to him now and even Joseph won't be able to save you. "I have already talked with James, the brother of Jesus, and some of his earliest disciples, such as Matthew, James, and Peter—"

"Agitators!" He snorted. "Sooner or later they will all follow their dead leader to the cross."

"I have also met with Caiaphas—"

"Caiaphas?" He interrupted again. "If you seek the truth, why are you wasting your time on that one?"

"But he is the high priest! He can—"

"High priest? Vitellius could remove him tomorrow and place a goat in his place, and we'd probably be far better off. Caiaphas is not to be believed on anything concerning this business of Jesus. I should know!"

I didn't dare respond to his vindictive outburst. All I could do was play the interview like a good fisherman and just keep letting him have all the line he needed. I hoped I wouldn't run out of line before he ran out of patience with my questions.

"Matthias," he said, using my name for the first time and with much less rancor in his tenor voice, "Joseph tells me that you are a close friend of Vitellius. Because I have great respect for my honored legate in Antioch, I will cooperate with you, as much as my memory allows, despite my distaste for that entire Jesus affair. Proceed with your questions."

"Thank you. When did you first become aware of Jesus? Was it on that night when Caiaphas came to you for soldiers to assist him and his guard in making the arrest?"

Pilate refilled his goblet, drained it slowly, and slouched back on the low couch, his eyelids drooping. "My friend, I have already managed to survive in this pesthole for ten years, policing the most difficult and unbending people on the face of our earth. I could not have done so without loyal and well-paid agents throughout the land, even in those provinces not under my jurisdiction. I knew about Jesus almost as soon as he began preaching in that village near the lake . . . what is it? . . . Yes, yes, Capernaum. I was kept constantly informed of his so-called miracles and his inflammatory discourses to the people and fully expected that Herod Antipas would put an end to his activities while he was still in Galilee, just as he had done with that one called 'the Baptist.' Then I was told that Jesus had allegedly raised a dead man from his grave in nearby Bethany, and I knew we would have our confrontation before long."

"You intended to arrest him at the first provocation?"

"Certainly. Anyone who dares to incite the people under my jurisdiction with promises of a new kingdom is clearly committing an act of sedition against Rome. From the time of Augustus, there has been only one punishment for that crime—death!"

"Then there's something I don't understand, sir. Five days before Jesus was crucified, I have been told that he rode into Jerusalem on a donkey accompanied by many of his followers, who created a great disturbance along the way by laying their cloaks and palm branches in his path as if he were royalty while the crowds going up to the city acclaimed him. Why didn't you arrest him immediately, for inciting the people?"

Pilate's face was blank. "Your information regarding such a grandiose entry into the city must have been supplied by his own followers, who never hesitate to magnify every event in his life far out of its proper proportions. Had there been any disturbance, beyond the normal expected from pilgrims coming from the north, I would certainly have known about it and taken the proper steps to subdue it. I do remember being told that Jesus had entered the Temple, and hoping that I might get a glimpse of this man of wonders I climbed our southeast tower, which overlooks the Temple courtyard, in order to see him. He did not disappoint me, I must say. With a few dozen followers at his back, he entered the yard and immediately began tipping over the tables of the money-changers. Then he drove them off with a whip of some kind and returned to smash countless cages until the sky was filled with doves. There was great havoc among the people, but to my surprise none of the guards moved to arrest him. As I watched, one of my officers came to me and said he was dispatching his men immediately, to seize the offender before a riot broke out. I stopped him."

"Why?"

"Jesus had committed a serious crime against the Temple. It was the responsibility of the Jewish authorities to arrest and punish him. During my time here I have found it necessary to put down trouble by spilling Jewish blood on more than one occasion. Whenever I have, the chief priests have always complained to Vitellius or Rome, claiming that I abused my power. Tiberius, for reasons I have never understood, insists on our coddling these miserable people, even to the point where they are exempt from military duty. I suspected that if I moved against Jesus in that crowd, composed of many Galileans as uncouth as himself, a riot might follow, blood would be spilled, and the priests would complain to Tiberius once again. Arresting Jesus under those circumstances was not worth the price to me, and because he had desecrated their precious Temple I was certain that the Jews would be forced to punish him on their own. Thus I would be rid of a dangerous man who threatened the peace of my province without so much as lifting a finger."

"Very clever," I said. "But I understand that these people do not have the right to execute any criminal they find guilty of a capital offense, such as defiling their Temple, without your permission."

The procurator placed his hands together, spread his fingers, and tapped one set against the other. "So long as their own courts found the man guilty and condemned him to death, the responsibility would be entirely theirs. I would then grant sanction to their verdict, as I customarily do, and they could take him out and stone him to death or whatever else they wanted to do with him."

"But according to Caiaphas, you finally did get involved. He said that he requested your assistance to arrest Jesus and you supplied him with soldiers."

"Caiaphas came here, late at night, rousing both me and my wife from our sleep. He sat there, where you are sitting now, in a state of great agitation. He pleaded for my help as he had never done before, saying that he knew where Jesus could be taken, away from the crowds, but his Temple guards were afraid to arrest him, just as they had been in the courtyard."

"Afraid? Of Jesus?" I forced a halfhearted smile.

"I, too, laughed at him," Pilate recalled, "but Caiaphas said that his men feared that Jesus might work a miracle and destroy them, for if he could make a dead man come alive, they believed he could certainly make one who was alive fall dead. He begged me to lend him a few of my troops, for he was certain that if my soldiers were present his men would have the courage to fulfill their duties. At first I refused, telling him that false prophets were his business, but finally I agreed since it would still be his responsibility for the actual arrest and trial and execution. I even promised to grant him my sanction, early on the following morning, to what he assured me would be a verdict of guilty by the Sanhedrin, punishable by death, so that they could do away with Jesus before their Passover and Sabbath began at sundown. Then I returned to bed."

"So the two of you had *already agreed* that Jesus would die?"

"A well-deserved fate for such as he. Yes."

"Caiaphas told me that he only requested a dozen or so soldiers but you supplied him with a small army. Why?"

Pilate's raucous, high-pitched laughter filled the room. He sat up and clapped his hands together as if he were applauding himself. "Several months earlier, a report had come to me that Jesus had fed many thousands in the wilderness of Galilee by multiplying five barley loaves and two small fish into enough food for all. According to my informer, the people were so impressed with his magic that they wanted to make him their king. Since some of the Jews considered this man powerful enough to be their ruler, I thought the least I could do was dispatch an army to arrest him that was worthy of his exalted position. The privileges of rank, you know." He snickered, still enjoying his practical joke on Caiaphas after all this time.

"Sir," I said, "according to Caiaphas, the Sanhedrin found Jesus guilty of blasphemy and agreed unanimously that he should die. They brought him here, early the next morning, as you and the high priest had agreed, for your approval to execute him—by stoning. What happened? What happened after they arrived that made you take the case out of the Sanhedrin's hands, find Jesus guilty of sedition, and crucify him, considering what you have just told me about not wanting to get involved? The high priest will not discuss any of that with me. He maintains that his jurisdiction ended at the gates of this fortress and that any information concerning what happened that morning within these walls will have to come from you."

"That wretch!" he roared. "If Caiaphas implies that his mouth is sealed, it is only because he has sealed it himself. He has never had the courage to admit that he betrayed me, before the people and my superiors, and forced me to act!"

Now we were getting somewhere! Thieves do fall out. Confide in me, Pilate. I'm on your side. See the purple stripe running down my tunic? We Romans must stick together.

Pilate continued. "I was awake before sunrise, as is my custom, and already waiting below in the Hall of Judgment when the Sanhedrin arrived with their prisoner. Rome, in their infinite wisdom, does not consider Judaea important enough to have a quaestor sitting in judgment on criminal cases, so it is necessary that I handle those matters myself. Since I had held court on the previous day, I had no other obligations that morning except to fulfill my promise to Caiaphas. Three tribunes from our headquarters in Antioch, here on their annual inspection tour of our fortress, were with me, delaying their departure so they could witness the simple procedure involved in sanctioning a Sanhedrin verdict for a capital offense. Caiaphas, curse him forever, made me appear as a fool in their eyes that morning."

"How?"

Pilate stood and gestured for me to follow. He opened a door and I followed him out onto a balcony overlooking the parade grounds. There it is, there it is! I kept repeating to myself between my galloping heartbeats. The pavement, the place where Jesus had been tried and condemned by Pilate— the *Gabbatha* in Aramaic, the *Lithostroton* in Greek, the square of sadness for every Christian who has relived the agonies of Jesus for two thousand years! I blinked several times

157

at the glare from stones polished by countless boots and horses' hooves parading back and forth across fifty square yards of immortality.

The procurator pointed to a spot on the pavement almost directly below us. "Caiaphas and the others had brought their prisoner through the entranceway in the wall, passed between the alley of the two buildings to our left, and stood there, outside the hall. When they did not enter, I sent one of my soldiers to invite them in but they told him that they could not or they would be defiled in such a way that they would be unable to purify themselves in time to fulfill their Passover functions at sundown. Think of it! They were ready to take a man out and stone him to a bloody pulp, and yet they could not bring themselves to enter the place of a gentile, even their procurator. I was furious. If the three tribune inspectors had not been with me I am not certain what I would have done to vent my anger. As it was I ordered that my platform and curule chair be brought out and placed on the pavement, vowing to myself that Caiaphas would regret he had ever crawled out of bed that day."

"How many had accompanied the prisoner here?"

"I have long had a policy that our pavement and Hall of Judgment are public areas on those days when I am holding court. All trials conducted before me are open to anyone who wishes to attend. It was still early, however, and so I would estimate that not more than fifty or so stood before the platform, including several worthless guards from the Temple, when I went out to them, accompanied by my own staff and the three tribunes from Antioch."

"What was your first impression of the prisoner?"

Pilate grinned. "I thought that if this was the Messiah who would deliver his people from their so-called oppressions, neither Tiberius nor Vitellius need lose any sleep. As I remember, his hands were tied behind him and his face had patches of dried blood on one cheek. His lips were puffed and his eyes were half closed as if he were nearly asleep. A rope was around his neck, and an old red woolen robe was draped on his shoulders. He was taller than most Jews, but with his beard and in his condition I could not estimate his age. All in all, he was not a pleasant sight as Caiaphas led him to the edge of the platform. I commenced by asking, as is customary, 'What accusation do you bring against this man?' expecting Caiaphas to tell me, as we had planned, that the Sanhedrin had found him guilty of blasphemy, under their laws, and had judged him deserving of death. I was prepared to grant them my permission to proceed, sign the execution certificate, and quickly adjourn the hearing. Instead, in response to my question, Caiaphas said, 'If he were not a criminal, we would not have handed him over to you.' I was speechless for a moment, before I realized what that worm in priestly vestments had plotted behind my back."

"I think I do too," I said. "He was passing the—I mean, he wanted *you* to try Jesus, find him guilty, and execute him. Then the burden of responsibility for his death would pass from the Sanhedrin to you, and if the people rioted, all the blame would be yours."

"Exactly," Pilate replied. "Caiaphas had tricked me, and with the three inspectors looking on I had to fight with myself to keep from leaping down from the platform and strangling him with my bare hands. Instead I said, 'Take him yourselves, then, and judge him according to your law.' I rose and prepared to adjourn the meeting, but Caiaphas and two or three other priests cried out, 'It is not lawful for us to put anyone to death.' "

"They did not inform you that they had already tried Jesus and found him guilty of blasphemy, under their laws, and were already prepared to execute him with your permission?"

"No. But they immediately began to accuse Jesus of other crimes, crimes against Rome rather than against their laws. One shouted that he had forbidden the payment of taxes to Caesar, and finally I remember Caiaphas repeating, over and over, 'He says he is Christ, a king; he says he is Christ, a king!' With those accusations made public, I had no choice. Caiaphas had outfoxed me, and since all the charges they presented, as legal witnesses, were against our empire, I was forced to sit in judgment of Jesus or the report Vitellius would receive from the three visiting tribunes would have ended my days as procurator. But now, even though from all my reports I was certain that Jesus probably deserved to be punished for sedition, I was determined to free him, at least for the present, if only to rub the high priest's face in the pavement. I ordered my soldiers to bring Jesus up here, to my quarters, in order that I might interrogate him privately."

I turned and looked back into the elegantly furnished room with its richly paneled walls, agate floor, and marble and gold statuary, and tried to picture Jesus in such a setting. "What did you say to him when you two were alone?"

Pilate stared skyward. "I simply asked him if he was the king of the Jews, but he turned the question back on me."

"How?"

"He looked me directly in the eyes and asked if I was speaking from my own observations or from what others had said about him. I had to admire his courage. He was obviously exhausted and in pain, and most prisoners facing the death penalty become little more than wailing infants, pleading for their lives, kissing my robe and my sandals, begging, screaming. Not that one. 'Am I a Jew?' I asked him, already growing impatient with the whole affair. 'How would I know about you? Your own people and the chief priests have delivered you to me. Tell me, what have you done?' "

"What did he say?"

"He began to speak about his kingdom not being of this world, because if it was his followers would have kept him from being delivered to the Jews. 'Then you *are* a king?' I asked and he replied, 'You have said it, I am a king. This is why I was born and why I have come into the world, to bear witness to the truth.' I asked him, 'What is truth?' but he refused to answer. I've always wondered what he meant. . . ."

"What did you do next?"

"I had already heard enough to convince me that Jesus presented no danger to Rome or to the peace of the city. At worst he was a dreamer, perhaps slightly deranged with devils and delusions, but harmless compared to the many evil zealots and murderers I had crucified in the past. I ordered that the prisoner be taken back downstairs and made him stand next to me on the platform. Then I announced that I had found no guilt in the man."

"You found him innocent of all charges?"

"Yes."

"But you didn't release him."

"Before I could, a great cry arose from the crowd. Accusations of all kinds against the prisoner filled my ears, with many of the priests and Sanhedrin members shouting that he stirred up the people in all parts of the country, beginning in Galilee and even here. Hearing Galilee mentioned was like a special message from Jupiter."

"I don't understand."

"Since Jesus was from Galilee he was a subject of Herod Antipas, and I knew that Herod was in the city to observe the Passover, staying, as always, at the nearby palace of the Hasmoneans. Against the loud protests of the chief priests, I told the crowd that Herod should be allowed to judge one of his own people. Jesus was then led away by my soldiers, with Caiaphas and his assistants following behind, while most of the crowd sat down on the hot stones. I returned here to my quarters to await Herod's decision."

"The crowd did not leave?"

"On the contrary, it grew larger and noisier as the sun climbed into the sky, for that was the Day of Indulgence, an old Passover custom established by an earlier procurator who should have known better, the day when I was to release to the Jews one condemned prisoner, with a full pardon, as a gesture of Roman goodwill. By the looks of the motley ruffians gathering on the grounds I knew the prisoner they would request, and I was not anticipating the moment when I would ask them to name their choice. Earlier in the week we had arrested and convicted another Jesus, called Barabbas, who had led a band of brigands against one of my patrols outside the city, killing three of my auxiliaries before he was taken. Barabbas would have been crucified immediately, except that we were hoping to extract information from him as to where his murderous group was headquartered."

"Torturing him?"

Pilate smirked. "Encouraging the prisoner to cooperate by any means at our disposal, would be a better way of putting it. In any event, sometime before the sixth hour I was informed that Herod had returned Jesus to me, and when I went down to the pavement he was now wearing a bright silk cape such as is worn by royalty. Herod had apparently mocked Jesus regarding his claims of kingship, but he would not touch the case. My centurion in charge of the guard reported that although Herod had questioned Jesus at length, the prisoner had remained silent, and even when he was cursed and ridiculed and punched he had uttered no sound."

" 'He was oppressed, and he was afflicted, yet he opened not his mouth.' "

Pilate scowled, "What did you say?"

"Just recalling an old quotation. And now that you had Jesus back, what was your next move?"

"I called Caiaphas and the others close to the platform and told them, once again, that although they had brought me a man they accused of perverting the people, I had examined him and found no guilt. I reminded them that even Herod had confirmed my verdict, for he had found no offense in the man deserving of death or he would not have returned him to me. I then told them that I would have Jesus scourged and release him."

"Why would you want to scourge a man whom you had already announced, not once but twice, as innocent of any wrongdoing?"

Pilate hesitated, "As a . . . a warning to the man to exercise greater care in what he said henceforth."

"Is this standard procedure for those found innocent in your court?"

"Of course not," Pilate replied, raising his voice, "but that was a most unusual trial."

"Obviously your decision didn't please the priests."

"It did not," the procurator said regretfully, "and Caiaphas, crafty, snakelike Caiaphas, immediately began to turn the crowd to his purpose. He and the other priests began to shout, in unison, 'Away with this man and release the prisoner Barabbas to us!' Soon the entire mob took up the cry and the noise was deafening; 'Barabbas, Barabbas, Barabbas!' I raised my hands until the clamor subsided and asked, 'What then am I to do with Jesus?' and Caiaphas led the others in crying, 'Crucify him, crucify him!' "

"From what you have told me," I said, "it was exactly the reaction to be expected from that crowd. Barabbas was undoubtedly considered a brave and colorful patriot, willing to risk his life against the forces of Rome, while Jesus preached love and meekness and turning the other cheek and even rendering unto Caesar the things that are Caesar's. Barabbas, to that crowd, was probably closer to their conception of a Messiah than Jesus."

Pilate agreed. "Your appraisal of the situation is accurate. Had the three tribunes from Antioch not been witnesses, I would have turned my soldiers on the mob and ended the madness swiftly. I did not relish freeing Barabbas. But I was still not defeated. See those two wooden posts on the parade grounds, separated by a distance of thirty paces or so?"

"Yes."

"They are used, on special occasions, by some of our more courageous soldiers who are bold enough to compete in a contest called the Circle of Death. I issued orders that Jesus be taken to that nearer post, there below us, where his clothes were to be removed, his hands and feet tied to the wood, and thirty-nine lashes administered. By the time my two expert lictors had finished inflicting their punishment, I knew there would be little of his body that was not covered with blood or open wounds from the leather thongs and chains.

"I waited here until they finished, and when I returned to the pavement it was almost impossible to recognize the battered face of the prisoner as belonging to Jesus. On his head, one of my soldiers had forced a crown of thorns woven from a dried desert plant used for kindling, and the cloak of Herod's was once again about his shoulders. In his hand someone had placed a bloody reed to simulate a royal scepter, after beating him with it. The soldiers were still spinning him around, prodding him with the points of their javelins and shouting, 'Hail, King of the Jews!' while the crowd cheered.

"At a signal from me he was lifted up onto the platform beside me, and he looked so pitiful that I was certain the priests would have mercy on him. I raised one of his bloody hands above his head and shouted, 'Behold the man!' It was all in vain. Once again the high priest shouted, 'Crucify him!' and the crowd echoed his words, again and again."

"Was there any reaction from Jesus?"

"None. No crying, no begging for mercy, not even any moans because of his pain."

"Did you know," I asked, "that by that time he had gone more than a day and a night without any sleep, and probably little food and water?"

"No," Pilate admitted, "and whatever else he may have been, I will say that I have never seen another prisoner, under even far less trying circumstances, conduct himself with such . . . such dignity."

"And with the crowd yelling for his execution, you finally gave in to their demands?"

"Oh, no! My patience with them had reached its limit. I told them that if they wanted him crucified they could take him and crucify him themselves, but I still found no fault in him."

"That was the third time you announced your innocent verdict."

"Yes."

"What did they do?"

"The crowd grew very quiet. Remember that most of them had come only to ask that Barabbas be freed. Caiaphas consulted with the other priests for a few moments and then he said, 'We have a law, and by our law he ought to die, because he made himself the Son of God.' When I heard that I wanted to spit on the high priest for his treachery. Had he made that allegation in the beginning, I would have sanctioned the Sanhedrin's verdict of death for blasphemy and the matter would have been finished hours ago. Now it was too late, as far as I was concerned. I ordered that the prisoner be brought back here to my quarters once more. Since he was no longer able to climb the stairs, two of my soldiers carried him up and leaned him against the wall, just inside this balcony. Later, it took many scrubbings to remove all his blood from the panels."

Both of us turned, as if on signal, and stepped down from the balcony into the room. Joseph looked up anxiously as we assumed our previous seats. I nodded toward the wall against which Jesus had been placed. "What did you ask him, this time?"

"I asked him where he came from—"

"Why? What difference did that make? And didn't you know? Nazareth, in Galilee—"

"No, no, Matthias, that is not what I meant. If Jesus believed he was a god I wanted to hear, from his lips, where he thought his spirit had originated and what he envisioned as its purpose. Just as Vulcan protects our fire and Fornax our corn for baking and Janus our entranceways and Juno our soul and Cuba our sheep, I wanted to know what he imagined his godly duties to be, here on earth."

"What did he say?"

"Nothing! His sad brown eyes just stared at me, with compassion and pity, as if he regretted the trouble he was causing me. I had the strangest feeling that he was prepared to go to the cross and did not appreciate my efforts to release him because I was hindering his desire to die, if you can believe such madness. I said to him, 'Why don't you speak to me? Don't you know that I have the power to crucify you and that I have the power to release you?' "

"Did he answer?"

"Yes, finally. He said that I would have no power at all over him if it had not been given to me from above. Then, as if he were forgiving me—as if I were receiving a pardon *from him*—he said that the person who had betrayed him to me had the greater sin. I could endure no more and had him brought downstairs to the platform, where I told the crowd that I was going to release him."

"For the fourth time," I said.

"Yes, but Caiaphas immediately leaned forward and pointed to this ring on my hand, bestowed on me by Tiberius, and said, 'If you release this man you are not a friend of Caesar's!' The crowd began to chant 'Crucify him!' once more, and I shouted, 'Shall I crucify your king?' Then it was that Caiaphas delivered his thunderbolt. He cried out, 'We have no king but Caesar!' and I dared not respond lest anyone present might accuse me, an admiring friend of Caesar's, of being less loyal than a mob of Jews."

"What did you do?"

"I asked for a bowl of water, and when my servant delivered it to me I dipped my hands in it and said, 'I am innocent of the blood of this just person. See to it yourself.' Then I ordered that Barabbas be released, as the crowd had requested, and passed formal sentence on Jesus with the words, 'To the cross you shall go!' The soldiers removed his robe of royalty, replaced it with his old red garment, and brought me a pine board on which I inscribed, 'Jesus of Nazareth, the King of the Jews' to be posted above his head on the cross. When Caiaphas and the others saw what I had done they wailed that I should not write 'the King of the Jews' but 'He said he was King of the Jews.' I told them that what I had written, I had written, and the sign would stand as I had made it. Then the soldiers led Jesus, and two others I had condemned to death on the previous day, outside the city to the northwest, to a place called Golgotha, for execution."

The procurator's voice was calm and matter-of-fact, as if he had just described what he had consumed for breakfast. A quiet fell over the room. I inhaled deeply and said, "Pilate, I don't believe your story!"

Joseph of Arimathea's mouth flew open. Pilate said nothing, but I could see that all the blood seemed to have drained from his face. He was within reach of me so I braced myself, fully expecting a backhand slap or worse for my insulting declaration. There was none. The most powerful and feared man in all of Judaea sat motionless, as if my words had suddenly transformed him to stone.

His unexpected behavior gave me the courage to continue. "I believe there was another and far more compelling reason why you wanted to release Jesus, one that had little to do with your desire for revenge against the high priest and, even less, with your own sense of Roman justice in dealing with a man who had obviously never preached the overthrow of the empire." I waited for a reaction, any kind, but there was none except for a furiously twitching left eyelid that I hadn't noticed before. "Tell me, sir," I said, "is your wife with you here, on this visit to Jerusalem?"

The procurator fumbled with his corded belt, removed a blue silk square of cloth, and coughed into it. I heard a muffled "No."

"She was here with you, was she not, during that Passover time when Jesus was executed, six years ago?"

"What has she to do with Jesus?" he snarled.

"As I recall, sir, you told me that when Caiaphas came to you in the night, to beg for soldiers to assist his guards in the arrest of Jesus, *both* you and your wife were awakened from a sound sleep, is that correct?"

He nodded. It was obvious that he had no idea where I was heading with my questions. Neither did Joseph, from his puzzled frown.

"After Caiaphas and you had completed your arrangements and he departed, you no doubt returned to your bedchamber?"

"Of course," he growled.

"And your wife"—I smiled understandingly—"if she is anything like most wives, was probably still awake, curious to know what strange business that could not wait until morning would bring the high priest to your quarters so late at night, am I correct?"

The procurator almost returned my smile before he caught himself. "She was awake," he sighed.

"And she asked what had taken place between you two, and you told her?"

"I did."

"Is it your habit to arise earlier than your wife, in the mornings?"

"Always. Especially when duty brings me to Jerusalem, where there are so many official obligations to fulfill."

"On the morning of the trial, were you dressed and downstairs before she had risen?"

"Yes. Caiaphas had promised that he would have Jesus before me soon after sunrise."

"Then you and your wife had no conversation whatsoever, before you left your bedchamber at dawn?"

"None."

Now I could hardly hear him. I leaned forward. "Pilate, is it not true that early in your trial of Jesus you were delivered a note from your wife, Claudia Procula?"

He slumped back in his chair, the lower part of his body sliding forward until our knees were almost touching. "How do you know such things?"

How could I tell him that I had read it in the Gospel According to Matthew, chapter 27, verse 19? How could I explain that I had labored over that anecdote from the trial, reported only by Matthew, for more than two decades? I had always wanted to accept it as fact, for it was the only logical explanation of why a ruthless and callous leader, with no

166

compunction about turning the swords of his men on the people he ruled but despised, would have suddenly turned into a spineless character bowing to the will of a high priest and his lackeys whom he had always before treated with the greatest contempt.

"Pilate," I bluffed, "there were many in that crowd who saw your servant deliver a message to you while you were on the platform. The sender of the message is only an assumption on my part, but who else would dare interrupt the procurator while he was sitting in judgment, except his wife? What did the message from your wife say?"

"She had written, 'Have nothing to do with that righteous man, for I have suffered many things this day in a dream because of him.'"

"Do you believe in dreams, sir?"

"Is there a Roman who does not? I believe, as Augustus did, that dreams are the means by which our gods most often communicate with us. When I read my wife's message I could not ignore it, since there had already been many times, in the past, when the things she dreamt had come to pass. Then I remembered how Julius Caesar had been told by his spouse, Calpurnia, that she had been warned in a dream that Caesar must not venture forth on the Ides of March. He ignored her words, as you know, and fell that morning under the assassins' daggers. Later in the trial, when I heard the high priest accuse Jesus of claiming he was the Son of God, I had him brought here to this room, again, as I told you, to ask him where he had come from. Because of Claudia's dream I was no longer certain who he was or what he was."

"Your wife is now at the palace in Caesarea?"

"No," he said stoically. "She packed her trunks and returned to Rome four days after the crucifixion. She told me that she could not live another day with the man who had murdered the Son of God, and now that he had risen from his tomb she had no desire to be near me when he came for his revenge."

"She knew about the empty tomb?"

"Claudia was with me when I first received that bad news." He smiled ruefully, sitting up in his chair as if relieved to have finally unburdened his secret to someone after all these years, even to a historian.

"Concerning that tomb: late on the afternoon of the crucifixion, Joseph, as I understand it, came to you for permission to bury the body of Jesus, rather than have it thrown in a common grave. You granted his request?"

"Yes, but only after I verified that Jesus was dead. A crucified one very often survives for several days on the cross, and I was surprised to hear that Jesus had expired so quickly. I dispatched Cornelius to Golgotha while Joseph and I waited together, and he soon returned with the report that Jesus was indeed dead."

"Cornelius?" I gasped. "By any chance would he be the same Cornelius who brought us here to your quarters from the gate?"

"The very same. He has been not only my most loyal officer but my closest friend and adviser for many years. We first served together under Germanicus."

"Would you have any objection to my speaking with him later?"

"None."

"In any event, when you were certain that Jesus was dead you allowed Joseph to claim the body?"

"Yes. I have made it a common practice, except in extreme cases, to return the bodies of executed criminals to their families or friends for burial. I knew Joseph of Arimathea as a man of honor, who always paid his taxes in full and on time, and so I had no objection to his receiving the body, although I was surprised that he, a highly respected member of the Sanhedrin who had condemned Jesus, would dare compromise his position on the high court of the Jews by coming forth, in public, to claim his body. In retrospect," Pilate said, glancing at the old man with chagrin, "I should never have released the remains to him."

"Why not?"

"If the body had been thrown in a common grave, along with the other two who were crucified that day, Jesus of Nazareth would have been long forgotten by now. Our friend here, as you know, proceeded to bury the body in an elegant tomb, and when it was discovered empty it was not difficult for the ignorant and gullible to be convinced that Jesus had risen from the dead. Without that tomb's false testimony we would not have that rabble, who now call themselves Christians, causing us more trouble with each passing day."

"From what you say, Pilate, I take it you believe the body was removed from the tomb so that the people could be misled."

"I do."

"But didn't Caiaphas come to you, on the day after Jesus was buried, warning you of what might happen? Didn't he ask you for a guard to be posted at the tomb so that the followers of Jesus could not remove his body in order to claim that he had risen from the dead as Jesus had prophesied would happen?"

"I should have listened to him. Instead, because I was still raging at his treachery during the trial, I reminded him that I had washed my hands of the whole affair. I told him that my men had more important things to do than guard a dead man's tomb, and if he wanted the grave watched he could use his own people."

"In retrospect, then, you regret that decision too?"

"I do. When I first heard the news that the tomb was empty, I assumed that Caiaphas had not bothered to post his own guard. Still, I sent Cornelius to the high priest, demanding an explanation. The high priest sent his regrets," Pilate said scornfully. "He told Cornelius that he had posted a guard but that they had grown weary because of their long day of duty in the Temple and had fallen asleep during the night, and while they slept the disciples of Jesus must have come and removed the body. Can you imagine any soldiers of *ours* sleeping on watch, knowing that Roman punishment for such a dereliction of duty is death?"

Our host was pouring more wine into our goblets when we heard four sharp raps on the door. He shouted, "Enter!" And Cornelius appeared to remind the procurator that it was time he began dressing for his weekly inspection of the barracks.

Pilate motioned for Cornelius to come into the room. "Why don't you have your talk with the centurion now," he said to me, "while I prepare myself for this time-wasting necessity of army life?"

Cornelius accepted my invitation to sit but his face registered uncertainty as to what we sought from him even after Joseph explained our mission and assured him that he had nothing to fear by answering me truthfully.

"Cornelius," I began, as soft-key as I could get, "do you recall that afternoon, six years ago, when Pilate asked you to go to the hill called Golgotha to check on whether or not a man called Jesus, who had been crucified that day, was already dead?"

The centurion nodded hesitantly. "Joseph wished to claim the body for burial," he said, "but Pilate had expressed doubts that Jesus had expired so quickly. We have long had an agreement with the high priests that no Jew convicted of a capital crime would hang on a cross during their Sabbath. For those who are crucified on the day before the Sabbath, which begins always at sundown, our procedure is to hasten their death as sundown approaches, by breaking their legs. By the time I arrived on the hill, Fabius, who was in charge of our execution detail, had already broken the bones of the criminal hanging on one side of Jesus. The man was still moaning but the sounds were already growing more and more faint and we knew he would be dead before long. Just as Fabius began to swing his heavy club at the legs of Jesus I stopped him, saying that it was unnecessary for one could see that Jesus was already dead. Fabius then proceeded to the third crucified one, who was unconscious but alive, and smashed his bones before he returned to stand beside me under Jesus. I could see that he resented my interference, since Fabius is a good man who follows his orders implicitly, so I took the javelin from a nearby soldier and thrust its pointed head deep into the right side of Jesus, bringing forth a large issue of blood and water. 'See, Fabius,' I remember saying, 'that man is already dead. Why waste your strength on a corpse?' I then told him that his men could remove the other two from their crosses and dispose of their bodies in the common grave but he was not to leave the hill until Joseph of Arimathea arrived to claim the body of Jesus. Then I returned to Pilate and reported that the Galilean was dead, and Joseph was handed the procurator's written permission to take possession of the body."

I stared at the tanned centurion, handsome despite an ugly birthmark that crossed from his left ear to his mouth, and I continued to stare until he began to shift nervously in his seat. Several minutes passed before I said, "Pilate informs me that you two have known each other for a long time."

"Yes, sir," he exclaimed, obviously relieved to have the subject changed. He threw out his chest proudly, the epitome of every top sergeant who has ever lived. "We fought together under Germanicus!"

"You are not stationed here, am I correct? You come down from Caesarea, with Pilate, for the Jewish feast days?"

"Yes, sir."

"Do you live at the headquarters in Caesarea?"

"No, sir, with my family on the outskirts of that city."

"Did you ever live in or near the village of Capernaum?"

"Yes, there had been a period of considerable unrest, many years ago, concerning the taxes imposed on fishermen of the lake, and during that time Pilate maintained a century of men in Capernaum, under my command, to enforce law and order. Even during that duty, however, I still accompanied

170

the procurator whenever he came here to Jerusalem for any occasion."

I leaned toward Cornelius until we were almost nose to nose. "Tell me, centurion, is it true that you knew Jesus from those days?"

"Yes, I knew him," he said, his voice trembling.

My shot in the dark! Now I was almost certain that I was in the presence of that unnamed centurion from Matthew and Luke whose servant had been healed by Jesus. "Did you ever speak with Jesus?"

"Yes."

"Tell me about it, as best you can recall."

Cornelius cupped his large hands over both knees and shook his head as if to clear it. He said, "I had heard many stories of the good deeds and wonders performed by this man among the poor of the waterfront, even his curing of many who were sick and infirm. When my beloved servant, Linus, became ill with palsy and none who tried could help him, I went to the waterfront in search of Jesus and begged him to intercede with his god in behalf of my friend. To my great surprise he placed his arm around my neck and said, 'I will come and heal him.' I told him that I was not worthy of his coming under my roof, but from what I had heard of his great powers I knew that if he just said the word my servant would be healed. I explained that I understood such things for I was a man with authority, having soldiers under me, and if I said to one man, 'Go,' he would go, and to another, 'Come,' he would come, and to my servant, 'Do this,' and it was done. I thought that Jesus might be able to do the same thing without having to defile himself, as a Jew, by entering my house."

"What did Jesus do?"

Cornelius rubbed his right hand across his eyes, several times, and said, "First he made those who were with him angry because he embraced me, and I need not tell you that most Jews would rather eat the meat of a pig than touch a Roman. Then he turned to the others and said, 'Verily I say unto you, I have not found so great a faith as his in all of Israel.' After that he turned to me, touched my cheek lightly with his fingers, and said, 'Go your way; and as you have believed, so be it done unto you.' By the time I arrived at my house there was already a celebration, for the palsy had departed from the body of Linus and there was great joy in my family. To show my gratitude I contributed heavily to the village's treasury so that they could erect a synagogue. If you

171

should have the occasion to visit Capernaum, anyone will direct you to it and tell you that a Roman centurion is responsible for their place of worship."

The centurion bowed his head, and when he did I saw a familiar glint of metal. Without thinking of the possible consequences from this tough fighting man, I reached down inside his tunic and removed a heavy gold amulet hanging from a thin leather cord. I turned it toward the window until I saw it had the same markings as the one Joseph had given me four days ago—including the unmistakable outline of a fish!

"Does Pilate know?" I asked gently.

He shook his head.

"And he'll not know from me, Cornelius," I heard myself saying. "Tell me, are you absolutely convinced that Jesus was dead when you departed from Golgotha?"

"He was. Positively. I have seen many dead men in my years of service, and I have taken many lives in battle. There was no longer a spark of life in Jesus, and in truth his flesh was already beginning to grow cold and hard to the touch."

"If he was dead, why did you pierce his body with the spear?"

"I don't know for a certainty," he half sobbed. "At the time I remember thinking it was the very least I could do for my Lord, for I could not bear the thought of his bones being smashed. Somehow I knew he would understand my wanting to save him from that shame even if it had to be at my own hands. . . ."

I shuddered and looked away, recalling that in both the Book of Exodus and the Book of Numbers, the prescribed preparation of the Paschal lamb for the Passover feast, after it had been slain for sacrifice, specified that *no bones of it should be broken.*

"Well"—Pilate's voice interrupted us—"have you managed to uncover any more truths, historian?" The procurator marched toward us with a touch of insolence, head high, his confidence apparently restored by his change into uniform. Now he stood before us as a warrior of Rome, from his polished breastplates to the belted harness around his waist with its many leather strips studded in silver. Clothes always make the man, I guess. He walked us to the door and down the long musty hallway.

"Tell me, Matthias," he said in that small-talk tone hosts assume while they are repeating farewells to their guests, "does Vitellius still ride his Arabian horses every morning?"

172

"Just as always," I assured him. "One could have worse vices, you know."

"Yes." He grinned, dripping with charm. "And most of us do."

"Pilate, do you still stand on your statement made at the beginning of our talk today?"

"What was that?" he asked wearily, as if the interview was over so far as he was concerned.

"As I recall, you said that in your opinion any mention of Jesus in my history was only deserving of a sentence or two, if that."

He released his hold on my arm and muttered, "I don't know, I don't know. I do know I wish I had never heard that name!"

We approached the landing with its cluttered array of statues. I stopped and asked, "Did you, by any chance, have the body of Jesus removed from the tomb, either to embarrass Caiaphas and the Sanhedrin or for any other reason?"

His laugh reverberated down the empty corridor. "If I had, you can be certain I would have produced it long before this. Do you realize that within a few months after the crucifixion there were thousands running around this city, agitating and stirring up trouble, all claiming that Jesus had risen from the dead and would return soon? Ever since then I have had to station four additional centuries of men here, just to keep order, and I could use more during the feast days if Vitellius would only give them to me. No, my friend, I have no idea who took the body, but I would pay dearly for information as to its resting place."

I couldn't resist one final shot. Turning to point down the long, lonely corridor that had not heard the voice of his wife, Claudia Procula, for more than six years, I said, "Jesus has already cost you dearly, hasn't he, procurator?"

Joseph stared morosely out the carriage window on his side as we rode through the busy streets back to his home. Finally, and without turning his head, he asked, "Whom would you like to visit next, Matthias?"

"The apostle John and then Mary Magdalene, if possible."

"You are in luck," he replied, but not with his usual enthusiasm.

"Why?"

"Since the crucifixion, John has lived in the large house of the widow Mary, where Jesus ate his last meal."

"Those two are now married?"

"No, no," he said unsmilingly, finally turning toward me. "Mary is a much older woman than the apostle and not in good health. Her home has become a virtual headquarters for Peter and James and the other leaders of the movement, here in the city. The place is maintained for their needs under John's supervision, with the help of Mary's son, Mark, and the Magdalene woman, who lives nearby, tends to Mary's infirmities, and prepares meals for those who gather there to confer. With a single visit you may be able to talk with both John and Mary Magdalene, and I believe we should do it today for I fear that your time is running out."

"But I still have three days," I protested.

"Perhaps not," he said solicitously, patting my knee. "Look out the rear window."

I did as I was told, squinting through the dust from our wheels at the turbulent stream of humanity we left in our wake as we ascended to the upper city. "We're not being followed, Joseph. I see no bald-headed or black-hooded man on a gray horse—or anyone else, for that matter, who looks suspicious."

"Exactly."

"What do you mean?"

"Matthias, it is now no longer necessary for Pilate to have us followed. Do you recall your little conversation with him, in the hall, just before we departed, especially about Vitellius and your confirming that the governor is still riding his Arabian horses every morning?"

"Yes, why?" I asked with a sickening foreboding that I knew exactly what Joseph was about to say. Unfortunately, my premonition was absolutely correct.

"Vitellius was seriously injured nearly five years ago. One morning, while racing, he was thrown from his favorite mount and landed on a boulder with the base of his spine. Ever since then he walks with a pronounced limp, usually with the help of a cane, and he has never been on a horse since the accident. Now Pilate knows that, at the very least, you are an impostor."

Belching hot blasts of searing dust, riding the desert winds, forced their way into our open carriage, but suddenly I felt very cold.

174

eleven

BILLOWING DARK SMOKE floated lazily over Hell.

From Joseph's palace, high in the city, I could see the infamous Valley of Hinnom far below, beyond the south wall, as we climbed into the carriage after a brief lunch of hot bread and honey. That valley, as I knew, was also called Gehenna, or Hell, not for the offal and garbage that was burned constantly on its lifeless slopes but because of the countless children who had been sacrificed there, in furnaces during Solomon's time, to satisfy the deity known as Molech.

Curling through the desolate wasteland, around craggy rock mounds that rolled like placid waves to the horizon, was a thin strip of magenta-colored road that led to a small village.

"Bethlehem," Joseph said reverently, in response to my questioning glance.

"Will there be time?" I asked hopefully.

"I'm afraid not, Matthias. Not only will there not be time for sightseeing, but I must urge you to make this visit and any others you have in mind as brief as possible."

The road from Joseph's place to the house of the widow Mary descended at such a steep angle that only Shem's great strength, applied constantly to the hand brake, prevented our carriage from gathering downhill speed until it was completely out of control.

Our vehicle finally came to a grateful and creaking halt before a walled courtyard fronting on a large two-story stone house at the bottom of the hill. No more than thirty yards away was the city gate used by travelers coming from or going to Bethlehem, or Hebron, fifteen miles beyond. Joseph was no stranger at this address. We were halfway across the courtyard before he stopped and pointed toward two dense pomegranate trees that dominated one corner of the small plot. Under the shady arches of their branches, reclining on a long wicker chair, an elderly woman was fast asleep.

"Mary," the old man called softly, "Mary."

175

The woman blinked her eyes several times before she recognized Joseph of Arimathea. Then she reached toward him with both arms and he went to her while I waited. After only a few minutes together Joseph kissed her lightly on the forehead and rejoined me, nodding toward the outside stone steps leading up to a second-floor open terrace.

"Mary says that John and her son, Mark, are at the Temple and the Magdalene woman has gone to the market. We can wait for them in the upper room. Come, let us walk up the same steps that Jesus ascended to eat his last supper," he said casually, turning to watch the expression on my face. I didn't disappoint him. There were fourteen steps. I took them all on my toes, and I was still walking that way when we entered the room.

Dominating the large, cluttered chamber was a huge table, rising no more than a foot above the mat-covered floor. It was at least ten feet long and four feet wide, and its dark, polished surface was free of the ubiquitous dust one usually finds on all desert furniture. At the head of the table was a tall, thick candle, set in a stone base, casting its flickering light across the burnished wood and the thick green cushions that were partially tucked beneath three sides of the tabletop. I didn't need Joseph to tell me that this was the table where Jesus, with his twelve, had taken the Paschal lamb on that fateful night when he was eventually arrested in Gethsemane.

"Many years ago," Joseph said, "it was the custom of our ancestors to eat the Passover supper in haste, while standing. But now that we are no longer in bondage or in an alien land, we recline during the holy meal and eat it leisurely."

The old man lowered his body until his feet extended behind him, away from the table, and his left elbow rested on one of the cushions. "This is how one partakes of the meal, Matthias, with the right hand always free to dip the bread into the common pot."

I motioned toward the candle. "Jesus sat there?"

"Yes, with John on his right and Judas on his left and the others along both sides. This fourth side, here, was where the food was placed when it was brought from the kitchen below."

"Judas was on his left?"

"That is what I have been told."

"Is the table used now?"

"Many times each week. Usually by Peter or James, the brother of Jesus, when they wish to take counsel with others.

176

However, no one ever sits there," he said, nodding toward the cushion behind the candle.

"Does Pilate know that this place is being used as . . . a virtual underground headquarters?"

"There is little that takes place in this city without the procurator's knowledge—or the high priest's either, for that matter. But the movement has grown too large to hide."

I kept staring at the table until Joseph read my thoughts, which no longer even surprised me.

"It doesn't look much like da Vinci's setting for his painting, does it, Matthias? However, as a writer you certainly must understand that while truth may be stranger than fiction, life is rarely as dramatic as art. While there is much to be said for that master's composition and brilliant arrangement of figures, in reality it was actually quite different."

The entire guest chamber was a sorry letdown after da Vinci. Piled high along one wall were bundles of clothing and crates filled to overflowing with sandals of countless variety. Wicker baskets, beneath the room's three small windows, were bulging with squash, ears of corn, figs, grapes, and several fruits I couldn't identify. Rows of thick round cheeses, wrapped in cloth and decidedly pungent, towered high in another corner, while several small carcasses, surrounded by buzzing flies, hung suspended from hooks attached to the heavy roof beams above.

"Many mouths are fed in this room," Joseph reminded me as he followed my gaze. "Come, sit with me and rest awhile until the others arrive."

It took every bit of my willpower to sit on one of the hard cushions, next to the old man. Hesitantly, I reached forward until the palms of both hands were resting on the smooth wood. I had to be dreaming. None of this was real. None of it. I could not possibly be sitting at the table where Jesus ate his last supper! The candle's flame suddenly went blurry until I wiped my eyes. The old man watched me. He said nothing.

Loud slapping of wooden-soled sandals on stone eventually announced John's return just before he rushed into the room and greeted Joseph. This "son of thunder" was smaller and far more frail than his brother, James, and also much younger. His light brown hair was clipped so that it did not quite reach his shoulders, and his sparse beard irregularly edged a fair-complexioned face whose protruding cheekbones gave him an almost emaciated appearance. As I studied him it was difficult for me to realize that here was the "beloved disciple" who, six long years ago, had been one of the inner circle of three, along with his brother and Peter, chosen by Jesus to be near him during so many of the most significant moments in his life. First impressions again. He sat across from Joseph and me, listening intently as the old man described the purpose of our visit, smiling and nodding frequently to both of us.

"My brother and Matthew have already told me about you, Matthias, and said I should be expecting a visit. Someday," he said earnestly, "I hope to write a history too, but only of our Lord."

I liked him. For an insane moment I wondered how I could assure him that he would indeed write that history, eventually, and unlike the others he would have many years to reflect on his experiences before he assembled what the world would come to know as the Gospel According to John.

"You will help me then?" I asked.

"Ask. What I know I shall tell you. Joseph, here"—he grinned—"can vouch for my honesty."

"Thank you. John, I have already spoken to many who were close to Jesus, as you know, and also to some of his enemies. You were with him almost from the beginning of his mission, and I have been given to understand that you were the only apostle at his crucifixion. Where you can be of the greatest assistance to me is by providing information to fill some of those gaps in his life on which I have no firsthand testimony, either because none was available from the others or because I was too ignorant to ask the proper questions of them."

"I understand."

"Do you also understand that I do not believe that Jesus rose from the dead?"

No change of expression. None of the bigot's customary cold animosity dulled his eyes. His lips curled into a half smile, and he said, "Your belief is shared by a great majority of our people, not only here but even in his own village. We still have much work to do."

"The more I hear about his final days," I began, "the stronger grows my conviction that Jesus came to Jerusalem, that last week, not only for the purpose of celebrating Passover but to rally all the people to his cause, somehow expecting to be able to convince them that he could lead them to a better life, a new kingdom here on earth. Since even his most bitter foes are in agreement that he was neither foolhardy nor ignorant, I find it difficult to understand how he expected to

178

impose his will on this great city with only a dozen or so unarmed Galileans to help him."

"Matthias, there was much that was puzzling about that week, even to those of us who were closest to him. None of us had any stomach for going up to Jerusalem to celebrate the Passover that year, for we knew that the chief priests and the Sanhedrin had agreed to put Jesus to death, after he had raised Lazarus, because they feared that all men would soon believe in him if he were allowed to continue working his miracles."

"John, why did Jesus enter the city, on that first day of his last week, riding on a lowly ass, of all animals?"

"As our party neared Bethpage, on our journey to Jerusalem for the Passover, Jesus sent two of us ahead to secure for him an ass, saying that it was necessary that he ride one into Jerusalem in order that the prophet's words be fulfilled."

"Did any of you understand what he meant?"

"None of us. We were not as proficient in the words of our prophets as Jesus. Only later, much later, did we learn that Zechariah had written, 'Rejoice greatly, O daughter of Zion; shout, O Daughter of Jerusalem: behold, thy King cometh unto thee: he is just, and having salvation; lowly, and riding upon an ass. . . .'"

"Was Zechariah describing the Messiah?"

"Yes, he who was to come to free the people from Alexander, more than three hundred years ago."

"Since Alexander died with the entire world in his hands, I take it that Zechariah's liberator never came. Then Jesus, riding upon an ass, intended this to be a sign to the people that he was entering Jerusalem as their Messiah? That makes no sense at all. If you and the other apostles did not understand the sign, how could Jesus expect the rural and uneducated crowds on the road to recognize it?"

John shrugged his thin shoulders. "Other than his words that the prophecy should be fulfilled, Jesus did not explain his reasoning to us, nor did we ask."

"And yet some of your party, according to what I've been told, apparently attempted to incite the crowd along the way by shouting, 'Hosanna to the son of David: Blessed is he that cometh in the name of the Lord.' Doesn't that acclamation have special significance for all Jews?"

"It does. It is a prayer to the anointed king, the Messiah, for salvation and deliverance, and it is as old as our people."

179

"But if none of you recognized the significance of Jesus' riding on an ass, who was shouting the Messiah acclamation from your group?"

"Peter, and with his encouragement the rest of us soon joined in, at first softly and then louder and louder."

"You did more than that, didn't you? I've been told that some of you also threw your garments and the fronds from palm trees in his path as if he were visiting royalty. Did all this commotion cause the crowd to fall in behind Jesus for a triumphal entry into the city?"

"No," John replied quietly. "Some, especially the most coarse, laughed at us, calling us 'fools from Galilee.' "

"Didn't any of the people, out of curiosity if nothing else, ask you and the other apostles the identity of the man who was riding on an ass and receiving such homage from your group?"

"Some did."

"And what did you tell them?"

"We told them that he was Jesus, the prophet of Nazareth of Galilee."

"Why didn't you tell them that he was the Messiah?"

John lowered his eyes and rubbed his fingers aimlessly back and forth across the polished wood. "Even then, most of us were blind to the truth. Except Peter."

"Peter? Are you referring to that incident at Caesarea Philippi when Jesus asked all of you who he was, and Peter was the only one who said he was the Messiah?"

"Who told you of that?"

"Peter himself. He also told me that Jesus charged all of you to tell no man. Was it because of this command from him that you told the crowds he was Jesus the prophet instead of saying he was Jesus the Messiah—or was it because, except for Peter, the rest of you were not certain who he was?"

John remained silent. I pressed him.

"Is it fair to conclude that the others, including yourself, had not yet acquired the faith necessary to move mountains—or convert cities?"

"Your words are harsh, but they are the truth, sir. Only later were our eyes opened, after Jesus had been raised and—"

I reached across the table and clasped his hand gently. "Wait! Please help me to understand those events in their proper order. Only this morning I asked Pilate about any crowd disturbance caused by the entry of Jesus into Jerusalem on that day. He said that he had known of none or he would have taken steps to keep it from growing into something more serious. Undoubtedly he would have arrested Jesus for incitement. Now you, John, have just confirmed Pilate's statement that there was no great entry into the city accompanied by surging crowds of followers greeting their savior. Jesus may have ridden into Jerusalem as the Messiah, so far as *he* was concerned, and possibly Peter, but for the rest of you, as well as for the pilgrims on the road, he was only another rabbi or, at the most, a Galilean prophet, entering the city on an ass in order to observe the Passover. And instead of the people rallying to his cause, as he may have expected, they went about their business of preparing for the holiday as usual. Am I correct?"

John glanced hurriedly toward Joseph, who proved to be no more help to him than he was to me during any interview. "Yes," he finally admitted.

"Could it have been his disappointment in the people's lack of response that drove him to disrupt the business of the Temple soon after he entered the city? Did he believe that such a dramatic move against the authorities as tipping over the tables of the money-changers might rally the crowds to his cause in far greater numbers than he had been able to achieve through his words or his good works among the poor and the sick?"

"Jesus wept over the city many times," John replied, "sad that they could not understand those things which would bring them peace and happiness, for he could foresee a terrible day when not one stone of Jerusalem would still stand upon another because they had not recognized their visitation. When he had said those things, we had been too ignorant to understand his meaning."

"John, have you ever reflected on what might have happened had that tremendous crowd of pilgrims, gathering for the holiday, believed he was truly the Messiah? Without doubt, Jesus could have mobilized a citizen's army large enough so that even with only clubs and stones they could have captured the Fortress Antonia within a day or two."

John shook his head helplessly. "I realize that as a Roman you must find it difficult to comprehend that Jesus did not come to recruit an army against our enemies and the persecutors of our people. Please try to understand that he came only to gather his children together so he could teach them how to find and enjoy the Kingdom of God in love and peace."

181

"And this Kingdom of God: have you managed to find it? Where is it?"

Now it was John's turn to reach across the table. With his first finger he tapped boldly against my chest and said, "The Kingdom of God is within you, just where Jesus said it is!"

Suddenly I felt ill. Nauseated. I wanted to vomit. With only scant circulation from the three small windows, the upper chamber was a giant kiln, baking us slowly. I closed my eyes, and in the darkness I could see silver lightning bouncing from side to side. This whole unbelievable experience was beginning to take a physical as well as mental toll. I inhaled and exhaled as deeply as I could—again, and again—until I heard Joseph's concerned voice asking, "Are you ill, Matthias?"

I shook my head. There was little time to spare if Pilate was on to me. I waved both arms at the table and candle and asked, "What is your strongest memory of the last supper that Jesus ate here?"

John pondered for several minutes, and when he replied there was more joy than dejection in his voice. "Before the food was served, I remember Jesus rising from the table, removing his robe, and wrapping a large towel around his body. Then he poured water into a basin and began to wash our feet and dry them with the towel. All of us were too shocked to say anything except Peter, who asked him why he was washing our feet, and Jesus replied that we would understand later. Peter then stood and said, 'You will not wash my feet!' because he knew that none of us deserved such special treatment from our Lord. Jesus replied that in that case Peter could have no part of him, and Peter, having been chastised, sat and allowed our Lord to bathe away his dust."

"Did Jesus explain his unusual behavior?"

"He did. After he had finished he returned to his place and told us that if he, whom we called Lord and master, could wash our feet, we could also wash each other's, and what he had done was an example that he hoped we would never forget. Then he shocked us even more by telling us that we were not all clean and that one of us would betray him."

"What happened next?"

"There was great consternation and shouting in this room, and many were heard asking, 'Is it me, Lord?' I was sitting to the right of Jesus, and I saw Peter motioning to me from his place here on this side of the table to ask Jesus who it was. I placed my head on his breast and whispered, 'Lord, who is it?' and he replied in my ear, 'He it is to whom I shall give a sop, when I have dipped it.' Then he dipped the bread, wrapped around a small piece of lamb, into the dish and handed it to Judas, who was sitting on his left."

"Had anyone else heard what Jesus had said to you?"

"No one. Then he spoke to Judas in a voice that all could hear and said, 'Whatever you must do, do it quickly,' and soon Judas had gone out into the night."

"Did anyone else connect the departure of Judas with the betrayal that Jesus had mentioned?"

"I do not believe so. Judas was always having to run off on errands for Jesus or one of us since he was the keeper of the common purse. We continued with our meal but with little enjoyment, since each was now looking at the other with dark suspicions."

"What other memories do you have of that supper?"

John's face brightened again. "As you know, Matthias, we Jews have Ten Commandments which our forefather, Moses, received directly from God. Jesus, that night, gave us another, one far more difficult to obey than all the other ten together and yet one so powerful that if we all could live by it none of the others would be necessary."

I knew what was coming, but I still had to hear it from the best source any writer would ever have until the end of time.

"Jesus warned us that he would only be with us a little while, and where he was going we could not come. Then he said, 'A new commandment I give to you, that you love one another as I have loved you, and by this shall all men know that you are my disciples.' Then Peter asked our Lord where he was going, and Jesus repeated that where he was going we could not follow him now but later we could. Peter could not accept that. He asked why he could not follow Jesus now and insisted, 'I will even lay down my life for your sake!' I shall never forget our Lord's response. Neither will Peter. Jesus challenged him, saying, 'Will you lay down your life for my sake? Verily, I say unto you that the cock shall not crow, this night, until you have denied me three times.' Peter confided in me later that Jesus repeated those words to him, after the supper, on our walk out of the city."

"And that prophecy came true, did it not?"

"It did. When Jesus was arrested in the garden, Peter and I were also seized but we were released after being beaten with clubs and kicked until we could barely walk. I wanted to flee over the mount to Bethany but Peter would have none of that. He said that we could not desert our Lord in his time of need, so we followed the arrest party until they finally arrived at the home of the high priest, after first going to the home of his father-in-law. We waited in the courtyard, hoping to learn what they were planning to do with Jesus and wondering why members of our high court, the Sanhedrin, were arriving in the middle of the night. Three times, when we drew near the fires, those in the employ of Caiaphas accused Peter of knowing Jesus and having been with him, and three times he denied it. His third denial had no more than issued from his lips when both of us heard the first cock of the day. Peter moaned as if he had been impaled by a sword and fell at my feet. At first I thought God had struck him dead for his denials, but when I saw his chest rising and falling I tried to lift him to his feet and remove him from the courtyard for fear we might be seized by the guard again. I tried and tried to move him but I could not, so I ran to the house of Joseph. With the help of his giant friend and servant we managed to bring Peter here and lay him in Mark's bed, which is the only other room on this floor. By then I was exhausted, but after the widow Mary and the other women, including our Lord's mother, had been told that Jesus was under arrest, none of them were in any condition to tend to Peter so I did so myself."

"What happened next?"

"By dawn the women had recovered enough to bring me food. Peter was still in a faint, his skin as hot as fire to our touch. Again and again I wiped his body with water and aloe juice, also splashing much of it on my own face in order to remain awake. Then, later in the day, perhaps the seventh hour, I heard terrible screams and wailing from below and rushed down the stairs to see what was wrong, almost colliding with the mother of our Lord, who was standing on the first step. She fell into my arms and I could feel her body trembling, until she took my face in her hands and said quietly, 'I was coming for you. Word has just arrived that my son has been taken to Golgotha by the Romans to be crucified. I must be with him, John. Please take me to my boy. Mark and his mother will watch over Peter until we return.' "

John paused and covered his face with his hands. I could see his chest rising and falling as if he, too, was having difficulty breathing. Then he wiped his eyes and continued.

"I began to sob and soon the Lord's mother was consoling *me*, wiping away *my* tears, until I felt nothing but shame for my weakness when I should have been providing her with sympathy and comfort. Soon, Mary Magdalene and my mother, Salome, and Mary, the mother of James and Joses, joined us in the courtyard, and the five of us went out the city gate and walked on the road outside the wall until we finally arrived at the place of execution, a small hill northwest of the city."

"Was Jesus already on the cross by the time you arrived?"

"Yes, as were two others, one on each side of him. His body was so covered with blood and bruises that not even his mother recognized him until one of the women pointed to the sign over his head that said 'Jesus of Nazareth, the King of the Jews.' "

"Was there a large crowd on hand?"

"No. Only the soldiers and some priests from the Temple and a few pilgrims who had come up from the road out of curiosity. I wanted to keep the women back as far as possible, to spare them, but the Lord's mother would have none of it. She insisted that I bring her as close to the cross as the soldiers would allow."

"Was Jesus in any condition to recognize you?"

"When we first drew near his eyes were shut. Blood dripped from both wrists and feet where the nails had been driven through his flesh and bones and into the wood. I turned my head, unable to look on our beloved master. His words—I could hear his words from another day, as if he were speaking them again from the cross—'Behold, we go up to Jerusalem: and the Son of man shall be betrayed unto the chief priests and unto the scribes, and they shall condemn him to death. They shall deliver him to the gentiles to mock, and to scourge, and to crucify him.' My heart was broken. I wanted to flee—to run and run and never stop. Only the hand of the Lord's mother, firmly in mine, kept me there. And then I heard his voice and I opened my eyes and he was looking directly at his mother and he said, 'Woman, behold your son!' and then his lovely brown eyes stared directly at me and he said, 'Son, behold your mother!' I know I was sobbing and so was she, for he was so close and yet we could not lift a finger to help him or soothe his pain. In yet a little while he opened his eyes again and said, 'I thirst,' and they passed him vinegar on a sponge. Then we heard him cry, 'My God, my God, why have you forsaken me?' and soon thereafter he said, 'It is finished,' and he bowed his head and gave up the ghost, and when he did his mother collapsed in my arms."

"Were any of the other apostles at the crucifixion?"

"No, only myself and the four women."

"What did you do next?"

"With my mother's help I brought the Lord's mother back

185

to this house and then resumed my vigil with Peter, who was still delirious."

"And the two women?"

"Mary Magdalene and the mother of James and Joses remained behind to see where the soldiers would dispose of the Lord's body in the hopes that we might retrieve it later. Before sundown they returned to tell us that Joseph of Arimathea had claimed the body and was having it placed in a tomb located in a small garden near Golgotha. Since Joseph had been a friend of Jesus and many of us, we were relieved to know that our Lord was in good hands."

"How long did you remain close to Peter?"

"Until sometime during the morning of the day following our Sabbath."

"You didn't leave him for any length of time—to visit the grave, perhaps?"

"No, I left his side only to relieve myself."

"No sleep?"

"In a chair, with my head on the mattress near Peter's feet."

"When did you first learn that the women were planning a visit to the tomb?"

John frowned for the first time and sat up straight. "Mary Magdalene came to me during the afternoon of our Sabbath and said that although they had seen the place where Jesus was to be buried they had not entered the garden, since it was private, to see whether or not the body had been washed, anointed, and wrapped in accordance with our laws. The burial, she feared, might have been performed in haste since sundown had been fast approaching. She told me that she and some of the women were going to the grave, in the early morning, with spices and oils and linens to anoint our Lord properly, and she wanted me to accompany them so that I might move whatever stone had been placed against the opening. I told her that I dared not leave Peter, in his state, nor did I have the strength to walk to the city gate, much less to Golgotha, and she became very angry with me, calling me a coward and other names. They went in the morning without me."

"None of you knew that the high priest had sealed the tomb and posted a guard?"

"No. Caiaphas had apparently made those arrangements during the Sabbath. If the women had known, they would not have gone."

"What happened next?"

"Soon after they departed, Peter sat up in bed and asked for food. The widow brought him a bowl of hot soup and cheese, and because of his condition I waited until he had eaten his fill before I told him the terrible news that our Lord was dead."

"What was his reaction?"

"He listened quietly while I confided what little I knew, without dwelling at any length on the crucifixion I had witnessed. Then he embraced me and we both cried. The world, for us, had ended at Gethsemane. Finally he fell back on the bed and stared up at the beams, and I could see his lips moving in prayer. This continued until Mary Magdalene burst into the room looking as if all the demons that Jesus had once driven out of her had returned. She fell across Peter and began shaking the poor man, crying, 'They have taken away the Lord out of the tomb and we know not where they have laid him!' Spittle flew from her mouth and her eyes protruded from their sockets as she repeated the same words, again and again, until the widow came and took her away and comforted her. Peter crawled from the bed, put on his sandals and tunic, and asked if I knew where they had buried Jesus, and when I nodded he said, 'Let us go, let us see for ourselves.' We both ran most of the way, and to this day I do not know where either of us found the strength. I arrived at the tomb first, just as the sun's first glow appeared in the east."

"How could you be certain that you were at the tomb where Jesus had been laid? After all, you had not witnessed the burial, and I have seen many graves outside the city's walls."

"Matthias, there is only one small garden near that terrible place called Golgotha, and in that garden Mary had told me there was only one tomb, hewn from rock. Later, Joseph confirmed that we had not been in error."

I looked at Joseph. He nodded.

"John, did you see any soldiers—anyone—in that garden?"

"No one."

"A gardener, perhaps?"

"No."

"And the grave was open?"

"Yes, with the *golal*, the great round stone, rolled away from the opening and leaning against the side of the tomb."

"What did you do?"

"I was frightened. Tombs at any time, especially at dawn, are not conducive to regular heartbeats, even when they are

187

empty. My reasoning told me to wait for Peter, but he was still several hundred paces behind, so I gathered up what little courage I possessed and, stooping down, I looked inside. In the dim light I could see the white linen sheet resting on a shelf carved in the stone. The cloth was wrapped around and around as if it still contained a body, but I could see there was none."

"Did you enter the tomb?"

"Not until after Peter arrived and crawled inside. When he emerged, his face was so pale that I feared he would collapse again. Instead he fell to his knees and began to pray. Then I crawled inside and saw not only the sheet that had been wrapped around the Lord's body but also the napkin that is always placed on the face of the dead—and that napkin was on the shelf exactly where the head would have been in relation to the body linen. Then I believed."

"You believed what?"

"That Jesus had risen from the dead as he had prophesied. Until that very moment, in that small garden, the true meaning of his words had never penetrated my thick head."

I raised both hands in front of him. "I don't understand, John. What did you and Peter see at that grave that made both of you believe that Jesus had risen from the dead?"

"In our terrible state of mind," John explained slowly, as if he had previously overestimated my intelligence, "and with Mary Magdalene's words still fresh in our thoughts, we went to that tomb believing the body had been stolen. But all the evidence at the grave proved that it had not been stolen. Who would take a body from its grave, in the darkness of night, remove its long burial sheet packed with spices, and then rewind that sheet without spilling any of the spices and place it on the shelf again, as if it still contained a body? And who would be careful to replace the napkin on the shelf just where it would be if it were still on the head of Jesus? These were the questions that Peter and I could only answer with one name."

"Who, John?"

"God!"

I should have known. "You mean that God removed the body of Jesus from his grave cloth without disturbing it?"

"For God, nothing is impossible."

"Then tell me, why did God bother to roll away the stone? If the body was raised from the linens without disturbing them, couldn't God have just as easily removed the body from the tomb without disturbing the stone?"

For only a fraction of a second, John's eyes rolled helplessly toward Joseph of Arimathea. The old man remained silent.

"Why did God bother to move the stone, John?" I asked again.

"So that we, who had eyes but could not see, would have our vision restored along with our shaken faith—through the great silent witness of that empty tomb!"

I had no rebuttal, but I wasn't satisfied, either. When I had raised the same points with Peter and insinuated that all the evidence had been manufactured to make it look like a resurrection instead of a grave robbery, Peter had lost his temper with me. And now John was talking about faith—and I wanted facts. Would I ever learn the truth? Weakly, I asked John, "What did you do next?"

"When I came out from the tomb, I knelt beside Peter and gave thanks to God for his greatest of miracles. Then Peter told me to go to Bethany, for he was certain that the others were there in the house of Martha and Mary. I was to tell them the good news about our Lord but also to warn them to say nothing to any man, for Peter was certain that our lives were still in danger and if it reached the high priest that we had visited the tomb, he would probably accuse us of removing the body so that we could seduce the people with our story of the resurrection."

"Did you find the others?"

John smiled sadly. "It was not difficult. Martha led me to them, all huddled together like frightened sheep, hiding in a woods behind her home. Their spirits were already so broken that they listened to my tale of the trials and crucifixion and burial as if they had expected it. What they had not expected, and would not believe, was my announcement that Jesus had risen from the dead as he had said he would. I remember Thomas telling me to take my story to the women, for they might believe me, but he, for one, would have to see the grave and the linens with his own eyes and even then he would have serious doubts. Some of the others, as blind as I had been, ridiculed my story, asking how it was that Jesus could have the power to rise from the dead when he had been unable to prevent Caiaphas from arresting him and Pilate from hanging him on a cross. It did no good to reason with them or to remind them of all that Jesus had prophesied about his future. Sick of heart, I departed from them and returned to the city and this house."

Now my frustration was complete. John had certainly confirmed Peter's earlier testimony that the two of them had spent all the hours, between the burial and discovery of the empty tomb, here in this house. Neither of them could have possibly been implicated in the grave robbery.

Even more damaging, so far as my investigation was concerned, both Peter and John had corroborated the words of Matthew and James concerning the other nine apostles who had fled to Bethany. None of them, I was now positive, had been responsible for the empty tomb!

Scratch eleven apostles. And Pilate. And Caiaphas.

The one-man Christ Commission's list of suspects was dwindling swiftly—almost as fast as his confidence.

twelve

THE WIDOW MARY was no longer dozing on the faded wicker couch beneath the dense pomegranate trees when Joseph and I followed John down into the courtyard from the upper room. In her place, but occupying only the lower half of the couch, was another woman, busily shelling dried peas into a wooden bowl cradled in her lap by folds of a full-length black dress. She was a beauty. Her long flowing hair was the shade of antique bronze, and her skin was so fair that I found myself foolishly wondering why she had no freckles.

Mary Magdalene! Heroine of thousands of biblical novels throughout the centuries. Played a prominent role in the latter part of all four Gospels. The woman out of whom Jesus was reputed to have driven seven devils. A reformed prostitute, or at the very least a "sinner," depending on your source material, with the latter category such a fitting one for most of us that her appeal had been universal for nearly two thousand years. On one point, however, all the Gospels and early sources agreed. The Magdalene woman's love for her Lord, and her courage, had been surpassed by none in that small party who had accompanied Jesus to Jerusalem for his last Passover.

The three of us sat on the grass at her feet, and after both John and Joseph took turns patiently and unhurriedly explaining the purpose of my visit, she looked down at me and asked plaintively, "Will you promise not to hurt me if I tell you whatever you want to know about Jesus?"

"Matthias is a friend of mine, Mary. He would never harm you," Joseph assured her.

She pointed to the purple stripe on my tunic. "All Romans hurt people. They even tried to kill my Lord." Her voice was childlike in both tone and inflection, and the slow cadence of her words, all spoken in an emotionless flat monotone, indicated a condition for which neither the old man nor John had prepared me.

"She has not been herself for many years, Matthias,"

Joseph finally confided, as if the woman could not hear him, "ever since that morning when she returned from the empty tomb. However, her ability to recall even the slightest detail about her experiences with Jesus has not diminished. Just talk softly to her and keep your questions simple."

"I have only a few," I said.

I happened to look up into the branches above my head. One lonely symmetrical pomegranate dangled gently in the breeze. On a sudden impulse I got to my feet, leaped for it, plucked the dark red fruit from its stem, and handed it to Mary Magdalene. She clutched it to her breast and lowered her eyes as poignantly as any bashful schoolgirl.

"Mary," I began, "when did you first meet Jesus?"

"I was brought to him, by some scribes and Pharisees, while he was teaching in the Temple. They threw me at his feet, shouting that I had been taken in the very act of adultery and should be stoned under the laws of Moses. They wanted to know what Jesus had to say."

"What did he say?"

"He blushed and pretended not to hear them and stooped down and wrote with his finger on the dirt of the courtyard."

"Did you see what he wrote?"

"No, but they continued to press him for an answer, so he finally looked up and said, 'He that is without sin among you, let him cast the first stone,' and then he wrote on the ground again. I was furious with him, certain that he had sealed my fate and that I would now be taken outside the city and put to death. I covered my eyes with my hands so that I could not see the faces of those who mocked me in my shame, and I waited to be taken away, but soon I could hear no more laughter or insults and when I opened my eyes I saw that all the scribes and Pharisees had departed."

"What did you do?"

"I rose to my feet, certain that these men and Jesus were playing some sort of cruel game with me. He asked me, 'Woman, where are your accusers? Has no man condemned you?' and I replied, 'No man, Lord,' and Jesus said, 'Neither do I condemn you. Go, and sin no more.' Then he turned to the crowd who had watched from a distance and said, 'I am the light of the world. He that follows me shall not walk in darkness but shall have the light of life,' and from that day I followed him and tended to his needs when he would allow me—and I loved him."

"Tell me about that morning when you and the others went to the tomb."

192

She reached down into the basket by her side and removed another handful of dried pea pods, which she dropped in the bowl and proceeded to shell as she talked. "With Mary, the mother of James and Joses, I had watched as Joseph, here, and those in his company removed our Lord from the cross. When we saw that they were only taking his body to a nearby tomb, in a small garden, we were relieved and returned here. But on the next day, which was our Sabbath, I began to wonder whether or not our Lord's body had been prepared properly for burial, in accordance with our law. After our Sabbath ended, at sundown, I went to the marketplace and purchased spices and myrtle and aloe and oil, resolving to go to the tomb early on the following morning to anoint our Lord properly. Mary and John's mother, Salome, agreed to accompany me to the grave, but when I asked John to come, so that he might help us move the heavy stone that is usually placed at the mouth of tombs, he refused, saying that he dared not leave Peter, nor did he have any strength to walk such a distance."

"The three of you went anyway?"

"Oh, yes. Before sunrise, each of us carrying a sack filled with spices and other things passed through the gate nearby and walked the dirt road northward until we reached that ugly hill where the Lord had been crucified. Three upright poles were still standing, but the crosspieces on which the poor men's hands had been nailed had been removed along with their bodies."

"On that road north, did you meet anyone?"

"To our great disappointment, no. We had been hoping to find someone along the way who might help us move the stone at the tomb. After we had passed Golgotha we began to lose our courage, for the sun had not yet appeared and there were many strange shapes and shadows among the trees and bushes. Still, we entered the garden, jumping at every noise, and soon passed near a fire whose logs sent up sparks and smoke in the soft breeze, and we wondered who had been there during the night. Then we came upon the tomb, and we saw that the great round stone had been rolled away from the opening."

"Did that frighten you away?"

"Oh, no. At first we thought that perhaps Joseph had taken the Lord's body elsewhere, for final burial, but had he done such a thing we knew he would have come and told us. Then I told Mary and Salome that someone must have stolen the body, and holding fast to each other the three of us knelt down so that we could see inside the grave. Salome screamed first and I almost fainted. Sitting on the stone floor, inside, was a young man dressed in a long white garment, and when he saw us he cried out in fright! I remember jumping back and striking my head against the stone. All of us dropped our bags and ran, tripping and falling in the wet grass many times before we were gone from that place. Behind us we could hear the stranger in white shouting, 'Be not afraid. You seek Jesus of Nazareth, who was crucified . . .' and that is all I remember, because by then we were on the road and running as if wild pigs pursued us. I arrived back here before the others and went immediately upstairs to tell Peter and John that someone had stolen the body of our Lord."

Only the clatter of hard peas, tumbling from their open pods into Mary Magdalene's bowl, disturbed the quiet of the courtyard. Now I was struggling with myself, trying hard to keep my composure. I was close to important evidence, new evidence, and I could not afford to let my anxiety betray me, either through the sound of my voice or the look on my face.

For many centuries, saints and anti-Christs, scholars and philosophers, theologians and writers, dreamers and scoffers—all had wrestled with conflicting versions from the Gospels as to exactly what Mary Magdalene and the other women had experienced when they had come upon the empty tomb. Had I just heard the raw truth, long before it became layered over by decades of the well-intentioned faithful—or was a woman with a long history of mental problems just having her little game with me?

"You are certain, Mary, that you saw a young man inside the tomb?"

"We all did. In the faint light we could not see his face clearly, but I know he was a young man, and when he called after us, as we fled, his voice was that of a youth."

"Could it have possibly been an angel that you came upon?"

Mary's ripe lips formed a condescending smile, if ever I've seen one. "I have never viewed an angel, at least one that I recognized as such," she replied. "And would an angel of God have been frightened by our appearance at the tomb or allowed us to run away without calming our fears?"

There was no arguing with that logic. I tried to concentrate, to recall some notes I had scribbled long ago during my early days of research for "The Christ Commission." In the Gospel According to Matthew, the women at the sepulchre had come upon the "angel of the Lord." In the Gospel According to Luke, two men stood by them in shining garments

194

who later were referred to in that same chapter as "a vision of angels." In the Gospel According to John, Mary looked into the sepulchre and saw "two angels in white," but in the Gospel According to Mark, the women entered the sepulchre and "saw a young man sitting on the right side, clothed in a long white garment."

Had there really been no mention of angels in Mark's narration of that early morning scene at the tomb? Yes, I was positive. If Mark's Gospel was describing an earlier visitor to the tomb than the women, who was that visitor and what was he doing there? And had that mysterious individual been an accomplice to the removal of the body or even a witness to the robbery? Could it possibly be—?

"John, do you know if young Mark has returned yet?"

"Yes, I heard his voice. He is inside the house with his mother, helping her to prepare supper."

"Would it be possible for me to speak with him for a little while?" I looked toward Joseph for support. The old man showed little enthusiasm for this sudden addition to our agenda, but he finally gave me the benefit of a reluctant nod.

The young apostle was headed toward the house to summon Mark before I stopped him. "John, may I speak to him up there?" I asked, pointing to the uppper room.

"As you wish," he shouted.

I thanked Mary Magdalene for her help, and this time Joseph followed me upstairs.

John Mark's thin dark body was covered by a loincloth of animal skin that hung from his waist to below his knees. His black hair was a mass of curls swirling loosely around sharp, handsome features that were more Grecian than anything else. Despite his youth there was a strange intensity about him, and his brown eyes were much too sad and serious for his age. He entered the upper room slowly and uncertainly, responding to Joseph's warm greeting with only a brief, forced smile. When the old man invited him to sit, he glanced back at the door as if he would have preferred to leave, but he finally lowered himself timidly onto a cushion directly opposite me at the table.

"Mark"—I smiled, trying to put him at his ease—"has John told you the purpose of my visit?"

He nodded.

"What is your age?"

He swallowed and said hoarsely, "I am in my twentieth year."

"Do you remember much about Jesus? Six years is a long time."

No response.

"Will you answer a few questions about him, if you can remember?"

Silence—but the muscles in his arms tightened and he clenched his fists as they rested on the table. Helplessly I turned to Joseph, who only shook his head despondently. Then I remembered my amulet, that heavy, flat, curiously shaped piece of gold I had worn since Joseph had presented it to me on our first day's visit to the Temple. Already it had become so much a part of my body that I was no longer conscious of it hanging from its leather thong around my neck. I reached inside my tunic and removed the piece, turning its face so that Mark could see the outline of the fish.

"Will you please help me, Mark?" I asked, reaching across the table and placing my hand over his. His face brightened, and after a moment's hesitation he placed his other hand over mine and nodded. Joseph's loud sigh of relief filled the room, and I settled back on my cushion knowing exactly how Judas must have felt.

"Do you recall that last meal Jesus ate in this room?"

"I brought the food to him, from the kitchen below," he said proudly.

"And did you see Jesus and the others when they finally departed, or were you in bed by that late hour?"

"I was downstairs in the courtyard, waiting for them. I had not seen my Uncle Peter in many months and I could not understand why he had not played with me, that evening, as he usually did whenever he visited our home. I had also resented having to eat the Paschal lamb with the women while all the men feasted together upstairs."

"Did anything happen in the courtyard when the party came down from this room?"

"When my uncle saw me he must have felt guilty for his neglect. Without saying a word he went into the house, downstairs, and when he came out he said that my mother had given her permission for me to walk with him and the others as far as the Fountain Gate, in the southeast part of the city near the pools."

"It's a rather long walk to that gate. Do you have any memories connected with it?" I saw that Joseph was scowling at me. Apparently he was wondering why I was asking such seemingly unnecessary and innocent questions when time had become such a precious commodity.

"I have many memories of that walk," Mark replied wistfully. "The festive lamps shining from the windows of many houses as families prepared to go up to the Temple, whose gates would be opened at the sixth hour after sunset; the crowds and animals on the road as if it were day; the excitement of being with my uncle and Jesus for at least a part of the Passover celebration; and the hymns we sang as we walked."

"Were all of you together?"

"We were as close as a cluster of grapes until we approached the gate, when Jesus stopped and said, 'You shall all be offended because of me, this night, for it is written, "I will smite the shepherd, and the sheep shall be scattered."' His words put great fear into the men, even my uncle, and then Jesus said, 'But after I am risen, I will go before you into Galilee.'"

Once again, my heart was thumping too enthusiastically for my own good. "Mark, did anyone else hear Jesus say those words except the eleven apostles—and you?"

"No. He had spoken almost in a whisper, as if he was sharing a secret."

Was I close to resolving a mystery that had baffled so many great theological minds? Mary Magdalene had just told me that when the three women had come upon the young man in the tomb they had fled almost immediately, but not before they heard him shouting, "Be not afraid. You seek Jesus of Nazareth, who was crucified . . ." and that is all they remembered as they ran off in terror. Only in one Gosepl, that of Mark, the earliest known record of the life of Jesus, had the author specified that *a young man*, not angels, as the other three reported, had been seen at the tomb, and in the last chapter from Mark one can still read the full quotation of what that young man had said to the women, not knowing, of course, that they had heard only a part of his announcement as they fled. I reviewed those verses quickly in my mind: "Be not afraid; you seek Jesus of Nazareth, who was crucified; he is risen; he is not here: behold the place where they laid him. But go your way, tell his disciples and Peter that he goes before you into Galilee: there shall you see him, as he said unto you."

Success! At least one small part of the resurrection puzzle now fitted together perfectly. From what Mark had just told me there was only one person, other than the apostles, who had heard Jesus announce, on their way out of the city, that after he had risen he was going before them into Galilee.

And that person, by his own words, was *the same young man* now sitting across from me!

Obviously, either from fear of punishment or embarrassment or some other unknown reason, Mark had yet to confess to anyone that it had been he who had inadvertently frightened the women, and been frightened in turn, when they had come upon him inside the tomb that morning. But what was a youth of fourteen doing at a grave before dawn? How did he get there, and return, without his mother or the others knowing about it? Most important of all, at least to my investigation, what else had he witnessed in the garden before the women arrived? Somehow I had to draw it out of him.

"Mark, did you hear any other words from Jesus as you neared the gate?"

"No. My uncle kissed me and told me that I had come far enough and should hurry back to my mother so that she would not worry. I did as I was told and went to bed."

"And then," I said, "according to the others I have spoken with, something terrible happened here, is that correct?"

"Yes. I don't know how long I had been sleeping before I was awakened by pounding and loud voices of men in our house, and soon I could hear my mother and the other women screaming. Before I could jump from my bed two Roman soldiers kicked my door open, held lamps close to my face, looked under my cot, and ran out. Trembling, I stepped out on the terrace and saw that the courtyard was filled with soldiers, each carrying bright torches. Then more soldiers came out of the house and I heard a man saying, 'He must have gone to Gethsemane. Let us go there and take him,' and they all rushed across the street and out of the city gate. When I went downstairs I found my mother and the others all gathered in her bedroom, crying and consoling each other, and when I asked her why the soldiers had searched our house she told me that they had come to arrest Jesus. I said that I must hurry to Gethsemane, immediately, to warn him, but she took hold of me and forbade me to leave the house for fear that harm would come to me at the hands of the soldiers."

"But you went anyway, didn't you?"

I heard two cries: one from Mark, and the other from Joseph of Arimathea. The old man was the first to recover his voice. "How do you know such things, Matthias?"

What could I say to him in Mark's presence? How could I remind the old man of an incident described exclusively in the Gospel According to Mark, one that could have only been written by the individual who had been personally involved? How could I repeat the story that when Jesus was arrested and all the apostles had fled, there was another person in the garden, *a young man* wearing a linen cloth about his body, and when an attempt was made to seize him "he left the linen cloth and fled naked." I ignored Joseph's question and decided to gamble on another bluff.

"Mark, you did run to the garden, didn't you, going down those outside stairs from your bedroom up here, so that no one saw you? Then you took a direct route across the city, through the Temple, out one of its east gates, across the bridge over the Kidron, and into the garden. But you arrived too late. Jesus had already been arrested, and when some of the soldiers saw you they tried to catch you but managed to clutch only the cloth you had thrown around yourself. You ran off, leaving them holding the linen, didn't you?"

He buried his head in the palms of both hands and said, "Yes."

"And you had to come all the way home naked."

"To my eternal shame."

"Did you tell anyone?"

"No."

"Even to this day?"

"No, but now that you—"

"Your secret is safe with us, Mark, providing you are willing to tell me all you know about another important matter."

I hated myself. There were tears in his eyes, and I've never been able to deal with the tears of others without coming apart myself.

"Anything . . . anything you want to know," he sobbed.

"Sometime after you returned from the garden and went to bed you must have been awakened again, am I correct?"

His mouth fell open. I explained. "Your Uncle Peter has already told me how he lost consciousness in the courtyard of Caiaphas and was brought here by John and Shem, Joseph's protector. Since Peter was placed in your bed, where did you sleep?"

"Outside, on the terrace."

"Wasn't it cold out there? Peter said there had been fires burning in the yard of the high priest. Why didn't you sleep in here?"

"I have slept out there many times, in all seasons. It is

199

good to lie back under your warm blankets and look up at the stars and feel the breeze on your face."

"Will you show me exactly where you slept that night, if you remember?"

Joseph groaned impatiently but said nothing. We followed Mark outside and around the corner of the upper terrace facing toward the southwest. Directly below us was the road that led to the palace of Caiaphas and Joseph's place, higher on the hill. To my left I could look down on the traffic entering the city gate from Bethlehem, and to my right, northward, I could see Herod's palace. I pointed north. "That hill, outside the city's wall, far beyond Herod's old place, is that Golgotha where Jesus was crucified?"

"Yes."

"And the dirt road, outside this nearby gate, does it go all the way to Golgotha?"

"And beyond," Mark replied.

"Now, Jesus was crucified on the day after you tried to save him from being arrested in the garden. Did you sleep out here on that night?"

"Yes. Peter was still sick with fever and John was with him."

Another alibi confirmation for Peter and John, as if they needed it. "The following day was your Sabbath. Where did you sleep that night, do you recall?"

"Peter had still not stirred from my cot. I slept out here again."

"Tell me, Mark"—I smiled—"was it your habit to sit here often, in the dark, and watch the people pass below you as well as look at the lights of the city? I imagine any boy of fourteen would enjoy doing that."

He nodded. "I did it many times when I was younger, even when I was not sleeping out here."

"And you do recall doing it on that night after your Sabbath ended?"

He answered immediately. "No one was asleep in our house, that night, except my sick uncle. Downstairs I could hear my mother and the other women wailing and crying and calling out the name of our Lord, and every now and then, just as I closed my eyes, one of them would scream and I would be fully awake again."

"As the night wore on, did you notice anything unusual taking place in what you can view of the city from this spot?"

He hesitated, wary of me after my accurate description of

200

his near capture in Gethsemane. "Unusual? I don't believe so. What do you mean?"

I pointed toward Golgotha. "A fire—a fire burning near that hill, in the garden. Built by the guards sent from the Temple, by Caiaphas, to watch over the tomb of Jesus, as you know now but didn't then. Did you see that blaze and perhaps the torches of the guards as they stood their watch? And didn't you wonder why a fire should be burning so near the place where Jesus had been crucified and buried?"

Mark's wide brown eyes looked at me pleadingly. He turned toward Joseph as if expecting the old man to rescue him from his plight, but he received no relief from that quarter. Finally I placed both hands on his shoulders and squeezed them gently. "Mark, why don't you tell us, in your own words, what you saw and what happened afterward. It will do you good to share the burden you have been carrying by yourself for so long."

He turned his back on me and took several steps toward the edge of the terrace that was unprotected by any railing. As he stared down at the pavement below I moved toward him, but Joseph's arm restrained me. He knew Mark better than I ever would. After several anxious moments, at least for me, the young man turned and said, "I shall tell you, providing that what I say remains a secret among the three of us. No good will come, at this time, of my story by making it public, and it will only create doubt in the minds of those whose faith is not yet strong that Jesus rose from the dead, as we know he did. Perhaps later, when the foundations that Peter and John and James and the others are building become more solid, everyone can be told. Are my terms acceptable to you?"

It was more than I had dared to expect. I nodded, knowing that he would keep his word. Within twenty or thirty years, according to my research, Mark would write the first synopsis of the life of Jesus, with the help of Peter's firsthand recollections. And in that powerful but most brief of all Gospels he would include the story of the naked young man in Gethsemane as well as the white-garmented one at the tomb.

"Proceed with your story," I said, "and be assured that your words are safe with us."

"You were correct, sir," he began. "I did notice the fire near Golgotha and the torches moving back and forth. I even went down to tell my mother, but the women were finally asleep. Then I went to tell John, but he, too, was fast asleep in a chair next to Peter, from whom strange sounds could be heard. Alone I came back out here, sat down, and watched. After perhaps two hours or so my eyes grew heavy and I unrolled my blankets, ready for sleep, when suddenly our house began to shake, back and forth. I jumped to my feet but the vibration ceased almost as soon as it began and I gave it no more thought, because the earth had shook many times since the Lord had been crucified and my mother had told me it was God expressing his anger for what had been done to his Son. Then I glanced toward Golgotha and saw, to my amazement, four torches moving away from the fire swiftly, as if those who were·carrying them were running, and I watched as the lights came south, in this direction, on the road outside the city. Soon they were blocked from my view by the wall, but their glow lit up the sky as the torches came closer and closer until four men, in the uniforms of Temple guards, rushed through the city gate and passed directly below me on the pavement."

"Were there people in the street?"

"A few. Standing across the street from here was a man with his animal, and I heard him shout out, 'Are you fleeing from someone or in pursuit?' and one of the guards, without stopping, cried out again and again, 'He has departed from his grave, he has departed from his grave!' and they raced swiftly up the hill until I saw them enter the courtyard of the high priest."

"What did you think when you heard their words?"

"I was filled with great joy, for I knew of whom they were speaking. Remember, I had heard Jesus say, 'After I am risen . . .' and now I had just heard those men, whose light I had followed all the way from Golgotha, announce that he was gone from his tomb. In my excitement I raced down the stairs and out the gate and north toward Golgotha, not even stopping long enough to put on my sandals."

"What were you wearing?"

"Wearing? Oh . . . my nightshirt. I had undressed and was ready for sleep when the shaking of the earth startled me."

"And what color is your nightshirt?"

"Color? It is white."

"Did you meet anyone on the road north?"

"None that I can remember, and if I had I probably would not have seen them. My mind and my heart, as well as my eyes and feet, were all pointed toward the place where they had laid our Lord. Finally I reached the garden. The huge fire I had seen from this terrace was still burning, and beyond it I could see the tomb. I managed to remove one of the smaller logs that was aflame, and carrying it as a torch I approached the grave, not realizing until I was quite close that the stone had been rolled aside."

"Did you see anyone in the garden?"

"Once I heard noises behind some bushes and I almost ran away before a small dog walked across the grass and disappeared under the trees. But other than that animal I saw no one. When I reached the mouth of the tomb I pushed my torch inside and then stooped down and looked, ready to flee at the slightest provocation. In the sepulchre, on a ledge carved from the stone, was the linen cloth of burial, and although the cloth was still wound around itself I could see that it contained no body. I crept into the tomb, slowly, and sat on the right side against the wall and contemplated the great miracle that must have taken place. I cried, at first. Afterward I prayed, as Jesus had taught us to pray, and I thanked God for delivering our Lord from his enemies, and I was in such a state of elation that it seemed I could hear the sound of many angels, singing and laughing with joy. Then, because of the lateness of the hour, I must have fallen asleep with my head against the wall, and I do not know how long I remained in that condition before I was awakened by voices and turned to see figures moving at the mouth of the tomb. With the dim light of dawn behind their backs and my torch no longer burning I did not recognize them, and in my surprise at their appearance I cried out and then some of them screamed and I realized they were women. Quickly, they pulled their heads from the opening and I crawled out after them, but they had already turned their backs in flight when I told them not to be afraid."

"Did you recognize them once you were outside the tomb?"

"No. It was still more dark than light, in the garden with its trees, and I saw them only from the rear as they fled."

"Did you try to stop them?"

"Yes. I called after them, as I said, telling them not to be afraid, and more."

"Do you recall what you shouted at them?"

Mark scowled and tugged at his pointed chin. "I believe I said, 'Be not afraid: You seek Jesus of Nazareth, who was crucified: he is risen; he is not here: behold the place where they laid him. But go your way, tell his disciples and Peter that he goes before you into Galilee: there shall you see him, as he said unto you.' "

So much for angels at the tomb. Still, for a private grave

in a foreboding pre-dawn setting, there had been considerable traffic. John and Peter, of course, but preceding them had been Mary Magdalene and the other women. And now I knew, for a certainty, that Mark had been there before any of them! But who had preceded Mark? If I had that answer I'd probably also know the identity of my grave robber. I shook my head in bewilderment and caught the slight smirk on Joseph of Arimathea's old face as he watched me straining for a solution to the mystery that had brought me here in the first place.

"Mark, according to Mary Magdalene, both John and Peter ran to the tomb as soon as she brought them the news that someone had taken the body of Jesus. How is it that they did not meet you on the road or find you still in the garden?"

He grinned. "I returned through the streets of the city rather than the road outside the wall. Then I rushed upstairs, unseen, and crawled under my blankets and pretended that I was asleep."

Mark's mother was calling to him from the courtyard below. Wood was needed for the fire. He turned to me apologetically, but I told him I was finished with my questions anyway and thanked him for his help. His parting embrace momentarily surprised me before I realized that, so far as he was concerned, my gold amulet had certified that I was one of them. All at once I felt exhausted. Beat. A sleepwalker.

Joseph said consolingly, "Come inside, Matthias. Let us rest."

I followed him back into the large upper room and slumped down on the green cushions at the huge table with its perpetual candlelight. The old man leaned toward me, hands together almost in the prayer position.

"Matthias, it has been my great privilege and honor to have accompanied you during the past four days. After observing you and listening to you deal so skillfully with all manner of witnesses in order to uncover the truth, it is not difficult to understand why your books of crime and detection have won you worldwide renown."

I braced myself. Joseph of Arimathea continued.

"I told you, when you arrived here, that any results you achieved would be strictly through your own ability, knowledge, and skills and that I would stand by, solely to protect you and advise you as best I could. I regret that, to this moment, I have not fulfilled my small end of our bargain as well as you have met your great challenge. For while you have made tremendous progress in absolving many of those you had suspected of having been involved in the removal of the body of Jesus from the tomb, your life is now in great jeopardy and all the advice I have dispensed could be placed on the head of a nail."

"Joseph, you have been wonderful, just as you are. Too much advice from you and I would have suspected that you were trying to influence me or blind me with some facts so that I wouldn't see others. We have accomplished much together."

He shook his head sadly. "But our time remaining is short. Would you accept a suggestion or two, at this late hour of our mission, in order to bring you to a more hasty resolution of the mystery concerning the empty tomb?"

"Of course."

There was relief and gratitude in his warm smile. "In your novels, Matthias, what would happen if the person who had been murdered were to reappear alive?"

"Can't happen."

"Why not?"

"I wouldn't let it happen."

"Why?"

"Because if the murdered person was actually still alive I have no murderer for my detective to uncover."

"Exactly."

"What do you mean, 'exactly'?"

"What I mean is very simple," he said patiently. "Just as a book of yours would have no murderer if the person believed to have been murdered was still alive, so, too, would you have no grave robbers, in this case, if the body they are alleged to have taken was seen walking and talking and eating, here in the city, after the tomb was found empty."

I sighed. I should have known. We had to get to it eventually. "Joseph, certainly you must have noticed that in all my questioning—of Matthew, of James, the brother of John, of Peter and even young John, today, and Mark—I purposely ended our discussions with the discovery of the empty tomb."

"I noticed—and wondered."

"When I first arrived here, I told you that during those years of work on 'The Christ Commission' I had accumulated hundreds of questions and doubts and stumbling blocks about the life of Jesus, and I gave you scores of them. But I also told you that if I could satisfy myself that no one removed the body of Jesus from his tomb, and that he did rise again, all other questions would fade away."

"Yes, I remember."

"I am aware of every recorded alleged appearance of Jesus after his burial, but to ask any of his closest followers to describe some vision they personally had, or thought they had, as a natural sequence to the empty tomb, is contrary to every bit of common sense and logic that I have applied to my work for twenty years. As you have seen and heard, I have concentrated only on facts, facts that could be corroborated, and that's all the Christ Commission would be doing, if they were really here."

He stared at me until I began to feel uncomfortable as he muttered half to himself, again and again, "Facts . . . facts . . . facts." Then he stood, arched his old back several times to accompanying groans, and asked, "Will you grant an old man his whim?"

What could I say? "Certainly."

"Remain there," he said, extending his open palm toward me. Then he went out the door and was gone for perhaps five minutes, returning with a puzzled-looking John at his side. After they both were seated opposite me, Joseph placed his hand on the apostle's shoulder and said, "Son, my friend Matthias has need for a little more information that he neglected to obtain from you before. I believe you told us that when you brought the news to the others, in Bethany, none of them believed your story that Jesus had risen from the dead. Instead, they ridiculed you and you returned here, alone, with heavy heart."

"That is true, but later in the day, toward sundown, all of them came to this house to pay their respects to the Lord's mother and they were shocked to hear, from her lips, the same news I had brought them—that Jesus was not dead. But none of them believed that the Lord's prophecy had come true, and they said they were returning to their homes in Galilee that very night. Hearing this, the Lord's mother would not let them begin their journey until they were fed, and so food was brought up here for them and all the outside doors in the house were bolted shut, as well as the gate in the courtyard."

"Why were they locked?" I asked.

"Thomas and Nathaniel had heard, in the streets, that already we were being accused by the authorities of removing the body of Jesus from his tomb, and there was great anxiety that soon we would all be arrested."

Joseph of Arimathea made one of his rare interruptions. "Matthias, try to imagine that small band of men, crushed by

206

events, leaderless and frightened, hiding here behind locked doors. They were, every one of them, uneducated and penniless and, for all they knew, fugitives in a city where the authorities had already nailed their leader to a cross. For many months they had followed Jesus back and forth across the land, enduring abuse and privation and threats. And now, this sorry lot—having lost everything at Gethsemane, including faith in their master and hope of sharing his promised kingdom—were preparing to flee forever from this city of danger and broken dreams."

John took up the story line. "None of us ate the food that had been prepared for us. We sat around the table, as we had done on that last night with the Lord, and many cried in self-pity despite everything that Peter and I tried to say to convince them that there was more to celebrate than there was to grieve. Some even blamed Jesus for their predicament, saying he had deceived them with his promises and his miracles and they had sacrificed everything to go with him and now they had nothing. Others agreed he was a good man and had brought relief to many, but certainly he was not the Messiah, as Peter had announced at Caesarea Philippi, for no Messiah of the Jews would have allowed himself to be humbled and shamed as the Romans and the high priest had done to him. Peter, stubborn Peter, continued to remind them of the empty tomb until Thomas, in a fit of anger, rushed from the chamber saying that he intended to borrow a lamp from the widow Mary and go to the grave, that moment, to see for himself. After he was gone, I locked the door again and the words continued to fly back and forth until several of the men wearied of the bickering and prepared to leave, saying they would travel north, in the dark so they could avoid all patrols."

"Wait!" Joseph cried, rising from the table.

He beckoned to John and the two of them went out the door. The old man returned alone and sat opposite me, his eyes burning with an intensity I had not seen before.

"Matthias, can you truly visualize the defeat and despair that hung over this room on that night? Can you see those frightened men of the earth and the sea, their weary faces streaked with tears of sorrow and disappointment, their shocked minds thinking only of their own safety—cringing here just as they had done in the woods for two days?"

"Joseph, I *am* a writer, you know. Of course I can."

"Matthias, listen to me," he commanded. "As you have witnessed with your own eyes, this week, there are now thousands upon thousands of believers in the risen Jesus. Ten years from today, as you know, that number will have grown so large that they will begin to create serious disturbances in the city and the Temple. Twenty or twenty-five years from now there will be Christians in every city and village from here to Rome, within forty years they will have begun to undermine the swords and spears of the empire, and in less than three hundred years a Roman emperor will fall to his knees and adopt the teachings of Jesus for all his subjects. You always insist on facts, my son, and you know that what I have just said contains nothing but facts. You nod your head; you agree. Very well, great writer of books, explain to me, if you can, how those eleven miserable weaklings, instead of fleeing to their homes, were able to leave this room, that night, and bring the word of Jesus to the people with such power and force that within three centuries they and their disciples to follow were able to conquer the Roman Empire! Tell me! What happened in this room, before they had a chance to escape into a life of anonymity, that changed them from defeated little men into the greatest force for good the world has ever known? Tell me, what could possibly have occurred here to create such a change in these men, a change so strong and binding in their characters that eventually they would all lay down their lives for their faith? Speak, Matthias!"

He was a different Joseph from the man I had known for four days. I shrugged my shoulders and replied faintly, "You tell me, Joseph. I'm the one who is looking for answers, remember."

"I'll not tell you!" he roared and his voice cracked. "I was not privileged to be here."

He rushed to the door, threw it open, and called John, who must have been standing close by, on the terrace.

"John, please tell Matthias what happened in this room while some of the men were preparing to leave it forever, that night."

John slammed the heavy wooden door and threw the long iron bolt noisily into its socket. "This door was locked, just as it is now. Suddenly Jesus, wearing only a linen girdle, was standing—here," he said, moving forward several paces. "I was the first to see him, and I fell to my knees. Some of the others cried out and knelt, and a few ran to that back wall out of fear. Then we heard him say, 'Peace be unto you,' and he held up his hands and we could see the nail holes that had been driven in his wrists and also his feet and the open wound in his side where the legionary had pierced him. I wanted to run to him and embrace him but my legs had become useless. I could not move from my place. Neither did the others go to him while he spoke to us at length, commanding us to go out into the world, beginning in Jerusalem, and tell his story to all, for we were his witnesses, and great power would be given to us in his name. Then he was gone from the room, just as suddenly as he had appeared, and everyone knelt in prayer. Afterward they came to Peter and me and begged our forgiveness for their unbelief and lack of faith."

"Had Thomas returned from his trip to the tomb in time to share the . . . the appearance of Jesus?"

"No, and when we told him we had seen the Lord he laughed at us and suggested that we had consumed too much wine. I remember him saying, 'Except I shall see in his hands the print of the nails, and put my fingers into the print of the nails, and thrust my hand into his side, I will not believe.' Eight days later, in this same room, although the door was locked as before, Jesus appeared again and stood among us. He pointed directly at Thomas and asked him to come forward. Thomas was so beside himself with fear that he remained in his seat until Peter's great arms pushed him toward the Lord. Then Jesus said, 'Reach here with your finger, and behold my hands; and reach here with your hand, and thrust it into my side; and be not faithless, but believing.' "

"What did Thomas do?"

"He did as he was told and then he fell before Jesus and said, 'My Lord and my God,' and Jesus replied, 'Thomas, because you have seen me, you have believed; but blessed are they that have not seen and yet have believed,' and from that time, every one of us, even Thomas, has been witness to the Lord, as I am to you now and will be to another and another, each day, until the Kingdom of God has come to all people."

Inside the carriage, motionless because he had not signaled Shem to move on, Joseph of Arimathea, his face still flushed, said, "Tell me, Matthias, how many suspects would still remain on the list of the Christ Commission if they were conducting this investigation?"

For a kindly old man he was excellent with the needle when he tried. "Just two," I mumbled, "you and Nicodemus."

"Are you too tired to go on? This would be the ideal time to see Golgotha and the tomb, for it is almost the same hour that we removed Jesus from the cross and laid him in the sepulchre."

"I'm ready."

"Excellent. And from there it is a pleasant ride, on the road to Emmaus, to the home of my old friend Nicodemus. There you will have the pleasure of visiting the most impressive and beautiful garden of flowers since the days of Babylon, as well as meeting the wealthiest man in the nation."

"Wealthier than you?"

"It is like comparing an anthill to Mount Hermon." He chuckled. "And what will your next move be, if, after you have questioned both Nicodemus and me, you decide that we are not your grave robbers?"

Exactly what I had been wondering. "I don't know, Joseph."

"But your manuscript: what did you plan to have the Christ Commission do next, after their witness list was exhausted?"

"I can't tell you. Long before my writing of the book reached this point, I had abandoned the project as hopeless."

"Then after myself and Nicodemus, you have no others to question?"

"None," I replied hopelessly.

"Well," he mused, "perhaps I can find you one more."

thirteen

"THERE HAVE BEEN NO CRUCIFIXIONS here for several years," Joseph said. "As you can see, and smell, it has become no more than a dumping ground for those too lazy to cart their waste to the fires in Hinnom Valley."

The place was called Golgotha in Aramaic, meaning "the skull," but as soon as I had stepped down from Joseph's carriage I could see that its name had not derived from its shape, as so many biblical scholars had conjectured. The hill's sandy terrain, scarred by patches of giant weeds, animal droppings, and mounds of foul-smelling garbage, ascended gradually for fifty feet or so to a barren flat summit no more than twenty feet in elevation above the road. Even in the warm orange sunlight of midafternoon, the place was foreboding and the stench of death hung like an invisible gas above our heads. Rodents, chirping their ugly cries, scurried in all directions when the sound of our approaching footsteps disturbed their feeding.

"Why no more crucifixions?" I asked, ready to clutch at any straw.

"Pilate decided that this was not a public enough place to display the bodies of executed criminals as examples to the people. Now the crosses are usually raised near the main roads to the northeast of the city."

"And why is it called Golgotha?"

The old man nodded toward a large mound of loose dirt and stones on the city side of the hill. "That is where the common grave was established for those executed here whose bodies were not claimed. When the heavy rains come, many bones and skulls are often exposed."

At last we were standing on the hill's uneven crest. Joseph's tired eyes swept back and forth across the drab ground beneath us. He reached for my hand and I gave it to him, following as he marched off ten paces and stopped. "Here is where Jesus was raised on the cross, facing the road, with another cross on each side."

211

I crouched low to the ground, not for a better view but because my legs suddenly felt very unsteady. The soil was pliant against my knuckles, as if it had not yet recovered from all the wooden crosses it had supported through the years. Then I heard a voice—raspy, hoarse, and angry. It was mine. "Joseph, why have you and the others allowed this place to be desecrated? Why haven't you, with all your gold, erected a monument on this spot?"

"Matthias," he said, helping me to my feet, "you must not forget that the shame of a criminal's death by crucifixion is still fresh in the minds of all who loved Jesus. Why should one recall the bad instead of the miracle that followed?"

"How many were in your party when you took Jesus down from the cross?"

"Four. Shem and myself, also Nicodemus and his son, Gorion. Shem, with his great height, removed the nails from the wrists of Jesus with the claws of the same hammer, borrowed from the soldiers, that had been used to drive them through the flesh and bone. He then held the body firmly against the cross while Gorion removed the nails from the feet of Jesus. Then they carried the body, already beginning to stiffen, to the garden and placed it near the tomb, on the grass."

"Were there many onlookers?"

"As I recall, only Mary Magdalene and another woman. The soldiers paid little attention to us, after I had presented them with my order from Pilate, for they were hurrying to dispose of the other two bodies in the common grave so they could return to the fortress. Lying on the ground, near the cross, was the familiar red seamless robe that I recognized as belonging to Jesus. I retrieved it, while Shem and Gorion were removing the body, but one of the soldiers ran after me and tore it from my grasp, saying he had won it fairly in a game of bones. I told him that while I had no money on my person I would gladly pay him a gold aureus for it if he delivered it to my home later."

"Did he?"

"He was waiting at my place when I returned from the burial."

"And what about the sign that Pilate had ordered to be displayed above the head of Jesus? Did you leave that?"

"Oh, no. I have that also. In truth I have a small room containing only relics pertaining to Jesus."

"The one you keep locked?"

His old eyebrows flickered. "Yes."

"Would seeing them be of any help to me?"

"In your search for the truth?" he asked, eyeing me hopefully.

"Yes."

He started to speak but caught himself. After several minutes he shook his head sadly and said, "I do not believe so. If you cannot learn the truth from the living you will never learn it from objects."

"Some of our archaeologists haven't done too badly."

"Indeed!" He snorted. "So what do you know about Jesus that was not already known a thousand years before your birth?"

"Not much," I admitted. "But you will let me see that room, won't you?"

"If we have time," he said ominously. "And what of this place? Have you had enough?"

"Enough to last me a lifetime," I said, immediately regretting my choice of words.

Joseph's garden was less than a hundred yards from Golgotha, screened from the hill and the nearby passing road by tall stands of unkempt cypress. Approaching it, the old man turned to me apologetically and said, "I have had no heart for this garden and rarely visit here since the discovery of the empty tomb."

Neither had anyone else from the looks of it. Like Gethsemane, the grass was above our knees, the flower beds and walks were totally overrun with weeds, and the broken limbs of trees lay where they had fallen. Even the tomb itself, part of a large outcropping of limestone near the garden's eastern edge, was so covered with shrubbery and tall grass that Joseph had to point out its opening to me, an oval cavity no more than four feet high and two feet wide. Obviously the same feelings applied to the tomb as Golgotha. And why would anyone want to visit an empty grave, anyway?

"After his body was placed on the grass, here"—Joseph pointed—"Nicodemus and I cleaned it with aloe water and rubbed it with oil. Then, with the help of Shem and Gorion, we wound a fine linen cloth around his body many times, beginning at the feet, and between each layer, where the cloth overlapped, we placed myrrh and perfumed aloe wood and other spices until the sheet held nearly sixty pounds when we reached the neck. His head we left uncovered."

The old man was going too fast for me. "Joseph, there are many questions I would like to ask you about your relationship with Jesus before his death, but perhaps this is not the place."

"That will be no problem for you, Matthias. Since Nicodemus is also involved with that part of my life, you can ask both of us, together, about our earlier experiences with Jesus. For now, why don't we concentrate on the final hours here?"

I agreed, but I still wanted to backtrack a little. "Joseph, you knew that Jesus had been arrested because you and Shem had answered John's plea to go to the aid of the fallen Peter, in the courtyard of Caiaphas, correct?"

"Yes, but I did not know that Caiaphas intended to try him that night, in direct violation of our laws. I assumed there would be a trial after our Passover days had passed, and as a member of the Sanhedrin I had no reason to believe I would not sit in judgment with the others, as always."

"Then you had no idea, on the following morning, that Jesus had been brought before Pilate after being tried by the Sanhedrin?"

"No. Soon after sunrise I was at my warehouse, in the market area, supervising the annual taking of inventory. I knew nothing of the morning's events until Nicodemus and his son found me and told me that both the Sanhedrin and Pilate had condemned Jesus to death and that he had been nailed to a cross on Golgotha and was already dead. I remember sitting on a bale of wool, at first, and sobbing like a little child. Then Nicodemus said that the legionaries, if they followed their custom, would probably toss the body of Jesus in the common grave with the other criminals who had been crucified, and his words revived me. 'Never, never, never!' I shouted, so loudly that those in my employ came running to my aid, fearing I was being set upon. I instructed the overseer of my warehouse to select our finest linen and all the spices necessary to prepare a body for burial according to our laws. Nicodemus and his son were to take them to Golgotha while Shem drove me swiftly to the fortress, where I requested an immediate audience with Pilate and received it. The procurator was surprised to hear that Jesus had died so quickly, but he refused to release the body to me, as I had requested, until he had sent Cornelius to the hill to verify that Jesus was truly dead. As soon as Cornelius returned, Pilate gave me a written order which I took immediately to Golgotha, arriving soon after Nicodemus and Gorion."

"Did they know that you were planning to bury the body in the nearby tomb you had prepared for yourself?"

"Yes, I had told them before I went to Pilate. Nicodemus objected at first, saying that we should remove the body to his palace and keep it there until the most magnificent tomb in all Israel was built for Jesus. However, I did not agree. The honor of having Jesus buried in my tomb was the last opportunity I would ever have of doing for him, in death, what I had always lacked the courage to do while he was alive—publicly attest to my love for him."

"I understand that Caiaphas and the Sanhedrin were outraged when they heard you had claimed the body."

He smiled. "To this day they have not forgiven me, blaming me for all the troubles that beset them from the followers of Jesus, in the Temple and the streets. If I had not claimed the body, they insist there would be no such thing as a Christian in all the land. And when I remind the high priest that he, himself, posted a guard here, he becomes furious and repeats the same story: that the disciples came and stole the body while the soldiers slept—which, as you now know, the disciples did not do."

"Then Nicodemus finally agreed to your plan to bury Jesus here?"

"I gave him no choice. He realized that I was probably the only Jew in the city who could convince Pilate to release the body, because of our past business dealings."

"Could Nicodemus have returned later and removed the body, unknown to you?"

"Never!" the old man exploded. "Nicodemus, as you will see, is a good and honorable man. We have been close friends for many, many years. I would vouch for his integrity with my life."

"And he'll probably tell me the same about you," I said tartly.

"I certainly would hope so."

"What did you do after you completed your preparation of the body?"

"With the help of Gorion, for Shem was too large to pass through the opening, we carried the body into the tomb and placed it on the shelf that would have been my final resting place some day."

Joseph watched as I went to the mouth of the sepulchre, pushed aside the shrubs, stomped on the tall weeds, stooped down, and looked inside. It was considerably larger than the tomb of Lazarus, having a small inner room which led to another on which I could dimly see the shelf, hewn from stone, approximately two feet from the floor. Behind me I could hear Joseph, his words now punctuated by sobs.

"Nicodemus and I had shared many hours with Jesus, in

the darkness of night, listening to his wise advice and counsel. Now we shared the darkness of a tomb with him, and our grief was nearly unbearable. Finally, I placed a linen napkin over his bruised face, as is the custom of our people, and we came out of the grave and prostrated ourselves on the grass in prayer. Later, at a signal from me, Shem released the great stone, and it rolled down the trench until it came to rest in front of the opening, closing the tomb."

"By the way, where is the stone?"

"With my permission, Nicodemus removed it to a place of honor in his garden, two or three years ago. It was necessary for him to build a special wagon to transport it, because of its size and weight."

"Where was the stone when the tomb was discovered empty?"

"It was still standing, resting against the left side of the opening."

"Could one person have moved it away from the entrance, after it had settled in place?"

"Never. The trench on which it rolled downward until it covered the opening was at its deepest directly in front of the entrance. Once the stone lodged itself, there was little danger of anyone's ever tampering with the grave."

"Could Shem have moved it?"

"Not even Shem."

"How about three or four strong men?"

"Perhaps. Do you know of such men, Matthias, who would have risked their lives in the darkness, against the soldiers of the high priest, rolled away the stone, removed the body of Jesus without disturbing the linen sheet we had so carefully wrapped around and around the body, and then disappeared with the remains without being apprehended? If so, you certainly should interrogate them."

He had me—and he knew it. "Do you mind if I go inside?"

The old man tenderly cupped my face in his hands, shaking my head gently from side to side. "Who has a better right to go inside after the journey you have taken to view this place? Even Thomas came here to see for himself."

The vacant tomb smelled like a damp cellar. Once within the small alcove, I turned and bumped my head on the low ceiling before I was sitting on the right side of the shadowy room just as Mark said he had done after his initial discovery of the empty grave. Resting there, it was easy to appreciate the terror that must have seized the women when they ar-

216

rived at the grave in semi-darkness, expecting to tend to a dead man, and instead came upon someone dressed in white moving around inside. Anyone, superstitious or not, would have fled.

On my hands and knees I crawled beyond the alcove until I could reach the shelf where the body of Jesus had lain, wrapped tightly in a grave cloth and weighed down by more than sixty pounds of spices. No robust and healthy man, in top condition, could have survived under such conditions for more than a few hours when sealed in that space, much less one who had suffered all that Jesus had. I rubbed my hand gently along the cool shelf before crawling out of the abandoned tomb.

The palace of Nicodemus was everything that he was not. Situated well back from the winding road to Emmaus, only ten miles or so from Jerusalem, the building with its bright marble columns and red-tiled roof, still unfaded from the sun, had the unmistakable look of newness about it, whereas its owner looked older than Joseph. The estate was large and sprawling, while Nicodemus stood little more than five feet in height and in his simple brown tunic obviously weighed no more than a hundred pounds. Inside the mansion, the few rooms I saw were all gaudy, ostentatious, and overbearing, but Nicodemus seemed to be modest, unprepossessing, and almost shy. His outstanding facial features were a luxuriant full beard and shaggy eyebrows above warm and friendly gray eyes that immediately put me at ease even in the opulent sitting room, where we were served the finest red wine I had ever tasted. As I listened to the two old friends bringing each other up to date on their lives and their businesses, it was not difficult to sense a bond between them that went far beyond their public lives. Nicodemus did not seem at all surprised by our visit, nor did Joseph give him any explanation of my purpose for being there, other than stating my profession, historian, and repeating my desire to obtain some information about Jesus.

"What is it you wish to know, my son?" he asked.

Almost reluctantly, I put down my goblet of red nectar and said, "I have some questions for both of you. To begin: Nicodemus, I wonder if you would tell me how you first came to know Jesus?"

"For that great honor I am indebted to my only son, Gorion. He came to me one evening, filled with sadness. It seems that he had gone to the Temple that day, with his friend from rabbinical school, John Mark, to hear a man from Galilee named Jesus who in only a short time had attracted much attention from the people through his words and his healing of the sick. Mark's uncle, Peter, was one of a small company of men who had already forsaken their former lives in order to follow this young man from Nazareth. Gorion, when he heard Jesus speak to the crowd, was so impressed with the man's promises that the Kingdom of God was close at hand that he went to him, with Peter's permission, and asked what good things he should do that he might share in the eternal life. Jesus advised him to keep the commandments, and my son asked him which one and was told not to murder, not to commit adultery, not to steal, not to bear false witness, to honor his father and mother, and to love his neighbor as himself."

"Good advice."

"Yes," Nicodemus agreed, "but not good enough for my brash son. He assured Jesus that he had always obeyed those commandments and wanted to know what else was necessary. Jesus told him that if he wanted to be perfect, if he wanted to have his treasure in heaven, he must go and sell what he had and give the money to the poor. 'And after you do,' said Jesus, 'come and follow me.' "

"And Gorion came to you for advice after his meeting with Jesus?"

"Not for advice, for consolation. He said he wanted to see the Kingdom of God but he could not bring himself to sell the Arabian horses I had bought for him, through the years, and he was grief-stricken for he truly believed what Jesus had told him. Always being accustomed to having his way, he hoped I could supply him with a solution so that he might have his stable *and* the Kingdom of God. Unfortunately I could give him neither advice nor consolation, having devoted too much of my own wasted life to the acquisition of gold and silver with little thought for others. Still, even though my party, the Pharisees, had already denounced Jesus as a troublemaker, I promised Gorion that I would go to him that very night, to learn if there were other ways by which a man might enter the Kingdom of God. Of course, I wished to learn for my own benefit, as well as my son's."

"That I cannot understand, Nicodemus. Why would a man of your great wealth, power, and education bother to visit an uneducated Galilean for any reason? What could he possibly have to say that would benefit you, a learned councilor, a

218

doctor of the law, and a member of the supreme judicial body of the land?"

"Matthias, if he was a true prophet of God I knew there was much I could learn from him, despite his lack of formal education. God does not choose his messengers by the titles they hold or the gold in their vault or the studies in which they excelled in school. And even if he were not a prophet, I was curious to meet the man who had made such a strong impression on my son and who was already causing great concern among the authorities because of his revolutionary ideas as well as his miracles."

"And your visit to Jesus was at night for a reason?"

"For the most obvious one," Nicodemus said, lowering his head. "I did not want to be seen in his company, for fear that my motives might not be understood by others and my good name would suffer."

"Did Jesus meet with you?"

"He met with both of us," Nicodemus exclaimed, placing his hand on Joseph's shoulder and pulling the Arimathean toward him. "I am not a man known for my courage and I was concerned about going to Jesus alone, so I asked my old friend, here, to ride with me to Bethany where Jesus was staying."

I should have known. Another minor biblical mystery had just been cleared up. The third chapter of John deals with the visit of Nicodemus to Jesus without mentioning that he had any company, but John quotes Nicodemus as having said, "Rabbi, we know that thou art a teacher come from God. . . ." *We*, not I.

"And you went with him, Joseph?"

"I did, Matthias. I too wanted to meet this man who had already been the cause of several meetings of the Sanhedrin. Shem accompanied us for protection, but none was needed and Jesus received us cordially."

"Did he know he was in the company of two of the wealthiest and most powerful men in Jerusalem?"

"He knew, but it made no difference in his treatment of us. So far as he was concerned we were just two more children of Israel seeking the truth. We told him that we knew he must be a man of God, for no man could do what he had done unless God was with him. Then Nicodemus asked him how we could share in the Kingdom of God, and Jesus said that unless a man was born again he could not see the Kingdom."

"At first," said Nicodemus, "I did not understand the

meaning of his words. I asked him how a man could be born again, once he was old. Did Jesus expect us to enter the womb of our mother for a second time? Patiently, he explained that to be born again meant to be born from above, with the spirit of God entering into our very being, no matter what our age or position. Joseph and I had great difficulty with his words, and Jesus grew angry at our blindness and wondered how we had managed to become masters of Israel when we understood so little about the greater Kingdom of God."

"Did you two go to him often?"

"Many, many times and usually together. Always under the cover of darkness. As the months passed, we developed great love and respect for him, and it was not long before we were both contributing heavily to the purse of his small group in order that Jesus and his disciples would not have to seek alms in the streets when their time could be better spent bringing solace and hope to the people."

"You two financed them?"

"Their party was growing in followers, day by day, yet they received little in the way of contributions from the poor who always flocked around. It was the least we could do. Although we dared not support him in public, we could help with our gold—and we did."

"Did any of the other authorities suspect that you two had become secret followers?"

"In my case," said Nicodemus, "I do not believe that any suspicion was aroused until I attended a meeting of the chief priests and Pharisees after some of our Temple guards had been dispatched, on one occasion, to arrest Jesus for stirring up the people. The guards returned empty-handed, saying that they dared not lay hands on him. I argued against any such future action, saying that it was unlawful to judge any man before he was tried, but Caiaphas became enraged at me and asked, 'Are you from Galilee also? Search and look, for out of Galilee there comes no prophet!' "

Joseph nodded. "As for me, I don't believe that anyone suspected my friendship with Jesus before I went to Pilate and claimed his body for burial. Even the procurator expressed surprise at my request. Of course, after the tomb was found empty, all the authorities, especially the high priest, blamed both Nicodemus and me for not allowing the body to be tossed into a common grave."

Nicodemus smiled. "We were treated like lepers at first,

until it came time for our next yearly contributions to the Temple funds."

"After the burial, where did you both go?"

Joseph spoke first. "As you know, Matthias, I have no family. I prevailed on Nicodemus to come to my house, where we spent the following day, our Sabbath, in prayer and meditation while consoling each other over our great loss. After sundown, when the Sabbath had ended, Shem took Nicodemus back to his place, here, and I retired very early."

Nicodemus nodded. "I, too, went to bed soon after my return from Joseph's house. The torment and anguish of burying our beloved Jesus had taken a great toll from my old heart and body."

"And neither of you went out of your homes again that night?"

Nicodemus looked puzzled until Joseph explained. "Matthias believes that the body of Jesus was removed from the tomb so that those of us who followed him could claim that he had risen from the dead, on the third day, as he had prophesied. You and I are on his list of suspected grave robbers—the last on his list, I must tell you."

It was impossible to fathom the looks that now passed between these two old patriarchs. Sitting there I suddenly felt like a child struggling futilely to break the code of an adult conversation with only limited faculties and knowledge. Finally Joseph said, "Nicodemus, I want to help Matthias in every way that we can."

Our host was silent for several moments before he said, "Then I believe it is about time that we showed him the garden."

The garden of Nicodemus was without any doubt the most magnificent display of horticultural artistry I had ever seen. When we stepped out onto the shaded colonnade I literally held my breath. Spread out before us, on a gradually sloping hill, was a floral mosaic of incredible beauty. For at least the next hour, walking on paths paved with colored stones, I was treated to shimmering visions of anemones in purple, white, delicate pink, and scarlet. There were beds of rock-edged daisies, cyclamens, tulips, lilies, short and stately roses, larkspur, jasmine, circles of burning bushes around gurgling fountains, stars of Bethlehem, and scores of other lush flora that were still unfamiliar to me even after Nicodemus identified them. Ponds were everywhere, shaped to fit the sloping contours of the hill, each filled with different varieties of water lilies and goldfish, while hedges, mediculously trimmed, ran through the entire grounds, providing a much-needed contrast of greens and yellows to the eye-boggling array of colors. If ever there had been a Garden of Eden I was now strolling through it.

On the north side of the garden, as we rounded a gradual turn past a tall clump of damask roses, I saw the great stone. It was leaning against the side of a dark outcropping of rock. Next to it an opening had been cut into the rock that looked identical in size and shape to the one in the tomb I had just visited in Joseph's garden. Joseph was standing next to me with a smug look on his face but he said nothing. Neither did Nicodemus, so I left them and ran ahead to the stone. It was round, stood nearly as tall as I do, and was a good foot in thickness. I leaned against its side and pushed. It refused to budge. I shoved harder. Not even an inch. I stooped down and looked inside the tomb. Then I fell to my knees. Incredible! Nicodemus had duplicated exactly, so far as I could see, the tomb in which the body of Jesus had been laid! Except for the great stone. I didn't have to be reminded that it was the actual piece that Mark and, later, Mary Magdalene had found rolled aside on that morning six years ago. I was still shaking my head when the two led me to a curved marble bench nearby.

"Well." Nicodemus finally broke the silence. "What do you think of my humble garden?"

"It's amazing," I marveled, "absolutely amazing, all of it!"

"I like to come out here and sit, as we do now, when the worries of the day become more than I can bear. Here, close to the great stone, it is possible to put everything in its proper perspective, and those things which seemed so important in the marketplace become as transitory and insignificant as a grain of sand."

"I have never seen its equal. Although my profession is words, I can't think of a compliment worthy of what you have accomplished here."

"Even if you could, I would not be deserving, Matthias. It is my chief gardener who has made this place his life's work."

"Perhaps Matthias would like to meet him," Joseph urged.

"I would indeed."

Nicodemus was gone for only a few moments, returning in the company of a giant almost as large as Shem. He was not a young man, and his dark, heavily lined face was marred by two ugly gray scars, one across his left cheek and the other beneath the mouth. Sword cuts? His long straight hair was tied into a ponytail, and his beard protruded from his chin as if all its hairs were made of stiff wire. When he saw us he slowed his walk and fell behind Nicodemus, staring self-consciously at the ground as if he were searching for any straggling weed that would dare to show itself in his garden.

"Matthias," Nicodemus said proudly, "here is the man responsible for all these gifts from God you see growing here. His name is Shobi."

"Shobi," I began, "this place is a miracle of—" Bang! Delayed reaction. Double take. Shobi? Where had I heard that name before? Shobi? Shobi!

I swung around toward Joseph. "Can it be . . . ?"

"It is he, Matthias. The Temple officer who ran, with the other three, to take the news to Caiaphas that the tomb they had been guarding was empty."

"The high priest told me that three of them took their own lives and the captain, Shobi, disappeared!"

Joseph nodded. "He has remained here with Nicodemus, secluded from the outside world, for six years. I promised you one more witness when we departed from the house of the widow Mary, remember? Shobi has agreed to talk with you, but there is one stipulation—mine, not his. Only two or three trusted friends know that he is still alive and in the employ of Nicodemus. Whatever else you may do, during your stay in Jerusalem, you must not violate his trust. If the high priest knew that Shobi was here, he would undoubtedly have him put to death under some pretense. Do you accept my terms?"

As soon as I nodded, Joseph rose and motioned for Shobi to sit next to me on the bench.

"We'll wait for you at the house," he called over his shoulder as he and Nicodemus walked away, leaving me alone with the only living witness to whatever might have taken place in Joseph's garden before dawn on that most mysterious of nights.

"Your name," I began hesitantly, "is most uncommon."

He spoke with dignity and fluency, articulating his words without the usual guttural quality common to Aramaic. "I was named after Shobi, the son of an Ammonite king who was instrumental in providing David and his troops with food and other supplies during his terrible battles with Absalom, his son. Without Shobi's assistance, Israel would have lost its greatest patriot and leader."

"How long were you a Temple guard?"

"For ten years. Caiaphas recruited me personally, during his second year in the office of high priest."

"Did you enjoy serving in the Temple?"

"Very much. During my eighth year I was promoted to the position of captain with more than thirty guards under my supervision. Since I had been raised as an orphan, in nearby Bethpage, I was very proud of the rank I had attained through hard work and devotion to duty. Who could ask for more than to spend one's days, and sometimes nights, in the house of God? Despite the difficulty in preserving peace there on occasions, I soon earned a good reputation for the manner in which I trained my guards to handle the large crowds in the courtyard."

"How did you feel when Caiaphas called upon you to guard a dead man in his tomb?"

He smiled ruefully. "At first it was a great struggle on my part to keep from laughing in his excellency's face. Then he explained that Jesus had told his followers, many times, that he would be crucified for his beliefs but would rise from the dead on the third day. Caiaphas was afraid that some of the disciples might come and steal the body and hide it, after which they would claim that Jesus had risen as he said he would. Convinced of the importance of my mission, I selected three of my most experienced men to watch over the tomb with me."

"When did you and your guards arrive at the garden near Golgotha?"

"At sundown, the end of our Sabbath."

"Everything was in order? The stone was in place, covering the mouth of the sepulchre?"

"It was. We then proceeded to seal the tomb, as the high priest had ordered."

"How was that done?"

"We placed thin strips of ribbon across the stone and sealed their ends, with wax, against the side of the tomb. After we were finished, no one could have moved the great stone without breaking the seals."

"Then what did you do?"

"The night air was cold, so we built a fire with some dead limbs that had been piled against one of the olive trees in the garden. I then assigned the hours of guard duty to my men, taking the third watch myself. Soon after the first took up his position, near the tomb, the others and myself were asleep under blankets, near the fire. Because of Passover we had al-

224

ready served long hours that day, in the Temple, and all of us were weary."

"From what Caiaphas has told me, apparently nothing happened out of the ordinary during the first two watches."

"That is correct."

"When your time came, did you take your scheduled turn?"

Shobi glared at me, and the blood rushing to his scowling face made his two scars all the more vivid by their contrast. "I did not earn my reputation for integrity and fairness by asking those under my supervision to perform duties that I would not do! I took up my place next to the tomb, prepared to serve my four hours just as the others had done."

"But something happened to cut short your watch."

"I shall never forget it!"

"Tell me."

"I had been standing watch for perhaps an hour when I heard a strange sound, a moaning of some kind. At first I thought it was an animal in the bushes or one of the sleeping guards having a dream, but as I walked back and forth in front of the tomb, the moaning seemed to be coming from inside! After a while it subsided and I put it out of my mind, thinking that it had been only my imagination or the wind. Then I heard it again, louder, sounding like someone crying out in pain. I ran to the fire, removed a burning branch to use as a torch, and searched in the vicinity of the sepulchre, looking for an animal or even a human who might be injured. I saw nothing. The noise continued, growing louder and louder until there was no doubt that it was coming from inside the tomb. I remember thinking that perhaps the man who had been buried, Jesus, was not dead. Now and then such a thing is known to happen. I leaned against the great stone, my ear against its side, listening, and then the ground shook, but only for a moment."

"Did the shaking disturb the stone—break the seals?"

"No. Nor did it awaken the three who were sleeping. Then I saw that our fire was in need of more wood, and I had started toward it when I suddenly heard footsteps behind me. I turned quickly, removed my dagger from its sheath, and assumed the battle crouch. Walking toward me was a man, and he appeared to be naked!"

"How far were you from the tomb when you first saw him?"

"No more than ten paces."

"Was he between you and the tomb?"

225

"Directly."

"And was the stone still in its proper position?"

"Yes."

"Not rolled to one side?"

"No."

"It was a man? Of that you are certain?"

He smiled faintly. "I am positive. The moon was bright and there was still some light from the fire. The man's body seemed to be giving off its own light, but I reasoned that what I saw must have been only a reflection of the moon and the fire upon the stranger's skin, as if his body had been covered with oil."

"What did you do?"

"Nothing. I had been in many battles and faced death often but never before had I known what it was to be afraid. I stood still, my feet rooted to the ground, as the stranger approached me without hesitation. When he was within arm's length he handed me a white linen cloth, a napkin of some sort, and I reached out and took it from him as if I was his servant."

"Was your dagger still in your other hand?"

"Yes, but it was a good thing I had no need for it because I do not believe I could have defended myself. My arms and my hands were as useless as my feet. Soon the man was lost from my sight in the darkness, beyond the trees."

"Did you see his face clearly?"

"No."

"Had you ever seen Jesus when he was preaching in the Temple courtyard?"

"Many times."

"Would you have recognized Jesus in that light?"

"No."

"Did the person speak to you?"

"If it had been Jesus and he had spoken to me I would have known him. Nothing was said. The napkin was handed to me in silence as if the man expected me to take it—and I did."

"After he disappeared, what did you do?"

"I tucked the napkin into my girdle and woke the others, telling them everything that had taken place while they slept. One of the guards, an old comrade of mine, told me there was no need for concern since the great stone was still in place, but my long years of service had taught me to take nothing for granted. I had to assure myself that the body was still inside. Two of us went to nearby Golgotha to see if the

226

Romans had left behind any of the crosspieces on which they nail the hands of those who are about to be crucified. We returned with a heavy timber and carried it to the tomb, where I placed a small boulder next to the great one, and using the crosspiece as a lever, the four of us, after much effort, finally managed to roll away the stone. . . ."

Shobi's words trailed off. He leaned forward and looked anxiously into my eyes.

"Are you ill, sir? Your face—it has a strange color. Perhaps the sun's heat has affected you. Come, let me take you back to the house."

It was an effort to shake my head. "Then it was *you and your men* who moved the great stone? You? You!"

"Yes, in order to see inside. Carrying my torch I stooped down and went into the sepulchre, crawling through the small outer room until I was close to the shelf on which the body must have rested. I could see that the grave cloth was still there, wrapped round and round, but inside it there was no body! I couldn't understand it. Then I shouted to the others to come and see, but none dared enter a place of the dead, even when I told them that the body was gone. I sat there alone, in the tomb, trying to collect my senses. What could I tell Caiaphas to convince him that we had not been derelict in our duty? All my years of loyalty and hard work would be wiped away as soon as the high priest was told that the body was missing. Never would he trust me again. Everything, for me, was lost. In anger and futility I remember pulling the linen napkin from my waist and throwing it upon the shelf near the larger cloth. Finally I decided that all I could do was tell Caiaphas the truth, as I had seen it, and hope that his wisdom would allow him to judge me as I deserved to be judged. I crawled from the cave and commanded the others to bring a torch from the fire and follow me, and we all ran from the garden, not stopping until we were back in the courtyard of the high priest."

"You told Caiaphas everything?"

"Everything, but he refused to believe my story. He slapped me and the others, many times, accusing us of sleeping on duty, screaming that we should all be stoned to death for our crime."

"You even told him about the stranger who passed near you at the tomb?"

"I did . . . and while we were still on our knees, not knowing what he would do to us next, he asked me to tell him about the stranger once more. Then he called for his or-

227

derly and ordered that four pouches be brought to him, each filled with silver coins. To our great surprise he presented one to each and warned us to say nothing of our experience, and if we were asked about the tomb we should only say that the disciples had come and stolen the body away while we slept. Then he excused us."

"What did you do then?"

"To this very day I cannot remember much of what followed. I know that I walked from the quarters of Caiaphas in shame, wishing that I was dead. As soon as I was out of the courtyard, after bidding good night to the others, I threw the coins in the street. Then I began to run until I found myself once again on the road outside the city, this time heading north toward the garden and its tomb, and all the while I was crying out at the top of my voice, 'Jesus is not dead—he has risen from his grave! Jesus is not dead—he has risen from his grave!' and that is all I can recall until I awoke, here, in the home of Nicodemus."

"Did you tell Nicodemus all that had happened?"

"Yes, but he did not seem surprised at my news. His servants fed me and bathed me and put me to bed, and I have remained here, in peace, ever since."

"And Caiaphas has never suspected that you are still alive."

"Nicodemus has protected me well. Few visitors come to this place, and rare is the person he will allow in this garden. Usually those who are permitted to view the flowers and the tomb, with its great stone, are brought here by Joseph of Arimathea, as you were."

"Oh! And how many, would you say, has Joseph brought here since the garden has been in your care?"

Shobi squinted up at the sky, rubbing his calloused thumb pensively against his lower lip. "In five years, perhaps ten—both men and women."

"Were you allowed to talk with all of them and tell your story?"

"Oh, yes. Of course they were all sworn to secrecy by Joseph, as you were, for the length of their stay in the city."

"Do you, by any chance, remember any of their names?"

"Some I can recall. One was called Tolstoy, another Augustine. There were men named Dante and Aquinas and Milton and . . . oh, yes . . . a lovely young woman by the name of Joan. Many, like yourself, came from lands beyond the sea."

Leaning toward the big man I hugged him and said, "Peace be with you, Shobi."

He returned my embrace, saying, "And peace be with you for all your days, Matthias."

fourteen

ALL NIGHT I PACED the floor of my room, reviewing in my mind every fact I had brought to light in my four days of investigation. To no avail.

Conclusion: case closed.

John's testimony yesterday, followed by Mark's convincing story, had brought me to the brink of admitting, to Joseph as well as myself, that I had been wrong. No one had removed the body of Jesus. There had been no hoax perpetrated on the people by the followers of Jesus. Shobi's climactic account had pushed me over the edge. I had failed to prove my case. I had, instead, proved that I had no case from the beginning!

But there was far more exhilaration than regret in my defeat, if it could be called that. For now I could do what no human had ever done before, describe in my writings exactly what had happened during those last days in the life of Jesus, using authentic eyewitnesses as my sources. And for those whose eroding faith constantly needed reinforcement I could even reaffirm the miracle of the resurrection! That few might believe me, especially after my declarations on the Carson show, never entered my mind. All I could think about was getting back to my typewriter and tackling the manuscript of "The Christ Commission" once more—this time with no doubts clouding my mind.

Still, there was something bothering me. I couldn't put my finger on it. What had I forgotten? The puzzle was nearly complete and the picture was plain to see, but a missing piece still marred the finished portrait. Who held it and where could I find it? I tried to concentrate even harder but the mind rebelled. Already overloaded, it had shut down.

After breakfast, I fell back on my cot and apparently dozed off, I don't know for how long, before the sound of loud knocking awoke me. Joseph was at the door, looking weary and haggard, his skin the color of ashes. It was obvious that the pace and strain of our last few days had caught up with him as they had with me. Even so, the old man made a valiant effort at joviality.

"And how does the great investigator feel this morning?"

I groaned and returned to the cot, where he sat beside me. "As if I had a terrible hangover."

"A hangover?" He frowned, shaking his head helplessly.

I tried to explain. "A hangover is a most repulsive and disabling condition, of both mind and body, in which one awakes after imbibing far too much wine during the previous night. It is a state of stupor for which there is no cure until the body has cleansed itself of the grape's numbing chemicals."

"You are familiar with this affliction through firsthand experience?" he asked solicitously.

"Oh, yes," I admitted. "There was a time in my life, many years ago, when it was almost a daily occurrence."

"No more?"

"No more," I said positively.

"What made you stop inflicting such terrible punishment on yourself?"

"One morning I regained consciousness in jail, remembering nothing of the hours that had preceded my imprisonment. I could have been accused of murder, or any other crime imaginable, and not been able to deny it or prove that I had not been involved. Fortunately for me, I had only been arrested for drunkenness, but the experience frightened me so much that I never forgot it."

He nodded understandingly. "So many of us must first fall into the darkest wells of despair before we learn to appreciate the sight of a single star. Were you writing your fine books during that time, Matthias?"

"I was writing but I was unable to interest anyone in my work. Failure and frustration are easily drowned, at least temporarily, with a few bottles of cheap wine."

"Did you ever pray for help during those sad times?"

"Never. I despised myself so much, for wasting my life and talent, that I felt I deserved no help. And if there was a God, which I did not believe, I was certain that my miserable cries would never be heard."

"You had forgotten those things you must have learned from your mother when she read to you at night—that not even a sparrow can fall to the ground without God's notice and that even the very hairs on your head are all numbered by him, as Jesus told us. What was it that finally changed your life for the better so that you were able to apply your

231

talents to earn worldwide renown? That must have taken more than merely sitting in a jail with self-pity and fear as your cell mates?"

"Three human beings changed my life, Joseph: the wonderful woman I married and the two handsome sons she gave me. Soon after she presented me with my second son, since I was still drinking heavily, she gave me a choice. I could have the bottles or my family, but not both. I quit drinking."

"Ah, ha!" he exclaimed. "Then it was love that changed your life! And with it you found God."

"I didn't say that, Joseph."

"But you did, Matthias, you did! When you discovered how much you truly loved your wife and sons, you found God. God is love! If we love one another, then God dwells within us. You cannot have one without the other. And when we know love we have also found the Kingdom that so many, who do not understand this simple secret, will never find. The Kingdom of God, Matthias, is not on a cloud. It is within you. That is what Jesus told the people, time and again."

"And they killed him for his efforts," I said cynically.

"Son," the old man said softly, "I did not come here this morning to preach to you. Your eyes have already been opened, I know. What you must learn to accept is that Jesus was murdered because he even loved those who would kill him and they hated him because he loved them. They could not comprehend his love, for it flew against all reason in a world that demands payment for all goods and services, and punishment for all crimes, leaving no room for charity or mercy or compassion. Sooner or later all mankind will realize that the greatest cure for all the ills and wrongs, the cares, the sorrows and crimes of humanity rests solely in acts of love. Love is the greatest gift from God. It is the divine spark that everywhere produces and restores life. To each and every one of us, love gives us the power, as it did to you, Matthias, to work miracles with your own life and those we touch."

Joseph stood and limped slowly toward the door, turning with his hand on the latch to ask, "Have you any plans for us, anyone else you would like to visit?"

"I'm afraid not."

"Good. Perhaps you should rest today, in preparation for your return journey. I too am weary."

"Is this your Sabbath?"

"No. Tomorrow is our Sabbath. Later today I must leave you for a short while in order to attend to some business in

232

my warehouse. Still, I can not allow you to depart from this house without first showing you those things of Jesus that I have managed to acquire. Yesterday, before you had spoken with Shobi, I told you, in response to your question, that I had doubts that your seeing my collection would help you to understand the truth. But now . . ."

Arriving in the lower wing of Joseph's palace, his cultural center, we had passed the studio of Hermogenes, the sculptor, and the three rooms filled with shelves of scrolls before we were standing in front of the only closed door in the area. Joseph fumbled in his tunic, removed a large silver key, and turned it in the lock. The door's hinges creaked noisily as he pushed it open and stood aside for me to enter.

"Kindly take no notice of the dust, Matthias," the old man apologized. "I allow none of my servants to clean in here, and I myself am a very careless housekeeper."

Compared to the other rooms in the palace it was little more than a storage place. Three long tables, standing parallel to one another, occupied most of the limited floor space, surrounded by stark whitewashed walls with two high windows along one side and a wide bronze door on the other. Dark green cloths covered the tables. I followed Joseph to the one nearest the wall. Without any preliminary remarks he pulled the green material down far enough for me to see his first exhibit.

"Pick it up, Matthias."

Even the sight of it repelled me. Joseph didn't need to identify the thing as a *flagra*, the Roman instrument used for scourging. I stared down at the ugly, long-handled object to which were attached a dozen or more small chains with curved rusty nails fixed to their outermost links. We have always been most ingenious in devising means for inflicting punishment on one another.

"Pick it up, Matthias," Joseph repeated.

I reached down hesitantly and took the rough wooden handle in my hand. After hefting it once or twice I stepped back and swung it through the air, watching the chains fan out with a swishing sound as each nail circled wildly within its own vicious trajectory. Punishment? This was an instrument of death! Joseph, once more, read my mind.

"Those trained in the use of that vile weapon," he explained, "can remove nearly all the skin from your body and yet still keep you alive for execution on the cross. Try to imagine being tied to a post, Matthias, before a jeering crowd, your naked body extended to the rear with your feet wide apart. Then imagine the chains and the nails smashing against your back and your ribs, each one tearing into your flesh to the bones, with every stroke delivered by men of great strength. Think of those nails tearing away at your private parts, at your eyes, your face, your chest. Try to conceive of a pain so terrible that you pray for death or unconsciousness, but just before you are overcome, cold water is thrown against your body and you are revived enough to feel the next blow and the next. There have been many, Matthias, who have bitten their tongues in two under the expert flogging of a Roman lictor! Imagine, if you can, anyone receiving so many horrible blows from that thing that his body was covered by his own blood while he stood in a pool of it and yet not cry out for mercy, as I have been told that Jesus did not."

I shuddered and dropped the *flagra* onto the table.

"Two of those were used on Jesus. The other, with leather thongs and weights, I was not able to secure."

He pulled the green cloth farther down the table, unveiling a crown of thorns. After I finally caught my breath, I asked nervously, "May I hold it, Joseph?"

"Of course, but be careful of your hands. It, too, is a terrible instrument. Jesus was crucified wearing that abomination, made by the soldiers from their kindling pieces. I removed it from his head myself, with great difficulty. Many of the plant's sharp spikes had become embedded in his forehead and above his ears."

Two strands of wood, each no more than a quarter of an inch thick, were wound around each other to form an imperfect circle with a diameter of approximately nine inches. Radiating from the gray stems, not more than half an inch from one another, were thin, needlelike thorns at least three quarters of an inch long. Their sharp points bit into my flesh as I raised the crown to my eyes with unsteady hands.

"You can still see the blood, Matthias, although it grows darker with the passing years. After the crown was placed on the head of Jesus, the thorns were driven deep into his flesh with this club."

He waited until I placed the crown on the table before handing me a heavy rod, approximately three feet in length.

"With that reed, the soldiers hit Jesus about the head, time after time, forcing the thorns down beneath the skin. Then they placed it in his hand, as if it were a royal scepter, and hung this cape on his shoulders."

He handed me a purple piece of finely woven cloth, perhaps silk, with braided twine at one end. "After they draped this on his body, they mocked him and spun him around, spitting in his face, kicking him, taunting him, and calling him the King of the Jews. When they tired of their sport they returned him to Pilate, who brought him, scourged and humiliated, once more before the people."

" 'Behold the man!' " I said, quoting Pilate.

"Yes," Joseph repeated softly, " 'Behold the man!' "

There were only two items on the second table. One was the roughly cut, unfinished pine board that had been nailed over the head of Jesus on the cross, crudely lettered in three languages, Latin, Greek, and Aramaic, "Jesus of Nazareth, the King of the Jews."

"That sign, according to Roman procedure, was carried by a soldier walking ahead of the convicted one on the way to Golgotha, so that everyone would know his crime. Pilate's words, words that he refused to change at the high priest's request, were his way of insulting the Jewish authorities. As you can see," Joseph said, holding up two pieces, "it was broken by Shem when he removed it from the cross."

I jumped back, pointing.

"What is the matter, Matthias?"

"Have you ever paid attention to how the wood broke, Joseph?"

He turned the two pieces and tears came to his eyes. The sign had separated down the center. The Latin on one piece read "Jesus," and under it was only one word: "Rex"—King!

We moved to the other exhibit on the table, a faded red woolen robe. Joseph placed it in my arms. "This is called an *abayeh*. Its type has been worn by shepherds here for hundreds of years. As you can see, it is seamless except at the shoulders. The mother of Jesus told me that he had this one in his possession even before he reached full manhood. All of us can remember him with this about his shoulders, walking in the streets and the Temple courtyard. I offered to purchase a new one for him once, saying that a man of his stature should be dressed in keeping with his position."

"What did he say?"

"He just laughed and told me that man should not be judged by what is outside the skin but what is inside, and he told me to take the money I would have spent on a new robe and give it to the poor."

I lifted the soft cloth and rubbed it against my cheek until I felt something hard and crusty. Along one side were several dark smears, brittle to the touch.

235

"More of his blood," the old man said.

We moved to the third table. Under the green cloth was a linen napkin and a large narrow sheet, folded over many times.

"This is the long piece of linen which we wrapped around his body, and this is the cloth that was placed over his face according to our custom. Shem retrieved them both for me, from the tomb, the day after it was found empty."

I nodded and Joseph replaced the green covering. Then he turned and clasped both my shoulders tightly. "You have just seen the entire material estate of one man, Matthias. He left behind no gold, no silver, no land, no wife, no children, no manuscripts, no works of art, and no position of authority or title. Furthermore, he was not even among us for very long. Most great men whose words or actions have changed the course of our world have required six or seven decades or more in order to accomplish their purpose. And even their deeds, so great at the time, soon fade from our memory. This man died while still in his thirties, and yet nothing he has done or said has ever diminished even a little."

He stared at me for several minutes, as if he were trying to make up his mind whether or not to continue. Finally he said, "One thing has puzzled me about your investigation, my son. Why is it that not once did you ask any of those you interrogated to describe the appearance of Jesus? Is that of no interest to you? True, it would not have brought you any closer to the facts regarding the empty tomb, but I would think that if you had spent so many years studying the life of a man you would have developed some curiosity about how he looked."

"I never thought about it, Joseph," I replied. "Since my youth, I have probably seen thousands of paintings and drawings and sculptures of him, as have most people, and I guess I just assumed that I knew."

Somehow I sensed he was toying with me. He had that now familiar twinkle in his old eyes. "But isn't it a mistake, Matthias, for anyone conducting an investigation to assume anything? Certainly, your famous detective creations would never solve their mysteries, in your books, if you allowed them to assume very much. Am I correct?"

I nodded, not knowing what to expect. Not even daring to guess! The old man reached into the folds of his tunic and removed another key, smiling broadly as he turned and walked toward the bronze door on the room's near side. He turned the key but waited until I was at his side before he pulled the door wide open. Inside what was no more than a closet, illuminated by a glass overhead window, was the statue of a man, life-size—in marble.

"Matthias, in my opinion this is the greatest work of my sculptor, Hermogenes."

"Jesus?" I cried out.

He nodded calmly. "It was done without my knowledge. Hermogenes would go of his own accord to hear Jesus in the Temple courtyard, and when he returned to his studio here he would make drawings from memory. Working from those drawings, in secret, he created what you see—a perfect likeness of our Lord."

The sandal-shod feet of the marble figure stood firmly on the floor, with no pedestal of any sort beneath them, so that when I moved closer I was face to face with probably the only portrayal that had ever been made of Jesus from life. Hermogenes had, indeed, done a masterful job. Even in the monochrome of white marble, the figure looked as if it might move and talk at any moment because of the diffused sunlight from overhead. I studied every feature, trying to burn them all into my memory.

The hair of Jesus was parted in the middle, flowing loosely down his back but pushed away from his face so that his earlobes were discernible. His forehead was wide, above full eyebrows and deeply set eyes. The nose was long with only a slight bend and the mouth was full. Both his mustache and beard were trimmed, if not too carefully, and his high cheekbones sloped down to a pointed chin. His height, if Hermogenes had been accurate in his scale, was the same as mine, approximately six feet—tall for a Jew of that time. More than any other likeness I could recall, he looked like the Jesus in an oil by Ralph Pallett Coleman. I had once admired a large copy of Coleman's work hanging in the chaplain's office at Scottsdale Memorial Hospital, and Arthur Howard had been kind enough to send me a smaller reproduction for my studio.

"What color was his hair, Joseph?"

"Brown—more a dark walnut, perhaps. His eyes also—and his skin, because of his days spent in the sun."

"His voice?"

"Not deep, more a medium range, and always soft. Even when he spoke in anger the words did not offend one's ears."

I stepped back, still trying to photograph that face through the lenses of my eyes. In the upper half of his face especially, I could see the resemblance to his brother, James. James?

237

Suddenly I remembered who held the missing piece to my puzzle. Turning to Joseph I almost shouted, "I must see James again!"

"Why?" the old man asked, his voice filled with concern.

"Don't you remember, Joseph? I asked him why, if he had refused to follow Jesus when he was alive, he was now risking his own life, every day, by preaching a philosophy that had brought death to his brother."

"Yes."

"And he refused to answer me at the time. He told me to come back and ask him that question again, after I had spoken to all the others. Well, I've spoken to all the others."

"Matthias, your time here grows very short. Remember, when you first arrived, I warned you that should something happen here, during your visit, that caused you to lose your life, I would be unable to revive you in order to return you to your own time and place."

"Yes, I remember."

"Is a visit to James worth such a risk? Are you not already convinced that you know the truth about Jesus without any further proof from anyone?"

"Joseph, don't send me back without my talking to James again, please!"

He sighed. "When do you wish to see him?"

"Today—now—the sooner the better, if, as you say, Pilate is ready to strike."

Joseph wrung his hands nervously. "I cannot go with you today, Matthias. I must soon be at my warehouse."

"Where would we find James at this hour?"

"Probably at his place of business. He has a stall in the market, where he builds and repairs furniture, wagons, and farm tools. In the afternoons he is always in the Temple."

"Is your warehouse near his stall in the market?"

"Beyond."

"Well, why not drop me in the market where James is located and then go to your warehouse. Allow me an hour with James and then send Shem for me. Please!"

"It can be very dangerous, my son."

"Don't worry. I can take care of myself. And it will only take an hour."

"Is it truly that important to you, Matthias?"

"Joseph, it means everything to me, especially after talking with John and Mark and Shobi yesterday. Through all my years of research for the book, I always wondered what it

238

was that made James change his mind about Jesus after the crucifixion. Twenty years, old friend."

"Most people spend a lifetime wondering."

"I know, but most people don't get the opportunity you gave me. He'll be my final interview, I promise you."

I had my way.

Despite Joseph's concern for my safety, he could not resist assuming his role as guide when we entered the squalor of the lower city, which inexplicably included the most ambitious and varied marketplace in the entire civilized world. No pilgrimage by the faithful to the Holy City was considered complete without a visit to the great market. On loosely cobbled streets, barely wide enough for our carriage to pass, Joseph, time and again, would command Shem to halt while he pointed out colorful sites and even more colorful strangers from distant lands. Jews from Babylon lifted their long velvet robes to avoid animal droppings while they jostled against their Persian brethren liveried in silk brocade. Worshipers from Anatolia wrapped their goat's-hair tunics close to their bodies to avoid the clutching hands of shrill vendors or the stumbling bodies of Galilean peasants who had eyes only for the gaudiest of merchandise, of which there was no shortage. I watched as a pair of Roman soldiers, probably Syrian auxiliaries, Joseph said, passed silently through the milling pre-Sabbath shoppers, their shining helmets and colored capes most prominent in the shifting maze of costumes. Visitors and natives alike looked the other way.

The market had something for everybody. Open stalls and booths, some so small that even the merchant stood outside, catered to any need or desire. One could have sandals repaired or a cloak mended or a tunic dyed or purchase a bracelet of the finest silver or a necklace of the basest metals or even exchange gold for an equal weight of silk. Rugs were woven before one's eyes by skilled artisans, while the next stall might display gross statues of Greek and Roman gods. Everywhere the din of raucous haggling could be heard as the headiest of perfumes and salves and fruits and oils and even livestock changed ownership.

Beggars, crippled, diseased, and even sightless, confronted every shopper. Only the menacing sight of Shem, sitting high in his seat with his whip in his hand, kept us from being overwhelmed by the mob. Meat and cheese, stacked on flimsy tables, collected swirling dust and sand as we rode by. Restaurants, Joseph pointed out, abounded on every street, serving a wide variety of lamb's meat and venison, partridge, quail, geese, yogurt, lentils, peas, lettuce, coarse bread, fresh fish, fruitcake, and fried locusts, with a wide choice of wines from Cyprus and Samaria and Canaan and also Egyptian beer. There were even prostitutes for the lonely traveler or soldier, all colors and all races, stalking back and forth in front of their stalls, whispering sweet words of seduction and promise to the wandering and wide-eyed pilgrims.

The sounds of the marketplace must have been deafening, if not terrifying, to rural visitors accustomed to the calm pastoral life of rustic villages. Accompanying the singsong clamor of bold merchants were the rhythmic poundings of craftsmen's mallets and hammers as they shaped wood, copper, leather, and silver. Sheep and cattle cried in braying choruses of fear as they were led under the whips and clubs of their new owners, hooves clattering and slipping on stone and wood. Holy criers, in sonorous tones, announced special messages from the high priest almost hourly, children screamed, pimps argued and bargained, dogs barked, and four times a day the priestly blast of seven silver trumpets reverberated throughout the squalor, driving all people to their knees. The inhabitants of the lower city, Joseph explained, were not only subjects of Rome but also prisoners of their own despair, and the pious injunctions of their priests offered them little hope of ever attaining a better life. They had almost rioted when they heard that Jesus had been crucified. He, like no other rabbi or teacher, had been accepted among them.

We found James on one of the many busy side streets, standing by his outside stall waving a hammer in one hand and gesturing furiously to a small crowd gathered around him.

"Even when he is supposed to be working at his craft," Joseph said admiringly, "he cannot forget his great mission in life." The old man turned to me and took my hands. "Be careful. Do what you must and watch for Shem. He will return for you in an hour. Go in peace. *Mizpah*."

"*Mizpah*? I know what that means."

"Tell me, son," he said, biting on his lower lip.

"The Lord watch between me and thee, when we are absent one from another."

He leaned over and kissed my forehead. "That is my prayer, Matthias."

I watched until the wagon turned left into one of the
240

crowded main streets. Suddenly I felt as insecure as any youngster who has run away from home.

"Matthias, welcome!"

I turned to see James rushing toward me, thrilled and relieved that he had recognized me. We embraced, and in his exuberance he almost carried me through the furniture-strewn lot into his small tent.

After several minutes of small talk, James asked, "What is it I can do for you? Certainly your visit here is not to see the sights, such as they are."

We were sharing the same unfinished bench. The smell of freshly cut pine filled the enclosure. "Do you recall your promise to me?" I asked.

His face clouded. "A promise—to you? No."

"You do remember that day I visited you in the Temple courtyard, in the company of Joseph of Arimathea?"

"I do. You asked many questions about Jesus, and I answered them to the best of my ability."

"You didn't answer all of them."

He started to rise. "Matthias, as you can see, I have no time for that now. Perhaps this afternoon, when I am in the courtyard—"

"James, I have only one question to ask, and I am here because you told me to come."

He settled back on the bench. "I do not understand."

"That other day, in the courtyard, you admitted to me that while your brother was alive you were filled with shame by his actions and you were certain that he was on a foolish path to destruction. I then asked you why, if that described your feelings truthfully, you were now his greatest advocate, risking your life each day in the Temple. You replied by telling me to speak to all the others, as I had planned, and then you would answer my question."

He nodded, grinning. "Now I remember. Well, have you questioned all those witnesses that you had intended to see?"

"All of them."

"And are you closer to the truth now than when you began?"

"I am, but you can still help me. If you, who did not believe, are now willing to risk the same death that Jesus suffered, then whatever you know, whatever it was that came into your life after his crucifixion, can also help me. It is one thing to see the truth through eyes that were once blind, but it is a far greater thing to understand the truth one sees."

James bowed his head until it was almost to his knees, rubbing the back of his neck furiously. I sat beside him help-lessly—hoping . . . hoping . . .

Finally he sat erect. Just as he opened his mouth to speak, a shadow fell across the floor and I heard the clanking of metal. James leaped to his feet, and so did I, but not before three legionaries were inside the small tent. One of them stepped forward, his face showing little emotion.

"Are you called Matthias?" he asked, pointing to me with his short sword.

"I am," I said hoarsely.

"Matthias, by order of the procurator, Pontius Pilate, you are hereby placed under arrest!"

fifteen

"WHO ARE YOU?"

I was once again in the quarters of Pontius Pilate. This time he poured no wine for me, nor did he invite me to sit on any of his plush couches. Pilate was in full dress uniform. Hands on leather-covered hips, he strutted back and forth in front of me, glaring—waiting.

"Who are you?" he demanded again.

"My name is Matthias. I am a historian from—"

"You lie!" he screamed. His right fist crashed against my face, his heavy gold ring tearing at the flesh just below my nose. As I pitched forward, the soldiers standing on both sides of me stepped out of the way. I was unable to break my fall, because my hands were tied behind me, and my head struck the floor. Dazed, I lay there until Pilate's studded boot slipped beneath my chin and tilted my head backward.

"Rise, imposter!" he roared. Already I could taste blood as it trickled into my mouth. I finally rolled over and managed to slide my feet far enough under me so that I could stand. My head was throbbing, and my tightly bound hands had already grown numb from lack of circulation. I was also terrified, but he was never going to know it. Silently cursing my stupidity for not following Joseph's advice, I braced my feet and waited for the next onslaught.

Now Pilate became the unctuous host. "Welcome, Matthias. I imagine you had not planned on our meeting again so soon."

"It's a small city, sir," I replied as bravely as I could through puffing lips.

"It is indeed." He chuckled. "Especially when compared with Rome."

"But the people here are more cordial, don't you think, sir?"

His fist landed again, a direct hit to my solar plexus. I doubled up in agony, gasping for air, but this time the guards expertly slid their hands under my armpits and prevented me from falling again. Head down, I watched as the blood from my mouth spattered on the tiles near my feet.

"Matthias," the procurator growled, "you have made a fool of me. I took you into my confidence, on the advice of Joseph of Arimathea, and answered all your questions openly and frankly. Now I learn that you are neither a citizen of Rome nor—"

"But I am!"

Pilate folded his arms and nodded mockingly. "Very well, show me your papers."

"They . . . they are not in my possession at this moment."

"Then tell me where you keep them and I'll send my men to retrieve them for you so that your identity can be verified. Where are your papers?"

I had no place to go with that dodge. And stalling for time by sending soldiers to Joseph's house to search my bedroom on a wild-goose chase would only get the old man in more trouble than he was probably in, already, for aiding and abetting me.

I sighed. "The papers were lost at sea, during a storm."

"Not a very convincing fabrication," Pilate sneered, "especially for an alleged historian. And did you not also assure me that you were a friend of our governor, Lucius Vitellius?"

"He is a longtime friend of mine."

His third punch landed flush against my left ear. "Liar!"

When I finally looked up, after my head stopped ringing, Pilate had been joined by another officer, also in full dress even to his cape.

"Tell me, Matthias, who is this tribune standing next to me?"

He was young and his black hair was trimmed close to his head. His nose had been broken, at least once, and his skin was as dark as Pilate's. Eyes, brown. Mouth, surly. Scars, none. Who could he be that Pilate thought I should know him if I were not an impostor? Someone from Rome? Or Antioch? From Vitellius, maybe?

In all my research on Vitellius, one man associated with him had especially intrigued me, probably because so little had been recorded about him. According to the Jewish historian Josephus, a council of Samaritans had gone to Vitellius and complained that Pilate had slain many of their people while they were gathering to conduct religious ceremonies on Mount Gerizim. Apparently this complaint, following so many others lodged against Pilate through the years, had been the final straw, because Josephus wrote that Vitellius dispatched a friend named Marcellus to relieve Pilate of his administration and to send the procurator back to Rome to account to the emperor for his misdeeds. In my unfinished book I had originally planned, before I had lost faith in the project, to make the historical Marcellus a member of my fictional Christ Commission, and I would have had him send Pilate back to Rome, at the end, not for his crime against the Samaritans but for his illegal actions against Jesus.

Was I actually face to face with the man who would have been the hero of my book, had I ever completed it? It was all so bizarre and unreal that I began to laugh despite my precarious position.

"You find this man comical, Matthias?" Pilate growled in surprise.

"No, no," I said. "To the contrary. He is one of Rome's finest soldiers and a friend of Vitellius. His name is Marcellus."

Pilate fell back as if I had struck him. He spun around and glanced at Marcellus, who shook his head in wonder. I decided to keep bluffing, even though I had a bad hand. I had nothing to lose. According to Josephus, Marcellus came to relieve Pilate in the latter part of A.D. 36 or early 37. Well, this was the latter part of A.D. 36! Was Marcellus here to assume command? Even more important, had he not broken the news to Pilate as yet? What would happen if I shook them both up?

"Pilate," I began, "you seem surprised that I should know this man's name. Do not be. I can do even more, by sharing a secret of state with you that affects your very future."

He waited, eyeing me with a combination of distrust and hate that did little for my confidence.

"I say to you, Pontius Pilate, that your days of command here are at an end! Did you not, recently, slay many Samaritans upon their arrival in the village of Tirathana before they could ascend Mount Gerizim for religious services?"

For a moment he forgot I was his prisoner. "They were gathered in that village," he whined, "not to worship their god but to mobilize a military force for rebellion against Rome!"

"My friend Vitellius does not agree with you. After being visited by a delegation of Samaritans, he has come to the conclusion that your conduct in that affair was little more than the murder of unarmed men, women, and children, and he has finally tired of your heavy-handed methods of dealing with the people here. Marcellus is in Jerusalem to relieve you of your procuratorship. He came to tell you that Vitellius has ordered your immediate return to Rome, where you are to give an account of yourself to Tiberius. Marcellus is to take command here pending the selection of a new procurator by the emperor!"

It was impossible to measure which face registered more shock. Both Pilate and Marcellus turned as pale as their skins would allow. Marcellus was the first to regain enough composure to speak.

"I can assure you, procurator, that the governor has no knowledge of this man. He is obviously a foreign agent sent here to stir up trouble. Perhaps a little time at the flogging post would encourage him to reveal his true identity and purpose."

Apparently Marcellus was not yet ready to relieve Pilate of his command. Perhaps the instructions from Vitellius had been that he conduct a thorough investigation into the incident near Mount Gerizim before he made his move. In any event, my ploy hadn't worked. The enemy had been divided—but not long enough for me to claim any victories. Despite the tribune's noncommittal response, color began to seep back into Pilate's face and his shoulders straightened. He marched toward me, eyes narrowed. I braced myself for the next blow.

"Are you just another believer in that dead rebel, Jesus, who was crucified?" he asked. "Is that why you asked so many questions concerning him?"

No one had to remind me that I was face to face with the supreme law of the land. If Pontius Pilate decided that I should be nailed on a cross, this very day, I would be crucified.

"No. I am only a historian, from Rome."

I suddenly remembered Peter and his three denials of Jesus in the high priest's courtyard. Self-preservation is an instinct that can turn nearly all of us into cowards.

"Does Joseph of Arimathea know your real identity?"

"Joseph is an old friend. He knows my only identity. I am Matthias."

Pilate raised his fist and I instinctively twisted my head to avoid the blow. There was none. Instead, I felt his hand sliding inside my tunic until he had my heavy gold amulet in his hand. A sly smile quickly blossomed into a victorious grin as Pilate turned the pendant over and over, gesturing with his head for Marcellus to come forward.

"See the fish, tribune! It is their sign, those miserable Christians. Now we know what he is."

Marcellus nodded. He too seemed pleased—and relieved. "After all the trouble he has caused you, sir, I would recommend that he be scourged until dead. These people will learn, eventually, that Rome intends to maintain the peace here no matter how many of them must pay with their lives."

Pilate tossed the amulet up and down in his hand, staring pensively at the ceiling. Then he carefully replaced it inside my tunic and patted it through the cloth.

"No, Marcellus, I have a better plan for this one. Tomorrow is the Jewish Sabbath, and on that day, because the city is quiet, we lock the gates of this fortress and enjoy a few games on the pavement below. It has been some time now since my men have been amused by any competition in the Circle of Death, and our expert in that contest, Porcius, only today was complaining that he is losing his skill for lack of adversaries bold enough to challenge him. Tomorrow he will have one."

When Pilate waved me away, I was marched across the parade grounds to the east wing of the fortress and thrown into a cell with James, who had been taken into custody with me. After taking one look at my face he made me lie down on the only mattress while he hurriedly ripped pieces from his tunic, soaked them with water from a small pitcher, and washed the blood from my face and neck. Then I had to tell him all that had taken place with Pilate.

With his calloused hand he began to stroke my forehead. "Matthias, do you know what the Circle of Death is?"

"When I first interviewed Pilate I vaguely remember his mentioning that it was a game played only by his more courageous soldiers. Why? What is it?"

"Do you recall seeing two wooden posts set into the pavement, perhaps thirty paces apart from each other?"

"Yes. Pilate showed them to me. He said that Jesus had been scourged on one of them."

"He was. In the Circle of Death contest according to what I have heard, two men are involved, each one chained to a post by an ankle. Each gladiator's chain is long enough to enable him to move from one side of the post to the other—a distance not greater than six paces. He can also, if he wishes, move around the post in a circle, thus giving the game part of its name."

Now I was up on one elbow. "And then what?"

"Each contestant is given ten javelins which are placed

within his own circle. At a signal, usually from Pilate, the two are allowed to pick up the javelins and begin hurling them at one another. Of course, since the chains allow some freedom of movement, they can move around and try to escape each other's throws."

James, bless him, was trying to make it all sound as casual as a walk in the country. "What happens," I asked, "when one has thrown his allotment of ten spears?"

There was a long pause. "If . . . the contestant is still alive, he is allowed to retrieve any spears thrown by his adversary that have landed within his reach, considering the length of the chain. However, from all I have heard, the duels rarely last through the hurling of ten javelins by both opponents."

"Why is that?"

"Because usually one of the two competitors is the same man, a famous legionary who is reputed to have killed more than three hundred opponents in that game since he arrived here at Antonia five years ago. With a javelin his throws are said to be so accurate that he can hit a sparrow from fifty paces, and he is so strong that his flings have killed a horse at that same distance."

"Do you know this soldier's name, by chance?"

"Yes. He is called Porcius."

Later in the afternoon we had a surprise visitor. Since our cell was no more than a room with a wooden door, bolted on the outside, we didn't hear him approaching until he knocked and called out my name softly.

"Matthias . . . Matthias, can you hear me?"

"Yes. Who is it?"

"Cornelius. Remember when we spoke after you had visited Pilate?"

"I'll never forget, centurion."

"I cannot stay, but I wanted to tell you that I shall try to get word to Joseph as soon as I am able."

"Thank you, but I'm afraid Joseph can't help me now."

"Never lose faith, Matthias. Pray. Pray with James."

"Believe me, Cornelius, I shall."

"One more thing. In your contest tomorrow, if you only release one spear at a time and then rest before you throw the next, you will have no chance against Porcius. What you must do is to hurl one, then a second, and then a third, as swiftly as you can. In that manner, there is far greater chance that while he is trying to dodge the first, one of the others may strike him. And be careful. He will try the same tactic on you."

"Thank you, Cornelius."

"God be with you, Matthias."

I kept my ear against the door, listening to his footsteps as they faded down the corridor.

"Matthias," James asked a little later, "have you any experience in throwing the javelin? I understand that most Roman youths have them as playthings."

"I have never thrown a javelin in my life," I admitted, gradually beginning to realize that tomorrow morning I was going to die and neither Kitty nor my sons nor anyone else would ever know what had happened to me. Then I suddenly remembered why I was in such a predicament. "I am so sorry I got you involved in this, James. It was nothing but selfishness on my part. Joseph had warned me of the risks, but I just had to talk with you again."

He pulled me close to him, stroking the back of my head to comfort me. "Do not concern yourself with me, Matthias. I have been here before. In a day or two, Pilate will give me another taste of the whip and then release me, always with the threat that someday he will hang me on a tree, just as he did my brother. Now, what was it that you came to the market to ask me? In all this confusion I'm afraid we both almost forgot that you visited me with a purpose."

We sat next to each other on the foul-smelling mattress. I struggled to put Porcius and his favorite sport out of my mind. Despite all the testimony I had heard from the others, even Shobi, I had to understand clearly what had changed this man, in particular, from a disbeliever while Jesus lived to one of his most ardent worshipers after the crucifixion. So ... I tested him.

"James, where have they hidden the body of Jesus?"

"Matthias, why do you ask such a question? If you have completed your investigation and done it thoroughly, you have already come to the conclusion that *no one* could have removed the body of Jesus from Joseph's tomb. For me, such an investigation was never necessary, even though, before his death, my own doubts were far greater than yours."

"Are you saying that faith alone became enough for you—blind faith?" I asked. "That would never suffice for me!"

James shifted his position so that he was looking directly into my eyes. "No. Faith alone would never have been enough for me either. To leave a comfortable, peaceful life

249

and a loving family behind in Nazareth, as I did, in exchange for the abuse, humiliation, aggravations, hard floors, crusts of bread—and, yes, even prison cells—which I now endure, requires far more than faith. Remember, Jesus was my brother. Together we played and raced and fought and worked and grew in each other's shadows. For many years we slept in the same cot. He told the truth, of course, when he said that for a prophet to find honor in his own house is difficult, if not impossible. Even Pilate's orderlies, I am certain, laugh behind his back when they bathe the powerful ruler. Familiarity breeds many things, but rarely respect and never adulation. No, Matthias, faith alone would never have changed me into what I am today."

All my imminent danger was temporarily forgotten. So far as my mind and heart were concerned, at that moment, we might just as well have been having our discussion in the crowded Temple courtyard or the greenery of Gethsemane or the small tent in the marketplace instead of in a makeshift dungeon in Antonia.

"If not faith, James . . . what was it?"

He hesitated. "If you should survive tomorrow's contest, do you intend to include what I tell you in your writings?"

"Yes, of course."

He shook his head pityingly. "If you do, they will laugh at you and scorn you."

"I've been laughed at—and scorned—before."

"Very well. Because of my younger son's illness, our family had not gone up to Jerusalem for that Passover when Jesus was crucified. We knew nothing of what had happened until our neighbor, Rehum, returned from the city with the terrible news. He also told us of the rumor that was spreading through the city, as swiftly as rumors always fly, that the tomb of Jesus had been discovered empty on the third day after his crucifixion and some were saying that his body had been stolen by his disciples."

"How did you feel when you heard about the crucifixion?"

"I was filled with a remorse so strong that I became sick. I wept for many hours—tears of guilt and shame and self-hatred for how I had treated Jesus during his last year when he was trying so hard to convince all of us that the Kingdom of God was very near. I could not eat. Everything that passed my mouth tasted like salt—"

The sound of trumpets from the adjoining Temple interrupted James. He cupped his hands over his ears to block out the sound.

"What did you do next?" I asked, as soon as the brassy notes subsided.

He cleared his throat and continued. "I tried to lose myself in my work, but that was to no avail. Even the smallest of hammers would fall from my trembling fingers. On the first night after we heard the news, I slept on the floor of the shop, not wishing to inflict my sorry condition on my wife, who was distraught enough between tending to our son and mourning her brother-in-law. The following day was no better. I tried to eat but it was hopeless. That night, once again, I slept in the shop until I was awakened by a voice calling my name. I knew that voice! Was I dreaming? Again it called to me. Now I was stricken for fear. I rose and stumbled about in the dark until I found a small oil lamp and lit it. Jesus was standing just inside the door. My brother! He was wearing nothing except a long shirt of bleached wool, and when he raised his hands to calm my terror I could see the ugly wounds on both his wrists. He came toward me, slowly, and I also saw the wounds on his feet. Then he stopped before I could reach out and embrace him and he said, 'Bring a table and bread.' "

"What did you do?"

"I ran to the house for a loaf of bread. When I returned he was still standing in the same place. I moved a small worktable from one corner to the center of the room and placed the bread on it. Jesus took the bread and blessed it. Then he broke it in two and handed me half, saying, 'My brother, eat your bread, for the Son of man is risen from among them that sleep.' Before I took my first bite I rose from the table and went to a nearby shelf on which I always kept a bottle of wine. When I turned . . . he was gone! Only the two pieces of bread remained as proof that he had been with me. But they were enough, for I knew I had seen and spoken with Jesus, who they had said was dead. So you see, Matthias, I need no further proof that his body was not stolen, nor am I in the Temple each day, exposing myself to ridicule and persecution, on faith alone. Jesus supplied me with all the proof I needed. Look! Look!"

He reached into the carpenter's apron he had been wearing when arrested. From it he removed two objects wrapped in soft linen and placed them both in my lap.

"Open them!" he commanded.

I unraveled both cloths. In my hands were two rock-hard blackened pieces of what had once been halves of a small

251

bread loaf, invaluable relics testifying to a biblical source that had always mystified and challenged me.

There are scattered records of an old gospel, supposedly written in Aramaic, perhaps before any of the others, called the Gospel of the Hebrews. Only a few fragments have been preserved. One of them had been read by me so many times, in my early years of struggling with "The Christ Commission," that I had memorized it:

Now the Lord, when he had given the linen cloth unto the servant of the priest, went unto James and appeared to him (for James had sworn that he would not eat bread from that hour wherein he had drunk the Lord's cup until he should see him rising again from among them that sleep).

Servant of the priest who had received the linen cloth from Jesus? Shobi—as he had told me, himself, only yesterday!

Appeared to James? I had just heard it from his own lips!

I tried to recall the end of that gospel fragment:

He took bread and blessed and broke and gave it unto James the Just and said unto him: My brother, eat thy bread, for the Son of man is risen from them that sleep.

Without knowing how I got there, I found myself on my knees, not on the mattress but on the stone floor. "James," I sobbed, "I have not prayed since I was a little boy. Will you help me with the words?"

"You?" he asked in dismay. "How can that be? What manner of prayer is it, from your youth, whose words you cannot recall?"

"The Lord's Prayer," I replied and instantly realized my blunder. Based on the life calendar of James, the Lord's Prayer, taught by Jesus to his apostles, had only existed for seven years or so, and therefore I could not possibly have known the words when I was a little boy!

"Who are you, Matthias?" he whispered softly.

I reached inside my tunic and held the gold amulet so that he could see the fish and the inscription and the anchor of hope. "I am no one of importance, James. Just a follower . . . like all the others."

He clasped his hands together and bowed his head. "Our Father, which art in heaven . . ."

And I repeated after him, "Our Father, which art in heaven. . . ."

sixteen

THERE IS NOTHING more difficult than to walk to one's own death. Only a few hundred legionaries were gathered on the western half of Antonia's parade grounds, laughing and shouting obscenities at me, when I was led stumbling from our cell on the following morning and marched across the dew-covered pavement.

As my ankle was being shackled to the chain attached to the post nearer the gate, the same one on which Pilate had said Jesus was scourged, I heard the procurator's unmistakable voice. He was on his balcony, half reclining on a white couch, flanked by Marcellus and Cornelius.

"Matthias?"

The balcony was ten feet or so above the ground and only twenty yards away. My first reaction was to ignore his call, but there wasn't very much stubborn bravado left in me after a sleepless night filled with self-pity and despair. They say that those who are drowning have their entire lives flash before them immediately before their death. I would have preferred it that way instead of the torturous hours I had spent dwelling on all the things I should have done and could have done with my life. I was afraid to die. I didn't want to die! Was it Twain who had written that each person is born to one possession which outvalues all the others—his last breath?

"Matthias, can you hear me?" Pilate shouted once more.

I nodded in his direction.

"Tell me who you are and what you are doing here, and you will be punished and set free. Otherwise your blood will fall on the same stones that were red with the blood of your friend Jesus, and you will die on the spot where he was scourged!"

I walked toward the balcony, as far as my chain would allow, and yelled, "But if I win this contest, will I not be released? Under the laws of Tiberius, even slaves who fight in our Coliseum are freed when they are victorious."

The sound of Pilate's high-pitched cackle was drowned by loud guffaws from those legionaries standing close enough to hear our exchange. When the merriment subsided, Pilate rose and extended both palms in my direction. "We violate no laws of the emperor here, troublemaker! If you are victorious, you have my permission to walk out that gate behind you, and you may take your rabble-rousing friend with you."

More laughter, suddenly interrupted by cheering from the opposite side of the parade grounds: Porcius had arrived, waving his arms and flexing his biceps for his comrades as he strutted confidently across the yard to his post and raised his fist in salute to his commanding officer.

The javelin sharpshooter never glanced in my direction as he stood, feet wide apart, and waited impatiently for the chain to be fastened to his ankle. Above his boots, laced with heavy leather straps to his knees, he wore only a loincloth and he seemed to be as large as Shem, God help me. Both his hair and his beard were long and unkempt, and when he smiled at one of the guards who had shouted down from atop the fortress wall, I could see, even from our distance apart, that he was almost toothless.

When the guards finished with Porcius, two more marched across from my right, each carrying an armful of javelins which they dropped at the base of both posts. Porcius picked one up and hefted it. So did I, after counting the weapons in my pile. Ten. Each was more than seven feet in length, with five feet of wooden shaft attached to a sharply pointed iron head two feet long. Heavy! Fifteen pounds, at least. I wasn't sure I could even throw one of them a distance of thirty paces.

Stooping down, I tightened the laces on my sandals as much as I could with trembling hands. I tried to remember what Cornelius had told me and lifted two spears in my left hand while holding a third in my throwing hand. I wiggled my left foot to make sure that the chain was free. Tripping could be disastrous. Pilate was now standing against the rail of his balcony, both hands raised in the air.

"You will commence as soon as I clap my hands together ... and may the bravest be victorious! Long live Tiberius!"

There was a unified roar from all sides, followed by silence. The wooden shaft now felt moist in the palm of my hand. I stepped back from the post as far as my chain would allow and tried to brace my right foot against a raised pavement stone. Porcius, unlike me, had taken up only one spear. Also, unlike me, he seemed perfectly relaxed, with a patronizing smile on his hairy face. A small whirlpool of dust momentarily came between us and I turned my head to keep from being blinded. As I did, I heard Pilate's hands coming together. I dived on my stomach—to the left. Just in time! The first spear from Porcius went by before I even saw it and continued in its low trajectory for many yards before it landed on the stones and danced noisily along their surface. Rising to one knee, I watched as Porcius casually turned his back and ambled slowly toward his pile of javelins. I jumped to my feet quickly and threw my first spear, then the second, and finally the third, each as fast as I could release them. They all landed short, accompanied by more laughter from the sidelines. I grabbed two more spears in my left hand and another in my right, watching Porcius as I did. Once more he selected a single spear from his pile.

"Finish him, soldier!" someone shouted, just before the big man let fly with a loud grunt. Again I dived to my left. Again, I guessed correctly. My first wrong guess would be the last. Porcius did not seem at all disturbed by his near misses. He grinned toward the balcony and knelt beside his remaining spears.

While he was still down, apparently unconcerned about my marksmanship, I hurled my next three, taking more time between each of the throws. The first went far to his right, and the other two were short. No velocity behind my tosses. And the two that landed in front of Porcius rolled, on their sides, close enough for him to reach them, giving him additional weaponry. He kicked both aside disdainfully and held up two spears for all to see. I took one from the pile, leaving three still on the pavement.

Porcius walked behind his post and held up the javelins again, but this time they were both in his right hand. He turned his back, spun completely around once, and let both spears fly. I could see them coming, their points glinting in the early sun and separating from each other as they came nearer. Turning, I slipped on the wet stone and fell backward. Lucky! Both spears swished directly over me, their carved wooden shafts sounding like a horde of bumblebees. Porcius had almost scored a double hit! I jumped up and flung my javelin, determined not to be short again. I wasn't. It arched directly over his head just as a stabbing pain along my right side made me think my arm had gone with it. Something had snapped in my shoulder! I had no feeling in my arm, my hand, or my fingers. If Porcius even suspected anything was wrong he'd cut me to pieces, a little at a time. I reached for two spears only seconds before there was a loud crunch of splitting wood. The heavy tip of his next spear had embedded itself into the post, only a foot from my head!

My mouth was so dry that my tongue felt as large as a cucumber. Sweat streaming down my face made it difficult to see. I was terrified and I was mad and mostly I was frustrated. It was hopeless and I knew it. There was no way out. I would be dead in the next few minutes.

With my two spears I tried to bracket him. I aimed to his left with the first and to his right with the second. A thousand long needles jabbed into my shoulder with each throw. My opponent didn't even have to move to avoid either toss. Now, he began taunting me. He leaned against the post with one elbow as if he were just passing the time of day. Without even a spear in his hand! The soldiers loved it.

Pilate, also, was obviously enjoying the match. I could hear his laughter above all the others. "Matthias," he screamed, "now we *know* you are not a Roman. No Roman has ever disgraced himself with the javelin as you are doing. You are a dishonor even to the miserable Christians you love, and now you will die for your Jesus!"

I scooped up my last three spears, and when I did, so did Porcius for the first time. The soldiers cheered, sensing that the end was near.

I gritted my teeth and let one fly. Short, but closer. I moved back, ran forward for all the momentum I could get, and threw again. The wooden shaft slipped from my sweaty palm and spun end over end in the air, landing on its metal tip halfway between myself and Porcius before it toppled over. Pilate's laugher filled my ears. Out of the corner of my eye I could see him holding his sides, his white head bobbing up and down on the couch. I turned in his direction, planted my feet firmly, and let my last spear fly at the balcony!

It was my best throw of the day, the heavy point burying itself in a beam no more than a yard above Pilate's startled face. The parade grounds grew deathly still, but the procurator quickly recovered and jumped to his feet.

"Kill him, kill him, kill him!" he screamed, pointing to Porcius and then to me.

Porcius raised his three spears. He exhaled deeply and threw, first one, then another, and finally the third. I dived for the post and tripped, instinctively grabbing its top for support as the first missile went by on my right and the second moaned past my left ear. I tried to move back to my right but my ankle had become tangled in the chain. Move!

Move! I pulled against the chain with all my strength. The third spear was so close . . . so close. I watched it approach as if it were all happening in slow motion . . . and then I felt its black forged tip smashing into my tired chest. . . .

The ringing persisted. . . .

Even when I buried my head under the pillow I could still hear it—imploring, insisting, demanding. . . .

I propped myself up on both elbows, reached for the noisy intruder, and put it to my ear.

"Good morning," said a lilting voice. "It's seven thirty—and the downtown temperature is seventy-one degrees!"

I let the receiver fall to the floor and blinked several times until my eyes were able to focus on a garishly framed print of a toreador hanging next to a mirror above a dresser. I blinked again and shifted my sights to close range. I was fully dressed—shirt, tie, Calvin Klein suit, shoes!

Next to the bed, the night-table lamp was on. In its light I could see my ring, gold Omega watch, and wallet. The watch was still ticking, and when I checked my wallet all the credit cards and cash were in place.

This is impossible, I thought. I can't be in my room at the Century Plaza!

I stumbled to the dresser, opened my attaché case, and found my promotional itinerary. Page four listed my appearance on the "Tonight Show" for September 8. I went back to the bed, retrieved the fallen phone, jiggled the receiver several times, and then dialed O. When a voice with a heavy Hispanic accent finally responded, I was still trying to figure out how to phrase my question.

"Miss, I'm a little confused. What day is this?"

She wasn't fazed in the least. People are always losing days in Los Angeles. "Thees is Septembair the ninth, sir."

I hung up without even thanking her. My jaw ached when I opened my mouth, and I had a dull pain in my chest. For God's sake, what had happened to me? Voices? I heard voices. Calm down, buddy, the television set is on. A man was talking. Strong Jewish dialect but loud and clear. What was he saying? I tried to concentrate. "Premier Sadat must recognize that Jerusalem is our nation's most precious treasure. We vill never . . . never . . . allow its land to be divided again. Never!"

Jerusalem? Easy transition, even for my foggy mind, from Jerusalem to Joseph of Arimathea. Had the old man kept his word? Had I been there with him, or . . . or had it all been a dream? I went back to the dresser and stared into the mirror.

Ugh! Eyes puffed and red. Hair askew. Skin blending perfectly with the color of the walls—sallow chartreuse.

The phone rang again. I jumped. A voice identified itself as the head of hotel security. "Are you all right, Mr. Lawrence?"

"Yes, I think so."

He chuckled. "You had quite a night. We have the name of the man who slugged you in the Granada Room, in case you intend to prefer charges. Also the names of a dozen witnesses."

I rubbed my chin tenderly. "No, no, I think it's best if we forget the whole thing."

"That's very considerate of you, sir. The hotel can do without that sort of publicity. Is there anything we can help you with, this morning?"

"No, just tell me how I got back to my room."

"Two of my men . . . ah . . . assisted you. Once you were inside your room, you told them you were okay so they left."

"Well, I want to thank all of you."

"Glad we could help out, sir."

I stumbled out onto the balcony, turning off Barbara Walters as I passed. At first the sun blinded me, but soon I could see, far below, a small figure in fatigues mowing the grass beyond the hotel's circular driveway. Across the street, workmen on ladders were slowly changing the letters on the marquee of the Shubert Theater. To the left, a light haze billowed lazily above the trees on the Avenue of the Stars. The air smelled strange, not like the air in . . .

Not like the air where? In Jerusalem? In A.D. 36? Wake up! The dream has ended. The big daddy of all dreams was just that—a dream. But how could that be? Is it possible to dream odors? How do I know they're different here from there? And what about Joseph and James and Matthew and Peter and Caiaphas and Mark and Pilate. Pilate? I reached for my right shoulder. Then I raised my right arm over my head. No pain. But didn't I throw those javelins? Didn't I almost nail the procurator? Fool! It had just been a dream, a wild and sensational technicolor special; twenty years of frustrated research on Jesus Christ all climaxing with some egotistical boasting on the Carson show plus too many scotch and sodas and a punch to the jaw.

But how could I remember so many details if it had been only a dream? Aren't dreams usually fragmentary bits of dialogue and action that rarely make any sense? When do they ever have a beginning and a middle and an end with all the

258

intervening chapters in their proper place and all the settings identifiable? I could still close my eyes and see Gethsemane and Golgotha and the Temple and the tomb, and if I concentrated I could even recall the fragrance in the garden of Nicodemus! Who has dreams like that? Was all of it just the product of an overactive mind accustomed to creating thousands of fictional plots and subplots, actions and scenery, and even smells in book after book?

I heard the flutter of wings. Three dingy-looking pigeons landed on the railing of the balcony, eyed me expectantly until I made no move to feed them, and then flew off. Now I was beginning to pick up the sounds of the city. Not trumpets blasting from the Temple tower or vendors screeching from their stalls in the market but automobile horns, screeching brakes, a 747 descending to the west, sirens. I leaned forward and watched an ambulance roar past, its lights blinking furiously.

What had happened to me? Can the mind play such tricks? Had it really been no more than a fantasy? If that was true, I'd never be able to write about it—or could I? God knows there are enough flakes cranking out books on subjects like voices from beyond, the transmigration of souls, and the transposition of bodies. Why couldn't I do the same? No! That I could never bring myself to do. Even so, perhaps I had better make notes of all I could remember while it was still fresh in my mind. Dreams fade fast, according to what I had read, and maybe someday it would be important to someone researching the unknown workings of our subconscious mind. I really should describe how Mary Magdalene had looked, Mark's early morning trip to the tomb, why Peter was not at the crucifixion, and so much more, especially the statue of Jesus in Joseph's palace.

Maybe I could still complete "The Christ Commission." But if I did, would I be accused of copping out—of trying to make amends for what I had said on the "Tonight Show." And how could I explain my conversion from a doubter to a believer? By writing in the book's forward that I had *dreamed* what I believed to be the truth about Jesus? Never! We have enough crackpots singing that song while they hustle dollars from nice, gullible people willing to clutch at any straw to make their faith meaningful. No. That line wouldn't play anywhere, not even in Marin County! But who would believe me if I told them that it had not been a dream and that I had actually talked with the Temple guard who had received the burial napkin from Jesus as he walked away from his tomb? Who would believe that the stone had been rolled away *after*, not during, the resurrection? No one! Including Kitty. Sooner or later some high-priced shrink would listen to my story, nod his head wisely, and prescribe a long vacation with plenty of rest.

I suddenly felt cold, even though the morning sun was shining on me. I touched my forehead and it was burning. I went back inside, dropped my jacket on the bed, and continued on to the bathroom. I turned on the cold water until the sink was nearly filled and splashed the stuff over my head and face. Felt great. Then I let it drain and brushed my teeth until the gums hurt. Head buried in the hand towel, I backed out of the bathroom. My thigh brushed against something hanging on the doorknob. It swayed back and forth, noisily bumping against the wood, sparkling in the glow from the fluorescent light above the sink.

I dropped the towel and fell to my knees, cradling the gold amulet tenderly in my hand. I was crying. When I turned the rough piece of hammered metal I could see the fish and the inscription and the anchor of hope all carved into the strange-shaped pendant attached to a looped leather thong! I held it close to my cheek, feeling its coolness against my skin. Then I kissed it before noticing that it looked different now. Much different.

In its center was a deep indentation, as if something sharp and pointed had collided with it at great force . . .

. . . something like the point of a spear from the hand of Porcius!

ABOUT THE AUTHOR

OG MANDINO is the author of eight books. His "greatest" series, including the enormously popular classic, *The Greatest Salesman in the World*, has already sold more than eight million copies throughout the world in more than seventeen languages. President of *Success Unlimited* magazine for twelve years, he retired in 1976, at the age of fifty-two, to devote all his time to writing and lecturing. His most recent success, *The Gift of Acabar*, was co-authored by Buddy Kaye.

Heartwarming Books
of
Faith and Inspiration

☐	13991	**LOVE AND LIVING** Thomas Merton	$2.95
☐	12963	**A SEVERE MERCY** Sheldon Vanauken	$2.50
☐	01184	**HE WAS ONE OF US: THE LIFE OF JESUS OF NAZARETH** Rien Poortvliet	$9.95
☐	14826	**POSITIVE PRAYERS FOR POWER-FILLED LIVING** Robert H. Schuller	$2.25
☐	20133	**REACH OUT FOR A NEW LIFE** Robert H. Schuller	$2.50
☐	14732	**HOW CAN I FIND YOU, GOD?** Marjorie Holmes	$2.50
☐	13588	**IN SEARCH OF HISTORIC JESUS** Lee Roddy & Charles E. Sellier, Jr.	$2.25
☐	13890	**THE FINDING OF JASPER HOLT** Grace Livingston Hill	$1.75
☐	14385	**THE BIBLE AS HISTORY** Werner Keller	$3.50
☐	14379	**THE GREATEST MIRACLE IN THE WORLD** Og Mandino	$2.25
☐	14216	**THE GREATEST SALESMAN IN THE WORLD** Og Mandino	$2.25
☐	14971	**I'VE GOT TO TALK TO SOMEBODY, GOD** Marjorie Holmes	$2.50
☐	12853	**THE GIFT OF INNER HEALING** Ruth Carter Stapleton	$1.95
☐	12444	**BORN AGAIN** Charles Colson	$2.50
☐	13436	**SHROUD** Robert Wilcox	$2.50
☐	14840	**A GRIEF OBSERVED** C. S. Lewis	$2.50
☐	14406	**NEW MOON RISING** Eugenia Price	$2.50
☐	14096	**THE LATE GREAT PLANET EARTH** Hal Lindsey	$2.50

Buy them at your local bookstore or use this handy coupon for ordering: